Created with Vellum

HEIRS OF ESRAN
BOOK 2

THE
PRINCESS
OF
MAREMER

HAYLEY TURNER

THE PRINCESS OF MAREMER

Heirs of Esran Book 2

HAYLEY TURNER

To those who work to create a world that's gentler than the one they've always known.

Content Warnings

The Princess of Maremer contains the following:

Graphic: character deaths, cursing, blood, violence, physical and psychological torture, sexual content, possession, sleep paralysis (one scene)

Moderate: memories of abuse (parent to child), depiction of panic attacks/anxiety, depiction of depression (side character, not POV), depiction of religious fanaticism/terrorism

Minor: alcohol use, sexual harassment, attempted suicide (self-sacrifice)

Note: the animals/pets are always safe, I promise.

CONTENTS

Summary of The Prince of Terrana   xvii

Acantha   1

PART ONE

1. Waking   7
2. Without the Moon   23
3. The Salt Bath   28
4. The Nature of Darkness   43
5. Greater Men   54
6. A Healer's Hand   66
7. A Claim   73
8. A Moment   83
9. A Cold Welcome   87
10. The Feast of Stars   95
11. The Shadows Return   108
12. The Shadow's Wrath   117
13. The Farmer's Help   125
14. Choosing a Path   131
15. Rage and Resolve   140
16. A Closed Door   148
17. The Market and the Manor   153
18. The Priests' Symbols   163
19. Testing Darkness   175
20. A Part to Play   184
21. The Freed Prisoners   192
22. The Heir's Servant   196
23. A City Square in Maremer   203
24. Beneath Parea   211
25. To Begin a Reign   220

26. A Form of Seeing   226
27. Something To Return For   234

Part Two

28. The Shadow in the Inn   249
29. The Summons   256
30. The Princess Returns   265
31. The Heir of Terrana   275
32. The Rescue   285
33. The Exchange   295
34. A Piece of Power   306
35. The Terranian Elite   311
36. A Vision of Death   325
37. Heart and Mind   332
38. The Order of the Eternal Flame   336
39. The Shadow and the Cat   343
40. In Dreams and Darkness   348
41. The Ruse   357
42. The Pretender   364
43. A Place to Hide   371
44. The Answer   378
45. The New Heir   384
46. Beneath the Sun and Stars   392
47. To Carry in the Morning   402

Epilogue   405

Acknowledgments   409
Character Glossary   411
Spice Rack   417
About the Author   419
Also by Hayley Turner   421

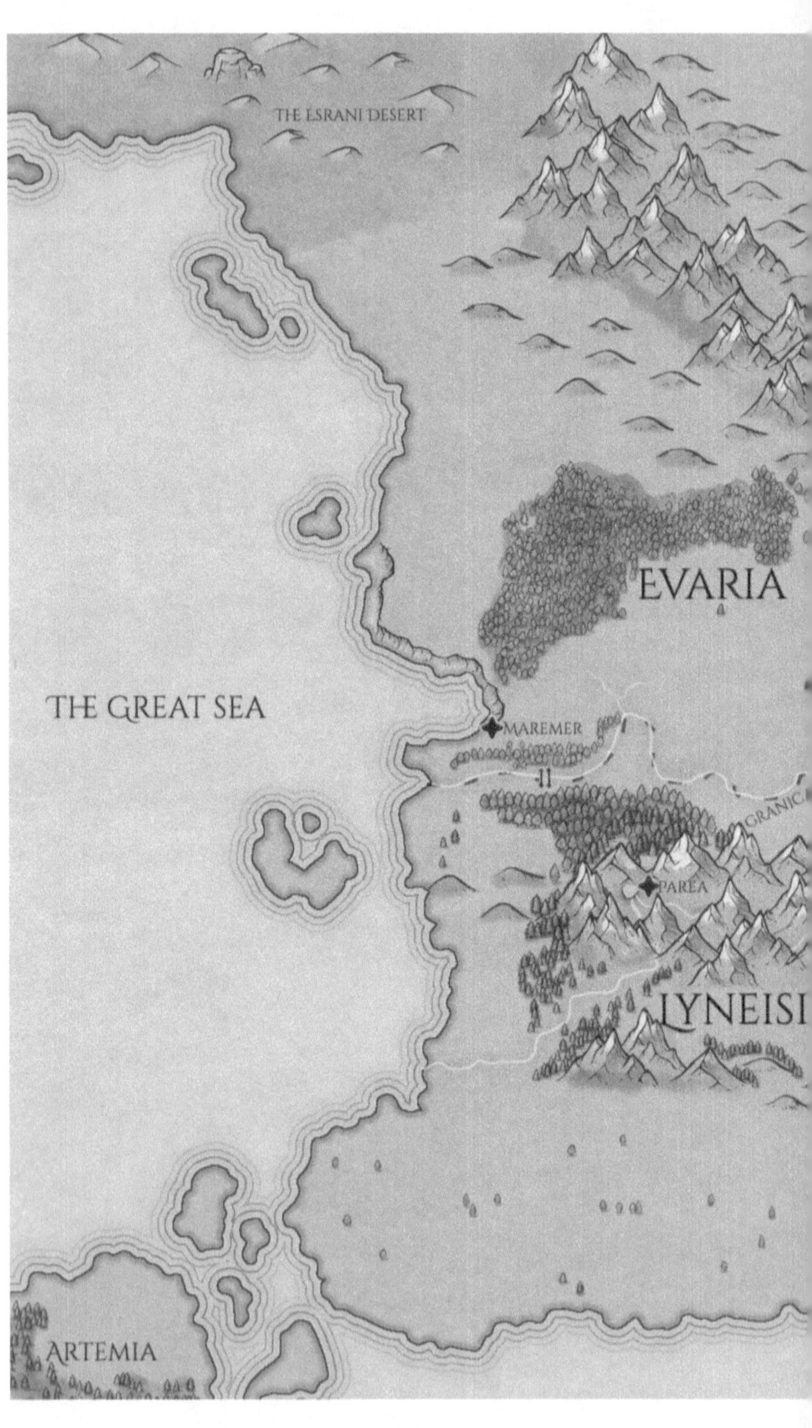

THE ESRANI DESERT
EVARIA
THE GREAT SEA
MAREMER
II
GRANIC
PAREA
LYNEISI
ARTEMIA

ESRAN
CRESTFALL
RIVENDYA
ELLYR
RYOS
THE CASPIAN FOREST
BANA
GRANICA RIVER
TERRANA
PERMARE
GRANGERTON
LUES
INMEDIO RIVER
BARLEO
THE BLACKWOOD FOREST

Summary of The Prince of Terrana

The Heirs of Esran series is meant to be read in order. This is a brief summary to refresh your memory after you've read Book 1.

The Prince of Terrana begins with our two protagonists meeting in Castle Alterna just as rumors begin flying that the Terranian Prince is somewhere in the capital of Lyneisia. Despite getting off on the wrong foot, Princess Relaina and Darren find themselves drawn to one another. They work together when a Terranian assassin infiltrates her father's guard and gets her best friend, Bracken, arrested, but it's soon revealed that Darren himself is the Prince of Terrana.

Despite who he is, Relaina doesn't believe Darren deserves to die just because he's the son of the Tyrant King. They escape Parea together and travel to Maremer, the capital of Evaria, where Bracken has been banished. There, they meet King Fabian Thercux and discover that Bracken has been working for him for years in an effort to protect Relaina from King Gabriel.

They don't know why the Tyrant King wants Relaina, but they all decide to join King Fabian's network of spies, or Shadows, to help Esran as a whole. As they explore the city, meet Evarian nobles, and track shady merchants, Relaina and Darren fall for each other.

But Relaina's uncle, Jeremiah, soon arrives in Maremer with grave news—nobles in Lyneisia have incited a coup and captured her brother, Aronn, and the Terranian army is marching on Maremer.

News of the army reaches Aronn, who was rescued from the traitors by Nehma, Rhea, and Thea, healers from the Caspain Forest. They, along with another healer named Catrin, set off to Maremer to help.

Alongside preparations for conflict in Maremer, they hold the Winter Festival. Fabian and Jeremiah rekindle a romance from twenty years prior, and Relaina, Darren, Jacquelyn, and Bracken head into the city...only to be met with dire consequences.

The Bay of Trade goes up in explosive flames, and Relaina is captured and whisked away on a ship headed for Terrana. Jacquelyn and Connor betrayed them all. In anger and grief, Jeremiah lets slip that Relaina is really his daughter, and her mother was a powerful healer and Seer named Talea.

After discovering she is a healer herself, Relaina manages to escape the ship as it explodes on the Granica River, and Darren, Bracken, and Jeremiah find her along with Aronn and the Caspian healers. Princess Annalise, Relaina and Aronn's younger sister, meets Relaina and Darren on the road, and they send her off to a Lyneisian village with healers to keep her safe.

The Terranian army arrives in Maremer, and Fabian challenges King Gabriel to single combat. Fabian is almost killed, but Jeremiah arrives at the last minute and saves him. The battle commences.

Darren realizes he must face his father and use the power he's feared and suppressed for years. They fight, Darren almost loses, and Relaina fights her way to him as magic draws her near. With their power combined, they subdue Gabriel, but at the last moment Gabriel attacks Relaina. Darren overuses his magic and lands himself in the realm of Calixtos. Relaina stabs Gabriel in the heart.

At the end of Book 1, Jeremiah and Aronn are headed for Parea with a host of Evarians. Queen Christine and King Stephan's fates are unknown, and Princess Annalise is in a remote Lyneisian village. Relaina agrees to sit on Fabian's small council in the aftermath of the battle, and after a week of nothing, she senses Darren's presence through a new mysterious connection they have. He has emerged from the realm of Calixtos.

Acantha

In the quiet of the snow-covered woods, she waited, impatiently twirling light around her fingers.

"Acantha, must you?" Kalmali asked quietly, his leather armor creaking as he edged away from her. She smiled slyly and threw a tendril of light in his direction. He yelped and jumped back.

"Poor Kalmali, afraid of a little light."

"I'd be stupid if I wasn't." He straightened himself, rubbing his neck where she'd managed to land a blow, one of few places his brown skin was exposed to the frigid air.

Acantha pouted. "I was only having a little fun. Waiting on these Lyneisian pricks is terribly boring." She approached her tenebrae devotee, ignoring his discomfort at her proximity as she palmed the pendant at his chest, turning it over several times. The smooth onyx stone was slick with condensation, the black shade stark against her porcelain hand. She smirked at him again, drawing his hazel gaze to her crystalline irises as they flashed white with her magic. "Besides, it's healthy for you to remember that you and your shadow exist at my mercy."

Kalmali blinked, his breath rapidly filling the frigid air. Acantha sighed and dropped the stone back to his chest. After all this time, tormenting him had grown rather dull.

"If these men don't show up soon, I'm going to kill one of them on their arrival," she huffed.

"Then I'm glad we aren't any later." The voice drifted through the trees a moment before the two men appeared, snow and pine needles crunching beneath their feet. They were both tall—at least to Acantha, who hardly reached Kalmali's shoulders. The tenebrae stiffened at the Lyneisian nobles' approach, ever wary and protective of his mistress. But these men were no threat.

One was nearly as pale as she was, with graying, cropped hair, while the other had a bronze complexion and black hair to his shoulders. Acantha smiled and shifted her white hair over her shoulder, the beast in her chest purring as confusion and desire flashed in the younger one's eyes. She adored the beautiful, greedy ones.

"Lord Norhen and Zarias Conclave," she said. "It's a pleasure to finally meet you."

"And you as well, Lady Acantha," Lord Norhen said, inclining his head. Zarias followed suit, his head dipping but his eyes roving over her unabashedly. She wasn't sure what he expected to see when she was covered from her neck down in winter furs; the Lyneisian winter was too harsh for any other apparel. Still, she offered him a wry smile in return, fighting a shiver as a breeze blew through her long tresses. If anything about her appearance should be admired, it was her hair. She expended much effort to draw the natural gold from its strands so it appeared as white as the snow around them, an homage to the goddess she served.

"Archan Conclave sends his regrets that he couldn't be present," Lord Norhen said. "We are still plagued with resistance in the capital."

"As would be expected," Acantha said, leaving Kalmali's side to approach the Lyneisian nobles. "The only advantage you possess is the captive king and queen, and you'll gain no love if you force the people to submit by threatening beloved rulers." She turned to Zarias. "This is why it was imperative that you married the heir."

Zarias's haughty expression soured. "How was I supposed to know she'd rescue the fucking Prince of Terrana and flee the kingdom?"

Acantha clicked her tongue. "I'm in a decent mood today, so I won't slit your pretty throat for speaking to me with that tone."

Zarias's scowl reignited, but he remained silent.

"We've heard she's in Maremer," Lord Norhen said, throwing a warning look at his fellow. "Surely it's possible to retrieve the princess, especially now that King Gabriel is dead."

"You're a fool if you think capturing her would be easy, or wise. We needed compliance, and you allowed that opportunity to slip away." Acantha examined a low-hanging branch that was coated in ice. "But what's done is done. We'll move forward with a different strategy. King Gabriel's death affords me the luxury of moving more freely in Terrana, and it will be easy to recruit his former supporters to our cause."

"What *is* your cause, exactly? What do you gain by aiding us?" Zarias narrowed his eyes at her before clearing his throat and adding, "My lady."

Acantha studied him, allowing him to squirm beneath her gaze before she closed the small distance between them. She played with the ties of his fur-lined cloak, considering his question. She needed this damned coup to work—the fewer contenders in her game, the better. Perhaps sharing part of her plan would instill trust. And motivation.

"I wish for worthy rulers to govern Esran," she said, lifting her chin. "And when I install them in their places of power, I expect gratitude and loyalty. I am the Heir of Elenia, and I will be the guiding light to all of Esran."

The gleeful hunger in Zarias's eyes made her heart sing.

"And from among those most loyal to me," she brushed a thumb along Zarias's jaw, "I will select a man to lead alongside me."

A grin split Zarias's face. She had him.

It took much of her strength to keep herself from laughing at him; she would never bind herself to such a feeble boy. No, the Heir of Elenia was destined for a partner of equal power.

She would have the Heir of Calixtos or no other.

Part One

CHAPTER 1

WAKING

Darren LaGuarde yelped in pain as the tenebrae prisoner slammed him against the dungeon wall. His power shuddered and grew. *No.* Even as he gritted his teeth against the throbbing in his head, he forced the darkness to heel.

"You're no king."

Darren flinched—his father's voice drifted from beneath the tenebrae's hood.

"You're unworthy of Calixtos's power."

Darren squeezed his eyes shut. *He's dead. He's dead.* He repeated it to himself even as the dark vapor coiled around his throat, pinning him to the wall, the cold so intense it burned his skin.

"Summon your little light-wielder, son. You know you want to."

Darren's eyes flew open.

"No," he growled, even as fear pierced his insides. Gabriel LaGuarde's face was half shrouded in darkness, his green eyes wild. A trickle of blood ran down the corner of the Tyrant King's mouth.

"Call her," Gabriel said. "She can help you. Isn't that what you want?" Gabriel wanted Relaina here, wanted to strangle her with this same darkness that drew tears from Darren's eyes and a cry from his throat.

"You're dead," Darren choked out. "Relaina killed you."

"Did she?" Gabriel's brow furrowed. "Are you sure?"

Darren pressed his back into the wall until the pressure turned to pain. "You're dead," he whispered.

"You can't kill me. Calixtos chose me. The god of darkness himself decided you are unworthy, and now I hold all of his power."

Darren shut his eyes again. *He's dead, he's dead, he's dead.*

"I'm right here, son. I am alive, and you will never see the outside of this dungeon again."

Relaina killed him. Relaina...

Darren shot upright in bed, his insides alight with panic. Cool, gentle fingers brushed his arm.

"I'm here. You're safe."

As Darren's breathing and heartbeat slowed, his eyes adjusted to the dark and his mind calmed. Another nightmare.

"Relaina," he said, his voice rough, and the bedcovers rustled as she sat up beside him. Her curls were tousled, her eyes tired as she studied him. "I'm sorry for waking you."

"You didn't, I was already awake."

Darren nodded. While his sleep had been plagued by nightmares these past two weeks, Relaina's had been difficult to come by altogether. He lay down once more, shifting closer to her.

"Do you want to talk about it?"

Darren sighed. "It was the same as before."

Relaina ran her fingertips along the scar over his heart, inhaling slowly.

"Today is the day," she said quietly.

"It is."

Relaina traced soothing circles on his chest. Her dark curls fanned out, resting on the pillow and tickling his neck. "I can be there, if you want."

Darren kissed the top of her head. "I'm not sure they'd react well to your presence. Otherwise I would want you with me."

They fell silent for a long moment, and Darren listened to Relaina's breathing and stared at the deep purple bed hangings above them.

"Darren." Relaina's voice was small, hesitant.

"What is it, love?"

Relaina twined her fingers through his as she sat up again, unable to meet his gaze. His stomach turned. *Is it my eye?* The left one had not returned to its original state. It was now permanently black around his brown iris, jarring him each time he'd seen his reflection over the past two weeks.

"I..." She traced his palm absently, biting her lip. "Just be careful tomorrow."

Darren sat up and brushed a curl away from her face before touching his forehead to hers.

"I will be." He still couldn't see her well in the darkness, but as he leaned in, finding her mouth with his, the softness of her lips and her hands on his chest was equally as familiar as her smile, as the gleam in her green eyes when they fought, or the way her hair fell in her face when she laughed. He resisted the urge to grip her more tightly, to deepen the kiss, unsure if he might scare her after what she'd been through the past month and her averting her eyes only moments ago. Darren leaned back.

"Relaina?"

"Hmm?"

"You're safe with me too. I hope you know that."

Relaina pressed her lips to his jaw. "I do."

Darren settled down again, and she draped one arm around his middle. He took her hand in his, holding it close to his chest. She kissed the back of his neck and began to hum softly, a melody he hadn't heard before. Her voice pulled him into a dreamless sleep.

~

DARREN COUNTED his breaths as he neared the inner perimeter wall of Seacastle, greeted in passing by various guards and Evarian nobles. He'd prepared himself for this day since he'd woken after the battle, but as he drew near the dungeons and the tenebrae prisoners that waited, it all felt rather foolish. What did he know of controlling tenebrae, of leading them?

He knew how to destroy a tenebrae's shadow, at least, if it came to that.

Standing at an iron door set into the stone wall was King Fabian, dressed in a red tunic with black cuffs at his wrists and warm, black trousers that covered most of his rich brown skin. The Maremer winter was proving to be far milder than the winters in Parea, but today the wind from the Great Sea whipped at Darren's cheeks and nose more insistently, and he blew hot air into his cupped hands as he approached the king and his guards. He'd worn a gray tunic made from the same fabric as the Shadow gear Fabian had gifted him, which kept out most of the cold.

"Good morning, Darren," Fabian said, his golden-brown eyes squinting against the wind. "I hope you slept well."

Darren shrugged. "I could do without the nightmares."

Fabian huffed a laugh, his breath appearing in a cloud before him. "They plague us all, it seems."

With a nod from the king, the guards nearby unlocked the door. It groaned as it swung open, and Fabian and Darren stepped inside and out of the wind.

"Are you certain you're ready?" Fabian asked, taking a torch off a nearby sconce.

Darren swallowed against the dry ache in his throat. "No. But we can't delay any longer."

Fabian nodded solemnly, and they began their descent into the dungeons.

"The healers have done well this past fortnight," Fabian said. "I'm pleased that we've avoided any issues of possession since the battle ended."

"Let's hope we don't change that today."

"You have my full confidence."

If only Darren held the same confidence in himself. *You're unworthy of Calixtos's power.* As they reached the bottom of the staircase, Darren pushed the memory of his nightmare away. Another guard greeted them by a second door, bowing before she opened it.

Torches lined the wall intermittently on the left side of the dungeon corridor, and every few feet on the right side stood thick, wooden doors with iron bars set into tiny windows. Darren took another deep breath—it had been years since he'd been in a dungeon of his own volition.

Still, as he and Fabian ventured toward the opposite end of the corridor, he couldn't deny that this was the most pleasant place of imprisonment he'd encountered. It was warm and dry, at the very least.

Thea and Catrin waited for them at yet another door, their faces set. Both healers had braided their hair back, Fabian's torch casting shadows that blended with Thea's dark brown hair and threw Catrin's fiery red into relief.

"King Fabian," Thea said, and both women bowed. "Prince Darren."

"The tenebrae are behind this door?" Darren asked, though he already knew the answer. The darkness in his veins shimmered, urging him in their direction.

"They are."

Darren nodded and braced himself. He'd been both eager and afraid to use his power since the battle—eager to know if he would hear the voices of the collective tenebrae again, and afraid of setting his shadows free, of losing control like he had before.

"King Darren!"

He whipped around. A pair of hands gripped the bars of the nearest cell.

"King Darren—Your Grace—please," the woman said, her face obscured. "I've been waiting to speak with you."

Darren stared at her. *King Darren.*

Fabian and the healers watched as he stepped toward the cell.

"Who are you?" he asked.

"Lady Mariana Delimont, Y-your Grace." She bowed clumsily, her face dipping below the window in the door. Darren's heart plummeted. *Katarina's mother.* He looked to Fabian, who nodded to the nearby guards.

The guards unlocked the cell and escorted Lady Delimont out, her wrists shackled. She slumped to the ground as they released her. Her gray dress was frayed at the hem, stained with dirt and blood, and her blonde hair fell limp around her face and shoulders. The Seacastle guards backed away several feet, keeping their hands on their swords.

"Please," she said, looking up at Darren. Her gaunt face was so different from what he remembered, he may not have recognized her had she not said her name. "I...my Katarina... they took her body for burial. I was unable to perform the rites."

Tears threatened to form in his eyes, but he mastered himself. "I ensured they'd been done."

"Your Grace, a feminine energy must be present—"

"There was."

Lady Delimont blinked at him through tearful eyes. "You have my thanks." She bowed her head again. "I only...could I... I wish to visit her."

Darren hesitated. "That's not up to me, Lady Delimont. You are King Fabian's prisoner, not mine."

"But you are my king."

Darren's power flared within, mirroring his disdain for the title. He'd made no claim to the Terranian throne. "There is no king of Terrana."

Lady Delimont's face contorted, all evidence of grief wiped away. "Then you are a *coward*, and my daughter died for nothing."

The crushing weight of fury and grief pressed on his chest, and some of his darkness broke free, appearing at his palms. Dozens of indistinct tenebrae voices emerged at the edge of his consciousness, now aware of his presence just beyond the door guarded by healers.

"Return her to her cell," Fabian said, his voice low and cold as Darren tried to refocus.

Just as the guards reached for her, Lady Delimont's eyes filled with darkness, and she dove forward, taking Darren tumbling with her to the ground. Her fingers closed around his forearm and slammed it to the stone with a sickening *crack*. Pain shot through his arm. With a well-aimed shove, he managed to free himself from her grasp using his uninjured arm and grabbed her throat, preparing to speak the words to banish the shadow. But his darkness moved faster than he could think, rushing down his arm and engulfing the woman. The tenebrae shrieked and snarled, desperate and disjointed, feral with rage, but it flew out of the woman's body where Darren's hand gripped her throat and vanished. Lady Delimont slumped to the ground, unconscious, and Darren shuffled away from her, cradling his arm.

He stared at her for a moment before realizing his darkness

was still smoldering up both his hands and arms. He breathed deeply, pulling the darkness back into himself, and the tenebrae voices went silent. Using his power was like flexing an underused muscle—stiff and uncomfortable, but not overly difficult. He winced at the pain that returned in full force with the absence of his darkness. Fuck, it hurt.

Catrin swore, and the Evarian guards came forward at Fabian's command and locked Lady Delimont away in her cell once more. Fabian knelt beside Darren.

"Are you all right?" the king asked.

"How the hell did we miss that she was tenebrae?" Catrin asked.

Darren leaned back on the dungeon wall, his face scrunched as he breathed through the pain. "She wasn't tenebrae," he said. "She was possessed by one."

"There's no way any imprisoned here escaped," Thea said.

"She must have been possessed before imprisonment." Darren cradled his arm, breathing through the pain. "The tenebrae felt...angry. And detached. The person it belonged to might have already been dead."

"Gods in hell," Fabian muttered. Darren started to stand, and the slight pressure on his arm sent a wave of nausea through him.

"Fuck. I think my arm is broken."

"I can heal it for you," Catrin said.

"No. I don't want to risk hurting you."

"We aren't going to leave you to question tenebrae prisoners with a broken arm," Thea said, tossing her braid over her shoulder before putting her hands on her hips.

"I'm worried I don't have enough control yet," Darren said, shaking his head. He'd reeled it back moments before, but how would it react so close to a healer's light? "And no one's tried to heal me since I fully connected with Calixtos's power. It may not even work."

"Relaina," Fabian said. "Could she help?"

"Again."

Relaina flopped onto the grass, exhaling sharply.

"This is impossible," she said.

"It's not. You're letting your frustration get the better of you," Nehma said.

Relaina sat up on her elbows and pursed her lips at Nehma, who sat a few feet away, legs crossed and eyes focused. Sunlight shone through the trees in the Seacastle greenhouse, adorning Nehma's dark brown skin with golden speckles.

"Your fear of allowing it to touch the darkness is likely what's making progress so slow," Nehma said.

"I'm not eager to feel that pain again."

"It hasn't happened since the battle, right?"

An icy feeling encased Relaina's chest. "Right."

"Release some of that fear, then."

Relaina tried to focus on what Nehma said as she kept speaking, but the dread in her gut drew her beneath a wave of despair as images of blood and smoke, shadows and death flooded her mind.

Darkness entered the world nearby, soothing and placid. *Darren.* It was the same feeling she'd had during the battle, and right when he'd woken. Now they had this strange new connection between them, though she couldn't hear his voice, exactly—only sense his emotions. He was nervous, and perhaps grieved, but who wouldn't be in a place like that, questioning prisoners?

"Did you hear anything I just said?"

Relaina shook her head as Nehma studied her. "I'm sorry, no. I was distracted."

"Hmm." Nehma's braids swished over her shoulder as she

uncrossed her legs and stood. The gold ornaments adorning the ends clinked together delicately. "I think that's enough for today. I can sense the darkness nearby."

Annoyance plucked at Relaina's insides as she and Nehma grabbed their cloaks and made for the greenhouse exit. Nehma wouldn't even mention Darren's name, even after they'd fought together against Gabriel.

"Ah!" Relaina gasped and froze mid-stride. Flashes of anger and pain flooded her mind, raising the hairs on her arms.

"What is it?" Nehma's dark brown eyes widened as she reached for Relaina's arm, careful not to touch the shadowfire scar that ran from her wrist to her elbow.

"Darren. Something's happened."

Relaina took off, Nehma on her heels. They'd made it halfway to the dungeons when Relaina's sense of the darkness disappeared, her connection to Darren severed once more. She willed herself faster.

Four guards stood at the top of the stairs leading into the dungeons, and a fifth emerged, lighting up in recognition as Relaina approached.

"Princess Relaina, I was just sent to find you."

"What happened?"

"Prince Darren was attacked by a prisoner, and his arm… it's broken. They thought you might be able to help him."

"Take us to them," Relaina said.

The guard led them deep into the dungeons. At the end of a long, torchlit corridor sat Darren, his back against the wall. Fabian crouched beside him while Thea and Catrin stood guard by another door. Relaina's black cloak pooled around her as she knelt and assessed Darren's face, his cradled arm. Nehma approached her healer sisters.

"What happened?" Relaina asked.

"Lady Mariana Delimont was possessed by a tenebrae and attacked me," Darren said. "I'm fairly sure my arm is broken."

Relief that he wasn't in mortal danger slowed her racing heart, but uncertainty still prickled Relaina's neck. "And you think I can help?"

"The way you did during the battle," Thea said, stepping forward. "He won't let us do it with the risk of the magics clashing, but you…"

"I have both," Relaina said quietly. She recalled all too vividly how excruciating it had been when the light and dark warred inside her, but Nehma was right—it hadn't happened since she'd connected her magic with Darren's at the battle. She returned her gaze to Darren, who closed his eyes.

"I want to try," she said. "But that was…different. I'm not sure how I did it."

"Follow your magic," Nehma said as she approached, stopping a few feet away from them. "And use what we've talked about in training. This may be a chance to truly test it."

Relaina nodded, but doubt remained pinned in her gut. Darren's eyes opened again and found hers.

"I trust you," he said quietly. He took a breath as he looked to Fabian and the healers. "The rest of you should leave. The darkness will be more difficult for me to control with Relaina's added to mine."

Relaina swallowed the impulse to protest as the others began the trek back down the corridor. She watched Nehma leave, wishing she would stay and guide her through this, but Darren was right—it wasn't safe for them to remain here when his power was so volatile and unpredictable. Their footsteps faded in a matter of seconds, and Relaina inhaled slowly, turning back to Darren.

"Ready?" she asked.

He nodded. Darkness filled both his eyes briefly and the vapor appeared at his hands, along his arms. It drew her in, and she reached for him. As soon as her hand touched his face, the darkness held in her scars gleamed and rushed to join his.

For the first time since the battle, Relaina's healer's light emerged, the glowing markings appearing along her arms. Darren's magic spread rapidly around the dungeon floor like dark wind. Relaina marveled at her light shining against their combined darkness, making the shadows' iridescence gleam. She pulled her focus back to Darren, visualizing her light gathering into her palm before touching his arm at the place where it was broken.

Without warning, emotion enveloped her so forcefully that she forgot Darren's injury for a moment. She nearly gasped as grief and despair roiled through her, wounds than ran deeper than muscle and bone. But there was playfulness, too, and a fierceness that filled her with fire and profound affection. As the emotions built and faded once more, Relaina took in Darren's alarmed expression, and a memory from months ago floated through her mind. *When we heal someone, we get a sense of their entire being.*

Is this what Ericka had meant?

"Relaina?"

She blinked, her own senses swiftly returning, and touched the hand he'd placed against her cheek.

"I'm fine," she said. "I just...wasn't expecting that."

The concern on his face thawed only slightly. "Expecting what?"

"I'm not sure how to explain. But let me try to heal your arm."

She focused again, her muscles wrought with tension as she willed the light to concentrate where she touched him. The bone slowly began to mend. It worked just as Nehma had explained in their training sessions.

You have flowers on your arms. Relaina looked up. Darren hadn't spoken, but his voice was clear in her mind. He traced the glowing markings on her left forearm. *Hydrangeas.*

Relaina stared at him and then her markings. She hadn't told him, but they'd become her favorite after—

"They're how you found me." Her voice was barely above a whisper. *The day Xavier attacked me.*

"Hmm." Darren closed his eyes again, letting his head fall back against the stone. "And here we are again, underground, with one of us injured."

"We ought to break that habit."

He chuckled, and Relaina refocused on his healing. Relief filled her heart as the pain melted away from his face; this was the first time she hadn't felt completely inept with her magic since the battle.

Before she was certain his injury was fully mended, her magic hit a block, dimming. Nehma had warned her of this, how healing had its limits, and how hers would have its limits, especially as she learned the basics. Relaina pushed forward, but the tension grew taut and snapped, the light falling back to her center and dissipating.

More easily than she'd expected, Darren drew his own power back to himself, and it drifted silently along his arms again. A bit of envy stirred in her heart.

"Thank you," he said, pressing his arm lightly with his fingers.

"Can you move it?"

He bent his arm and flexed his fingers. "There's a bit of soreness, but it's much better."

Relaina wanted to revel in her small success, but the lack of complete healing still diminished her hope that she'd achieved a breakthrough with her magic. Pushing that feeling aside, she helped Darren to his feet. The cool vapor still rolling along his arms spread over her hand gently, as if it recognized and welcomed her.

Strange.

Darren smiled at her, a question in his eyes, followed by his voice in her mind. *What's strange?*

"This connection," Relaina said aloud, her voice soft. His attention shifted before the smile faded from his face. He turned toward the door that stood between them and the tenebrae.

What is it? Relaina thought to him, still marveling at this new way they could speak to one another.

I can hear the tenebrae here. Not as clearly as I hear you, and not in words, exactly. But I think one of them wants to speak with me.

"Now?"

Darren nodded. He breathed deeply and the shadows around him disappeared, along with the mental tether between them.

"Then let's hear what they have to say," Relaina said. "I'll get the others."

Nehma, Thea, Catrin, and Fabian waited at the base of the staircase on the far end of the corridor, heads turning at Relaina's approach.

"He's healed," Relaina said, and Thea grinned at her, clapping her on the back as they followed Relaina back into the dungeons. She couldn't help but smile a little.

Soon the three healers were facing the door nearby, skin alight. For the first time, Relaina studied their light more closely—none of their markings created a discernible image or object, just indistinct shapes and swirls. She'd have to ask Nehma about that later.

"Darren, are you certain they aren't trying to deceive you?" Fabian asked.

Darren's brow furrowed as his eyes went black again. His power flickered to life, its presence ghostlike in Relaina's mind. "I believe they're sincere," he said.

Fabian nodded slowly and stepped back. The healers

unlocked the door and stepped inside. Relaina resisted the urge to take Darren's hand as they followed the healers through the door.

They turned sharply to the right, and beyond was a new corridor of cells, this time on either side of them. Relaina couldn't feel the tenebrae the same way Darren could, but the mood in this passage was different from the first, especially somber and menacing. The healers fell back, staying close to Fabian and allowing Darren to lead the way. He stopped at the third cell on the right. Relaina stood behind him.

"Greetings, my king," the prisoner said.

Relaina's heart skipped a beat. *My king.* The man's face was obscured in the dim torchlight, his voice ragged.

"Who are you?" Darren asked.

"Alaris Onnea," he said. "I was a member of Queen Arienne's personal guard many years ago, when we honored our vow to Calixtos."

Rage and terror shot through Relaina like thousands of icy needles.

"Are you a priest of Calixtos?" she demanded, stepping closer to Darren. The prisoner studied her, his blue eyes set deep into an aging face, now visible through the cell window.

"I am not. I was a reluctant soldier in Gabriel's army," Alaris said, studying her.

"You wanted to speak to me," Darren said.

Alaris returned his attention to Darren. "I did. I wish to serve once again under a ruler with just morals and a proper sacred bond to Calixtos."

Relaina glanced sidelong at Darren. She knew Darren's magic came from the god of darkness, but priests of Calixtos had committed such violence against them both and countless others. Was a *proper* bond with such a god even possible?

Darren took a deep breath. "What do you know of my bond to Calixtos?"

Alaris considered him for a moment. "When your power calls to us tenebrae, it does not feel corrupted the way your father's did."

Relaina could attest to that. Gabriel's power had felt like frozen knives ripping into her flesh, while Darren's was soothing, cool, like plunging into a mountain pool on a summer day.

"You seek freedom, then?" Darren asked.

Alaris nodded. "If I can prove my loyalty to you, could you grant me that request?"

Darren and Relaina both turned to Fabian. The king's gold circlet glinted in the torchlight as he nodded once, his face somber.

"How do we know we can trust you?" Relaina asked, narrowing her eyes at Alaris. He offered his hand through the barred window.

"See for yourself, King Darren."

Relaina almost shivered at the title. Darren hesitated a moment, then reached for Alaris's hand. Shadows appeared between them, Alaris's eyes going black. Darren released his hand after a few moments, turning to Relaina.

"He speaks true. I trust him."

Relaina nodded, and they both looked to Fabian.

The King of Evaria stepped closer, the healers close behind him, their light casting a bluish glow on the dark walls. Fabian studied Alaris for a moment.

"Tomorrow morning," Fabian said. "We'll have him released."

Chapter 2

WITHOUT THE MOON

"Still not a *whisper* of the king and queen's whereabouts, and you think now is the time to stage a full-scale attack?" Misenia demanded.

Jeremiah Andovier looked up from the map of Parea on the table before him, desperate to get away from the arguing nobles in the small meeting room in the healers' sanctuary. Misenia stood at his right shoulder, wrapped in silver furs that matched her braided hair and complemented her light brown skin. She stared daggers at Lady Elke, a broad woman covered in leather armor with annoyance on her pink face.

"The traitors have had the king and queen for six weeks," Lady Elke said. Misenia gripped the table with surprising strength. "Parea has been under their control for too long. We must *act* if we want to root them out before they establish a real foothold."

"Enough," Jeremiah said, and the room quieted. "We will not put King Stephan and Queen Christine's lives in danger. We cannot mount an attack on the city if there's any possibility of harming them or innocent Pareans."

Lady Elke pursed her lips but nodded. Jeremiah sighed and looked to the nobles, healers, and guards around the candlelit room. Aronn stood before one of the large windows with his arms crossed, his dark auburn hair cropped short in King Stephan's usual style. Behind him, the frost on the glass panes gleamed in the lanternlight, obscuring any view of the night and the forest surrounding them.

"We'll wait for the scouts to return before moving forward," Jeremiah said. "They're due back before dawn. We'll reconvene in the morning to discuss adjustments in strategy."

Aronn and Misenia remained behind as the others filed out of the room, returning to the main hall of the healers' sanctuary. Jeremiah was grateful that the healers had allowed them to stay here; it was only an hour north of Parea, and winter in the mountains of Lyneisia was brutal. Setting up a camp would've left them not only exposed to the elements but also more easily attacked by traitor soldiers.

"Captain Andovier," Misenia said quietly. "We have not had a successful mission yet."

"I'm well aware. I'm trying."

"I know you are." Misenia tapped her fingers on the table. "I just want to keep you apprised of the state of our people. Morale is low."

Jeremiah's back ached at the thought of it all. "Thank you, Misenia. Your council is appreciated."

With a tight-lipped nod and a bow, she left the room.

"Well, that went poorly," Aronn said.

Jeremiah huffed and turned to his nephew. But before he could speak, shouts echoed in the hall, startling them both. Moments later, Saheer burst through the door.

"Captain Andovier," the Evarian guard panted. "Our scouting location was sabotaged. Traitors found the old tower."

Jeremiah's exhaustion vanished. "The others?"

"Still fighting when they sent me off."

Jeremiah nodded, already leaving the room.

"Uncle—" Aronn started for the door.

"Stay here, Aronn," Jeremiah said, his voice sharp as he turned in the doorway.

Aronn frowned but nodded.

Jeremiah called three guards to join them, two Lyneisians and another Evarian who had traveled with them from Maremer. They stepped into the frigid night air with hardly a wince, mounted their horses, and raced for the tower. It wasn't far—minutes away on horseback, even in the few inches of snow, and set between towering pines. They'd cut a few branches from the trees to give a clearer view of the road to Parea. It had seemed like the perfect place to station scouts to avoid detection.

The fire from their torches cast an eerie glow on the blood-splattered snow as they arrived. Jeremiah dismounted and drew his sword. The tower loomed in front of them, unsettling as the wind momentarily died.

"You two, check the exterior," Jeremiah said to the Lyneisian guards. They nodded and set off, torches in hand. Jeremiah, Saheer, and the other guard made for the tower's entrance. Jeremiah stepped around a body on the ground, making his way toward the tower's heavy wooden door.

Winding stairs clung to the wall, crumbling in a few places. Before Jeremiah could assess the dark interior, a terrible cry rang out, and he raised his sword just in time to block the slice of another. The man's face was bloodied, his eyes wild, half-delirious as he attacked. As the others sprang into action alongside Jeremiah, two more assailants appeared from the shadows of the tower's base, swords in hand.

Gods in hell, they were relentless. He disarmed his attacker and ran him through. Shouts drifted from outside as Saheer and the guard finished off their own opponents, and they ran to aid the Lyneisians fighting two others. These traitors were heavily injured, too—at least if the loyalists who'd been stationed here were dead, they'd put up quite the fight.

Once they'd subdued the remaining traitors, Jeremiah wiped the blood from his sword onto his cloak, his breath hot against the frosty night air as his heart finally slowed. The forest had gone entirely still around them.

Saheer spat, her face gleaming with blood. She drove her sword into the snowy earth and swore. "Who are they?"

Jeremiah frowned at the bodies in the snow before them. "Erine Tarod. And one of the Norhen sons, I can't remember his name."

"Lyneisian nobles?"

Jeremiah nodded once. "Traitors."

"What should we do with our own dead, Captain?"

Jeremiah looked to the Lyneisian woman. "You found the others?" She nodded once. "We'll take the three of them back to the sanctuary."

Minutes later, after each dead loyalist had been retrieved and hauled onto a horse, Jeremiah approached Elodeus with a sigh, patting the palomino stallion's neck. As Jeremiah gripped the saddle to mount his horse, a twig snapped in the forest behind him. He swiveled, drawing his sword, scanning his surroundings and listening intently.

But nothing was there. The hairs on the nape of his neck stood up as his companions disappeared down the path, heading back toward the sanctuary. All that remained was snow and creaking branches. Jeremiah shook his head and turned back to his horse.

A fierce cold enveloped his feet and legs, sharper than the night air around him. He dropped to his hands and knees. He tried to scream, tried to move, but his body had frozen over, become beholden to some other force. The forest faded into the background as the cold spread more rapidly, squeezing the air from his lungs, choking him, shrouding his vision. A voice that filled him with horror slithered into his mind.

You shouldn't walk alone, Jeremiah Andovier.

Chapter 3

The Salt Bath

Relaina stood before the mirror in her washroom, frowning at the dark circles under her eyes as she freed her hair from its braid and shook out her curls. She sighed as she turned on the tap to the water basin, wetting her hands before retrieving the hair elixir Selene had given her months ago. In only a few moments, her curls showed more life again, shining in the candlelight.

Darren sat on the couch in the main room of their chambers, his gaze far away. He'd changed into a clean tunic and trousers, the red fabric reminding Relaina of the night she'd seen him at the Harvest Festival. He'd looked criminally handsome then, but this tunic's neckline dipped several inches below his collarbone, revealing more of his smooth, lightly tanned skin and part of the X-shaped scar that spanned the left side of his chest. He'd allowed his facial hair to grow in the last few weeks but kept it neat and short along his jaw and mouth. It was darker than the ash-blond tones of his hair, which had grown out an inch or more since their arrival in Maremer, yet suited him all the same. Tonight he'd pulled half of his hair into a small bun at the crown of his head.

Relaina glanced at her reflection once more before leaving the washroom, satisfied enough with her own midnight-blue tunic and fine black trousers. She paused a few feet away from the couch. "Ready?"

Darren pulled himself back to the present as he stood, nodding. His hand brushed her arm as they stepped into the hallway, his touch so light she almost questioned if he'd touched her at all. Gods, she *wanted* him to touch her, but now was not the time.

They arrived at the Seacastle's small dining hall later than the others, but no one commented as they took their seats, Relaina to Fabian's right and Darren directly to hers. The four healers from the Caspian Forest sat across from them, while Desiree sat to Fabian's left. A dull ache thrummed in Relaina's chest as she noted Bracken's continued absence; she'd have to check on him later.

"Good evening, all," Fabian greeted them as the first course was served. Relaina was hardly aware of what she consumed as she listened to Fabian discuss protocol for releasing the first tenebrae prisoner in the morning. She still didn't fully trust this Alaris Onnea.

"Desiree, I know we are meeting tomorrow afternoon, but is there anything imperative to report from the city?" Fabian asked, taking a sip of wine.

"Looting continues to decrease in the eastern part of the city as we find housing and food for displaced citizens," Desiree said, leaning forward in her chair. The more Relaina interacted with Nehma, the more resemblance she saw between the aunt and niece, in their eyes and facial expressions especially. "The artisan market we've set up in the old temple began business today."

"Excellent. I'll speak more with Lord Vontair tomorrow about the status of trade agreements."

As the conversation continued, Relaina's attention was

drawn back to Darren. His small smiles and answers to questions were halfhearted and distracted throughout dinner. The uneasiness in her chest only grew when Fabian requested she remain behind as dinner concluded. The others left swiftly, including Darren, who nodded when she assured him she'd follow him shortly.

"I wished to speak privately," Fabian said. He retrieved a letter from a pocket in his cloak. "There's been a letter from Jeremiah."

Relaina's heart leapt and sank in a single moment. "Is he well?"

"It seems so, but there has been little progress in determining the whereabouts of your parents."

He handed her the letter, which she scanned quickly.

Fabian,

I've arrived at the healers' sanctuary just north of Parea. Morale is low as the deep winter takes hold, and it makes gathering information more challenging. Still no word regarding where Christine and Stephan are being held, but the loyalists do believe they're alive.

I'll write again soon. Please tell Relaina that Aronn and I are safe. I miss her already. And I miss you.

All my love,
J

Relaina returned the letter and swallowed her disappointment. She was glad Jeremiah and Aronn had arrived without conflict or injury, but guilt nagged at her more persistently at the reminder of her parents' imprisonment.

"The Parean winter will pose a problem for weeks to come," Relaina said. "Travel will be grueling and slow."

"The only consolation is that the winter will be difficult for our enemies as well." Fabian placed his empty wine glass on the table. "Your sister is arriving in Maremer soon to be kept under our protection as well, and they're unlikely to find her on the road from that Lyneisian village. Without a Gienty heir in hand to rally more support, it would be ill-advised for the traitors to harm Stephan or Christine."

Annalise. Relaina had kept her word to her sister—once it had been deemed safe in Maremer, she'd had Fabian send for her. While Seacastle wasn't home, at least she would be far from Zarias and others who would seek to use her for their political gain.

"Let's hope they retain what little honor they have left," she said.

"They will if they don't want the Pareans to riot in the streets."

Relaina sighed. Zarias was a foul bastard, but she was confident Archan would try to avoid widespread violence. He was a traitorous piece of shit, but he wasn't a reaper of chaos.

"Thank you, Fabian," she said, rising from her chair.

"One last thing," Fabian said. He stood and approached a small, ornate table beneath one of the windows, retrieving a wooden box he then placed on the dining table before her. "I realize this is late, and given recent events it may not feel right to celebrate, but I couldn't let your birthday pass entirely unacknowledged."

Relaina blinked. She'd nearly forgotten it herself. It had come and gone during the Battle of Maremer, overshadowed by violence and pain and fear.

She opened the box, revealing two exquisitely crafted

white steel daggers resting on red velvet. The metal gleamed in the light of the chandelier overhead, the handles wrapped in black leather. Relaina removed one, studying the slightly curved blade more closely.

"Fabian, they're beautiful," she said. Beautiful and wickedly sharp, by the look of them. The balance was perfect, the grip comfortable in her hand. Relaina's mind drifted to the sword still stowed in her wardrobe, the one Jeremiah had gifted her before she'd left Parea. She hadn't used it in months, but fighting with dual daggers felt so natural to her now, so effortlessly ferocious.

"I'm not well-versed in daggers," the king said. "So I asked Darren for his input. Consider it a gift from us and Jeremiah."

"Thank you," Relaina said, her throat constricting. "They're perfect."

"I hope you and Darren both find rest tonight. I'll see you in the dungeons tomorrow morning."

Some of Relaina's worry lifted as she stepped into the corridor and found Darren waiting for her. His smile was small but sincere as she showed him the daggers, thanking him too.

"I'd forgotten about those," he said. "I'm glad you like them."

They walked side by side as they headed for their chambers, but his demeanor grew more subdued with every step. Where normally he spoke with her about their respective days, now he was silent, his face troubled when Relaina glanced at him. She grabbed his hand, pulling him off to the side of the hall.

"Are you all right?" she asked.

"I'm fine."

She fixed him with a pointed stare. "Darren."

He took a shaky breath. "It's just...this morning. All of it—"

A servant passed by, and Relaina nodded to them with a tight smile. After a quick glance around, she tried a nearby door, leading them into a disused storeroom. Through a high window, a shaft of moonlight shone on the empty wooden shelves lined against each wall, and a few discarded rags lay on the floor. Relaina placed the box with the daggers on a shelf as Darren leaned his back against the door, rubbing his face in his hands.

"I'm sorry," he said. Relaina reached for him, gliding her fingers across the roughness along his jaw.

"Darren, look at me."

His strange, striking eyes met hers.

"Don't apologize to me," she said. "We're all a fucking mess."

A glimmer of light reappeared in his eyes as he laughed, but the sound died on his lips as quickly as it had arrived. "I...I wasn't prepared for this morning. And not just the tenebrae attack. They called me king, and I don't know if I want—I don't even know how—"

Relaina took his face in her hands.

"You don't have to know any of that now," she said. "You will have to decide when the time comes, but you won't have to do it alone. The fallout of this upheaval does not rest solely on your shoulders, love."

He stared at her, as if that had only just occurred to him, and Relaina's heart ached. Darren dropped his hands to her waist as she drew him close, her face buried in his neck. If she could hold him forever and tell the entire world to fuck off, she would.

She pressed her lips to his neck, and his breath hitched, his grip tightening around her waist. Relaina leaned back, a heartbeat away from tearing his clothes off as her eyes met his again, her pulse skittering at the heat in his gaze. His lips found hers a moment later. Their kiss the night before had been gentle, comforting, but now Relaina's blood sang as Darren's tongue brushed against hers and his fingers knotted in her hair. She needed more of him. All of him.

Darren turned them around, pinning Relaina against the door with his body, and her skin came alive at every point of contact, at his unrestrained hold on her. He left a trail of kisses along her neck, his facial hair gently grazing her skin.

Coolness broke through the heat between them, and Relaina inhaled sharply. Darren pushed away from her, his back hitting one of the empty shelves as he panted, staring at the darkness creeping up his arms. Relaina cautiously stepped toward him, holding out her hands. His eyes flashed obsidian before returning to normal.

"Sorry," he breathed. "It startled me. I didn't expect it to…"

"It's all right," she said quietly. His darkness called to her, even the small amount drifting along his skin. After a moment of hesitation, Darren took her hands. Their power didn't connect as strongly as it had that morning, but as Darren's fingers glided over the scar on her forearm, she felt a more forceful pull. Magic acknowledging magic.

Can you hear me? Relaina sent the thought to him deliberately, and he exhaled.

Yes. He took several measured breaths, and the darkness receded once more. Relaina's mind quieted, the silence profound with the absence of Darren's voice and emotions.

"I'm not sure I'll ever get used to that," he said.

Relaina stared at their hands for another moment. "I still don't fully understand it."

"Can you hear me if I'm not using the power?"

She shook her head. "My darkness only manifests if yours does first. And I can't manipulate it the way you can, with the shadows extended beyond yourself."

A long silence passed between them as Relaina tried and

failed to make sense of their connection, her darkness, her light. Darren cleared his throat.

"Should we return to our chambers?"

Heat rolled through her again at all that was left unsaid in his question, but she shook her head.

"I need to check on Bracken first. I won't be long."

"Take as much time as you need."

Relaina started to kiss him again, stopped herself, and patted his chest instead. The wolfish grin on his face was the most beautiful thing she'd ever seen. If she spent another moment in his presence, her self-control would disintegrate. She handed him her daggers and set off.

Bracken was staying in a different room now, close to those the healers had been given on the second floor. She hurried up the stairs, nodding quickly to a guard who passed by. Soon she was standing outside the heavy mahogany door that led into his chambers. She knocked twice with no answer.

"Bracken?"

A groan sounded from within. Frowning, Relaina opened the door slowly, casting a beam of light into the dark room. A slumped figure lay upon the bed among the blankets.

Relaina's chest tightened. Jacquelyn's betrayal still stung, but she couldn't imagine how deep that wound ran for Bracken. He had barely left his chambers once he'd ensured Relaina was all right after the battle.

Grabbing a candle from a sconce in the corridor, Relaina stepped inside and approached the bed. Bracken's unkempt brown hair fell into his face as he stirred, his eyelids heavy. Relaina sat gingerly on the edge of the mattress.

"Hi, Bracken."

"Hey, Laines."

"Did you eat today?"

"Hmm." He stretched and sat up, his white shirt rumpled. "I had some breakfast. Or...fuck, it may have been dinner."

"Good. There's food downstairs still if you're hungry now."

His eyes met hers, candlelight dancing in their blue-gray depths alongside the dull, ever-present grief.

"I may go back to sleep."

Relaina nodded. "Did you talk to Rhea?"

"Not yet."

"Well, when you're ready, she'll help." Rhea had helped Relaina manage the worst of her episodes in the direct aftermath of the battle. *The body can be healed with magic,* she'd said. *But the mind is more complex.*

Relaina had almost laughed in her face. *No shit.*

Bracken settled down again, rolling over and pulling a blanket up to his chin. Relaina blew out the candle, patting his shoulder before leaving.

"Love you, Bracken."

He was already asleep again.

~

DARREN WASN'T in their room when Relaina arrived, and disappointment prodded at her until she spied the note he'd left on the bed.

Head for the third floor. I'll meet you at the end of the hall, by the stained-glass window with a phoenix.

Puzzled, Relaina tucked the note into the front of her tunic and set off.

Curiosity and anticipation urged her faster as she ascended

the stairs. With a huff Relaina reached the third floor landing and stepped into the hallway. The intermittent windows were narrow, but the torches lit her way as she made for the stained-glass window at the end. Darren waited for her there, barely suppressing a smile as he held out his hand.

"Where are you taking me?" Relaina asked.

"You'll see."

Her heart skipped a beat as he squeezed her hand and led her through a door on the left. The scent of lavender drifted through the air as they entered a narrow stone corridor lined on either side with doors and small torches. Darren opened the third door on the right, ushering her inside.

The room was small, the steamy air heavy with that same lavender scent. Before her was a stone bath set into the floor, surrounded by several candles that cast a low glow on the water, the stone floor, Darren's face. He released her hand and took a step back, grabbing the hem of his tunic and pulling it over his head. The X-shaped scar that spanned the left side of his chest stood out among the rest of his smaller scars, various healed wounds he'd acquired over the years. Another smile graced his face as Relaina looked him up and down. He was so gods-damned beautiful it hurt.

Relaina kicked off her boots and tossed them into the corner, snaking her arms around his waist before kissing his neck, melting into the warmth that radiated off his bare chest.

"We have a bath in our chambers, you know," she said, her voice low next to his ear. He laughed softly.

"We do, but not like this."

Relaina glanced at the bath again, at the steaming water that ran from a spout in the wall and exited into a little drain at the side of the room. "How did you know about this place?"

"I explore the palace while you train with Nehma." Darren drew her attention away from the bath again as he ran his fingers down the side of her neck, tracing the shadowfire scar that began at her jaw. The faintest hint of his magic tugged at her. Just as she began to pull away to discard her own tunic, he drew her back, his lips seeking hers almost desperately. Urgency colored their desire as their hands roamed, and Relaina broke away from him with a soft moan when he reached between her thighs. They fumbled to remove their clothing, impatient, and stepped into the bath.

Relaina sank into the hot water as he pulled her close again. It wasn't unlike their first time, when Darren had touched her carefully, almost reverently, but Relaina's very skin was on fire, and all she craved was *more*.

"Touch me, damn you," she half-whispered, half-growled as he kissed her neck, his fingers gliding across her slick skin, once again pulling at the darkness contained in her scars. Darren leaned back for a moment, breathing heavily, and then grabbed her waist, lifting her above the water and onto the stone floor.

He stood in the bath, kissing the skin between her breasts, and Relaina wove her fingers into his hair. Darkness appeared along his arms and hands. The coolness of the magic was a stark contrast to the warmth of his mouth, the roughness of his jaw, and he hesitated, his eyes uncertain as he searched her face. Relaina leaned down and kissed him again, reveling in the heat and cold surrounding them, drawing them together. Darren continued downward, his hands roving over her breasts before pushing her legs apart. The kisses he pressed slowly, deliberately to her inner thighs brought Relaina close to incineration.

"Darren," she said. "Should we be doing this here?"

He lifted his head, eyes locking on hers, and she forgot how to breathe.

"I don't see why not. You'll just have to be quiet, Princess," he said, dipping his head to lightly bite the soft skin of her left thigh. *Gods in fucking hell.* Relaina pulled at his hair before she could stop herself. He smirked. "Shall I continue?"

She nodded.

"Lie back," he said, and a thrill shot through her middle. She did as he said, and he dipped his head again, lightly flicking her clit with his tongue before increasing the pressure. She closed her eyes, whimpering softly. With the expert work of his tongue, lips, and fingers he brought her to the precipice of climax within minutes. Waves of pleasure built and spread down her thighs until they reached a crest, and release rushed through her, her back arching. Darren's strong hands gripped her thighs as her orgasm peaked and subsided.

"Darren," she gasped, tugging his hair so he would lift his head as she sat upright again. "Are you still taking the crían?"

"Every week." He pressed his lips to her sternum. When his eyes met hers again, they twinkled with lust and mischief. "Why do you ask?"

Relaina wrapped her legs around his upper body. "I think you know why."

Darren smirked as he placed his hands on the floor on either side of her and lifted himself from the bath, water running down his smooth, muscular arms and the planes of his chest. Wisps of darkness curled up his arms, floating gently as Relaina shifted and lay on her back again, allowing him room to fully emerge and climb on top of her. When they were eye-to-eye, he leaned down, his teeth grazing her ear.

"I want you to tell me," he said, his voice low. He brushed his thumb along her jaw, briefly touching the edge of her scar, and Relaina closed her eyes, her darkness responding to his. It connected them further, in its strange way, and Relaina felt his delight in what he was doing to her, his anticipation as he waited for her to speak. But she didn't need to speak now. She opened her eyes and held his gaze.

I want you to fuck me.

His eyes widened, a smile playing at his lips. "Out loud."

Relaina squirmed and lifted her hips as his erection pressed against her, and the contact drew a groan from him.

"You're awfully demanding today, aren't you?" she said, running her fingers through his hair. He grinned.

"You usually like it."

"Oh, I like it." Relaina hitched one of her legs around his waist, pinning him. *Just know next time, it's my turn.*

"I look forward to it." Darren reached between her legs, two of his fingers slipping inside her as his thumb rubbed her clit in gentle circles. Relaina dug her nails into his back. "But right now...tell me what you want me to do."

It took Relaina a moment to find her voice again. "I want you to fuck me."

Darren kissed her neck again, his breathing picking up as he slowly pushed into her until his hips were flush against her inner thighs. He began to move, and Relaina couldn't stop the moan that fell from her lips, lost in the feeling of him inside her.

"Quiet, love," he said in her ear, and Relaina clamped her mouth shut, muffling another whimper as he moved his hips. He knew *exactly* what he was doing to her. She closed her eyes as he continued working that spot with his fingers and thrusting into her again and again. Her hands traveled down his chest to the hair on his lower abdomen before reaching around to grip his ass. He kissed her as he sensed her impending climax. *Don't stop.* He didn't.

Her body shuddered and came undone. He climaxed shortly after, barely able to keep quiet himself. Breathing hard, he collapsed on top of her, the weight of his body pleasant as it pressed her to the floor. Relaina kissed his neck as the dark vapor receded again and disappeared.

Darren shifted onto his elbows, looking down at her.

"Gods," Relaina muttered, her skin still tingling, and he grinned again.

Any remaining tension melted from Relaina's body as they slid back into the saltwater of the bath, especially as Darren ran his fingers along her right forearm, tracing the shadowfire scar there. She breathed easily for the first time in a month.

"So my darkness truly doesn't cause you any pain?" he asked quietly. Relaina took his hand and kissed his fingers.

"No," she said. "But I noticed other tenebrae felt different, during the battle..." She lapsed into silence as those images played across her mind again.

"We don't have to talk about that if you don't want to," he said, snapping her back to the present. "I just...I've always been so afraid of my own power, and the healers still seem a bit uneasy around me too."

"You mean Nehma seems a bit uneasy around you," Relaina corrected, raising an eyebrow, and Darren laughed without humor.

"I suppose the others have been less fearful," he said.

"There's a lot we don't know about dark magic. But you seem to have decent control over it, which is more than I can say for my own."

Darren pressed his lips together, frowning before he said, "Unless strong emotions are involved, I suppose I do."

"If that's the case, what you did this morning was even more impressive."

"Well," he said, tugging her to him by the small of her back, "I always aim to impress you."

She laughed as he kissed her collarbone. They sat blissfully in the bath for a few minutes more before climbing out and toweling off, redonning their discarded clothes.

Relaina studied the scars on Darren's back as he pulled his

shirt on. At least a few of them had come from the torture inflicted upon him in Parea. Even now, months later, remembering his broken expression and battered body in the Castle Alterna dungeons brought hot anger to the surface of Relaina's skin.

Yet that anger was also tangled in warring emotions. King Stephan had given the order for Darren's imprisonment and torture, but he was still her father, still the man who had raised her to be a queen. And he was in peril now, wherever he was. Jeremiah and Aronn had been gone for two weeks, and knowing there was still no progress in locating her parents only added to her fears.

"What is it?"

Darren brushed his fingers along her shoulder, his brow furrowed. Relaina shook her head. She placed those worries aside for the time being and threaded her arm through his.

"Nothing," she said. "Let's go get some sleep."

CHAPTER 4

THE NATURE OF DARKNESS

Jeremiah stood in the snowy grove with no memory of arriving there. Had he slept somehow, or had the tenebrae pushed him away from consciousness?

"How *dare* you not consult me before possessing someone?"

A short woman with white hair and light blue eyes stood before him, her porcelain cheeks flushed as she snarled up at him.

"All I asked was that you keep watch on our allies, and now you've potentially revealed our presence to the loyalists. This may very well be the most foolish thing you have ever done, Kalmali. If your shadow weren't inhabiting him I'd rip into it until Calixtos himself appeared to put you out of your misery."

The tenebrae within Jeremiah recoiled, and panic took hold as the shadow forced his lips to move, speaking with his voice. "I saw it as my only course of action, my lady. My apologies."

"Save your flimsy apologies and let me *think* for a moment without you buzzing in my ear." The woman swiveled, her boots crunching in the snow as she paced. The tenebrae trembled, and Jeremiah tried lashing out at it in his own head. He cried out, doubling over, and the shadow shoved him back, taking his body firmly in grip once more. When the tenebrae looked up, the white-haired woman was inches from Jeremiah's face, fury blazing in her icy eyes.

"You will keep *focus*, Kalmali." She grabbed him by the front of his cloak. "You took him, and you will keep complete control, or I will ensure a very slow and excruciating death for you."

"Yes, my lady," the tenebrae said, using Jeremiah's own voice again.

"Where are *you* right now?"

"Hidden away near the tower."

The woman released him and stepped away. "You knew I'd be angry. Is that why you waited until morning to seek me out?"

Kalmali didn't answer. The sun peeked through the low-hanging clouds for just a moment, and the snow glittered before dulling once more. Jeremiah was trapped by the tenebrae's hold on him, but a small spark of hope ignited in his chest. He could fight it.

"We'll make this work to our advantage," the woman said, her tone cooler as she appraised the body Jeremiah no longer controlled. "Find some excuse to return to the Evarian capital."

The flicker of hope within Jeremiah transformed into fierce rage and terror. *No.*

"You want me to enter a place crawling with healers?"

"You accepted that and any other risk when you possessed Jeremiah fucking Andovier right near a loyalist hideout. You made a brazen decision and your assignment will match it. Did any of the loyalists suspect anything?"

"No, they had gone when I struck."

"Good." The woman stepped forward, grabbing Jeremiah's chin in her surprisingly strong hand. "Go to Maremer. Be discreet. Gather information on the Pretender."

Fear, raw and bitter, roiled through the tenebrae.

"How long am I to stay?"

"Until I send for you. I'm shifting my plans for this, so you'd better bring me information that makes me forget this mistake."

"My lady," the tenebrae said, and Jeremiah hated hearing it from his own lips, "It will be done."

The woman turned and stalked off, heading for a white horse that Jeremiah had only just noticed was standing among the trees beyond the grove. The tenebrae forced Jeremiah to turn away from the woman, forced his legs to move and traipse through the snow. He was present in his own mind, seeing everything the tenebrae saw, feeling everything his body felt, but he could not even blink of his own accord.

The tower appeared through the trees after several minutes of silent walking, and a man with warm brown skin and chestnut hair stepped into Jeremiah's path. His hazel eyes ran from Jeremiah's face to his feet and back up. He looked both annoyed and fearful at the same time. The man, whom Jeremiah could only assume was Kalmali, cocked his head to the side.

I suppose we'll be together for a while. The tenebrae's voice snaked through his mind. Jeremiah tried to push against the shadow again, to no avail.

"That won't work again," Kalmali said. His non-tenebrae voice was less menacing, less grating to Jeremiah's senses. Without another word, Kalmali turned, and Jeremiah was forced to follow. He'd heard the stories of tenebrae, of course, had seen Evarians possessed by them in the Battle of Maremer, but feeling it himself was a different type of horror.

Directly ahead, a familiar whinny greeted him. Elodeus was tethered to a tree branch by the tower.

"One horse won't do for our journey," Kalmali said, stopping several paces in front of Jeremiah's horse. Jeremiah walked on, the tenebrae making him soothe and then mount the beast. *We'll just have to steal one from your friends.*

As he rode back to the healers' sanctuary, Jeremiah tried to think of something, anything he could do to stop this, and a low laugh echoed in his mind.

I would save yourself the disappointment and give up now.

To any onlooker, he'd appear alone. Calm. He raged against it, against Kalmali, and the tenebrae merely gripped him tighter. Dread built within him at every familiar landmark on the way to the sanctuary. That one particularly knotted pine tree, the boulder that appeared to have split down the middle, and finally—

Here we are.

Loyalist guards spotted him immediately when he emerged from the forest.

"Captain Andovier!"

Panic overtook him, but there was no racing heart, no sweaty palms, no shaking hands. There was only Jeremiah stuck in his own mind, desperate to retake control and unable to grab hold of anything but endless darkness.

Saheer and several others met him as he dismounted, one taking his horse's reins.

"See he's given water and rubbed down," Kalmali's shadow said. "We'll be traveling soon."

"Captain Andovier," Saheer said. "Where have you been? You never returned last night and when we went back to check the tower—"

"I followed a lead into the forest after you left and it grew too cold to return," the tenebrae lied easily. "I found shelter in a nearby cave."

Saheer nodded, her face relaxing somewhat. "I know you're captain around here, but going off alone isn't wise. What lead were you following?"

"I thought another traitor had escaped last night's skirmish. I saw another set of footprints, but they circled back after I'd followed them deeper into the forest."

"Where are you planning to travel to, Captain?" one of the guards asked, watching the other lead his horse to the stables.

"Let's discuss inside, shall we? I'd like to warm up."

Jeremiah tried to calm himself as his comrades walked into the healers' sanctuary alongside him. They had no idea the danger they were in, and he was powerless. Perhaps, though, if he waited for the right moment, for an instant of vulnerability from the tenebrae, he could break the shadow's hold on him again.

"I'll be traveling back to Maremer," Jeremiah heard himself say as Saheer and the guard led him toward the meeting room. Saheer turned, an eyebrow raised.

"Maremer? Why so soon? King Fabian doesn't expect us for weeks or longer."

"What do you mean, traveling back to Maremer?" Misenia appeared, entering the meeting room herself.

"King Fabian and I had an agreement," the tenebrae made him say. "If we hadn't made any progress by now, I would personally return to seek additional reinforcements."

Misenia frowned. "Perhaps that would help."

"Uncle?"

The tenebrae turned Jeremiah, and Aronn stood in the meeting room doorway.

"Hello, Aronn."

His nephew frowned. "You're leaving?"

"I'm afraid I must. But not for long, I assure you."

Lies. All of it. Lies that would place everyone Jeremiah loved in danger.

Saheer sighed. "We'll send a guard with you."

"Very well," the tenebrae said.

Misenia stepped closer to Jeremiah. "Are you certain you're well, Captain Andovier?"

"I spent the night in a cave. I'll rest for a while and set off this afternoon."

That seemed enough to appease both Misenia and Saheer. Jeremiah's hope suffered another blow as they discussed who would lead while he was gone. *No missions without my approval,* the tenebrae told them. The two women left the room shortly thereafter, but Aronn remained behind.

"Uncle," Aronn said, approaching him. "I don't like this. It feels like a waste of time."

"I know you don't want me to leave," the tenebrae braced a hand on Aronn's shoulder, "but I must do this."

"But what about my parents? The longer they're with—"

"You've done enough, Aronn," the tenebrae said coldly, his fingers gripping Aronn's shoulder. "Perhaps you should leave this fight to those more capable than you." Hurt and guilt flashed in Aronn's eyes. He pressed his lips together.

That look on Aronn's face replayed in Jeremiah's mind as the tenebrae forced him to walk away.

~

FABIAN SAT QUIETLY in the portrait room on the first floor of Seacastle, quietly scanning the numerous faces in his presence. Nehma stood by the exit with Rhea, arms crossed as she glared at the old man seated in an upholstered chair across from Fabian and Desiree's couch. Darren sat on the smaller couch to Fabian's left, Relaina at his side. Anxiety radiated from the prince—or king, as some now referred to him— while deep mistrust set Relaina's face into a mask of scrutiny.

"Thank you for freeing me," Alaris Onnea said, his head

dipping low to Fabian. He'd been given the chance to bathe and put on fresh clothing, appearing less haggard than before. "And for your kindness."

"This is a tentative trust, and I'm sure you can imagine why," Fabian said, and Alaris nodded once. Every few moments, his blue eyes darted to Relaina and Darren. "You've agreed to share what you know."

Alaris's gaze shifted away from Relaina and Darren and to the healers instead. "Indeed. And I thank your light-wielders for giving me this chance as well. I hold much respect for you all." He inclined his head to Relaina, then to Nehma and Rhea. None of the women returned the gesture. "In the days of Queen Arienne's reign, tenebrae and healers both occupied the Obsidian Keep."

"And their magics did not harm one another?" Fabian asked.

"It was rare that a healer's light clashed with a tenebrae shadow," Alaris said. "But King Gabriel misused his power and drove away most of the healers, though I suppose he did keep one around for many years, before the raids."

Relaina shifted in her seat, her face growing pale.

"What did you know of this healer?" Darren asked.

"Only that King Gabriel kept her close and relied on her magic. She was a powerful Seer."

"And she was an advisor to my father?"

Alaris grimaced. "In a way. She came willingly to court, but in her final years there she was more or less a slave. I believe she disappeared around the time the healers in Terrana were driven to near extermination by King Gabriel."

Fabian's upper lip curled as he failed to mask his disgust. Gabriel had enacted a genocide against the Terranian healers from which Esran had yet to recover. Desiree's older brother and his wife had been killed in the raids, orphaning Nehma.

"While I am curious to know more of the dynamics of

healers and tenebrae in the Terranian court of years past," Fabian said, "we have met today for you to provide insight into Darren's power and how we can separate friend from foe as we navigate the interrogation of prisoners."

Alaris nodded, folding his wrinkled hands together on his lap. A furrow formed and deepened in Fabian's brow as Alaris explained the nature of the Terranian royal family's connection to the power of Calixtos. The origins, it seemed, were dubious.

"One thing we know for certain is that the tenebrae were meant to serve as an external vessel of Calixtos's power," Alaris said. "They are drawn to the main source of the darkness, the LaGuardes. Usually multiple LaGuardes hold a piece of Calixtos's power, so each tenebrae may choose which family member they wish to pledge their loyalty and strength to."

Fabian glanced at Darren, but his expression was unreadable.

"And if there is only one LaGuarde?" Darren asked, his voice soft.

Alaris inhaled. "I am not sure. That had not occurred until recently."

"What of healers with shadowfire scars?" Relaina asked. Alaris's eyes darted to the scar on Relaina's forearm, and she shifted and pulled at the sleeve of her green tunic.

"I'm not sure what you mean," he said.

"How do they manage the warring magics?"

Alaris's eyes widened. "Warring magics? You mean wielding both the light and the dark?"

Relaina nodded, and Fabian suppressed a sigh. More mysteries to uncover.

"I have never encountered such a thing," Alaris said. "Any healer I've met with those scars simply cannot access their light anymore."

"Are there sources you know of that might yield answers?" Fabian asked. "People, books, the histories?"

"Anyone helpful I may have known is long dead or back in Terrana somewhere. And I fear King Gabriel destroyed many historical texts during his reign. But I could search your collection here for books that may contain useful information. With your permission, of course."

Fabian had already scoured the library for answers about the tenebrae, but he was willing to allow this man to look all the same. Perhaps Alaris would find something he hadn't.

"So when questioning tenebrae prisoners," Darren said, his face still impassive, "will it be clear who I can trust, who has chosen to support me?"

"Yes. Some of King Gabriel's supporters will be outwardly hostile, as I'm sure you can imagine, and that will be simple, if unpleasant. But for any who attempt to deceive you, the darkness will reveal the truth."

As silence fell, Fabian caught Darren's eye. There was determination in his gaze, but also uncertainty—if the tenebrae loyal to Gabriel refused to support Darren, what did that mean for the power they held?

"Thank you, Alaris," Fabian said. "For your own safety, you may remain at Seacastle as a guest, and we'll assign a guard to accompany you at all times. You're free to use the library at your behest."

"You have my gratitude, King Fabian," Alaris said, standing and bowing deeply despite the visible stiffness in his joints. Fabian called for a guard to escort Alaris to a room on the third floor, and Nehma, Rhea, and Desiree left to attend to their daily tasks. Relaina took Darren's hand as he leaned forward and massaged his forehead. Fabian stood and approached a nearby window, gazing out at the rain-sodden gardens on the south side of the palace.

"We'll find answers," Fabian said, turning back to Relaina

and Darren. "I know it feels overwhelming now, but we have time. His knowledge gives us direction."

Darren looked up, the emotion he'd suppressed during their meeting now clear in his eyes. "Fabian, I...I have no idea what to make of all this."

"I'm unsure myself," Fabian said, striding back to the couches. "That Seer he mentioned. Do you both know to whom he was referring?"

Relaina and Darren exchanged a look before Relaina said, "It's possible that Seer was my birth mother."

Fabian blinked. Talea. Did Jeremiah know she may have worked for Gabriel?

"How is that so?"

Relaina shifted, and Darren held fast to her hand.

"Right before I killed Gabriel, he told me he knew my mother," she said. "He offered to tell me everything if I spared his life."

Fabian nodded. "I see. I'm glad you declined his offer."

"Declined his offer," Relaina said, shrugging a shoulder. "Stabbed him in the heart."

She spoke with nonchalance, but her free hand shook slightly. Fabian cleared his throat. "How are your sessions with Nehma coming along?"

Relaina grimaced. "Healing Darren's arm yesterday morning was the first time I'd been able to utilize the healing magic since the battle."

Fabian sat once more, resting his chin on his hand.

"It seems that the darkness clashes with the light unless it has somewhere to go," she said quietly.

"And this darkness...it is not the same power as the tenebrae?" Fabian asked. Darren shook his head.

"The tenebrae can utilize the darkness to bolster their own strength or project it to possess another person," Darren said.

"Or create shadowfire blades if they've learned how to do so. Relaina's magic feels closer to my own."

"I see. I will contact several of my Shadows and have them seek further information. In the meantime, we now know Darren can question tenebrae prisoners and easily tell who is a threat and who is not. Are you comfortable going into the dungeons to continue this work, Darren?"

The prince nodded, and Fabian smiled softly.

"Excellent. We'll see you at the Shadows meeting this evening. Relaina and I must attend a small council meeting."

CHAPTER 5

GREATER MEN

Relaina's mind raced as she sat at a table with Fabian, Lord Vontair, Desiree, and three Evarian nobles. She'd agreed to sit on Fabian's small council, but the confidence she'd held on her father's council in Parea was absent here. The eastern side of Maremer was littered with damaged buildings and homes, ship repairs had barely begun, and several Evarian holdings had been damaged or destroyed by the Terranian army, leaving some essential farmlands barren. Relaina stared at the tea on the table in front of her as Fabian discussed the crop yield for the coming year with Lord Elowen Rhoe.

"And the soil is stripped. We don't know how long these effects will last," Lord Rhoe said, his russet knuckles paling as he laced his hands together. Collecting her courage, Relaina sat up straighter.

"Darren was a farmer's apprentice in Parea for a year," she said, and all eyes turned to her. Her cheeks heated at their surprise; she ought to speak more in these meetings. She'd often resented her father for silencing her in Lyneisian council meetings, and here she was in Maremer, not utilizing the voice she'd been given. She cleared her throat. "I don't know the extent of his expertise, but he may be equipped to help in some way."

"Prince Darren was a farmer's...apprentice?" Lady Kenna Granger asked, raising a perfectly sculpted eyebrow. Her dark brown hair flowed in satin waves past her round, pink cheeks and rested at her elbow.

"Yes, he worked for Maurice Garnier in Parea," Relaina said. She pushed the thought of Maurice and Camille away before her emotions got the better of her. "He's now quite knowledgeable about farming practices."

"Then I'll gladly consult him," Lord Rhoe said. "But we should also consult farmers with more extensive experience. Are there any in the city?"

"It's likely," Desiree said. "I'll issue a summons."

"In the meantime, we must acknowledge that domestic food may be insufficient this harvest season," Fabian said. "This isn't a problem we can solve in mere months."

"We will need to import more grain and produce, then," Lady Jiteya Abara said, her voice quiet. She adjusted the embroidered blue scarf that kept her voluminous, fluffy hair in place as she took notes throughout the meeting. She was the only councilmember Relaina had trouble deciphering—her delicate features and dark brown eyes betrayed no emotion during these meetings, and her contributions were logical, if dispassionate.

"That poses another problem," Desiree said. "Most of our ships still need rebuilding, and many merchants have avoided Maremer since the fire and the battle. The Artemians are glad to trade with us, but their largest import is timber, not food."

Relaina knew it would be wise for them to send out envoys of their own to negotiate with other nations, but the repair needed for the ships combined with the impending food crisis seemed impossible to overcome. She fell silent again as the others discussed the issues in circles.

"I suppose we'll simply have to be patient," Lord Vontair said, sighing. "We cannot magically repair ships or restore healthy soil to the farmlands."

"What if we trained shipwrights from the displaced population or those who lost their business in the eastern part of the city?" Relaina asked. "Surely there are people who would be willing to learn those skills."

Lord Vontair's mustache twitched as he considered. "Perhaps."

"We could pay them," Relaina said. "I believe you mentioned that there are some unallocated funds remaining from repairs that are already underway."

"An excellent idea, Princess Relaina," Lady Abara said, looking up from her piece of parchment. Relaina smiled in return even as her heart tightened at the title. *I'm not a princess. I never was.*

"We should also halt repairs on city buildings until we have at least a dozen ships in sailing condition," Desiree said. "Let's move those workers to the docks and shipyard."

Despite Lord Vontair wringing his hands at spending the remaining funds, Fabian approved the plan and adjourned the meeting within minutes. He didn't ask Relaina to stay behind again, but she lingered by the fireplace as the others took their leave.

"Does something trouble you?" Fabian asked, joining her by the fire.

Relaina watched the flames for a moment. "What would happen if they find out I'm not a princess?"

"Hmm." Fabian removed the golden circlet from his head and placed it on the mantel, massaging his forehead. "I should think you are still a princess, even if not by blood."

"Even though I relinquished the crown?"

"In my eyes, all you relinquished was your status as heir. To be stripped of the title of princess, Stephan and Christine would need to make a decree. I don't believe they would do that."

The dull ache of her grief throbbed in her gut. "I don't believe they would, either."

"And even if you were no longer a princess of Lyneisia, you are, by blood, the daughter of my intended. Not to mention you've helped this city through a battle and its aftermath. You could simply be the Princess of Maremer, if you so wish."

Relaina felt a small smile tug at her lips. "That's a title I would be honored to carry."

DARREN HAD ARRIVED FAR TOO EARLY for the Shadow meeting. He sat in his usual place at the table, his eyes lingering on the chairs that were and would remain empty. Katarina's made his stomach twist with grief; Jacquelyn's filled him with contempt.

As the minutes passed, several Shadows of Maremer trickled in, wearing their Shadow gear and silent. Most of them did at least nod in Darren's direction, and their casual acceptance of his presence in each meeting wasn't something he took for granted. The Shadows never made him feel untrustworthy or feared.

The darkness in his veins rippled subtly, and his optimism faltered. But Relaina was right—he'd exercised plenty of control the day before, and even the healers hadn't seemed bothered by his darkness.

The doors opened again, and Relaina stepped inside, clad in the same green tunic as earlier that morning. Her eyes were dull with fatigue until they met Darren's, and she smiled. His heart softened at the warmth in her gaze.

"Early again?" she asked, taking her seat to his left. He leaned back, sighing.

"I tried to sleep some while you trained with Nehma, but after this morning..."

"Alaris gave us much to consider."

Darren studied her for a moment.

"Are you all right?" he asked, his voice just above a whisper. Relaina's smile was sad this time.

"As much as I can be."

Before Darren could respond, Bracken entered the room, halting their conversation. His brown hair was flattened on one side, his gray tunic and trousers wrinkled, but he was there, and that was better than the past five meetings. He trudged over to them and sat beside Relaina, his shoulders sagging as he sank further into the chair.

"Hello, Bracken," Relaina said, the surprise in her voice poorly disguised.

"Laines. Darren." He only glanced at them for a moment, but there was a hint of color in his fair cheeks, and lucidity in his eyes that hadn't been present for weeks. "Ah, here's the wine."

Servants distributed flagons and cups around the table with practiced efficiency before retreating once more, and Bracken poured himself a generous amount.

"Don't worry," Bracken said, waving his hand at Relaina's raised eyebrows. "I won't overdo it. *Some* people at this table know their limits."

Relaina rolled her eyes. "I won't be doing that ever again."

Darren's face flushed at the memory. It was the first time she'd kissed him, the first time she'd admitted she cared for him.

He reached for the wine in front of them, forcing his focus back to the imminent meeting. After conversing with Alaris, Darren wondered if any of the Shadows might have information that could help them find answers about his magic. And maybe even Relaina's.

King Fabian appeared moments later, clad in his usual red. The circlet resting on his forehead captured and enhanced the gold in his brown eyes. They all stood as he entered the room and settled in his chair at the head of the table.

"Good evening, all," he said, and the Shadows were seated.

He started to speak again, but a guard hurried toward him, bowing quickly before leaning down to whisper in his ear. Darren could hear neither the guard nor Fabian from where he sat, but Fabian's eyes shot to Darren.

"My apologies, our meeting must be postponed. Relaina, Darren," he said, omitting their titles despite their mixed company. "Come with me, please."

Darren's pulse quickened, his power shimmering beneath his skin in response. Relaina took his hand as they stood and followed Fabian into the corridor.

"Fabian, what's happened?" Darren asked, and Fabian slowed his pace and turned, frowning.

"Three Terranian nobles are here," he said. "I meant to tell you they were ahead of schedule for arrival, but it slipped my mind with the events of yesterday and this morning."

Darren stopped in his tracks, and Relaina and Fabian paused with him.

"Which nobles?" he asked, hating how afraid he sounded.

"Lord Delimont, Lady Tryali, and Lady Eyern," Fabian said.

Lady Eyern was neutral enough, but Lady Tryali and Lord Delimont had always supported Gabriel. And they'd shown Darren nothing but contempt or apathy when his father had tormented him in front of them.

"I'm sure Lord Delimont won't be pleased that his wife is in the dungeons," Darren said.

"Likely not. But if he and the others are sincerely here to

engage in diplomacy, we can have her released to return with him to Terrana."

Steeling himself, Darren nodded.

"I know this is earlier than expected," Fabian said, placing a hand on Darren's shoulder. "And I know how much I'm asking of you. I wish I didn't have to."

The warmth in Fabian's hand and voice slowed his racing heart.

"I can be there," Darren said.

"Should I be there?" Relaina asked.

They turned to her, and Darren didn't need to hear her thoughts to know what she was thinking. They hadn't discussed how to proceed with the Terranian nobles regarding their relationship, or whether it was even relevant. And while Fabian had ordered witnesses to keep quiet about the fact that Relaina was Gabriel's killer, it was safe to assume that information had still traveled.

"You are one of my most trusted advisors," Fabian said. "Your presence is not only acceptable but necessary."

Darren took a deep breath, attempting to assuage his concern for Relaina in a room of Terranians. But a new fear took root inside him as they drew closer to the entrance hall—would he be able to mask and control his magic in their presence? He'd proven himself capable of reining it in, but there was no way to know what would happen when he faced them. During the battle, his raw fear and determination to protect Relaina had shattered his control and landed him in the realm of Calixtos for a week.

Before he could ruminate on these thoughts for too long, they arrived at the entrance hall. A heaviness settled in his chest as he stared at the doors. Fabian looked to Darren, his eyes full of resolve and encouragement. Darren nodded, and the Evarian king signaled the guards to open the doors. Relaina squeezed his hand once before dropping it.

Fabian swept into the room, exuding authority before he'd said a word. Darren forced his feet to follow, Relaina at his side. His heart picked up speed even before he looked at the Terranians' faces, and the darkness leapt beneath his skin. He tamped it down hard.

All three nobles were rain-soaked and travel-worn. Lord Leonardo Delimont glared at Darren. Even as sodden as he was, his appearance was gut-wrenchingly similar to Katarina's, with his golden hair, tawny skin, and brown eyes. Darren's chest ached. He forced himself to take in his surroundings. The sconces with torches, decorated with seashells. The sound of rain just outside the doors. The smell of balmy sea air that had wafted into the hall. His heart slowed, his breathing evening out. Beside him, Relaina said nothing, her attention locked on the nobles as Fabian spoke to them.

"Welcome to Maremer," Fabian said. "I fear you've arrived during our rainiest season."

Darren blinked at the other faces before him, now in focus and horrifyingly familiar. Lady Ines Tryali stood shorter than Lady Eyern and Lord Delimont, her bronze skin slick with rainwater, her black hair wet and limp on her sharp shoulders. She frowned at the mud on the hem of her blue skirts before turning her gaze to King Fabian, then to Darren. Her eyes widened, and Darren looked away.

Lady Lucia Eyern, the only one of the three who'd ever shown Darren any kindness, removed her fine leather gloves and tucked them into her gray cloak, her eyes darting around the entrance hall. Her dripping trousers clung to her thick thighs, and her silver hair rested in a braid down her back. She wiped the remaining water from her fair face, her full cheeks lifting as she plastered on a diplomatic smile.

"My apologies for our lateness," Fabian continued. "We are not prepared to discuss anything at length tonight, but perhaps tomorrow we can meet."

The moment Fabian finished talking, Lord Delimont stepped forward.

"I want my wife released immediately," he said, lifting his chin. "We will not be treated as lowborn miscreants."

Darren's insides went cold as Lord Delimont's words sank in.

"You will not enter my palace as nobility from a hostile nation and demand anything of me, Lord Delimont," Fabian said. The guards by the entrance tensed, almost imperceptibly, at the change in the king's tone. Lord Delimont took a step back, but his scowl remained intact as his attention shifted to Darren.

"I should have known you would hide behind men greater than yourself. It's what you've always done, isn't it, Prince Darren?"

Darren's eyes flashed with darkness, vapor curling between his fingers, and Relaina's responded, a glimmer along her scars. Lord Delimont blanched.

"You're on Evarian soil, Lord Delimont." Fabian's voice cut through the air, sharper than freshly hewn steel. "Mind your tongue, or I'll entertain no diplomacy with you or any other Terranian delegation."

Lord Delimont's lips flattened as his eyes narrowed. As the shadowy vapor disappeared from Darren's hands, a strange feeling settled in his chest, earnest and steady.

The Terranians held no power here.

"You certainly found me capable five years ago, Lord Delimont," Darren said. "When you begged my father to have me murder your cousin. And when you schemed to ensure I married your daughter."

The Terranian noblewomen eyed Lord Delimont. The nobleman's face reddened with rage.

"Miskah will show you to your rooms," Fabian said, his voice low. "Dinner will be delivered to you shortly, and guards will escort you throughout your stay to ensure your safety."

Lord Delimont started to speak again, but Lady Tryali grabbed his arm, her fingers squeezing.

"Thank you for your hospitality, King Fabian," Lady Tryali said, smiling tightly. "When can we expect to meet with you?"

"Tomorrow evening. I'll summon my council members."

The three Terranians bowed, Lord Delimont with no shortage of chagrin, and the guard, Miskah, led them out of the entrance hall.

Something within Darren loosened and snapped free, and his knees nearly gave way. Relaina exhaled loudly and took his hand.

"I'm all right," Darren said, his voice trembling a bit.

"You did well," Fabian said. "I'm sorry he was cruel."

"I wanted to throttle him," Relaina muttered.

"If he speaks to me or either of you in that way again, he can take his wife's place in the dungeons."

Darren forced himself to breathe deeply. "Thank you, Fabian."

The king's voice softened. "They're likely to speak directly to you during the meeting tomorrow evening. And likely to ask questions."

"I'll be prepared," he said, and Relaina's fingers tightened around his. "If they're here to speak diplomatically about the aftermath of the battle and my father's death, I'm at least willing to hear what they have to say."

Fabian nodded.

"What about the Shadow meeting?" Relaina asked.

"I'll find another time for that soon," Fabian said, grimacing. "I need to go speak with Desiree about these nobles."

Fabian bid them both goodnight, and Darren breathed in slowly again, his thoughts a blur.

"I'm going to find Bracken before bed," Relaina said, turning to face him. "He'll want to know what happened. Will you be all right for a few minutes?"

Darren rubbed his face with his free hand. "I'll be fine."

Relaina kissed his cheek. "I'll be quick, I promise."

Darren removed his boots the moment he entered their rooms and shrugged out of his clothing before collapsing onto the bed. He clutched a pillow to his chest and stared at the gently flickering candles on the bedside table.

True to her word, Relaina arrived shortly after him. She pulled her tunic off, retrieved a nightgown from the wardrobe, and climbed into bed with him. She leaned against the headboard behind him, drawing him somewhat upright as she wrapped her arms firmly around his chest and pressed her legs into his on either side.

"Will you talk?" he asked. "Or sing?"

Relaina kissed the top of his head. She began to hum, and on the second pass of the melody, she started to sing.

Oh, lend me your ear, love,
And know that I speak true:
There's power in the morning,
But also night's dark hue.
The sky is ever turning and the world is ever new—
If ever you know anything,
Know the depth of my love for you.

Her voice soothed the worst of his worries, and he turned his head to kiss her shoulder.

"I don't think I've heard that one before," he said.

"I haven't heard it in years, but it was in my head when I woke up this morning."

Darren inhaled slowly, focusing on the pleasant tingling that trailed after Relaina's nails as she glided them along his bare chest.

"It's lovely," he said. "You're lovely."

She ran her fingers through his hair. "You're going to be the end of me, saying things like that."

"Would you like me to stop?"

"Absolutely not."

Darren chuckled.

"Do you think you'll be all right tomorrow?" she asked.

Darren breathed in once, twice, then exhaled slowly. "I have to be."

Relaina tightened her hold on him, increasing the pressure across his chest and back, and another knot within him loosened.

"I hate this," he whispered. "I hate how much even seeing them affects me."

"I can't imagine how that must feel."

Darren sat up, lifting the blankets so she could settle down beside him. She rested her hands on his chest as she pressed her lips to his. Her mouth tasted faintly of wine, but nothing like it had the first time they'd kissed during her drunken stupor two months prior.

Part of Darren wanted to indulge in the kiss, to slip the straps of her nightgown off her shoulders and lose himself in the softness of her skin, but exhaustion nagged at him. Relaina's lips slowed against his, leaving one last lingering kiss before she pulled away, turning over so her back was against his chest.

"I love you," he said, his lips brushing against her neck as he draped an arm across her middle. Relaina took his hand and kissed his fingers.

"I love you, too."

CHAPTER 6

A HEALER'S HAND

Relaina's chest heaved as she straddled Darren, one of her new daggers at his throat. With a grin, he thrust his hips upward, grabbing her wrist to remove the blade from his skin. Relaina rolled on the sparring hall floor to avoid the swipe of his dagger.

"You're better than that, Princess," Darren said, flipping the dagger in his hand as he crouched, watching Relaina as she settled into her new stance. She was wearing her new Shadow gear, which Fabian had commissioned after her return to Maremer. The black fabric was reinforced with armored material at her torso, arms, and legs, and it contained numerous pockets and holsters for concealed weapons.

"You keep teasing me, and I'll kick your ass," she said.

"That's what I'm hoping for."

Relaina lunged at him, an exhilarated laugh leaving her breathless as they continued to fight. They hadn't had much time to spar with one another in recent weeks. She'd missed it, this familiar song of metal scraping, hearts racing, feet dancing. The playful spark in Darren's eyes brought her back to the first time they'd fought in the Parean underground—how had she not recognized him immediately, with those stunning brown eyes and that infectious laugh?

She couldn't bring herself to be disappointed as Darren pinned her, holding her left wrist at her back in one hand and a blade at her throat in the other.

"You're normally far less tolerant of losing," he said in her ear, just before releasing her. Relaina retrieved the dagger he'd knocked from her hand and sheathed both of them at her hips. She blew a loose curl out of her eyes as they stepped out of the ring, making room for two Evarian guards to practice. The guards' fellows surrounded them, egging the two on.

"I'm just glad to do something where I don't have to think," she said. "I can just *move*. Nothing else feels like it comes naturally to me lately. I'm frustrated with myself a lot of the time."

Darren opened the door to the armory, and the sounds of the sparring hall dulled as they stepped inside. He quickly put away the daggers he'd been training with and turned back to her, taking her face in his hands. His calloused fingers brushed her cheeks, his eyes soft as they met hers.

"Remember what you told me the other night?" he asked. "We're all a fucking mess?"

"Oh. Yes."

"Don't rob yourself of the same compassion and understanding you afford others."

Relaina placed her hand on his, keeping it pressed against her cheek as she sighed.

"Relaina," a voice called across the room.

Relaina and Darren both started and turned. Nehma and Thea stood in the armory doorway.

"Shit, am I late?" Relaina asked. Nehma shook her head.

"I wanted to talk to you about our session today," Nehma said, her usual steady confidence upended by the shifting of her eyes and the furrowing of her brow. "I think you should bring Darren with you." She looked at Darren for the first time. "If you feel you're able, that is."

Relaina looked to Darren, raising an eyebrow.

"I'm able," he said, his expression betraying his own bewilderment at Nehma's invitation.

"Good," Nehma said. "Relaina, I think it will be helpful to practice accessing the light more freely first, and then we can learn to navigate it around your scars."

"Oh," Relaina said. "That makes sense."

"Do you think it's a good idea to be so close to my power?" Darren asked.

"We discussed it," Nehma said, nodding to Thea, who smiled brightly. "From what we've seen, you have enough control that it's a minimal danger to us. Everyone was fine in the dungeons."

Darren looked to Relaina for confirmation, and she nodded.

"We'll meet at the usual place, then," Nehma said.

"The usual place," Relaina agreed, and she and Darren left the armory and sparring hall, passing by guards fighting and heckling one another.

"That was unexpected," Darren said as they stepped into the corridor.

"Nehma's nothing if not practical," Relaina said. "I've made almost no progress since the battle. If there's a chance something could help, she'll pursue it."

"Even if she doesn't like who it involves."

Relaina opened their door and let him walk through first.

"You certainly didn't meet on the best terms," she said. "But maybe she's warming up to you now."

Servants had already delivered a spread of roasted meats, smoked cheese, bread, and fruit to the dining table in their rooms. After their lunch, Relaina took a moment to lounge on the couch with a cup of kahvi for a few minutes. She'd first tried some a week ago when she'd arrived especially early to a council meeting and found Fabian there with breakfast laid before him. It was slightly bitter, but rich and invigorating, and the effects made her feel more refreshed than she had in weeks.

She changed into ochre pants and a black shirt with laces down the front, eager to be comfortable during training. After tying her hair in a high bun, Relaina approached Darren in the washroom where he re-tamed his own hair in the mirror. A small smile settled on her lips. The blond strands were soft and dynamic, capturing the light in their cool, ashen tones. He gathered the top half of his hair at the crown of his head in a small bun and tied it off with a black ribbon.

"I like your hair this length," Relaina said as he turned. "You look handsome."

Darren smiled softly before kissing her fingers.

Relaina opened the doors leading to the massive central garden, a gust of sea air enveloping them, already warmer than it had been the previous weeks. A winter without frigid cold and snow wasn't something Relaina had ever experienced.

Thea held the door open for them as they arrived at the greenhouse on the far south side of the palace interior, smiling and nudging Relaina excitedly after she followed them inside. They all settled in Nehma and Relaina's usual spot, on a patch of grass by a cluster of flowering shrubs.

"All right," Nehma said, placing her palms on her knees. Her eyes shifted from Relaina to Darren. "Let's try you two connecting your power first, and I'll guide Relaina through the rest."

Nehma and Thea both summoned their light, illuminating the markings running up their hands and arms. Beside Relaina, Darren took a deep breath before releasing his darkness. The healers' light was warm and pleasant, but the light magic did not pull at her the way the dark did. After a moment's hesitation, Relaina took Darren's hand. Coolness raced from her scars to their hands as her power joined his. His grip tightened on her fingers, but he held the shadows steady, keeping them from spreading more than a foot away on the grass.

"Call upon the light," Nehma instructed, and Relaina did so, her arms lighting up with her own markings. This time, they were indistinct swirls like Nehma and Thea's, no flowers in sight.

"Now what?" Relaina asked. Beside her, Darren was calm, focused. Nehma moved closer to her.

"Focus on the light, the warmth in your chest and hands."

Relaina closed her eyes. Warmth pulsed in those three places.

"Now visualize it all moving to your palms."

Their training continued for another hour, Darren patiently sitting by Relaina as she struggled to manipulate the light. It was easier with him holding the darkness, but the exercises Nehma led her through were still a challenge. She practiced moving it all to her chest, then back to her hands, and by the time the session was over, both Relaina and Darren were exhausted.

"That was the most progress we've made yet," Nehma said. Relaina squinted at her from where she lay sprawled in the grass. "And Darren...thank you. Are you able to return for magic training again?"

"I'll be questioning tenebrae in the morning, but as long as nothing unexpected happens, I can be here."

"Excellent," Thea said, offering Relaina a hand. She took it, and Thea hauled her upright. Nehma's arms remained crossed over her chest as Relaina helped Darren to his feet, her dark brown eyes still cautious.

"Will you two be at the meeting this evening?" Relaina asked.

"What meeting?" Thea asked.

"With the Terranian nobles."

"Oh, gods." Thea turned to Nehma, eyebrows raised.

"Hmm." Nehma frowned. "Maybe at least one of us should attend."

"The more allies we have there, the better," Relaina said.

"I'll see you tonight, then," Nehma said.

With the afternoon ahead of them and the sky darkening with clouds, Relaina ventured to the kitchens to retrieve some pastries while Darren went to find Bracken. She met them in the library shortly after, pleased to find Bracken speaking with more energy than she'd seen the previous night.

"Don't know how you read books that long," Bracken said, gesturing to the tome in front of Darren. At Relaina's approach, Darren shifted a stack of books aside, making more room on the table.

"I'm not reading it cover to cover," Darren said. As soon as Relaina set down the various scones and layered turnovers, Bracken reached for one. "Just scouring these old myths since they might have information about...well, anything that could be helpful. My power, light magic—"

"My frustratingly unique situation," Relaina finished, picking up a book and a cinnamon orange scone. The pastry was Fabian's favorite and was fast becoming hers too. Bracken nodded as he devoured the raspberry scone in his hand and opened his own book, turning to a marked page.

"Then I'll scour one too."

Relaina had just immersed herself in a myth involving a quest through the Esrani desert when a servant arrived, handing her a letter with a quick bow. She found herself torn between excitement and worry as she read it.

"Annalise is arriving in two days," she said.

"You sound almost disappointed," Bracken said, peeking over the spine of his book.

"I'll be glad to see her, but...I don't know. I'm afraid she's leaving one unstable situation for another."

"At least there's a certain familiarity for her here," Darren said. "The village I told them about is friendly, but the accommodations are certainly not something a princess would be accustomed to."

"That's true," Relaina said. She leaned her head back in the cushioned chair, staring at the rain outside as it pattered against the high windows, troubled as she left her true concern unsaid.

How could she possibly take care of Annalise and be the protective sister she knew when she was barely holding it together?

A moment later, the same servant returned to the library, bowing at the three of them again.

"Apologies, Princess Relaina," he said. "There is a second message I must relay."

"Oh?"

"Lord Vontair wishes for you to accompany him into the city."

Relaina looked to Darren and Bracken. Darren gave her an encouraging nod, and Bracken shrugged. Relaina stood, closing her book.

"Tell him I'll be along shortly."

CHAPTER 7

A CLAIM

Gulls called overhead by the waters of the Bay of Trade, and Relaina stood at the rail of a small stone bridge overlooking the empty docks alongside Lord Vontair. The first two weeks following the Battle of Maremer had been spent hauling the burned remains of ships from the water and replacing the scorched wood of the docks.

"Foreign ships can now approach the docks for trade," Lord Vontair said, leading Relaina across the bridge and back toward the cobbled streets. Several buildings had been singed in the explosions that set the bay aflame, but most had escaped unscathed. Relaina followed the lord back to the guards that had accompanied them and held their horses while they viewed the bay. "Let's visit the trade market."

Relaina patted Amariah's neck, brushing her hand along her sleek black coat before mounting up. She tugged her Shadow hood over her head again. She wouldn't don the mask while venturing into Maremer in broad daylight with a council member, but the protection the rest of the garb provided was unmatched, even if it made her look less like a princess and more like a sellsword. Her daggers, at least, were less visible where they were holstered behind a layer of armored material at her sides.

But as Relaina and Lord Vontair rode through a merchant neighborhood and approached the open-air trade market on the western side of the city, none of the people seemed bothered by her appearance. The few who remained in the market stood at their stalls as they normally would, selling household items or tools to the occasional customer. Relaina dismounted when they reached the edge of the market, once again handing Amariah's reins to a guard who stood by the entrance, and followed Lord Vontair inside.

A long table had been set up at the back of the market, where three shipwrights sat before a long queue of people. Lord Vontair led the way past the line and stepped around the side of the table, greeting one of three.

"Lord Vontair, Princess Relaina," the woman said, standing abruptly and bowing. She had a fair, freckled face and fiery red hair. Relaina's stomach lurched. She longed for the day she could see someone with Jacquelyn's features and not have such a visceral reaction. She still sometimes started when she saw Catrin, and the healer had crossed paths with her numerous times over the past weeks.

The two other shipwrights stood and bowed. Several people in line craned their necks at the mention of Relaina's name.

"We are grateful for your interest in our work, Princess," the redhead said to Relaina. "My name is Osha. I'm the head shipwright of Maremer."

"I'm glad to meet you, Osha," Relaina said. "Lord Vontair and I don't want to delay you. We just came to see if you needed any additional support."

"Of course," Osha said. The other two returned to their seats and those waiting while Osha stepped away with Relaina and Lord Vontair. "We have found thirty citizens since this morning who already have some skills in building and twelve more who can be trained easily enough."

"That's excellent news," Lord Vontair said brusquely. As he and Osha continued to speak, Relaina glanced at the line. It stretched almost to the edge of the market, and more people were joining it. It would take hours for them to record the information of each person.

"Thank you, Lord Vontair," Osha said, bowing her head. "My apologies, but I must continue taking down these names."

"Can I help?" Relaina asked, turning from the line to Osha. She didn't have anything to do until the meeting that night, after all. And this was small, but a real, tangible way she could help the rebuilding efforts.

The shipwright smiled at her, and Lord Vontair's perfectly sculpted eyebrows lifted.

"Well, certainly, Your Highness," Osha said.

"I'll stay to help too," Lord Vontair said, nodding at Relaina.

Osha quickly explained the information they were to record on the parchment and gestured for them to sit in two vacant chairs to the left of the others. Guards instructed those next in line to approach them. Relaina greeted the man who scurried forward with a gentle smile, asked him his name, and began to write.

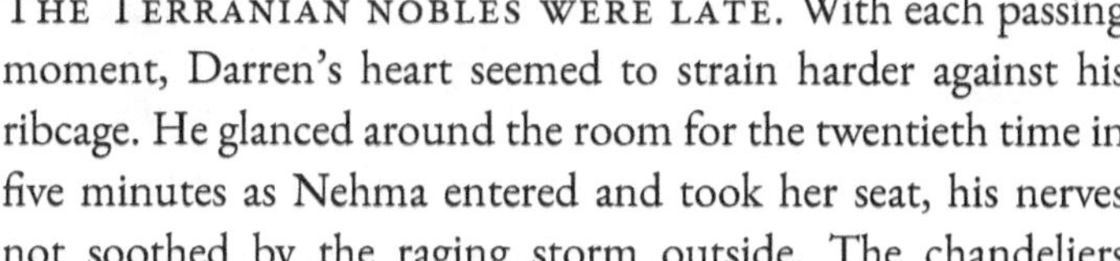

THE TERRANIAN NOBLES WERE LATE. With each passing moment, Darren's heart seemed to strain harder against his ribcage. He glanced around the room for the twentieth time in five minutes as Nehma entered and took her seat, his nerves not soothed by the raging storm outside. The chandeliers reflected brightly in the windows against the stormy night.

At the head of the table, Fabian spoke softly with Desiree, who wore her usual armor over a deep red dress. Relaina sat to Darren's right, holding a glass of wine and answering Lord Vontair's questions about the aqueducts in Parea. She wore a long-sleeved black chiffon gown with gold embroidery at the neckline. She sat beside Darren with quiet power, the shadow-fire scars on her neck and collarbone shining obsidian in the light of the chandeliers.

Darren wasn't sure why, but he breathed easier as he glanced between Relaina's gown and his own attire, which the tailors had created to match. Darren's black jacket was fitted perfectly, with the same gold embroidery stitched across his chest that matched the gold buttons on the left front side. He hadn't worn anything this fine since the Winter Festival.

"...And you think we could build them even with the cliffs?" Lord Vontair asked.

"I don't pretend to be an expert in architecture, but if they could build the aqueducts along the mountains in Parea, I assume the same could be done by these cliffs," Relaina said, taking a sip of wine. *Parea.* He'd only spent a year there, but he missed it, and he missed Maurice and Camille. He could only hope they hadn't gotten tangled up in the coup.

Lord Vontair nodded as Relaina finished speaking, scribbling on a piece of parchment, and Relaina turned her attention back to Darren. Her kohl-lined eyes watched him carefully as he reached for the wine on the table before him. The dryness of the red liquid burned his nose as he finished it off.

The Terranian nobles, now totaling four, finally stepped inside. Lady Tryali and Lady Eyern glanced at Darren briefly before taking their seats, and Lord Delimont appeared behind them, his wife on his arm. Fabian had released Lady Delimont earlier that day as a gesture of good faith, and her gaunt face and dulled blonde hair stood out among her well-groomed fellows. The Terranians sat at the end of the sixteen-seated table, only a few feet away from Darren's place in the center. Nehma sat closest to them on the opposite side, her expression unreadable but her posture stiff. None of the other healers were in attendance.

Darren braved a look at the Terranian nobles. The last time he'd been in a formal meeting with Lady Tryali and Lord Delimont, he'd ended up on the floor of the banquet hall in the Obsidian Keep, his bloodied face pressed into the stone as his father called for the priests of Calixtos to take him into the catacombs. Darren breathed through it. Beneath the table, his hands were steady.

"Good evening, all," Fabian said. "Let us begin. Lady Tryali, I understand you wish to begin our conversation."

The noblewoman stood, smoothing the skirts of her velvet navy gown. Darren didn't trust her placid smile.

"Good evening, King Fabian, nobles of Evaria, and other council members," Lady Tryali said. "We extend our most gracious thanks to King Fabian and the rest of you for your hospitality. We have come as representatives of the Terranian nobility and the court of the Obsidian Keep to build a new relationship with Evaria that will be prosperous for us both, and cement a peaceful future for our nations."

"And you have the full support of every noble house in Terrana?" Fabian asked. Lady Tryali frowned.

"We have enough that our leaving Terrana was unhindered," she said. "But there is much uncertainty and unrest, as you might imagine."

"Forgive me, Lady Tryali," Fabian leaned back in his chair, folding his hands in his lap, "But I will need assurance that the negotiations we agree upon are legitimate and will not dissolve amid inter-kingdom disputes. There is already conflict with nobles in Lyneisia that led to a coup."

"That's why we're here, Your Majesty," Lady Eyern said

quickly, standing. "No one has claimed the Terranian throne, though we expect several nobles may do so, and soon, unless a stronger claim is made."

Her eyes settled on Darren, and every gaze in the room followed her lead. Darren breathed deeply again. He'd practiced questions to ask—all he had to do was remember them now.

"I'm not well-liked among the Terranian nobles," Darren said. "Why do you think my claiming the throne would settle the current unrest in Terrana?"

"As the only living son of the last king, your claim is naturally strongest," Lady Tryali said. "Many nobles will bow to historical precedent."

"And many nobles were complicit in your father's...disdain for you...only out of fear," Lady Eyern said.

The three nobles fell silent, awaiting his response.

"Several powerful noble houses abandoned historical precedent when my father made slavery legal again," Darren said. "I wouldn't expect those houses to fall at my feet simply because I am the most-legal heir to the throne."

"We have ideas for how to ensure their cooperation," Lady Tryali said, her eyes darting to Darren's right for a moment. Darren's power came to life beneath his skin. *What does she want with Relaina?*

"Such as?" Darren asked, his eyes narrowing. Lord Delimont sat forward in his chair.

"Houses Reyes, Artea, and Maez each have daughters close to your age," he said. "Announcing a betrothal to any one of them would easily sway that house to our side."

Darren's heart took off, and Relaina went rigid beside him. Lady Tryali began speaking again, but his mind was moving too quickly to hear the first part of what she said.

"...And Corta Artea is twenty-two. But you may select

whomever you like, as long as she is a Terranian woman of noble birth."

"No," Darren said. Lady Tryali's tight smile remained in place, and Darren fought the urge to recoil. *Breathe.* For the first time since waking after the battle, he hoped the appearance of his darkened eye was intimidating, or at the very least unsettling, as he fixed the noblewoman with his gaze. "That's out of the question."

"It would be the simplest way to—"

"I haven't even decided whether I'll make a claim to the throne, and you've already made that prospect less appealing," Darren said. "There are other ways to gain loyalty and form alliances besides marriage."

"There are, indeed," Fabian said, his voice carrying through the hall. Darren's eyes met the king's, and the steady calm in Fabian's expression reassured him further.

"Of course," Lady Tryali said, her smile tight as she bowed her head.

"When will you need my answer?" Darren asked.

"As soon as possible," Lord Delimont said flatly. Lady Eyern shifted where she stood, folding her hands together.

"Lord Delimont speaks true," she said, her eyes apologetic. "We expect Houses Artea and Kratos will make claims soon. Within the week, possibly."

A week. He had a week to make a decision that would alter the course of his life and the lives of countless others.

"It would take longer than a week for word to reach Lues that a claim has been made," Relaina said. The firm clarity in her voice eased his mind. "Even if he made a decision tonight, it may not stop these potential claimants."

All four Terranians stared at Relaina, and every part of Darren ached to shield her from their eyes.

"But claiming the throne might still prevent challengers

from gathering additional supporters," Lady Eyern said. "We traveled here because we believe that with Prince Darren's claim to the throne and an established alliance with Evaria, much of the unrest in Terrana can be resolved without further violence."

"Rather than continue to speculate, it's best that we adjourn this meeting so I can speak with my advisors and Prince Darren about what you've proposed," Fabian said.

Lord Delimont's face reddened at the abrupt close of conversation, but he held back whatever snipe was on the tip of his tongue.

"There is still the matter of the Terranian prisoners in Evarian custody," Lady Tryali said, leaning forward on the table. The king appraised her with an impassive expression.

"While there is no sovereign of Terrana with whom I can negotiate, I will take action regarding those prisoners as I see fit," Fabian said, his voice low. "They aren't being mistreated, but they pose a danger to my people and are being thoroughly questioned."

Lady Eyern bowed her head once, and Lady Tryali followed her example.

"Of course, Your Majesty," Lady Eyern said, though something had shifted in her face, something Darren couldn't quite decipher. Was it sadness? Remorse?

"Tomorrow evening is the Feast of Stars," Fabian said, standing, and the rest of the table followed suit. "We won't be feasting this year while food supply is uncertain, but there will be a meal and music. You all are welcome to attend. We will reconvene to discuss this further the following day."

Two guards came forward and waited by the Terranians, who bowed to Fabian before they were escorted from the room. Darren fought the urge to grab Relaina's hand the moment they were out of sight.

"Relaina," Desiree said, stepping around Fabian and Lord

Vontair as they spoke quietly by the head of the table. "I need to speak to you about your sister's arrival."

Relaina looked at Darren apologetically.

"I'll meet you back in our rooms," she said, and he nodded, standing. It had been a long day—he planned to return to the dungeons tomorrow and was eager for a respite from these nobles.

But just outside the doors, Lady Eyern had lingered with one of the Evarian guards. She bowed quickly at Darren's approach.

"Do you have a moment, Prince Darren?" she asked. Darren nodded, and Lady Eyern stood taller, her face set. "I don't want us to leave here without achieving what we set out to do. I want to see you as King of Terrana, and so do my fellow nobles, even if they may seem less...congenial."

King of Terrana. And a week to decide.

"What I mean to say is, I want to make the prospect more appealing to you," she said pointedly. "Am I right in my assumption that Princess Relaina is your lover?"

Darren's face heated. She was more than that, but he didn't know what Lady Eyern wanted, or how much he should reveal. "She is."

"And do you intend to marry her?"

Darren's power stirred beneath his skin again. "That hasn't been discussed yet."

Understanding lit Lady Eyern's face. "I see. Well, if that would be your choice, you would have my support. There is much to be gained from marrying a member of the Lyneisian royal family. I would expect many past troubles between Lyneisia and Terrana may be alleviated."

Darren schooled his face into neutrality. "Thank you, Lady Eyern."

"I have a request for you, if you're open to it," she said, her eyes flashing with that same sadness he'd seen in the meeting.

"I know the aftermath of the battle must have been quite chaotic, and I heard you were even incapacitated for a week after."

Darren nodded again, cautiously curious. Lady Eyern took a deep breath.

"I received word that my wife, Ihara, fell in the battle," she said, her voice thick with suppressed emotion. "But it was only through whispers. I know you are questioning tenebrae prisoners, and I would humbly ask to be informed if she is among them."

Darren's eyes widened. "She's tenebrae?"

"She is. I know you must question them all for yourself, but if she is down there, I can assure you she never fought for Gabriel willingly."

Darren studied the woman, her clasped fingers, lifted chin, and solemn eyes.

"I'll find out if she's there," he said. "And I'll tell you what I discover."

Lady Eyern thanked him profusely, and he took his leave, unsure why his hands were beginning to tremble as he walked off.

CHAPTER 8

A MOMENT

Mere steps away from his and Relaina's rooms, the grip Darren had on his distress and his power shattered, and the darkness broke free, filling the corridor around him. The shadowy wind whipped around him with almost the same level of force it had in the battle, and he sank to his knees, reaching fruitlessly into the void to regain control. A startled voice broke through the blackness, and a warm hand found his shoulder.

"Darren!"

Bracken's face appeared before him, blue eyes wide with fear, his hair blowing away from his face in the wake of Darren's power. He had to regain control, or—

"Breathe, mate," Bracken said, placing his free hand on Darren's other shoulder. Darren nodded and did so. His throat felt tight, but he pushed past it. He exhaled, then inhaled again. Fear that wasn't his own flickered at the edge of his mind. *Shit.* He'd have to find Relaina, tell her he was all right, but first he had to get a grip on this darkness. He closed his eyes and gritted his teeth. Breathe in. Breathe out. *Pull it back.*

He reined it in slowly. The darkness finally fell back to just his arms and hands, drifting gently along his skin. He slumped against the stone wall of the corridor. Bracken joined him, settling to his left.

"Thank you," Darren said.

"I've felt similarly lately," Bracken said. "The rest of you bastards are lucky. If I had dark magic it would've engulfed the entire gods-damned palace."

Darren laughed and let his head fall back against the stone, staring at one of several torches he'd extinguished.

"I never wanted any of this," he said, his voice quiet. "This power, this responsibility…"

Bracken patted his shoulder, and some of Darren's shadows billowed around his hand. He blinked at the darkness creeping along the floor.

"I don't envy your position, but if someone must wield the power of Calixtos, I'm glad it's you," Bracken said.

Darren met Bracken's tired gaze.

"That means more than you know, Bracken."

Before Bracken could reply, running footsteps echoed down the corridor, and Relaina appeared, slowing to a walk as she drew nearer, Nehma close behind.

"What happened?" she asked, breathless. "I felt Darren's power…are you both all right?"

"Fine, fine," Bracken said, standing and offering Darren a hand. "Just having a moment, is all."

As he stood, Relaina's eyes darted to Darren's arms and the vapor still gliding along his skin. It was too much to draw it all back within himself for now.

"I'm headed upstairs, if you're both unharmed," Nehma said, adjusting the displaced sleeve of her bone-white dress. "Bracken, are you going up as well?"

"Actually I came down here to find out about the meeting," he said. "If Relaina and Darren are up for it, of course."

All three of them looked to Darren, Nehma eyeing the darkness drifting around him with a frown. Darren nodded.

"I'll leave you all to it, then," Nehma said, turning.

"Do you want to join us?" Relaina asked, and Nehma stopped short. She glanced at Darren and Bracken, then back to Relaina.

"I appreciate the offer, but I'm sure my sisters are eager to know about the meeting as well. I should speak with them."

Nehma strode off, the gold bands in her braids clinking together delicately. Relaina faced Bracken and Darren once more, her brow knit together and her mouth curved into a frown.

"She'll come around," Darren said softly as they stepped into their rooms. It only took a few minutes to fill Bracken in, but the lingering pang of fear in Darren's chest faded as they spoke. By the time Bracken left, the darkness had disappeared from his arms and hands, present within him but steady and calm.

A servant brought up a tray of tea, and Relaina joined Darren on the couch by the fire, thanking the girl before she left. The warm burgundy liquid tasted of rose and orange. Relaina removed the various pins fastening her hair, shaking out her dark curls before nestling closer to him beneath a shared quilt.

"How are you?" Darren asked. Relaina took another sip of her own tea.

"I'm frustrated," she said. "And overwhelmed."

Darren's heart picked up speed again, and he worried she could feel it. His conversation with Lady Eyern drifted through his mind. If he chose to make a claim, would Relaina still want this? She leaned back and looked him in the eyes.

"But more than anything, I'm proud of you."

Darren's worries shuddered to a halt.

"You spoke to them and stood your ground," Relaina said,

smiling against the rim of her teacup. "I know that wasn't easy."

Darren reached for her, letting his fingers linger on her neck, his thumb brushing her cheek. Relaina put down her cup and shifted so she could rest her head on his chest. He drew her close and kissed her hair.

"I would do anything for you," he said. He tightened his hold on her. "I...I know we haven't really discussed what would happen if I agree to claim the throne." His bravery faltered. Relaina took one of his hands, kissing his palm.

"A few months ago," she said, "I thought I would spend the rest of my life with some man I did not love, sharing his bed and bearing children for the sake of a crown. A crown I now know was never meant to be mine."

The future she described, the one she'd narrowly escaped, filled Darren with a profound sadness.

"And now I'm sitting in the palace of a foreign king, with a foreign prince, and magic abilities that make no fucking sense," she said, and Darren couldn't help but laugh. "I don't know what's going to happen in Parea. I don't know the nuances of what's happening in Terrana, and I have no idea what to make of the possibility that Talea worked for your father." She leaned back again, resting her elbow on the back of the couch. "But none of that changes this," she gestured between them. "I want to be by your side, whatever comes."

Darren rested his forehead on hers, closing his eyes. "That's good to know," he whispered. He didn't know what he was going to do, but this was enough for now.

CHAPTER 9

A COLD WELCOME

Relaina shifted in her saddle as she waited at Maremer's southern gate, scanning the grassy plain beyond for any sign of approaching travelers. Amariah huffed and shook her wavy, black mane, and Relaina patted her neck with a gloved hand. To the west, the water of the bay rolled gently to the shore. Its blue-gray depths reflected the overcast sky above, and Relaina sighed.

"I hope the rain holds off until we return," she said to Rhea, who sat beside her on a brown stallion with white markings. Rhea tossed one of her two dark brown braids over her shoulder, her face pink from the sea air. She'd elected to forgo armor, wearing only a long burgundy tunic and black cloak. But Rhea was an accomplished healer, and Relaina wasn't going to venture into Maremer without wearing the Shadow gear, not while she still struggled to control her magic when she was injured.

"We could find a pub or tea lounge in the meantime if it doesn't," Rhea said, craning her neck to look at the sky.

In the distance, four horses appeared, approaching the gate from across the field. Relaina's heart leapt, her previous worries about Annalise's arrival dispelled for now. Amariah shifted beneath her, sensing her anticipation.

As soon as Annalise's face was discernible, Relaina dismounted and walked closer to the gate. Her sister's eyes lit up at the sight of her. Relaina couldn't help the grin that spread across her face as Annalise jumped down from her horse and ran into her arms, laughing even as she cried.

"I'm so glad to see you," Annalise said, her voice muffled by Relaina's shoulder. Her golden hair was falling out of its braid, strands hanging loose around her dirtied face as she pulled back. She wiped the tears streaming from her gray eyes as the healers dismounted behind her.

Relaina looked her over fully, ensuring she was unharmed, and marveled at her. Their brief reunion in the forest hadn't given Relaina enough time to really study her sister—or time to tell her the truth of her own parentage.

She pushed that thought aside for the time being and looked to the healers coming up the path. Karra and two others she'd met before approached, one of whom was the healer Relaina had nearly stabbed for attacking Darren. The woman narrowed her eyes at her, but Relaina couldn't find it within herself to care.

"Thank you for watching over her," Relaina said.

"It was our duty and privilege to do so," Karra said, bowing. Her eyes flickered over Relaina's shoulder and her brows lifted. Rhea appeared on Relaina's left.

"Sister," Rhea said, offering her hand, and she and Karra clasped forearms.

"May Iros guide us," Karra said. "You're from Caspian?"

Rhea nodded. "And you near Parea?"

"Indeed. We must go there now."

Annalise hugged Karra, and the healer stumbled slightly before patting her on the back.

"Thank you, Karra," Annalise said. She turned to the

others to say her goodbyes, and Relaina took a tentative step forward.

"Have you had any word from Parea since you left?" she asked. Karra's eyes met hers hesitantly.

"No," she said. "Our sisters there were unaware of our changed plans, and I'm certain the winter makes travel even more challenging."

Relaina's throat constricted. She'd known it was unlikely to receive news from the healers, but between their lack of knowledge and Jeremiah's limited correspondence, her hope that Christine and Stephan were still unharmed dwindled.

She forced herself to smile as Annalise returned and the healers mounted their horses.

"Surely you all must rest tonight before journeying back to Lyneisia?" Rhea said, and Karra shook her head.

"We'll stop and camp later," she said. "But we must return to the sanctuary north of Parea with haste."

As the healers set off onto the grassy plains again, Annalise, Relaina, and Rhea climbed onto their own horses and ventured into the heart of Maremer.

The southern part of the city had escaped most of the destruction. Shops and inns and pubs lined the streets that wound for miles, and citygoers bustled along. Rhea led the way past colorful awnings jutting out from buildings, and music drifted from a pub just ahead. The sound of a jaunty fiddle tune made Relaina's heart ache all the more for Jeremiah's presence.

The streets quieted somewhat as they walked along, their horses' hooves echoing off several abandoned buildings on the right. Very little damage was visible from this street, but another block to the east would reveal the scars of the battle.

A cold, heavy raindrop landed on Relaina's forehead. She looked up just as several more hit her face.

"Shit," Relaina said as the deluge began. They led their horses to the closest pub, taking refuge in the warmth within.

"Welcome to Maremer," Rhea quipped, and Annalise grimaced. They found a table by a window while Relaina approached the bar. The door opened behind them again and three others stalked in out of the rain. The barkeep handed two other patrons their spirits before turning to her.

"What can I get for you?" he asked.

"Three ginger beers, please."

"You sure? We've got the best ale in Maremer."

"Another time, perhaps."

Relaina leaned on the bar while the man retrieved three tankards and filled them from a barrel against the wall. As Relaina waited for their drinks, wet footsteps came to a halt directly behind her. She turned, coming face-to-race with a man dressed in a damp black tunic. A small symbol was stitched into the front over his heart, a silver hand with a diamond floating over the palm.

"Can I help you?" Relaina asked, tensing at his proximity.

A cry sounded from her left, and Rhea hit the ground by their table, another man in a matching tunic standing over her unconscious form with a large bottle of whiskey. Annalise scrambled back, directly into the grasp of the third person, a woman nearly as tall as Rhea and twice as muscular. Before Relaina's fingers could close around the hilt of her dagger, the man in front of her grabbed her forearm, and the one who'd knocked out Rhea dove at her. Three patrons fled the premises as Relaina flung herself backward onto the bar, twisting her arm out of the man's grasp and avoiding the second man's attack. They collided with one another as Relaina regained her feet, drawing both her daggers and holding them aloft. The barkeep scurried down a back hallway.

Relaina circled the men as they faced her. She didn't have a clear opening to get to Annalise. The woman kept a firm grip on her sister by the table, her fingers digging into her Annalise's arms.

"You *can* help us, in fact," the first man said. "Our master will be very pleased to speak with you."

"I don't know who the fuck you are," Relaina said, her bewilderment narrowing to steely focus at the sight of the terror in Annalise's eyes. Relaina looked to the woman. "Take your hands off my sister."

"Or what?" the man asked. "You're outnumbered."

Instead of answering, Relaina lunged, her dagger drawing blood from the man's upper arm. He yelped and stumbled back, cradling his wound, while the second man drew a knife of his own. Relaina knocked his blade to the side when he struck at her, twisting forward with her other dagger to swipe at his chest. She cut through his tunic and flesh with ease, and a deep gash bloomed beneath his collarbone. Out of the corner of her eye, by the table, a white glow began to shine.

Before Relaina's opponent could notice, she had her daggers crossed at the top of his blade and sent a knee to his groin. He dropped the knife and crumpled to the ground.

Just before a broken glass hit her in the face, Relaina threw up her arms, stumbling back as pain erupted in her right forearm. With a growl, she brandished her daggers and stepped over the man with a gash in his chest, who lay unmoving on the floor.

"Not another step."

The woman had drawn a knife and held it at Annalise's throat. A small bead of blood appeared, running down Annalise's neck and staining the collar of her gray tunic. The first man breathed heavily, spitting blood onto the floor as his eyes darted between Relaina and his ally. Rhea hadn't woken yet, but her healing light still glowed on the floor by the table.

"Put down the knife," Relaina said to the woman, her grip on the daggers tightening.

"Come with us quietly and I'll release her," the woman said. Her voice was soft, almost gentle, but her hand was steady as she kept the blade pressed to Annalise's flesh. Relaina's throat went dry as warmth began to fill her chest. *Not now.* She tensed as she grappled to hold the light at bay, to keep it from growing and reaching her scars.

"Last chance," the woman said. A groan sounded by the table, and Rhea stirred.

"Tana," the man said, alarm in his voice. Rhea got to her feet, a bit unsteady, but her eyes focused quickly as her light continued its work on her head. The left side of her face was sticky with blood. With a look from Relaina, they both moved. Relaina leapt back as Rhea flung out two arcs of light that struck the woman's forehead and the man's chest. Both of them went down.

Relaina sheathed her daggers and Annalise ran to her, embracing her sister as she studied the figures slumped on the ground. The symbol on their tunics was familiar, somehow, but she couldn't place it.

"Are you all right?" she asked, looking at Annalise's neck, and her sister nodded, her mouth twisting as she held back tears. The warmth within Relaina began to grow again as her arm throbbed. She was losing her grip on her light. She turned to Rhea, releasing Annalise.

"Rhea," she said, and the panic in her eyes must have been enough. Rhea rushed forward, placing her hands on Relaina's shoulders.

"Breathe," she said, her light blue eyes calm. "Focus only on the light. Draw it back."

Relaina closed her eyes and visualized the inner light as she had in her training with Nehma. The warmth resided in her chest, mostly, not yet forming in her hands. She focused on its energy and took hold of it, clumsily at first, then with greater conviction.

"Good. Pull it back to your center."

Gritting her teeth, Relaina forced the light to heel and dim until it was nothing more than a faint speck, the flame of a candle deep within her. Her eyes opened slowly as she released the light, and it remained dormant. Rhea exhaled sharply.

"Fuck," Rhea hissed as she dabbed at her face, grimacing. "Who the hell are these people?"

"I'm not sure, but let's get out of here," Relaina said, taking Annalise's hand and unsheathing one dagger again. "We need to get to Seacastle and alert the city guard."

FEAR AND HOPELESSNESS gnawed at Jeremiah's soul as he rode along the silty path beside Kalmali. He'd been unable to regain even an ounce of control since the first time he'd lashed out against the tenebrae, powerless when Kalmali had killed the guard they'd sent with Jeremiah.

"Gods, being in your head is excruciating," Kalmali said from his stolen horse. He spoke to Jeremiah mostly in his own mind, but occasionally he'd speak aloud. "You worry about everything, don't you?"

Jeremiah tried his best to ignore the tenebrae. His thoughts weren't safe. No one he loved was safe. The shadow turned Jeremiah's head so he was looking directly at Kalmali.

"You have a secret." *You've been trying to hide it. I know it has to do with the Pretender.*

Jeremiah didn't know what he meant by that name. That white-haired woman had used it too.

"That niece of yours is who we mean," Kalmali said, his eyes narrowing. Niece. Jeremiah's gut wrenched at the word, and panic overtook him as Kalmali's eyes lit up with glee. "Your *daughter?* My gods. We'd wondered who Talea fucked all those years ago."

The shadow seemed to feed off the turmoil it caused Jeremiah. Cloud-diffused sunlight filtered through the trees around them, the gentle warmth an agony as he fought against the tenebrae's hold. Kalmali only chuckled.

"That explains how Talea convinced you all to take the child. Gods. Her birth is disastrous on all sides, a bastard child of magic *and* nobility."

Rage built within Jeremiah, but he kept it close this time. Expending that energy would do nothing.

"Ah, you're learning." The tenebrae made him face forward again. *Good, because we're due to arrive in Maremer very soon, and I'd prefer it if your attempts at regaining control weren't constantly grating my nerves.*

Unable to watch as Maremer drew ever nearer, Jeremiah tucked himself away into a corner of his mind. Perhaps no part of it was safe from the tenebrae, but he would try.

CHAPTER 10

THE FEAST OF STARS

Darren trudged up the dungeon stairs toward the waiting rain, fatigue nagging his every step. He hadn't found Ihara Eyern in the dungeons, but he had questioned five others, two of whom tried to attack him before he banished the tenebrae back to the realm of Calixtos. The others had complied quietly, proving they held no ill will toward him and that their magic supported his.

Pulling up his hood, he dashed through the rain, crossing the grounds quickly before entering the southeastern side of the palace. Guards and servants greeted him as they passed.

As he started to pass the doors to the entrance hall, panicked voices drew his attention.

"...They followed us into a pub and attacked." *Relaina.*

Darren flung one of the doors open. Relaina stood at the opposite end of the hall with Annalise and Rhea, speaking with Fabian, Desiree, and four guards. Blood stained the side of Rhea's face, Annalise's collar, and Relaina's arm, smudged where the rain had tracked through it.

"What happened?" he asked, walking forward just as Relaina noticed him. Fabian and Desiree turned.

"Three people attacked us in a pub," Rhea said, her eyes tired. Darren stopped a few feet away from them.

"Are you—?"

"We're all right," Relaina assured him quietly, her smile as soft as it was unconvincing.

"My sincerest apologies for this attack, Princess Annalise," Fabian said. "Maremer should be a place of safety for all."

With as much dignity as the young princess could muster, she sniffed and said, "No apology necessary, Your Majesty. Relaina and Rhea beat them, and I am glad to meet you. And glad to be able to freshen up."

Everyone except Desiree offered an appreciative chuckle. Rhea stepped to the side with her, Fabian, and the guards to give more details of the attack while Relaina turned to Annalise. Darren approached them, taking the hand Relaina extended toward him wordlessly.

"I want you to teach me how to fight," Annalise said before Relaina could speak.

Relaina frowned. "You want to fight?"

"No, but I don't want to be helpless in dangerous situations anymore."

Relaina exchanged a look with Darren. Sadness touched her eyes before she sighed and looked back at her sister.

"All right. I'll teach you."

DARREN LEANED against the back of the couch in his and Relaina's chambers, his arms crossed and brow furrowed as he waited for Pemma and Selene to finish Relaina's hair for the Feast of Stars. It was a minor holiday, an acknowledgment of midwinter and the spring to come. But even a modest dinner seemed excessive right now.

"There you are," Selene said, her voice drifting over from

the vanity. They stepped back from Relaina as she stood, gathering the skirts of her silver gown. "How do you like the braids?"

"They're beautiful," Relaina said, her smile grateful but her eyes tired. Darren had lost count of how many braids they'd done, but they were woven together in an elegant twist at the back of Relaina's head. "Thank you both."

The two women left swiftly, and Relaina remained in place, staring blankly at the closed door. Darren fidgeted with the cuffs on his midnight-blue jacket before approaching her.

"Are you sure you want to attend tonight?" he asked, brushing his fingers along her bare arm. The velvet sleeves of her gown lay gently on her shoulders, one partially covering the shadowfire scar on her collarbone. She met his eyes.

"I would much rather peel this gown off and crawl into bed," she said. "But I won't show any weakness to those nobles, and I need to be there for Annalise."

Darren knew she was going for his sake, too, and he was grateful.

"Will you help me with Lady Eyern?" he asked.

"Of course. You think she'll be easier to speak to than the others?"

Darren nodded. "She spoke to me the other night. She... doesn't disapprove of our relationship."

Relaina smiled. "I'm glad to hear that. What is it you'd like to discuss with her?"

"I'd like to know more about which nobles still have slaves."

"Slavery isn't widespread, is it?"

"No, it didn't have time to really settle in most places. Most Terranians agree it's a vile practice."

"What about brothels? Would they participate?"

"I would be surprised." Darren frowned as they approached the door. "Terranian brothels and parlors are well established and keep their workers safe and compensated."

"Good. Well, then, let's go find out more."

He kissed her temple before they ventured out of their rooms and toward the large banquet hall where they'd first met all the Evarian nobles. Every crystal chandelier was lit when they arrived, and a fire roared from the stone wall at the back of the room. Darren and Relaina took their seats on the left side of the table, greeting Annalise and Bracken as they sat. The Terranians were seated at the far end of the table, much like they'd been in the council meeting the previous night.

The dinner itself was cordial, full of light conversation as everyone ate and avoided the topics of war and politics. The Delimonts both wore black and spoke little, and Lady Tryali engaged Lord and Lady Vontair in conversation. Lady Eyern spent most of her time eyeing the room. Darren and Relaina would have to seek her company later, when everyone would depart the table and socialize over the feast's traditional sparkling wine. Beside him, Relaina remained cheerful with her sister, and Bracken said something under his breath that made Nehma try and fail to stifle a laugh.

A group of servants entered, carrying large silver trays with thin glasses filled with pink sparkling wine. After each guest was served, everyone stood with Fabian.

"To the promise of winter's end and spring's coming," Fabian said, holding his glass high. "And to finding our way toward a new beginning."

Darren lifted the glass to his lips alongside the others. He didn't much care for the taste, but the effervescence was pleasant on his tongue.

Chatter began anew, and several Evarian nobles swiftly left their places to approach others around the room. Darren exchanged a look with Relaina. She nodded almost imperceptibly.

Lady Eyern stood alone at the far end of the table, still quietly observing everyone else. Before any other nobles could claim their attention, Relaina and Darren approached the Terranian woman.

"Lady Eyern," Darren said, and the noblewoman flinched delicately. "Apologies, I didn't intend to startle you."

"Oh it's quite all right, Prince Darren," she said, smoothing her pale green skirts. Her eyes were nearly the same color as her dress, bright with curiosity as she studied him and Relaina. "Quite a gathering this evening, no?"

The pleasantries of nobles still grated his nerves, even after over three years of avoiding them. What was the point of meaningless conversation when there were more important questions to ask? Surely she wanted to know if he'd found her wife.

"It is indeed," Relaina said, saving him with her disarming smile. "Though admittedly more somber than usual. I hear those in the city are celebrating in any way they can."

Lady Eyern frowned. "I saw much of the damaged farm-lands on the journey from Terrana. Perhaps my house could provide supplemental crops. I own some of the most fertile land in the kingdom."

"I'm certain that would be deeply appreciated." Relaina offered a slight bow of her head, and Darren fought to keep his face unreadable. With only a few words, Relaina may have made a connection that would aid hundreds of Evarians.

She was far better at this than he was. At a subtle nudge from her, he cleared his throat.

"Speaking of farmland, Lady Eyern," he said. "I know you manage your lands fairly, but are there other nobles who still utilize slave labor?"

Lady Eyern took a sip of her wine before answering. "House Gerratt certainly had a few household slaves, though that was mostly the younger Lord Gerratt's doing. Since he's dead now, I imagine his parents would have freed them."

Darren stopped breathing. "My—the Gerratts are alive?"

"As far as I know. Reese had King Gabriel declare him Lord Gerratt after Queen Kacelle died." Lady Eyern's eyes widened, horrified. "Apologies, I did not mean to speak so bluntly about her passing, may the gods rest her soul."

"It's all right," Darren said, though his mother's name had sent a pang of sorrow through his heart. "So my father gave him the lordship and he took over their lands and holdings?"

"Essentially." Lady Eyern took another sip of wine. "Lady Carmen and Lord Kastor were all but prisoners in their own home, but I've heard they were both so grief-stricken that it hardly mattered anyway."

"I see." Darren took a deep breath. "What other houses would push against the banning of slavery?"

"You would find resistance with House Kratos and Maez. The rest of us have always found the practice appalling."

"I'm glad it hasn't become more established these past four years."

"So you would seek to abolish it?"

Darren nodded, and Lady Eyern granted him a smile.

"That is good to hear, Your Highness. I look forward to speaking more on this matter."

"And Lady Eyern," Darren said. "About your request...I have only questioned a few tenebrae thus far, and I haven't found anyone called Ihara, but I'll keep asking."

Lady Eyern's smile turned sad. "Your efforts are greatly appreciated, Prince Darren."

With a bow of her head, she stepped away, and Darren could have slumped into a chair with relief.

"Does she know a tenebrae prisoner?" Relaina asked quietly, nodding and smiling at an Evarian noble who greeted her in passing.

"She thinks her wife may be among them."

"Oh, gods."

Relaina was summoned away to introduce Annalise to Lord and Lady Vontair, and Darren stood by a vacant part of the long table and finished off his wine. As he placed the glass down, Lady Delimont timidly approached him, her face drawn.

"Your Highness," she said, bowing slightly.

"Lady Delimont," he said, inclining his head.

"I am sorry for what happened in the dungeons." Her brown eyes filled with tears that did not fall. "T-there were tenebrae sisters, you see, in Gabriel's war tent..."

"You aren't responsible for what a tenebrae forced you to do," Darren said, surprising himself with the steadiness of his voice. "I don't hold it against you."

Lady Delimont's mouth opened and closed several times before she swallowed, nodding. "Thank you... for ensuring my Katarina had a proper burial."

Darren nodded. "It was the least I could do. Several healers assured me they knew our customs and carried them out." Darren's eyes landed on Relaina, who accepted a glass of wine from a servant's outstretched platter. Lady Delimont turned to follow his gaze.

"Is it true?" she asked, stepping closer as she lowered her voice. "Did she kill King Gabriel?"

He stared at Lady Delimont, pushing down the fear that crept up his neck before answering.

"What if she did?"

Lady Delimont's features melted into relief for the first time since her release. "Then I would thank her and tell her I wish I could've done it myself."

She walked off, returning to her husband's side as Lord Delimont spoke with Desiree. Darren barely had a moment to exhale before Nehma and Bracken approached him, a conspiratorial twinkle in both their eyes. Bracken's lopsided grin widened as he leaned in.

"Meet us upstairs in a few minutes. Thea took two bottles of whiskey from the kitchens."

"Excellent," Darren said. The last time he'd gotten properly drunk was at the bonfire after the Harvest Festival. Even after she'd allowed him to be unceremoniously thrown out of the castle, he hadn't been able to get Relaina's flushed face and smile out of his head. And what he wouldn't give to see her punch Zarias Conclave in the face again.

Grinning at the memory, he turned to find her, and his heart dropped. Lady Tryali was speaking to Relaina by the banquet table, and Relaina's expression was murderous. Darren headed straight for them, but Lady Tryali left in a huff before he was in earshot. Relaina's eyes followed her, no shortage of loathing in her glare.

"What did she say?" Darren asked.

"Nothing of fucking importance," Relaina muttered, but her eyes could've burned a hole in the door even after Lady Tryali left the room. Darren wanted to press further, but Relaina's tone suggested he wait.

"Bracken and Nehma invited us to come upstairs for drinks."

Relaina's eyes brightened, her ire slowly dissolving. "Oh, thank the gods. Let me say goodnight to Annalise and Fabian."

Annalise had been given the chambers just across the hall from Relaina's. After a quick detour to allow Relaina to change into a comfortable dark blue shirt and tan trousers, they made their way to the second floor and knocked on the door to the healers' suite.

It flew open, and Thea nearly stumbled into them. Relaina steadied her shoulders as the tall healer grinned, her eyes glazed over. Darren suppressed a laugh. How long had they been up here that she was already so drunk?

"Finally! Come in, come in!"

Terrible, offkey singing floated down a short hallway with two doors on either side, emanating from the open door at the back left. The window at the end revealed nothing but the blackness of the night. Thea led them through the door and into a room outfitted with two plush couches and several chairs gathered near the fireplace. Empty whiskey glasses were strewn on end tables and the thick woven rug. Nehma, Catrin, and Bracken were all piled on one of the couches, bellowing a drinking song Darren hadn't heard before. Rhea was settled on the rug in front of the fire, her eyelids droopy as she took another sip of whiskey.

Oh, when the hour is late and calm,
I feel the urge to sing
Of love and loss that's come to me—
The joy and sorrow they bring.
So bring me whiskey and bring me wine,
And more I'm bound to share.
It burns away my hesitance
And shoulders all my cares!

"Relaina! Darren!" Bracken said, standing and leaving Nehma and Catrin to finish their song alone. Nehma had changed out of her banquet dress as well; each of the women present wore trousers and soft, billowing shirts of varying colors. It was the most relaxed Darren had seen any of them. Bracken squeezed between Relaina and Darren and threw his arms around their shoulders.

"Gods in hell, you're already halfway to the floor," Relaina said, stooping beneath his weight. "How many glasses of wine did you have at dinner?"

"Three, and then some whiskey before you got here. You two need to catch up."

Thea plopped onto the couch to their left, sprawling out and reaching blindly for her own drink on the table beside it.

"Oh! Now that Relaina and Darren are here, we can play the game!" Catrin said, her red hair loosening in its bun as she stood.

Darren fought a grimace. Relaina threw him a sympathetic look as Bracken herded them to the dining table behind the couches, handing each of them a glass and Darren a half-empty bottle of whiskey.

"I thought you said Thea took two bottles?" Darren said, smirking at the three others he saw on the table.

"I found more!" Thea said from her couch, nearly sloshing her drink onto the red upholstery. "We finished the first bottle while you four were at that dinner."

"It went on far too long, holiday or no," Nehma said as Relaina and Darren joined Thea on the couch. The whiskey burned as he swallowed, leaving behind an earthy aftertaste laced with something sweet he couldn't place. Thea shuffled to the floor beside her twin, nudging her lightly and drawing a smile from Rhea. Were it not for their starkly different personalities, it would be difficult to tell them apart most of the time. Darren gazed at them and the others, wondering at Nehma's sudden thawing and the healers' acceptance of his presence here. Thea had never been anything but friendly, but the rest of them finally lowering their guard around him was comforting.

"All right, what's this game you've been on about, Catrin?" Bracken asked, plopping down in the chair across from Relaina and Darren with a full glass.

Catrin's hazel eyes glittered in the firelight. "It's called Drink or Spill."

"That sounds messy," Darren muttered, taking another sip. Relaina smirked before leaning against him.

"All right," Catrin said, pulling her legs up onto the couch. "Someone will ask a question, and you can choose to either spill your secrets, or you have to drink. Simple, yes?"

"Simple, yet agonizing," Nehma said, slumping into the back of the couch.

"Only for those too afraid to share," Rhea said, a laugh suppressed in her gentle voice. Nehma stuck her tongue out at her.

"I'll go first!" Catrin said. She placed her glass down and rested her chin on her fists, her eyes traveling to the ceiling as she contemplated. "Ah! First question: Have you ever stolen anything, and if you have, what was it?"

They went around the room, starting with Bracken, who admitted he had stolen all of the Castle Alterna dressmaker's pins when he was ten. Relaina laughed, her side shaking against Darren's as she recounted how furious Lucinda had been. Rhea denied stealing.

"Five bottles of whiskey," Thea said, her face deadly serious. Everyone stared at her for a moment before she grinned, and they all laughed. Darren had stolen before, but the explanation was far too complicated and rather depressing, so he downed the whiskey in his glass to a chorus of disappointed groans. Catrin retrieved one of the whiskey bottles and refilled his glass as all eyes shifted to Relaina. She paused for a moment, then pointed to Darren.

"Does stealing a person count?"

Bracken howled, and the room erupted into laughter. It was nice to be able to laugh at something from the last few months, and she *had* technically stolen him from the Castle Alterna dungeons. Warmth bloomed through Darren as the alcohol slowed his ever-whirring thoughts, and he draped an arm over Relaina's shoulders as her body sank further into his. Nehma shrugged and drank.

"Oh come *on*, Nehma!"

"Not all of us are an open book, Cat," Nehma said, grinning smugly.

The night wore on with continued questions, each eliciting indignant yelps or roaring laughter at one answer or another. Nehma had refused to answer so many that she'd slumped lower and lower into the couch cushions before drifting off to sleep, snoring lightly as the rest of them prepared to disband for the night. Rhea hauled Nehma off the couch and bid them goodnight as Relaina and Darren made their way to the hallway.

Relaina walked ahead of him as they turned the last corner before their chambers, swaying as she went, and Darren sped up to take her elbow. She smiled and leaned against him.

"I love you, you know? I think I already did the last time I was drunk in this hallway," she said, her words slurred. Darren opened the door for them, ushering her inside. "Gods, I'm so glad to see Bracken smiling again. Did you see him tonight?"

"I did. And it's good to see you smiling too." Darren wrapped his arms around her, breathing in the sweet citrus scent of her hair.

"That whiskey was fantastic. I haven't had any in ages, though I thought about it nonstop for *weeks* when tailing—" Relaina leaned back, silent for a moment. "Those *fuckers*."

"Who?"

"The people who attacked us today in that pub. They were Quentin's."

He thought for a moment before the memory came to him. "How do you know?"

"The hand symbols on their tunics. I saw them on ledgers in his manor. Gods damn it, that means he's still in the city somewhere."

Darren tucked a loose curl behind her ear. "Then perhaps I'll pay him a visit."

CHAPTER 11

THE SHADOWS RETURN

"*Y*our Majesty. *Your Majesty.*"

Fabian peeled his face from his desk, the muscles in his neck protesting as he beheld Calliope standing before him. Her brow was furrowed, her hands on her hips. Not a single strand of her braided silver hair was out of place, neat plaits wrapping around her head in a crown. She pursed her lips.

"If I find you asleep at your desk again, I'm going to start checking on you in the evenings."

"That's not necessary, Calliope."

"You will work yourself to an early grave, my king."

Fabian frowned at the book he'd left open, full of more useless information that had gotten him nowhere in his search for answers about the nature of light and dark magic. All of it was the same as what he'd already learned. The tenebrae could project their shadows to attack or possess others, and, as Alaris had explained, they were connected to Calixtos, but not the same way the LaGuardes were. The LaGuarde family had been wardens of Calixtos's power for a millennium, with many calling them *death-keepers* or worse yet, *death-bringers*.

Records grew murky beyond that, and further details were infuriatingly absent.

Light magic, in contrast, was not bound to a larger source, but it was dispersed among a select few chosen by Iros. Only in the past five hundred years did the practice of light magic seem to have evolved, allowing light-wielders to manipulate their power for purposes other than healing. Nehma and her healer sisters were a testament to that.

"I find it difficult to find rest these days," Fabian said, leaning his head to one side to stretch the stiffness out of his neck. He glanced through the open door to his bedroom, studying the gentle beam of morning sunlight illuminating the rug by his bed.

Calliope opened the curtains as he stepped into the washroom to freshen himself and don his newly made protective clothing, fashioned by the same tailors he'd commissioned for the Shadow gear. This attire had taken more time to craft, as the goal was to disguise its true purpose. He didn't want it to be overtly obvious that he was essentially wearing armor at all times, and the red fabric and black stitching concealed the reinforced material well. While he was confident in the security of Seacastle, he also heeded his advisors' requests to maintain his own safety at all times following the battle. Prior to his departure, Jeremiah had agreed with them.

Thoughts of Jeremiah only deepened the ache of missing him, so Fabian tucked them away. He retrieved a leather band from his ornate vanity and began pulling his locs back as Calliope placed a cup of kahvi on the small table by his bed. "Remind me of my schedule today, Calliope?"

"Breakfast with Prince Darren, a private meeting with Lady Eyern, lunch, which should be used to *actually* eat lunch, if I may be so bold." Fabian sighed, nodding. She was right. "Then the meeting with the Terranian nobles this evening."

Calliope handed him his favored plain golden circlet, and he placed it over his hair.

"Holding these meetings with the Terranians makes me uneasy," he said, frowning at his reflection in the mirror. His beard was still neat, shaved close to his face, a single silver hair on his chin standing out among the black as one of very few signs of his forty-two years. "I'm not accustomed to so much uncertainty."

"I trust you to make the best decisions for Evaria, even with that uncertainty," Calliope said, bowing. "I will see you this evening, Your Majesty."

Fabian thanked her and downed the kahvi after she left. He pulled on a pair of boots before heading for the small council room on the first floor. Darren was already waiting for him when he arrived.

"I hope last night was a small respite for you and Relaina," Fabian asked as they took their seats at the small dining table. "Especially after the events of the past week."

"It was," Darren said, smiling gently. "She seemed shaken after what happened yesterday."

"Where is she now?"

"Sparring with Annalise." Darren picked up his own mug of kahvi and inhaled the scent before taking a sip.

"Oh?"

"Just teaching her the basics. Relaina told me she was frustrated after they were attacked yesterday and wanted some instruction."

Fabian sighed. "Desiree has guards questioning the pub owner and barkeep today. That incident was deeply concerning."

"Relaina thinks they worked for Quentin."

"I see," Fabian said, eyebrows raising. He hadn't heard a whisper of the man in weeks. "I'll have Desiree informed as soon as we're done here. But let's discuss the meeting tonight. What concerns do you have regarding the Terranian nobles?"

Before Darren could utter a word, a series of knocks sounded on the door to the small council room. A guard opened it, and a Shadow called Iryan hurried inside, smelling of horse and sweat.

"Your Majesty," Iryan said, bowing quickly after stopping at the head of the table. "My apologies for the short notice, but Lord Andovier has entered the city."

Confusion, concern, and joy tangled within Fabian at once. "Jeremiah is in Maremer?"

"Yes, my king. He is headed up the road to Seacastle as we speak."

Fabian stared at Iryan for a moment, baffled.

"Fabian," Darren said, warmth in his strange eyes. "We can reconvene later. I'll be in the dungeons until midafternoon."

Fabian nodded, exhaling. "Thank you. I'll send for you later."

Fabian's anticipation grew with every step he took toward the entrance hall, two guards close on his heels. What could have happened to make Jeremiah return with no warning?

The question tumbled around his skull as he paced for what felt like hours in the entrance hall. The moment the doors opened and Jeremiah appeared, travel-worn but unscathed, Fabian's jaw unclenched, his entire body nearly melting with relief. Jeremiah grinned and Fabian forced himself not to sprint for him, keeping his pace steady. Without a word, Fabian pulled him close before looking him over.

"You're back so soon," he said, smiling even as his brow furrowed in confusion. Jeremiah took his hand. Something strange flashed in his eyes, there and gone in an instant.

"I'm sorry I didn't write before I came." Jeremiah brushed Fabian's cheek with his fingers. "We've managed to gather some information on the usurpers, but we've reached a stalemate that will require additional support."

Fabian's smile faded. "Support from Evaria?" Jeremiah nodded. Fabian looked at the guards stationed around the room and lowered his voice. "I'm afraid I don't have additional resources to offer. Has something happened to the loyalists? To the Evarians I sent with you?"

"Many of them died in a skirmish shortly after our arrival."

"Gods. Saheer?"

"She's alive. I left her in charge."

Fabian pressed his lips together, backing away from Jeremiah as uneasiness took hold. "Have any of the Caspian healers come to your aid?"

"They have not. The only healers are those who live at the sanctuary near Parea."

Gods. If they lost Parea entirely, it could mean war with Lyneisia, and Stephan and Christine would surely be killed. Fabian took a deep, steadying breath.

"I need time to think," he said. "To plan. Why don't you get cleaned up and rest? I'll have someone bring you food."

"That's much needed. Thank you, dearest."

Jeremiah stepped forward to kiss him, his hand resting on Fabian's shoulder. As he watched Jeremiah exit the entrance hall, Fabian blinked, disquiet bubbling in his chest. *Dearest.* Jeremiah had never once called him that.

He left the entrance hall himself, bound for his meeting with Lady Eyern with a head that was anything but clear.

～

"Fuck!"

Relaina gaped at her sister as Annalise landed on the ground in the sparring hall and quickly sat up with a frustrated huff. Annalise's scrunched face relaxed somewhat when Relaina burst out laughing.

"What?" Annalise asked. "*You* swear all the time!"

"I do," Relaina said, wiping a tear from her eye. "But I've never heard you do it. It just sounds funny."

Despite herself, Annalise cracked a smile as Relaina joined her on the floor. The sparring hall was nearly vacant, at her request, so she was able to instruct Annalise with relative privacy.

"It's going to be frustrating for a while." Relaina patted Annalise's knee. "You just have to embrace that you'll be awful at first."

Annalise sighed. "We've practiced that one move twenty times."

"And we'll practice it two hundred times before you feel good about it." Relaina stood, offering her hand. Annalise took it and stood. "That's enough for today. Want to get some lunch?"

"Don't you want to eat with Darren?" Annalise asked. The sisters headed for the sparring hall exit, two guards nodding at the doorway as they passed and stepped into the interior gardens.

"He'll be busy questioning prisoners until later," Relaina said. She could sense his power even from here, on the opposite end of the palace grounds. It grew and dissipated every few minutes.

"He's brave," Annalise said.

"He's the bravest person I know."

"And to think you didn't like him at first." Annalise bumped Relaina with her shoulder.

"Don't remind me."

Relaina smiled at her sister as they walked by a large blue and green mosaic fountain, its design matching the colors of the pool close to Relaina's chambers. The fountain spanned down one side of the path, a thin sheet of water falling quietly down the tiles and into a drain below. Annalise paused to study it for a moment, and when she looked up, her eyes widened.

"Uncle?"

Relaina whipped around. Stopping in his tracks by the end of the fountain was Jeremiah. Her heart jumped into her throat. She grinned and dashed for him with a laugh, and he pulled her into his arms.

Relaina yelped—icy cold shocked through each of her scars, nearly as potent as the pain when they were first inflicted. She flinched back, and shock filled Jeremiah's eyes moments before the darkness did.

She pivoted to face her sister just before he grabbed a fistful of Relaina's hair and flung her to the ground. She broke her fall with the side of her arm, pain smattering up her skin.

"Annalise, *go!*" she screamed, barely able to get the words out before Jeremiah hauled her up by the fabric of her tunic. Annalise bolted down the path, yelling for help.

Jeremiah slammed her against the fountain wall, water soaking her hair as he took hold of her throat and squeezed. Her tears joined the fountain water as she gasped for air and looked into the obsidian eyes of the tenebrae that had over-taken her father.

"Jer—" she choked out. His grip tightened, and her hand flew to his, grasping at his fingers. Dark splotches filled her vision.

With a cry, Jeremiah released her, stumbling backward. Relaina crumpled to the ground, wheezing and coughing as air filled her lungs once more. She tried to scream, but the only sound that came out was a hoarse cough, accompanied by punishing pain. Jeremiah moved toward her as though he were fighting against his own body, his gait erratic. One of his eyes had returned to its normal brown. His face was anguished as he drew a knife from his belt, and Relaina scrambled away from him before realizing he wasn't pointing the weapon at her.

He'd turned the blade on himself, aiming for his heart with a trembling arm.

"*No!*" Her cry was weak as she regained her feet and tackled him to the ground, knocking the knife from his grip. He threw her off, and she collided with the edge of the fountain, her ribs barking in pain. Jeremiah's eyes rapidly changed between void-like darkness and brown, his expression caught between fury and fear. Warmth glowed in Relaina's chest as she struggled to her feet, her inner light beginning to spread.

"*Run*, Relaina," Jeremiah said, his voice breaking as he stood once more. Relaina shook her head. She would not leave him to bury a knife in his own heart. Darkness filled his eyes again.

"Pretender bitch," the tenebrae hissed, and Relaina winced at the sound of her father's voice. "How do you wield both magics?"

The tenebrae attacked, trying for her throat again, but she moved enough that his grip found her upper arm instead.

Cool darkness flooded through her as Darren's power manifested again, followed by gut-wrenching fear. Darren knew she was in trouble—she just needed to hold out for a few minutes. Relaina's shadowfire scars shimmered alongside the light she desperately fought to keep at bay. Without thinking, she grabbed Jeremiah's arm and pushed her darkness toward him, hoping it might flow outward the way Darren's did.

Nothing happened.

The tenebrae threw her to the ground several feet away. Her head hit the stone path, sending pain reverberating through her skull and down her arms.

"You cannot channel power to a tenebrae who doesn't accept it, Pretender. You truly know nothing of magic."

Jeremiah stalked toward her, barely discernible through her blurred vision. *No.* She rolled onto her stomach, attempting to crawl away from him, but he easily caught up to her. He shoved her onto her back with his foot and grabbed her by the collar of her tunic, flipping the knife in his hand. Relaina let out a strangled sob.

She was going to watch her father smile as a tenebrae forced him to kill her.

"It's—" Her voice broke and died before she could say the rest. *It's not your fault.* She hoped he knew that. She lost her grip on the light within her.

Pain worse than the throbbing in her head or her battered throat tore through her body as her magics collided. She thought she'd recalled its intensity, but this—how had she survived it twice? Perhaps the tenebrae would kill her quickly and it would end.

Garbled, distant shouts pressed against her ears, and she hit the ground again. The pain grew, reaching its peak, and Relaina tumbled into unconsciousness.

CHAPTER 12

THE SHADOW'S WRATH

Darren tore through the palace with wind and darkness in his wake.

Rhea and Catrin had followed him from the dungeons and were close behind. Nobles, guards, and servants passed by in a blur. He couldn't sense anything past the panic and agony that drew him toward the interior gardens, a cacophony of terror in his head that didn't belong to him.

He was paces from the entrance to the gardens when it stopped all at once, the silence more horrifying than the wordless despair. He burst through the doors, the healers at his back, and kept running—past the pool, past leafless trees, until he saw them.

Jeremiah stood over Relaina's body, shaking as he brandished a knife. The energy emanating from him was wrong, corrupted, razor sharp and icy cold. *Tenebrae.* Catrin swore, and Rhea shouted for guards. Darren didn't think—he threw out a hand and his darkness erupted, engulfing Jeremiah and throwing him off-balance. The knife slipped from the tenebrae's hand. Jeremiah hissed as he faced Darren, body tensing to attack, but his face went slack with shock before morphing again into rage.

"You've chosen wrong, Heir of Calixtos," the tenebrae said.

Darren lunged.

With the power of the shadow added to Jeremiah's strength, Darren had to employ all his training to avoid his attacks. He narrowly avoided a blow to the head, dancing back several steps on the path.

"Get down!" Catrin shouted, and he did. A beam of light shot over his head, narrowly missing the tenebrae, and Darren slipped through his defenses to land a kick to his side, cracking a few ribs. The tenebrae shrieked and growled. Relaina lay unmoving behind Jeremiah. Her scars shimmered with darkness, but Darren sensed nothing from her.

As Catrin and Rhea threw more light at the tenebrae, Darren let his fear bleed into his power, ignoring the instinct that he was overexerting himself. He let the darkness extend past his hands again as he ran at Jeremiah, who was attempting to retreat down the stone path. Darren's darkness almost solidified, wrapping around Jeremiah's upper arm. Darren stopped, clenched his fists, and flung him to the ground with a hard yank. He ran forward and pinned Jeremiah by the shoulders.

As soon as the intention to destroy the tenebrae entered his mind, his power pulled the shadow from Jeremiah, the darkness enveloped by Darren's. There was unbridled fury in the tenebrae's final wail.

Jeremiah's body went limp, and Darren released him before pushing to his feet. Rhea and Catrin ran forward as he approached Relaina, and four guards appeared, one barking orders to find Desiree.

Relaina's hair was sticky with blood, and bruises were already blooming around her neck. Darren's breath grew shallow. Darkness still shimmered along her shadowfire scars. He took her face gently. He'd stopped this once before, in the forest before the healers had attacked them. But just like banishing a tenebrae, the spoken words weren't necessary anymore—at his touch, her power quieted. Gritting his teeth, Darren pulled his darkness back, huffing as it settled within once more.

Rhea knelt beside them, placing glowing hands on either side of Relaina's head while Catrin rushed to Jeremiah. Darren took Relaina's hand and turned as the guards parted to make way for the king, who looked between Relaina and Jeremiah, horror etched across his face. Annalise and Desiree stood just behind him, the young princess clutching the captain's arm. For several moments, the only sound was water running from the nearby fountain.

"Where shall we take him, Your Majesty?" Catrin asked. Fabian's eyes lingered on Jeremiah.

"Take him to the dungeons," he said, his voice shaking.

With Catrin's help, two guards lifted Jeremiah and carried him off. Relaina stirred, and Fabian stepped forward. "Relaina?"

Her eyes opened slowly, unfocused, before settling on Darren. Rhea whispered something in her ear, and Relaina's face crumpled as she burst into tears, gripping Darren's hand. Fabian dismissed the guards as Relaina's sobs echoed around the gardens and tore into Darren's soul. His power surged and appeared at his palms again as his throat constricted.

Darren's darkness drew Relaina's in, allowing her light to emerge and speed up her healing process. Once she was healed enough to keep her light from engaging uncontrolled, Rhea scurried off to find Nehma and Thea, and Fabian asked Desiree to place additional guards near his own chambers and Relaina and Darren's. Darren leaned close to Relaina's ear.

"Can I carry you?"

She nodded, her eyes closed. He lifted her, his arms sure and steady with his power still aiding his strength. She wrapped her arms around his neck and buried her face in his chest.

"Darren," Fabian said, and Darren paused. "The shadow... has it been destroyed?"

"I believe it has," he said. "It happened faster than before, but I don't sense it anymore."

Fabian nodded, his expression hard. "Thank you."

She's going to die. You're going to kill her.

Jeremiah shot upright, metal digging into his wrists. Images of his hands on Relaina's throat and her cries on the garden path were slow to fade from his mind. He looked down at his shackled wrists, flexing his trembling fingers. He might be in a dungeon cell, but he was in control. There was no darkness, no cold shadow whispering horrible things in his mind.

The cell door opened, and Jeremiah flinched. Fabian stepped inside.

"Relaina?" Jeremiah choked out.

"She's alive."

Jeremiah dropped his face into his hands and wept. The door to the cell shut again, and chair legs scraped the floor.

"Jeremiah," Fabian said, his voice strained.

"I failed her," Jeremiah sobbed. "I failed us."

"Jeremiah, *please*." Fabian's voice broke. "I must ask you some questions."

"I'm sorry, I'm so sorry." Jeremiah repeated it over and over again, unable to say anything else, unable to breathe.

A warm hand gripped his left shoulder, and Jeremiah looked up. Fabian knelt before him, his face torn between caution and grief.

"I need you to listen to me," he said quietly, firmly. "Darren believes that he destroyed the tenebrae, but I have to be certain."

Jeremiah sobbed again and nodded. Fabian drew back, returning to the small chair several feet away. He took a shaky breath.

"How do you sign your letters to me?"

"With my first initial."

"What was the name of the healer who kept our secret twenty years ago?"

Jeremiah stifled another cry. "Corra."

Fabian nodded, his face twisting. "And what did you say to me the night of the Winter Festival this past year?"

Jeremiah forced himself to breathe. "I told you that Relaina was my daughter. And I promised you I would come back."

"And later that night...what did you say you were going to do when you returned to Maremer?"

Fabian's eyes shone in the dim light of the cell as he clasped his trembling hands together over his lap. Jeremiah swallowed against the dryness in his throat.

"I said I was going to take an axe to the wall between us."

Fabian's shoulders slumped as he exhaled. He called for a guard, and a man appeared promptly to remove Jeremiah's shackles. As soon as the guard was gone again, Fabian dropped to his knees and pulled him into an embrace. Jeremiah ignored the pain in his ribs and clung to him, his fingers gripping Fabian's cloak. The scent of vanilla and cinnamon enveloped him, overpowering the damp dungeon air. It smelled like Fabian always did. It smelled like home.

"I'm so sorry," Jeremiah said again.

"It's not your fault," Fabian whispered.

"I wasn't strong enough. And I left the Pareans and Evarians with no direction. I've already failed in my duty to protect your people."

Fabian shifted back, taking Jeremiah's face in his hands. "Jeremiah, look at me."

He did, and Fabian wiped the tears from his cheeks, his eyes molten ochre in the torchlight. Sorrow and love mingled in their depths, just like the last time Fabian had held Jeremiah in a dungeon cell over twenty years prior.

"Hear me when I say this," Fabian said. "Some of my strongest warriors succumbed to the tenebrae on the battlefield. You are not at fault for anything it forced you to do."

Another sob wracked Jeremiah's body, and Fabian pulled him close again.

"The Evarians and Pareans will be fine," Fabian said. "Did the tenebrae speak true of the death toll?"

"No."

Fabian leaned back, his smile sad. "See? They will be fine. Saheer is more than capable of managing things for a few weeks."

Jeremiah inhaled, then exhaled slowly. Again. He still trembled, but the terror waned.

"I need to tell you what happened."

Fabian studied him for a moment. "Do you think you're ready?"

"It doesn't matter if I am. Others' safety is at risk the longer I wait."

Fabian brushed the back of Jeremiah's hand with his thumb and nodded. "Very well. But let's speak in my chambers. There's no need to remain here."

Fabian helped Jeremiah to his feet, and two guards came forward once they exited the cell. It was the first in the corridor, only several paces from the stairwell. Jeremiah's whole body ached—whether it was an aftereffect of tenebrae possession or fighting two healers and Darren, he couldn't say.

The guards followed Fabian and Jeremiah closely as they made their way out of the dungeons and across the palace grounds. Night had fallen, and Jeremiah gripped Fabian's arm more tightly when a chill breeze crossed his face. They walked in silence until they reached Fabian's chambers.

Once they'd settled on a plush green couch in Fabian's bedroom, Jeremiah started at the beginning, with the attack on the tower. Though it was jumbled and somewhat out of order, he managed to tell Fabian everything he'd learned while possessed by the tenebrae.

"So this Kalmali is somewhere in the city?" Fabian spoke only after sitting in silence for a few moments.

"Last I saw him, he was headed into the northeastern part of Maremer."

"Can you tell my Shadows what he looks like?"

"Yes."

"Then I'll be back shortly."

When Fabian returned with two Shadows, Jeremiah described Kalmali as best he could, down to the onyx pendant he wore around his neck. They listened intently and bowed to both Fabian and Jeremiah before donning their masks and leaving. Numbly, Jeremiah bathed, scrubbing the dried blood from his skin. His ribs ached, though not as badly as they would have if Catrin hadn't partially healed them while he was unconscious.

By the time Jeremiah emerged, Fabian had removed his various kingly articles of clothing, wearing only soft, billowy trousers as he lit a candle by the bed. Jeremiah crawled beneath the bedcovers on the opposite side. His swollen eyes ached and itched.

"The white-haired woman," Fabian said, joining him. "Kalmali never mentioned her name?"

Jeremiah shook his head against a pillow. "He only ever

referred to her as 'my lady.' Whoever she is, she's a powerful light-wielder."

"And she knew Talea."

"She and Kalmali both did, as did whatever group they belong to. For all I know, Talea was part of the group herself."

Fabian drew Jeremiah to his chest, his skin warm and smooth, his heartbeat slow and steady. He ran his fingers through Jeremiah's hair.

"We will learn the truth," Fabian said. "And we will keep Relaina safe."

Tears again filled Jeremiah's eyes, shame and fear suffocating him.

"How can I face her again?" he whispered.

Fabian's embrace tightened. "You'll both need time to heal. But she loves you, Jeremiah, and neither of you will be destroyed by this."

He couldn't see past it all, not now. But gods, he hoped Fabian was right.

CHAPTER 13

THE FARMER'S HELP

Clouds obscured the moon and stars as Aronn Gienty crouched on the perimeter wall of Parea, studying the progress of the traitor guards patrolling the gate. To his left, the outermost rows of Maurice's orchard ran along the wall.

"Looks like the traitors aren't venturing this far down the wall for a while," one of the loyalists said behind him. The man was Lady Elke's brother, Hektor, who was close to Jeremiah's age. He was muscular and broad, not suited for sneaking into the city, but well-suited for hauling two people back up the wall.

"We've already established that, Elke," the other man, Mazin, said, his voice clipped. Mazin was one of the few dozen Lyneisian guards whose loyalty hadn't been bought by Archan Conclave and who'd managed to escape after the coup.

"Watch your tone when speaking to me, boy."

"I answer to Captain Andovier, not to you."

"Captain Andovier left us here with no indication of when he'd be back."

Aronn whipped around to motion for his companions to be quiet.

"Apologies, Prince Aronn," Mazin said, his dark eyes just visible over his own face covering. "I became distracted."

Aronn sighed, his breath puffing in front of him even through the cloth. "It's all right. Let's hurry up and get to Maurice's."

Aronn's uncle had left them days ago with a vague explanation about needing more soldiers from Maremer and orders to pause resistance efforts. But Aronn had to do *something*. He would not sit idle while Archan and the other traitorous bastards lorded over his people and kept his parents locked away.

It wouldn't have happened without your foolishness. A small voice, deep within, was persistent enough to spur him to action despite Jeremiah's absence and lack of approval. Aronn had allowed Zarias and the others into Castle Alterna; he'd befriended them, trusted them when he shouldn't have. And now they sat in the castle, in Aronn's home, planning gods knew what.

"Prince Aronn?"

Aronn shook his head and shivered. "Sorry. Let's go."

Aronn and Mazin dropped over the side of the wall, the few inches of snow softening the impact. Aronn had always loved the snow, but as the cold crept into his boots on their trek through the orchards, that fondness morphed into intense dislike.

Aronn approached the back of Maurice's shop, inching toward a window. A light from inside cast a low glow on the frosty panes as he looked through the glass. He and Maurice jumped at the sudden appearance of one another's faces. A muffled, "Gods in hell!" sounded as the farmer stepped away from the window. Aronn and Mazin hurried toward the front door a few feet away. In seconds, it opened, enveloping Aronn in welcome warmth. Maurice ushered them both inside.

Aronn hurried past the farmer, greeting both him and his

wife, Camille, with a timid smile. Mazin closed the door behind them, stamping the snow from his boots.

"Prince Aronn, it's dangerous for you to be here," Camille said, brushing snow from his cloak as she gripped her wool shawl with the other. The smell of baking bread wafted down the hallway, and Aronn's mouth watered. She turned to Mazin. "And you are?"

"Mazin." He inclined his head.

"Welcome to our home, Mazin. I am Camille, and this is Maurice."

"It's a pleasure to meet you both."

"What brings you here?" Maurice asked, chauffeuring them toward the front of the shop.

"We're here to see if either of you have new information on the usurper nobles." Aronn leaned on the shop counter and accepted a cup of hot tea from Camille gratefully. "And if you might know where they're keeping my parents captive."

Maurice and Camille exchanged a look, both frowning.

"We know very little of what the traitor nobles do day-to-day," Maurice said. "They are often holed up in Castle Alterna. Before that, some Pareans tried attacking them in the streets. One of the nobles' sons was killed in a brawl at Alterna Tavern. The man who did it was hanged."

Aronn blanched. "Gods."

"As for King Stephan and Queen Christine, no one has seen them," Maurice said. "The underground market and fighting ring have been shut down, and few of us are venturing outside our homes now, anyway."

Aronn had expected as much, but it was still discouraging.

"I'm sorry we don't know more," Camille said, her voice soft. "But Prince Aronn, you must leave this place. If they capture you alongside your parents…"

"They think I'm being held captive elsewhere, or dead, so they aren't actively searching for me." Aronn stood, downing the rest of his tea. "It's Annalise they want, and she's safe in Maremer."

After hesitating a moment, Camille asked, "Have you heard anything from Relaina?"

Aronn smiled sadly. "She's safe. And Darren...well, they think he will be."

Both Camille and Maurice tensed.

"What happened to him?" Camille asked.

"I..." Aronn stared at them. "Have you heard no news from outside Parea?"

"Only rumors," Maurice said. He lowered his voice. "Is it true King Gabriel is dead?"

Aronn took a deep breath and looked to Mazin, who nodded.

"We ought to sit," Aronn said, motioning for the little table by the fire.

Aronn recounted everything he could remember of Relaina and Darren's tale, hardly believing it himself when he told them about Darren's dark power and Relaina's apparent healing abilities. They both stared at him in stunned silence once he'd finished. Tears fell from Camille's eyes in earnest.

"So Darren is free of his father," she whispered.

"You knew?"

"We did," Maurice said. "He told us about a month after arriving here."

Aronn could see why Relaina and Darren were fond of these two. "I have just a few more questions for you both, if you don't mind, and then we'll take our leave."

"However we can help," Maurice said. And help they did; Aronn and Mazin prepared to leave minutes later, armed with additional information about traitorous guard movements. Camille insisted they both take some bread, which they accepted gratefully before they ventured back outside into the snow.

"Do you think their information was worth the trip?" Mazin asked, his golden-brown skin covered once more by a thick cloak.

"I do."

"They didn't know where the king and queen are being held."

"No." Aronn stepped past the edge of Maurice's shop, following the same path they'd taken into the village. "But I think I do."

"Excellent, because you'll be joining them shortly."

The new voice shot terror through Aronn so sharply he no longer felt the cold. He and Mazin pivoted toward the voice. Three men stood by the front of the shop, swords drawn and cloaks draped around their muscular frames. *Castle guards.* Mazin drew his own sword and stepped in front of Aronn.

"Go, Prince Aronn," he said. With a shaking hand, Aronn pulled out his own shortsword.

"No."

"You'd do well to stand aside, Mazin," the man in front said. "And maybe we'll let you live."

Mazin tensed. "Go to hell, you honorless fucks."

The man sighed. "Very well."

Before he could attack, the castle guard stumbled forward, coughing dark blood onto the snow as his fellows swiveled and faced the city square behind them. He wheezed, grasping at his chest before collapsing, revealing an arrow protruding from his back. The remaining traitors turned back to Aronn and Mazin and ran at them.

Another arrow flew, and a second castle guard went down with a yelp, face-first into the snow. Lanterns were lit in homes across the square as Pareans emerged to investigate. Aronn stumbled back as Mazin met the remaining man head-on, the collision of their swords piercing the frigid air. Another traitor guard started toward them, but he stopped in front of

Maurice's shop, yanking the farmer into view and knocking a kitchen knife from his hand.

"Put your fucking weapons down!" The guard held the knife at Maurice's throat.

"Put *me* down, you traitorous ass," Maurice bellowed, but Mazin and Aronn both froze.

"I said, put them *down*. Or I'll cut his throat."

Aronn dropped his shortsword to the snow, but Mazin didn't budge, his sword held aloft and ready to re-engage in battle with the other guard. Aronn opened his mouth, but a metallic *clunk* cut him off as a shovel struck the skull of the knife-wielding guard. He slumped to the ground as Maurice scrambled away from him, and Mazin disarmed the other guard in seconds. Aronn's stomach turned as he ran the man through. More guards appeared on the opposite end of the square, and Camille, who had dropped the shovel into the snow, shouted at them.

"*Go!*"

Mazin took Aronn by the collar and yanked him back.

"Wait, I—"

"These people have given us a chance to escape and we will not waste it," Mazin hissed. "Let's *go.*"

With one last glance at Maurice, Camille, and the guards bearing down on them all, Aronn swore and sprinted with Mazin back to the perimeter wall.

Chapter 14

Choosing a Path

Relaina stared at the purple and gold canopy above her bed, gritting her teeth while Thea finished healing her head. They'd all thought Rhea had done enough the day before, but Relaina's light had emerged of its own volition again, attempting to heal lingering injuries. While Darren met with Fabian and the Terranian nobles, Relaina had never been so grateful that guards were assigned to stand watch just outside her door. They'd found Thea in minutes.

"That should do it," Thea said, withdrawing her hand and her light. "How do you feel?" Relaina met her blue-eyed gaze soberly, and Thea grimaced. "How do you feel *physically*?"

Relaina sat up in bed, and her head didn't swim, her body didn't ache.

"Better," she said. "Thank you, Thea."

After hesitating a moment, Thea pulled her into an embrace, and Relaina returned it.

"Try to get some rest, okay?" Thea said, her smile sad. Relaina knew she meant well, but gods, she didn't want to be pitied.

A knock came at her door, and Relaina called, "Enter."

Annalise appeared, picking up the skirts to her dark blue dress as she rushed to Relaina's bedside. Thea excused herself as Relaina's sister took her hand.

"You're healed now?" Annalise asked, her face pale. Relaina nodded. "Thank the gods."

"Thank *you*, Anna," Relaina said. "You were brilliant to get to Desiree and Fabian."

Tears filled Annalise's eyes. "I've never seen a tenebrae possess anyone. And for it to be Uncle Jeremiah...it was horrible."

A lump formed in Relaina's throat. She swallowed hard. "There's something I've been meaning to tell you. Let's go sit."

Relaina was healed, but a deeper ache settled into her body as she led Annalise to the couch by the fire. She took her sister's hands and started to speak, but the words got caught in her throat. She cleared it and tried again.

"You know that Fabian and Jeremiah are together," she began. "And that they were together over twenty years ago?"

Annalise's brow knit together. "Yes..."

Relaina took a deep breath. "After they were separated, he met a Terranian healer and Seer named Talea. I don't know the details but I know they spent a night together, and months later she showed up at Castle Alterna with a baby in her arms."

Annalise stared at her, waiting.

"That baby was me," Relaina said.

Understanding crept into Annalise's eyes, followed quickly by confusion. Relaina did her best to explain it all, how she wasn't a Gienty by blood but had been passed as such for her own protection and to secure an heir to the throne. Annalise stood and paced in front of the fireplace. Her lips pressed together into a tight line as she fiddled with the end of her braid.

"Are you angry?" Relaina asked, her voice soft. Annalise turned sharply.

"I...not about any of that," she said, shaking her head. "You will always be my sister. But I have been kept in the dark these past few months, separated from you, and then from Aronn and the rest of our family. You *left* me, Relaina. You didn't even say goodbye."

Relaina stood and approached her, taking Annalise's hands in hers. "I know. I know I did. I'm so, so sorry, Annalise."

Annalise stared at her, taking a few deep breaths before she said, "Just...please don't hide things from me anymore. I'm not a fighter like you, but I'm not fragile."

Relaina pulled her close. "I know you aren't. I promise I'll be honest with you from now on."

Annalise squeezed her back. "Good."

"I love you dearly, Anna."

"I love you too." Annalise leaned away from her. "I'm glad you're healed."

Relaina exhaled slowly as she watched Annalise go. Every part of her felt ragged and raw, even if her body was healed. She looked at her hands, studied the black scar on her right forearm. She clenched her fist. If she wanted to help those she cared about, she needed to be able to fight like she once had. She had to figure out this gods-damned magic before it got her killed.

She pushed away every emotion as she opened her wardrobe and extracted her Shadow gear. Every emotion except rage—she let that grow and burn away the rest.

DARREN FURLED and unfurled his fingers on the table while

he waited. Just a few hours of focus and he could get back to Relaina.

Fabian entered the small council room, a guard following closely behind him. As soon as he was seated, Fabian propped his elbows on the table and let his forehead fall against his folded hands.

"I know what weighs heavily on both our minds," he said quietly. After taking a deep breath, he met Darren's eyes. "But should we discuss it now, I may not be able to complete my duties today."

Darren swallowed against the lump in his throat and nodded.

"The situation in Terrana," Fabian said, his posture straightening. "I cannot deny that you will need to answer them soon, so we must plan accordingly."

Darren knew that, but it didn't make it any easier to decide.

A clear future dictated for him, or one of uncertainty, but also of freedom?

"What do you think I should do?" he asked. Fabian tilted his head to the side.

"You must make that decision based on what you want." Fabian's gaze traveled to the nearby window, to the gray sky outside. "And I don't mean base desire. What is it you genuinely care about in all this? What is at stake?"

Darren frowned at the dark wood of the table, his mind a cluster. What wasn't at stake?

"I care about the Terranian people," he said finally. "I care about living in a world where I don't have to be afraid every moment. But that doesn't make me fit to be king. I don't know how to lead a kingdom."

Fabian studied him for a moment. "Relaina does."

Darren couldn't deny that he'd considered it, but the moment he imagined Relaina in the Obsidian Keep, it was difficult to breathe. She had only just relinquished her title as heir in Lyneisia, and was no longer bound to a throne or a crown. How could he take that freedom from her?

"I'm not sure she would want that."

"Then perhaps you should ask her." Fabian offered him a small smile. "Under normal circumstances, it would be ill-advised to speak of such things so soon. But if her path in life is one you wish to travel, and if you'll choose a direction based on her steps, you must ask her where she's going."

Fabian was right. He and Relaina had danced around the subject several times now, and approaching it directly terrified him. It was one thing for them to assure one another of their mutual affection and commitment, but it was another entirely to discuss exactly what that would mean if Darren chose to claim the Terranian throne.

Marriage.

Darren didn't dare let himself dwell on the idea. He couldn't allow the possibility of marrying her to take root inside him if Relaina ultimately decided the role was too much.

"Think about it," Fabian said, drawing Darren back to the present. "Now, what are some non-negotiables you believe I should lay out for the Terranian nobles when it comes to diplomacy and trade?"

～

"A tenebrae has breached your palace, and you wish to delay the decision still?" Lady Tryali hissed, halfway out of her chair. Darren fought the urge to recoil. "It's almost certain they were an agent of one of the usurper families in Terrana. We must act now."

"There is no evidence of that," Fabian said, his voice cold. Darren's discomfort grew with every passing moment. He kept an iron grip on his power, not allowing even a whisper of it to appear.

"The tenebrae have been a scourge on our court for decades," Lord Delimont said. "You should be taking this incident seriously."

"For you to suggest I am doing anything but that is rather insulting, Lord Delimont," Fabian said, his fingers clenching into a fist on the mahogany table. "And I'm not a king to take advice from men who use others like pawns to gain more power. Or did your daughter flee Terrana because she was glad to be betrothed to a sadist twice her age?"

Lord Delimont's face flushed. "Don't you dare speak of my daughter!"

Fabian's eyes burned with anger and pain he'd never displayed in Darren's presence. The darkness beneath Darren's skin pulsed, clamoring for freedom as his heart picked up speed.

"We're in my kingdom, in my home, and you have the audacity to tell me what I should do?" Fabian demanded. Lord Delimont opened his mouth again, but Fabian cut him off. "If you speak to me with such disrespect again, Lord Delimont, you'll be headed back to Terrana far earlier than you intended."

Silence permeated the room, giving Darren several moments to calm himself and allow his power to settle once more.

"Let us turn to the reason we originally called this meeting," Fabian said, and Lady Eyern visibly relaxed in her seat. Lady Tryali sat with narrowed eyes and pursed lips, her hand resting just below her chin. Darren caught Fabian's eye and nodded once.

"I'm not giving you my answer about claiming the Terranian throne today," Darren said. "But I would like to discuss hypotheticals."

The Terranians sat in silence, their expressions varying degrees of curiosity.

"*If* I were to make a claim," he said, "exactly which nobles can we count on for support?"

The list provided was better than Darren had anticipated, but there were several names that made his skin crawl.

"And the Terranian Elite," Darren said. "Who controls them now? Or have they gone rogue?"

Lord Delimont exchanged a look with Lady Tryali before answering. "House Artea announced a summons for them. We don't know how many will respond."

"Another reason for us to provide them incentive to take our side," Lady Tryali said, her voice sharp. "I must insist you set aside your feelings for this Lyneisian princess as we discuss the future of our kingdom, Prince Darren. Marriage to Corta Artea would be a boon to our cause and to your claim."

Darren's eye twitched. "Is that what you said to Princess Relaina at the banquet two nights ago?"

For the first time, chagrin touched Tryali's features. "More or less."

Cold, seething ire settled in Darren's chest. Shadows snaked from his palms and up his arms slowly as he fixed Lady Tryali with a stare he hoped was utterly terrifying.

"You want me to feel nothing," he said, his voice calmer than he'd expected. "To trust your word without argument. You don't want a king. You want Prince Darren, the boy assassin who bent to his father's will and was beaten into submission when he didn't." Darren stood, placing both palms on the table as his darkness spread. "I am not that boy anymore. I will not *set aside my feelings*. Honoring what I feel is why I am still a man and not a mindless killer. The fucking priests of Calixtos couldn't take that from me, and neither will you, Lady Tryali."

Somewhere in the back of his mind, a familiar presence

flickered to life, a single candle in the darkness. He couldn't hear Relaina's voice, but irritation and frustration dominated her emotions. He pulled his power back as he took his seat.

"My apologies," Lady Tryali said, her eyes narrowing as she folded her hands on the table.

"I'll hear no other arguments for that strategy," Darren said. "And you will not speak to Princess Relaina about it again, either."

Lady Tryali's face remained set, but she nodded once. To her left, Lady Eyern looked as though she were fighting a smile.

"Surely there are other ways to secure House Artea's loyalty," Fabian said.

Darren breathed freely again when the meeting concluded after another hour of discussion. He stayed in his seat as the Terranians left the room.

"I'm going to check on Jeremiah," Fabian said, dropping his air of kingly authority once they were alone.

Darren nodded and stood.

"Thank you," Fabian said, and Darren paused, turning back to him. More of that pain Darren had never seen from the king crossed Fabian's face. "For what you did yesterday. Your actions saved them both."

Darren couldn't think of anything to say, so he simply placed his hand atop Fabian's still-clenched fist for a moment. Fabian bowed his head slightly, and Darren set off.

Right outside the doors, Darren nearly ran into a man he didn't expect to see.

"Good day, Your Majesty," Alaris Onnea said, bowing even as his face turned red. Had he been eavesdropping? "I was quite grieved when I heard what happened yesterday."

Darren tried very hard not to sigh.

"It was horrific, to say the least," Darren said. "My apologies, Alaris, but I must go."

The old man bowed again. Darren walked quickly through the corridors that led back to his and Relaina's shared rooms and stopped short a few feet from their door. Only one of the two guards Desiree had assigned here stood outside.

"Princess Relaina left a short while ago," the other guard explained. "I believe she went to the healers' quarters."

"The healers?" Darren asked, and a moment later he knew. He thanked the guard and made for the second floor.

CHAPTER 15

RAGE AND RESOLVE

"Relaina, you need rest," Rhea said gently.

"What I need is to figure this out," Relaina said, standing with her arms crossed just outside the door to the healers' suite. Nehma was shaking her head, and it grated Relaina's nerves. The guard that had followed her from her chambers stood down the hallway in silence.

"Pushing yourself right now won't help anything," Nehma said.

"I'm *fine*," Relaina almost growled. "But I won't be if I keep needing help every gods-damned time I get injured."

"Relaina?"

She and the healers turned. Darren approached, passing her guard, concern plain on his face. Had he followed her?

And *why* did that irritate her so much?

"Relaina wants to train right now," Nehma said, "And we both told her she needs to rest."

"I don't need to rest," Relaina insisted. Darren stopped next to her, brushing her arm with his fingers.

"It's only been a day," he said. "Rest today and I'll help you tomorrow."

"I don't *want* your help!" Relaina snapped, yanking her arm away. "And *don't* touch me."

Darren's face went blank with shock. Silence fell. He dropped his hand to his side before turning to leave the same way he'd come. Shame washed over Relaina as she watched him disappear.

"Fuck," she whispered, closing her eyes. When she opened them, she glanced at Nehma and Rhea. Nehma's face was unreadable, and Rhea looked equal parts empathetic and exasperated. Without another word, Relaina followed Darren, and her guard followed her.

Darren was washing his face in the washroom when Relaina entered their chambers. She stood in the doorway as he vigorously dried his face with a towel.

"Darren," she said. He hung the towel on the side of the wash basin and turned, leaning against it with his arms crossed. Hurt and anger were etched into his face. "I didn't...I only meant that I didn't want you in my head right now."

He stared at her for a moment, then shrugged. "I'm not sure why that matters when you clearly say what you're thinking anyway."

Relaina bristled, that rage she'd allowed to take over earlier preparing to do so again.

"You have no idea how frustrating it's been for me," she said, stepping into the washroom. "You have this natural control of your power, and I cannot even access mine safely without your help. I almost *died* yesterday because of it, and you want me to rest?"

"You can't fix this problem with your magic by running yourself into the ground in training."

Relaina turned and stalked out of the washroom. "I won't fix it by fucking sitting around either."

"Relaina—."

She ignored him and began peeling off the armor of her

Shadow gear by the wardrobe. No one was going to train with her today, so fuck it. She'd go to the library and get back to researching.

"Relaina, would you stop seething for five seconds and look at me?"

She tossed one of her boots to the floor and huffed, looking at him expectantly.

"Look, I understand—"

"You *don't* understand!" she said. "I have never felt so incapable in my life. I want to be able to use this magic without relying on you or anyone else to keep it from getting out of control."

"Gods in hell, Relaina," Darren said, rubbing his forehead with his hand. More darkness appeared along his arms, calling to her, pulling at her. And in that moment, it was infuriating. "You don't think I understand how it feels to wield power that terrifies you? That could burst free any moment and hurt you or those around you? I lived for *years* in fear of that."

"And now you wield it like you were born to it."

"Well fuck me, then!" he said, throwing up his hands, and the darkness pulsed. "I'll try to be terrible at it from now on. Or would that also be too *helpful*?"

"Ashima fucking smite me," Relaina muttered.

"There's nothing wrong with needing help. Especially when I *want* to help you."

"Can you restrain your magic now, then? It's pulling at me, gods damn it."

Darren pinned her with a look as the anger faded from his face and the shadows receded. "I didn't realize it pulled at you so forcefully."

"It's just a frequent reminder that I have made almost no progress in wielding this magic I never asked for or wanted."

"I never wanted this, either."

"Then I suppose we're both fucked."

Darren choked on a halfhearted laugh, but Relaina couldn't even dredge up a smile.

"I'm going to the library," she said.

"Relaina—"

"I need some time."

He started to speak again, stopped, and nodded. He returned to the washroom while Relaina changed into a pair of tan trousers and a black shirt with laces down the front. She retrieved a book from her bedside table, clutching it to her chest as she headed for the door.

DARREN DUCKED as the prisoner before him attempted to throw a punch, a puff of air floating past his nose. The now-former tenebrae lost his balance and fell to his knees on the dungeon floor.

"You're no king," he said, spitting at Darren's feet. Perhaps it was frustration with Relaina's outburst, perhaps it was yet another prisoner staunchly supporting his father's ideals, perhaps it was everything and everyone who had shoved him to the ground up until that point—no matter the reason, wrath exploded in his chest, a blaze that ignited faster than a wildfire. He reached down and grabbed the man by the front of his tattered shirt, slamming him against the cell wall.

"You're right, I'm no king," Darren said. Cold filled his veins, his power appearing much like it had in the council meeting, slowly and deliberately filling the room. "No one has made a claim to the Terranian throne, and I'm not feeling terribly inclined to do so. You know why?" The prisoner recoiled as Darren's power drifted over his neck, and Darren tightened his grip on the man's shirt. "Because of fuckers like you. You're a disgrace to the god you claim to serve."

It was a truth he knew deep in his bones, ever since

Calixtos had appeared to him the night the bay had been set aflame, ever since he'd realized his power hadn't hurt Relaina or anyone else the way his father's had hurt him. The prisoner's eyes widened as he pressed himself harder into the wall, desperate to get away.

Darren's anger dissipated as fast as it had come, and he released the man, letting him crumple to the ground as he strode out of the cell. An Evarian healer, Nadia, greeted him with a nod and locked the door behind him. He still had two more tenebrae to question today if he wanted to stay on schedule and get through them all over the next few days. He and Fabian had agreed that he should know where their loyalties lay before he made his decision about claiming the throne.

Another healer whose name he couldn't recall unlocked the next cell down. Two tenebrae scrambled to their feet and bowed as he entered the cell. Neither of them said a word, just trembled at his approach. One was a slight woman who looked barely older than he was, and the other was tall, spindly, and especially pale. As subtly as he could manage, he released a bit of his power, letting the shadows coil lazily from his hands. He took a deep breath.

"May I?" he asked, holding out one of his hands to the younger woman. He couldn't make out her features clearly in such dim lighting, but he could sense her fear. Her hand shook as she lifted it and placed it in his. Her eyes flashed obsidian.

Darren could've crumpled with relief at the cool, gentle darkness that met his. The tenebrae woman's shadowy voice grew clearer in his mind amid the chorus of others, but her thoughts remained indistinct and panicked. He hadn't been able to hear any of the tenebrae the way he heard Relaina, but their emotions were easy to sense if they touched him.

Darren dropped her hand. He wanted to assure her that he knew she meant no harm, but he had to test the other woman first. She took his hand with a firmer grip, eyes locking on his as they flashed with her power. She, too, radiated darkness that soothed, that matched Darren's. It almost shimmered in his mind's eye as her voice grew louder than the rest. She was determined, if not a little fearful.

Darren stepped away, pulling his power back once more. Each day it felt easier, like an extension of himself, the same way his daggers felt in his hands. Relaina was right about that —it had come rather naturally to him once he'd stopped repressing it, once he'd felt confident that he wouldn't accidentally hurt people.

"I trust you both," Darren said. The younger woman slumped in relief while the other nodded. "How did you come to be in my father's army?"

Darren listened intently while each tenebrae explained their experience with Gabriel, and his heart sank ever lower. They had both been conscripted from their homes as teenagers, the older one over ten years prior. Gabriel had torn families apart for years. He'd known this, but it felt heavier now.

Because he now had a chance to do something about it.

"Please, Your Highness," the younger woman said, clasping her hands together as she fought back tears. "I never wanted to fight. I just want to go home."

Darren's heart cracked. "What are your names?"

"Mari," the younger one said.

"My name is Ihara," the tall woman said, and Darren's heart faltered.

"Ihara Eyern?" he asked, and she nodded, her eyes brightening. Darren looked to Mari, then back to Ihara. "Lady Ihara, your wife has asked after you. She feared you were dead."

"Lucia is here?" Ihara asked.

"She is. I must speak with King Fabian," Darren said, resolve forming in his chest. "But I promise you won't be kept down here much longer. Neither of you will."

"Thank you," Ihara said, and Mari echoed her, both of them bowing as he turned to leave.

He headed down the dark corridor that led back to the main dungeon, passing by Catrin and Thea. Thea gave him a friendly wave, and he inclined his head.

Darren squinted against the sunlight as he emerged from the dungeons and crossed the grounds. Once inside Seacastle's southeast corridor, he approached a passing servant who was holding fresh linens.

"Do you know where I might find Lady Eyern?" Darren asked the man.

"I hear she spends much time in the old temple in the north wing," the man said.

"Apologies, Prince Darren," another servant approached, bowing her head quickly. "But Lady Eyern just left a meeting with Lord Vontair in the small council chamber."

"Thank you," Darren said, already hurrying off. That room wasn't far.

Sure enough, Lady Eyern was bidding Lord Vontair farewell by the chamber door. Her eyebrows lifted gently when she turned and caught sight of Darren.

"Prince Darren," she said.

"Good evening, Prince Darren," Lord Vontair said.

"Good evening to you both," Darren said. "Lord Vontair, may I have a private word with Lady Eyern?"

"Of course, I was just headed home for the evening. I will see you both at our next meeting."

Lord Vontair headed for the entrance hall, and Darren gestured for them to enter the small council chamber. It was quiet and empty as they took two seats at the table.

"I found your wife, Lady Eyern," Darren told her. Lady Eyern blinked rapidly, her hand reaching for her chest. "She is well, or as well as a prisoner can be."

Lady Eyern's lip trembled as she closed her eyes, fighting to keep her composure. She took a shaky breath and wiped at her eyes.

"You have my gratitude, Prince Darren."

"I'll see that she's released soon," he said. And he meant it. It was the least he could do after the kindness and support Lady Eyern had shown him.

"Thank you," she said quietly, bowing her head. Darren started to stand again but hesitated.

"Lady Eyern," he said, and she straightened herself, blinking away more tears. He had to ask this, despite what he'd said to the prisoner who had attacked him earlier, despite his argument with Relaina. "If I should make a claim, do I still have your support in marrying Princess Relaina?"

The Terranian noblewoman smiled wryly. "You do."

Another brick of resolve fell into place in his heart.

CHAPTER 16

A Closed Door

The forest grove was familiar. Relaina gazed at the browned grass and leafless trees—the last time she was here, the forest had been covered in verdant foliage. A single figure stood in the center, white hair matching her flowing gown as both floated in the chilled breeze. The heaviness in Relaina's heart lifted.

Elenia!

The goddess didn't turn, so Relaina stumbled toward her, anticipation filling her chest. Perhaps Elenia could explain it all—perhaps she would have the answers about her magic.

But just as Relaina reached her, hand outstretched, the goddess turned. Her skin was pale white instead of azure, her middle-aged face devoid of compassion, and her stature too small. The woman's blue eyes widened, her upper lip curling in rage.

"You!" she snarled at Relaina, and lunged.

Relaina cried out as she awoke, her clammy cheek nearly ripping a page out of the book she'd fallen asleep on.

"Don't need rest, eh?" Rhea pulled out a chair at the

library table and sat across from her, folding her hands together. "Nightmare?"

Relaina's heart slowed as she nodded. "It was...vivid."

"Not uncommon for a light-wielder."

"Really?"

Rhea nodded. "It's stronger in some than others. Wasn't your mother a Seer?"

Relaina could only stare at her. She hadn't even considered the possibility that the Seeing aspect of Talea's power had also been passed down to her.

"I don't have visions of the future," Relaina said.

"That's the rarest form of Seeing," Rhea said. "Most healers simply have vivid dreams. Thea and I sometimes have visions of each other in the present moment if something particularly distressing or emotional is happening."

Memories of a burning healers' village filled Relaina's mind, of Talea's frostbitten fingers and fury-filled death.

"What about visions of the past?"

"Not common, but not unheard of." Rhea's brow furrowed. "You've had a vision like that?"

"After the explosion on the river."

Rhea nodded. "Three elders of the Caspian Forest are Seers. Aaresh has had visions of the past, but it's usually only after something triggers it. Shiva and Tolera have occasional visions of other places in the present."

Relaina's burgeoning hope deflated. "So there's no way to control it?"

"Unfortunately no, not that I know of."

Relaina groaned and let her forehead rest against the table. A warm hand covered hers, and Relaina looked up, meeting Rhea's gaze.

"We'll figure it out. There must be answers."

Rhea's soft determination was more encouraging than Relaina expected.

"I need to apologize to Darren," Relaina said, pushing her hair back from her face.

Rhea pressed her lips together. "I'd agree with that. And so would Nehma. You were rather harsh."

"I was." Relaina grimaced. "He didn't deserve that."

"No, he didn't. He and the rest of us only want to make sure you're safe. What happened to you yesterday was horrible."

"I know." Tears threatened to form in Relaina's eyes as flashes of the tenebrae's attack ran through her mind. She closed the book in front of her and stood. "Thank you, Rhea. I'll find you later."

Rhea nodded as she headed for the door.

Midday sunlight shone through the intermittent windows as she trudged back to her rooms. If guilt and shame were the only emotions she felt, it would be easier. But grief and terror still lingered from yesterday, exacerbating her frustrations with everything she faced. Everything they all faced.

Her steps slowed as she passed by a staircase. Jeremiah was recovering in Fabian's chambers and hadn't come to see her. Perhaps seeing him would ease her mind. She doubled back, nearly bumping into the guard trailing her, and bounded up the stairs before she could change her mind.

She'd only been up here once before, to meet Fabian in his study first thing one morning before a council meeting, and she almost forgot the route. The last thing she wanted to do was ask the guard behind her which way to go, but she was spared—the next corner she turned led to the large red doors of the king's chambers. As Relaina approached, the guards on either side of the doors bowed to her, and her determination wavered. She swallowed.

"Is the king present?" she asked one of the guards.

"No, Your Highness," the guard said, shaking her head.

"Am I able to see J—Lord Andovier?"

The guards exchanged a glance.

"Are you certain, Your Highness?" the guard asked. Relaina nodded. "Very well. We will be outside should you need anything."

The second guard moved to open one of the large red doors, and Relaina stepped inside, her legs trembling as she went. She walked around two plush chairs and a chaise on her way to the green bedroom door. Trepidation swirled and built within her as she stopped before it, one hand suspended midair.

Was this wise? Should she be here?

Wise or not, she had to see him. That gods-damned tenebrae would not take him away from her. She knocked.

"Jeremiah?" she called. There was no answer beyond a muffled shuffling on the other side of the door. Relaina knocked again. "Jeremiah, it's me. I just..." Tears welled in her eyes and spilled over, and she let her hand and forehead fall against the painted wood of the door. "Please, I just want to see you."

She sank to the floor, her forehead still pressed against the door as her hand clenched into a fist.

"Relaina." She looked up as more tears leaked out of her eyes. His voice was strained as he spoke from the other side of the door. "Relaina, I'm sorry, I...I can't. Not yet."

"Please," she whispered. "It wasn't your fault. You have to know that."

Silence grew as she waited for his response, hoping the door would open.

"I'm sorry," he said again. "I just can't."

Relaina sobbed once before dragging herself to her feet. She should have known it was too soon. With her arms wrapped around herself she hurried for the door, ignoring the guards completely as she pushed past them. When she reached the stairs again, she nearly barreled into Fabian.

"...And tell the kitchens we'll need a—oh."

Relaina gaped at him, fumbling over her words. "I'm sorry, I didn't mean...I wasn't sure..."

"Leave us," Fabian said to the guards, who followed the king's order immediately, footsteps rapidly retreating and doors opening and closing again. Fabian opened his arms, and Relaina fell into them gratefully.

"I'm sorry," she said again.

"No, don't apologize," Fabian said, his own voice thick with emotion. "After all you've endured, it's astonishing that you're still standing." He leaned back and placed his hands on her shoulders. "And you're not only standing, you've helped manage rebuilding efforts in Maremer and you've offered valuable insight when speaking with the Terranian nobles. You have persisted despite every challenge, every horror thrown your way, and I know you will overcome this too. You and Jeremiah both will."

His voice broke on the last sentence, and Relaina embraced him again.

"Thank you, Fabian," she said, her voice soft.

"I hope you know that I wish I didn't have to involve you or Darren in any of this," he said. "I would offer you both nothing but peace and safety if I could."

Guilt nagged at her as her thoughts drifted to Darren, but before she ventured downstairs, she craved a few more moments of comfort, of someone else holding her burdens and assuring her she wasn't a failure. *There's nothing wrong with needing help*, Darren had told her. She closed her eyes and inhaled slowly.

"I know."

CHAPTER 17

THE MARKET AND THE MANOR

Darren's churning thoughts came to a halt as he stepped into his and Relaina's chambers. Relaina was in bed, curled up beneath the blankets, her dark curls splayed across her pillow. He didn't speak as he removed his weapons belt and washed up before climbing in bed beside her. For a moment he wondered if she was asleep, but she turned over and looked at him through puffy, swollen eyes.

"I'm sorry," she said. Her voice was thin and hoarse.

"I know."

She reached for his hand, and he took hers, pressing his lips to her fingers.

"You didn't deserve what I said earlier."

Darren smiled sadly at her. "I know you're frustrated and angry. You have every right to be. And you can rage all you like, but not at me."

"Not at you," she agreed softly.

"Now if I ever do something to deserve it..." Darren shrugged one shoulder.

"That's difficult to imagine."

"I've said and done plenty of things I regret out of anger

and fear," Darren said. A dark alley flashed into his mind, a scene of fury and grief that led to the indiscriminate spraying of blood. He brushed a curl out of Relaina's eyes. "It sometimes led me to actions that were...less than honorable."

Relaina searched his face. "Do you want to talk about it?"

"Not particularly. But if we—" the words caught in his throat. *If we marry.* He took another deep breath. "You deserve to know about my past. About everything I've done. Everything I'm capable of."

Relaina pondered for a moment, her green eyes tired but full of empathy, and despite the anxiety simmering in his veins as he prepared to tell his story, he trusted her to listen and not find him abhorrent.

"I want to know," she said.

"Now?"

Relaina nodded. Darren closed his eyes and kissed her hair. She twined her fingers through his as he began.

"I was given my first assignment when I was fifteen."

Darren was brave enough to relay his tale without holding back, but he couldn't bring himself to look Relaina in the eye while he did so. She stopped breathing a few times, and her grip on his fingers tightened when he told her about the guards he'd slaughtered in that alleyway.

"There are many deaths that weigh on me," he said, his voice shaking. "But this...I don't want to justify what I did and how I felt. But it was the day I realized that my father saw me as nothing more than a weapon, and that everything I had done under his orders was for the sole purpose of giving him more power. I'd been wandering the streets of Lues and ended up cornered in an alley by Obsidian Keep guards and I just...I went into a rage. They were all dead in moments. Five of them, and I felt no remorse. I still don't. And part of me is ashamed that I don't feel regret."

Relaina went still beside him, and a small bit of fear crept into his chest. Had he finally revealed something about himself that scared her?

"I've felt that way since the battle." Silence grew for several moments before her eyes met his. "I've thought part of me was just broken, or that I was pretending as though I didn't kill more than twenty people that day."

Another piece of Relaina's long list of frustrations and worries fell into place. "That's why you've been reluctant to speak about it."

Relaina nodded. Darren took both of her hands in his and kissed her calloused palms.

"You never have to hide from me," he said. "I meant what I said after we found you by the Granica River, and it still stands now. Nothing you've done could turn me away or make me think less of you. And needing my help or Nehma's or Rhea's won't make me think less of you, either."

Relaina exhaled. "What could I have possibly done to deserve you, Darren LaGuarde?"

He brushed his thumb across her cheek and said, "You loved me despite that name."

THE NEXT MORNING, Darren gently disentangled himself from Relaina as she slept on, adjusting the blanket around her shoulders before tending to the fire. He'd sent servants away when they arrived to see to the task and was glad he had; the simple work of ensuring the flames didn't extinguish grounded him after the events of the past two days. He breathed deeply and reveled in the flaring heat before setting the iron poker on the stone hearth. His pulse jumped as he glanced at the fiery red end of it. Another unpleasant memory. But his time in the dungeons of Castle Alterna had at least ended with relief. He would never forget how it had felt when

Relaina had shown up to save him. No one had ever been so full of rage on his behalf.

He was already bound to be hers after their fight in the ring and their conversation in Maurice's shop, but nothing could've stopped his foolish heart from falling for her when she spirited him out of Parea.

With a small smile, he kissed Relaina's forehead and made for the kitchens. He'd hoped to steal down there with little notice, but as he descended the final step into the dining area, he found himself facing Fabian. The king was speaking quietly to one of the kitchen workers. Darren recognized the man from the Shadow meetings.

"Oh," Fabian said, catching sight of Darren. The Shadow bowed swiftly and scurried off. "Good morning, Darren."

"Morning, Fabian," Darren said. "I'm sorry, I didn't mean to intrude—"

"It's no intrusion. Have you come down for breakfast?"

Darren nodded. "Relaina is still asleep, and I didn't want to wake her."

"Ah," Fabian said, sadness touching his eyes. "I'm glad she's getting some rest. Please, don't let me keep you."

Fabian started to walk past Darren for the stairs. Darren hadn't intended to speak to him now, but—

"Fabian?"

The king turned, expectant.

"I wanted to ask you...the prisoners I've questioned who are not loyal to Gabriel. Can we release them?"

Fabian's brow lifted. "Do you feel confident that we can trust them?"

Darren stood a bit straighter as he said, "I do. Many of them were forced to fight for my father and simply want to return home. Lady Eyern's wife is among them."

"Gods," Fabian said. A long moment passed as Fabian

studied him. "Very well then. I'll speak to the healers and my guards, and we can arrange for their release."

Darren exhaled. "Thank you. I wouldn't have asked if I wasn't certain."

There was that look in the king's eyes again, the one that made Darren feel like Fabian was peering right into his soul. "I know you wouldn't. You have my trust and my support, Darren."

"I'm grateful for both," Darren said. Fabian bid him good-bye, and Darren shook his head, refocusing on his original task.

He ate breakfast quickly and hurried back upstairs, a plan forming in his mind. He still needed to question other prisoners today, but first, he had business in the city. The two guards stationed outside their chambers nodded to him as he entered quietly. Relaina was still buried in the blankets. It was the most rest she'd gotten since the battle.

Darren stalked to the wardrobe and extracted his Shadow gear. Relaina didn't wake as he donned the form-fitting black pants and shirt and buckled the additional layers of protective material across his torso. He sheathed a set of six small knives across his chest and tucked several more in various concealed places. Satisfied with the number of blades, he headed for the entrance hall.

"No need to follow me," Darren said to the guards by the palace entrance. "I'll be in the city."

"Prince Darren, I'm under orders to—"

"I'll take the blame if King Fabian or Captain Fontaine questions you about it," Darren said. "I'm not taking the main roads, so unless you'd like to chase me across rooftops, I suggest you stay here."

The young guard opened and then closed his mouth, nodding as he stepped back. Darren pulled up his hood and mask before dashing outside.

Halfway to his destination, an old temple of Ashima stretched along the street. It had become a space for displaced artisans to sell their wares, and Darren stepped inside, curious. He wove between citygoers in the large space with ease. Limestone pillars rose at regular intervals, resolute and slightly worn with age. Jewelers lined an area that was well-protected by city guards.

He approached one of the tables with a collection of earrings and necklaces, examining the displays. One of the artisans collected payment from a customer and met Darren's gaze with a start.

"Prince Darren," she said, her eyes wide as she bowed, and several other vendors craned their necks to look at him. *Shit.* He'd forgotten about his eye. Even with the Shadow gear, nothing concealed the obsidian darkness that surrounded his brown iris. "How can I be of service?"

Darren prepared to politely decline assistance when a sparkling gemstone set into a silver ring caught his eye.

"Could I see that ring?" he asked, pointing it out.

"Ah," she said, retrieving it from the small, black velvet box where it lay. "A lavender moonstone." She held the ring out to him, and he took it carefully, studying the iridescent purple hues in the teardrop-shaped gem. It was delicate but sharp, and Relaina's favorite color.

Did she wear rings? Uncertainty made heat creep up his neck. But it reminded him of her, and it might lift her spirits.

"It's beautiful," he said.

"A gift or a self-indulgence?"

He swallowed. "A gift."

"If you're uncertain about the size, that can be adjusted after purchase. I can also remake it into another type of jewelry." The artisan's eyes were kind, her smile soft.

"How much?"

Darren paid for the ring and tucked the small box into a

pocket beneath the top layer of his Shadow gear. It rested above his heart, pressing lightly on his X-shaped scar.

He wandered around the temple for several more minutes, glancing at each table. At the very back, curtains had been strung between several pillars, and a couple emerged, speaking to a small woman who was wiping ink from her hands. They listened to her intently before setting off, holding up their arms to compare their fresh tattoos. Darren couldn't see the design from here, but they both smiled brightly before exchanging a kiss and lacing their hands together. *Betrothal tattoos.* His face heated. It wasn't a Terranian custom to get the tattoos, but Relaina was half Evarian. Would she want to get them?

Darren shook his head. He couldn't speculate on that when he hadn't even asked her yet. He passed by the city guards at the temple entrance and focused on his initial objective: Quentin Eriver's manor.

Darren couldn't track Kalmali now that he'd destroyed the shadow, but Relaina had been attacked twice in a matter of days, and he couldn't help but wonder if they were connected.

And he couldn't deny that there was part of him that wanted to find Quentin anyway. It was a different kind of darkness that stirred within him as he made his way through the streets, unrelated to his magic.

He'd discerned the manor's location weeks before, not long after Relaina had broken in and fought Quentin. The events that followed had overshadowed Darren's desire to find the man and bring a number of painful consequences to his door, but there were too many enemies on too many fronts now. If he could take care of this one quickly and quietly and perhaps learn some information in the process, why wouldn't he?

Darren disappeared behind an old building and scaled it, landing silently on the roof. A quick glance around told him he hadn't been seen. Shadows grew deeper as clouds parted and the sun emerged, and Darren's power vibrated softly beneath his skin.

After leaping across half a dozen rooftops and onto the outer wall of Quentin's manor, he assessed the grounds and the massive building that rose above him. He quickly located the study Relaina had mentioned on the second floor, illuminated by lanterns from within. He vaulted over the garden wall, his route decided.

With deft hands, Darren picked the lock on the balcony doors and slipped inside. Quentin stood from the chair behind his desk, cursing the weather as he moved to shut the doors again. The merchant made no more than a scuffling sound as Darren grabbed him from behind in a chokehold. His struggling slowed as Darren lowered him to the floor.

As soon as Quentin was unconscious, Darren retrieved a strand of rope from one of his many pockets. He shoved it between Quentin's teeth and tied it off before dragging the man to a wooden chair by a bookshelf, making quick work of binding his wrists and ankles to the chair arms and legs. It was all done in less than a minute, the method still second nature to him. He didn't have time to dwell on how he felt about that.

As expected, the merchant gasped awake, glancing around wildly for a moment before his panicked eyes landed on Darren. Darren pulled a small knife from his belt, studying the lightweight blade as he leaned casually on the desk.

"You know who I am?" he asked. Quentin nodded, his face paling. Darren bent down, holding the knife at Quentin's throat.

"I hear you have a problem with Princess Relaina," Darren said, his voice laced with silky venom. He'd mastered the tone years ago—soft and articulate, as if his teeth were made of knives, his tongue poisonous. It still had its intended effect.

Quentin trembled, his jugular bobbing against the blade as he swallowed. "Which means I have a problem with you."

Quentin tried to speak, but the rope muffled his voice almost entirely.

"Oh, I don't need an explanation or excuse. I'm not here to negotiate." Darren shoved the knife in Quentin's upper arm, and Quentin's howl barely made it past the thick rope. Darren watched Quentin carefully, but no darkness filled the man's eyes. He let a bit of his power drift from his right hand to be sure. His magic sensed no tenebrae nearby.

"I'm going to remove this," Darren said, gesturing to the rope in Quentin's mouth. "If you shout for help, the next knife goes in your heart."

Quentin nodded vigorously, his face scrunched up in pain. Darren removed the gag and stood in front of him, pulling another knife from his belt.

"Who do you work for?" he asked.

"Whoever pays me most," Quentin croaked. His chest heaved as he breathed rapidly. "Last man was called Gerratt."

Darren's uncle. "He's dead now."

"I know."

"What did he promise you?"

"Money, of course," Quentin wheezed. "And safety in King Gabriel's new empire."

Darren watched him for a moment. "So you supported Gabriel?"

"I supported surviving."

More of Darren's power appeared at his hands, but he held back the insults on his tongue. A man like this wasn't capable of shame.

"Do you know of any magic wielders who worked with Gerratt or Gabriel?" Darren asked. "Tenebrae or healers?"

Quentin nodded. "Tenebrae, but no healers. Gerratt was tenebrae."

"Is the name Kalmali familiar to you?"

"No," Quentin said, shuddering.

Darren leaned down again, his knife at Quentin's throat. "Whatever transgression you feel Princess Relaina has made against you is now forgotten. If you or your lackeys ever touch her again, I will end you all. Slowly. Same goes if you've lied to me today. Understood?"

With a small squeak, Quentin nodded.

"Good." Darren replaced the gag between his teeth. He took a step back and channeled all his strength into a kick that landed halfway down Quentin's shin, resulting in a satisfying *crack*. Quentin's muffled shrieks followed Darren for only a few moments before he vanished from the manor, melting into the shadows of the garden.

CHAPTER 18

THE PRIESTS' SYMBOLS

No one bothered Relaina all morning—Selene had stopped bringing her crìan contraceptive tea daily after Darren began taking the herbs himself, and no one expected her to show up at meetings or training today. Darren was likely in the dungeons again or at another meeting with the Terranians.

She stared at the gardens outside their chambers as a lack of urgency and obligation washed over her for the first time in weeks. It was probably still too soon to visit Jeremiah, and the memory of his broken voice sent a pang through her stomach. The events of the past few days and months still weighed on her, but as Relaina pulled on her Shadow gear and riding boots, determination thrummed through her bones.

She'd been a force of nature during the battle; she would figure out how to harness that power again. It wasn't wrong to want to reclaim that feeling. But Darren and the others had been right. Pushing herself until she broke wouldn't solve anything.

So rest it was. No meetings. No magic sessions. No sparring.

After retrieving a late breakfast from the kitchens, Relaina headed for the palace stables, greeting Amariah with a sugar cube. She rested her forehead on the mare's snout for a moment, stroking her soft neck.

"Want to go for a ride, beauty?" Relaina asked, and Amariah snorted and pawed at the ground. Relaina smiled. "I thought so."

Relaina waved off the stable worker who offered to help saddle Amariah, glad to have something mundane and familiar to occupy her hands and thoughts for a few minutes. She thanked him as she rode out of the stables, two guards riding just behind her. She donned her hood and mask. It was comfortable enough outside when walking, but once Amariah reached a gallop, the temperate air would turn frigid against her cheeks.

"Princess Relaina."

She halted Amariah and appraised one of the guards as they rode up beside her.

"Are you heading east?" she asked, adjusting her red cloak around the sword at her belt.

"I am. Not too far."

"Very well. We'll be right behind you."

With a grateful nod, Relaina nudged Amariah forward. The gloves, mask, and hood did wonderfully to keep her warm as she exited the palace grounds at the eastern gate and took off, passing the old Evarian ruins where Fabian and Gabriel had fought. She wished she could have seen the look on Gabriel's face when Jeremiah had disarmed him.

Just over the cliff by the ruins, scars of the battle still marred the ground, leading directly to the eastern city wall. Relaina was glad they'd evacuated that part of the city prior to Gabriel's arrival, or many more lives would have been lost.

Fabian himself had nearly died, as had Darren. Countless others were dead. As a blur of trees whipped by on either side of the path, Relaina lamented how quickly she'd killed Gabriel. If she could have inflicted every cut, wound, bruise, and burn upon him that he'd inflicted upon Darren over the years, she would have done so. And she'd have smiled as she did it.

Anxiety prickled along her scalp. Darren had admitted to his own questionable deeds, but did he truly have thoughts as dark as hers? It was difficult to imagine his gentle eyes hardened into a cold, heartless stare or him smiling with satisfaction at harm he'd caused.

But his father had sharpened him into the ultimate tool of death, and perhaps that part of him was something he kept tucked away. She'd seen glimpses of it when he fought. *I am merciful. But you don't deserve it.*

Relaina shivered. Was it wrong that she reveled in both his gentleness and his violence?

As if her thoughts summoned him, a whisper of darkness pulled at her from the west, accompanied by a touch of surprise. It faded, wordless and fleeting, and the urgency of learning more about their connection settled in her mind again.

"Your Highness! *Your Highness!*"

Relaina blinked as the forest path came back into focus.

"Princess Relaina!"

She slowed Amariah to a walk, allowing the guards to catch up.

"It's beginning to rain," the guard said, squinting as a few drops hit her in the face. How long had she been trying to get Relaina's attention? "The clouds gathered quickly."

"Ah." Relaina looked wistfully at the damp forest around them, full of leafless trees occasionally punctuated by an evergreen. "I suppose we ought to return, then."

By the time they reached the stables, all three of them were soaked through. The rain came down in unrelenting sheets as

Relaina dismounted. She offered profuse apologies for having them out in such weather, but the guards insisted they were fine. After ensuring Amariah was taken care of, Relaina dashed through the rain back to the palace.

Darren wasn't in their rooms when she arrived, and after changing into dry clothes, she sat and ate lunch halfheartedly, her mind wandering as she stared at the rain in the gardens. Just as she reached for an orange slice, the silver title of a face-down, open book caught her eye, and she picked it up from the table. Darren must have been reading it. She glanced over the page he'd left off on and flipped to the following pages with little enthusiasm until familiar markings caught her eye.

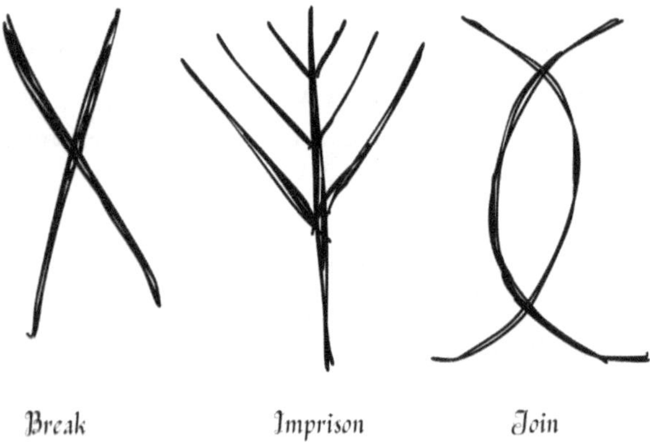

Relaina stared at the page for a moment before reading the description below, so eager to digest the information that she nearly ripped the page as she turned it.

Shadowfire blades inflict excruciating pain, but the wounds heal more quickly than those caused by nonmagic blades. Surviving victims relayed that their wounds healed within a week, but the scars themselves refused to fade. While many priests of Calixtos believe these symbols to enact some magical effect based on what each represents, there is little evidence that they do anything beyond permanently scar the victim.

The door to their chambers opened, and Relaina started, dropping the orange slice in her hand as Darren entered, his wet hair plastered to his face and neck. They spoke simultaneously as their eyes locked.

"I found something."

"I have something for you."

Darren approached the table, then thought better of it as he dripped water onto the floor. He must've gotten caught in the rain as well.

"Let me get a towel, then you first," he said, heading into the washroom. He returned moments later, drying his hands and hair. Relaina showed him the page, and he studied it more closely, plopping into the chair next to hers as he scanned the pages.

"What are your thoughts on this?" he asked, his brow furrowing.

Relaina bit her lip. "What if the symbols don't work on normal people or dark magic wielders?"

Understanding touched his eyes. "But they work on light-wielders."

Relaina nodded. "Shadowfire only leaves black scars on healers, right?"

"As far as I know."

Relaina stood and strode to the nearby vanity, unlacing her red tunic and dropping it off her shoulders so she could see the symbol on her back in the mirror. It almost precisely matched the middle drawing. Darren joined her, holding up the book as he compared the two.

"I knew what the symbols meant to the priests," he said. "I thought it was nonsense because it didn't break me the way my father wanted. He thought it would detach my heart from my mind. But if it works on healers..."

"It's not an answer for how to fix it, but it's something. Where did you get that book?"

"I found it in the library. I hadn't gotten to the page you read yet."

Relaina pulled her shirt back onto her shoulders. "I'll see what the healers think about it tomorrow. But what have you been doing today?"

Darren placed the book on the vanity and turned to face her. "I went into the city. Made a detour to the artisan market, then stopped by a certain merchant's manor."

Relaina raised an eyebrow. "You went after Quentin." Darren nodded. Relaina studied him, counting at least four knives attached to his still-wet Shadow armor. "What did you find out?"

"His loyalty lies with the highest bidder, and he wasn't connected to Kalmali or the white-haired woman as far as I could tell. He worked for my mother's brother, who's dead now."

"Hmm." Relaina frowned. "Did you kill him?"

"Just a knife wound...and a broken shin."

"Impressive restraint."

They both laughed softly, and her skin tingled pleasantly as he brushed his fingers against her cheek.

"Oh," he said, reaching for a pouch on his chest and extracting a small velvet box. It was slightly less damp than the rest of him. "I found this today. Well, I bought it, I mean."

Relaina took the box and opened it with an encouraging nod from him. An intricately carved silver ring rested inside with a shining lavender stone set into its center, shaped like a teardrop. She lifted it carefully and gaped at it, speechless.

"I knew it was your favorite color," he said, "and it reminded me of you as soon as I saw it. The jeweler said if it doesn't fit we can go back and have it adjusted."

Relaina slipped it onto her middle finger with no issue, holding it up to the light.

"Do you like it?"

Relaina looked at him. His wrinkled brow and hopeful face were too much—despite his wet clothes, she wrapped her arms around his neck.

"It's beautiful," she said, and he exhaled, warmth enveloping her as he returned her embrace. "Truly, I love it. Thank you."

"Oh, thank the gods."

She leaned back, her fresh clothes no longer dry. "Now I'll have to change again."

Darren's eyes traveled down her torso and back up again, and her stomach flipped pleasantly.

"I can help with that," he said. "Though I'd like to clean up first. And I may delay you putting clothes back on."

Relaina sighed dramatically and began walking away from him. "How will I ever stand it?"

Darren caught her wrist to draw her back, and with a smirk she twisted out of his grasp, grabbing his arm and pushing him against the wall by the vanity. Shock and a touch of amusement colored his features.

"Is this okay?" she asked, brushing his arm with her thumb. Darren's mouth twitched.

"You did say it was your turn next time."

Slowly, he reached for her hand and wrapped her fingers around his wrist. He didn't break eye contact as he did the same with her other hand and then raised both of his arms over his head. The movement drew her closer, so her body was flush against his, and her eyes widened as his arousal pressed against her thigh. His arms went slack, and she held his wrists in place against the wall above his head.

"You're in control," he said. Relaina's breath caught as waves of heat rolled through her center and between her legs. "I'll tell you if it's too much."

Relaina released his wrists as she leaned in to kiss him softly, holding his face instead.

"I'll need my hands to get your clothes off," she said, and he shivered. Relaina reached for his top layer, her fingers gliding against the hilt of a small knife. She pulled it from its holster and tossed it onto the vanity, lightly brushing her lips along his. He pressed forward and she pulled back, teasing him before pulling the protective material over his head. At the sight of all the knives strapped to his chest and waist, she burst out laughing.

"Gods in *hell*, Darren."

He shrugged. "I like to be prepared."

Relaina kissed him again, thoroughly this time, and pressed her palm to the bulge in his pants. He broke away with a moan. "*Fuck*, Relaina."

"Just making sure it wasn't another knife." She peeled off her own shirt and tossed it at his feet as she walked to the bed. "Clean up and dry off. I'll be waiting."

DARREN EXITED the washroom with nothing but a towel around his waist. He approached the foot of the bed, perplexed at Relaina's absence before soft footsteps padded behind him and Relaina embraced him, kissing his back. Her bare breasts pressed against his skin as her hands glided down his chest. He turned around and marveled at her smooth skin, her scars, her breasts, her mouth...

"You're the most beautiful person I've ever seen," he murmured, threading his fingers through her dark curls. Relaina smiled and kissed him, her tongue teasing his upper lip before she pressed her palms to his chest.

"Get on the bed," she said. His erection pressed against the towel at the order. Relaina's eyes roved over him shamelessly as he stepped back and sat on the mattress, the towel tightening around his hips. His skin heated and buzzed with anticipation. She approached him, taking his face in her hands and lifting his chin.

"You're beautiful too," she whispered. She pushed him back onto the bed gently. She kissed his chest, then his sternum, her hands following the progress of her mouth as she traveled ever lower. She tugged at the towel and let it unravel, revealing his hardness fully. His heart picked up speed. Was she going to—?

"I want to do this first," she said. "Is that okay?"

Darren's voice nearly failed him. "Yes."

Relaina's mouth closed around his tip, and he melted into a blissful haze as her tongue traveled along his length and sent waves of pleasure through him over and over. As she continued, his power threatened to appear, and he reined it back in.

"Stop," he gasped at last, and Relaina emerged from between his legs, a question in her eyes. "Wait. I need you. All of you."

Relaina kissed his abdomen before crawling on top of him, straddling him at the waist. She reached between their legs, stroking him a few times before guiding him to her entrance, and slowly lowered herself onto him.

"I'll be still for a moment," she said, and Darren breathed deeply, closing his eyes. Relaina left tingles along his skin where she traced his largest scar.

"It was shadowfire that did this?" she asked, and Darren

opened his eyes again. Her dark curls cascaded over her bare shoulders, a few ringlets ending just past her breasts.

"Yes," he said. "Four years ago."

Relaina leaned down and kissed the raised, white-pink flesh right where it crossed over his heart.

"I'm glad it didn't work," she said.

"So am I."

With a glint in her eyes, Relaina sat up and threw her hips forward, and his hands flew to her thighs, gripping them tightly. She rode him for a minute or so before grabbing his wrists and pinning them above his head on the bed.

"You like that?" Her voice was huskier than normal, and his eyes rolled back in his head as he moaned his assent. His breathing grew uneven as his climax drew nearer, but Relaina slowed down, taking her time sliding up and down every inch of him. When she quickly thrust her hips down again, it drew a groan from him.

"Fuck," he ground out, and Relaina laughed softly near his ear. He huffed as she stilled, trying and failing to hide a smile. "Are you laughing at me?"

"I just...enjoy seeing you so undone," she said, sitting up so she could see his face. Darren bucked his hips, drawing a surprised gasp from her.

"The feeling is mutual." He grinned as she narrowed her eyes and leaned forward, pinning his wrists again. He lifted his mouth to one of her nipples, flicking it with his tongue, and she whimpered, grinding against him. Her grip on his wrists tightened as she started moving again, and Darren surrendered himself to her entirely, allowing his power to freely manifest, allowing her to bring him pleasure and chase her own. She bent down and nipped at his ear before kissing him again.

"You are *mine*," she growled, and Darren's hands twitched, aching to touch every part of her he could reach, to claim her in return. But Relaina held fast, keeping him firmly in her control. She needed this—deserved to feel as powerful as she was. And gods, he *was* hers. They were connected in a way he didn't fully understand, and he was utterly, unconditionally hers. Her lust-drunk eyes found his as his shadows drifted around them and her voice entered his mind. *And I'm yours.*

Relaina released his wrists and took one of his hands, keeping eye contact with him as she put his thumb in her mouth before guiding it between her thighs.

"If you need all of me," she said, "then take all of me."

Darren sat up, drawing one of her nipples into his mouth again, and she threw her head back as he rubbed her clit and began thrusting into her. *Harder,* she thought to him, and he whisked her into his arms to flip them over, giving him better leverage as she wrapped her legs around his waist. Soon Relaina's moans reached a peak, and she shuddered, her inner walls tightening around him so forcefully it sent him over the edge. He kept thrusting as Relaina came, the fingernails of one hand digging into his back, the other hand gripping his hair. As his release barreled through him, he sank his teeth into her shoulder, and her gasps continued until he stopped moving. They lay there for several moments, dazed.

"Fuck," Relaina said, her breath cool against his sweaty shoulder. He rolled over, gently pulling out of her. He caught his breath for another moment and then kissed her neck before retrieving the towel they'd discarded at the foot of the bed. Relaina quickly cleaned herself and then flopped back onto the mattress, sidling up to him and tracing the various scars on his chest. He pressed his lips to the top of her head.

"I want to bathe, but I also don't want to move," he said, and she giggled. She kissed him again, her lips soft and gentle.

Several minutes later, they were both partly submerged in the bath, and Relaina lathered soap on Darren's chest, her face tranquil.

"Relaina." Darren hesitated for a moment.

"What is it?"

"...Can I show you?"

He held out his hand, and Relaina nodded, taking it. Their darkness connected with cooling sweetness, and she rested her head on his shoulder as the hot water lapped around their waists. He didn't send her any particular thoughts, but he wanted her to feel what he felt, to know what it meant to him that he could be so undone, as she'd said, that he was safe to be so vulnerable with her.

"Oh." The word fell from Relaina's mouth with a deep exhale as the gravity of what he wanted to convey settled on her. She wrapped her arms around him and held him close. *I feel the same way with you.* And she did. He could feel that too.

Darren traced the shadowfire scars along her back as they lapsed into silence. He knew he needed to talk to her about answering the Terranians, and what that meant for them both. The courage to do so was just out of reach as he held her in the warmth of the bath.

A knock sounded at their chamber door, and both of them jumped. Relaina sighed, climbing out of the bath and toweling off quickly before tossing a scarlet robe over her shoulders. Darren sank back into the bath as he waited for her to return, closing his eyes.

"Darren."

His eyes flew open again, and his heart jumped into his throat when she drew closer.

"What is it?"

"They found Kalmali," she said. "But Alaris is dead."

CHAPTER 19

TESTING DARKNESS

Fabian stared at the body before him in the inn cellar as two healers completed their work and stood back. He'd watched in stony-faced silence as they'd mended a deep slash across Alaris's chest. The man's face had been left untouched and appeared almost peaceful now, but one of his hands was broken, and there were six stab wounds to his belly.

Footsteps announced Darren's arrival, and the prince's eyes widened at the dead man.

"He snuck out of the palace," Fabian said, still staring at Alaris's face. "One of my guards said he'd overheard him say something about finding Kalmali himself."

"Kalmali isn't tenebrae anymore," Darren said. "He probably thought he could fight him."

Fabian shook his head, closing his eyes. "Foolish man. Is there a way for you to ascertain if the shadow has gone?"

Darren's eyes flashed black for a moment, and Fabian watched in quiet awe as his power appeared in his palms. In the darkness of the cellar, he could see tiny flickers of iridescent light within the vaporous shadows. Darren stepped closer to Alaris, then turned back to Fabian, his power fading.

"I don't sense any tenebrae nearby," he said. "It's likely the shadow died with him."

The two of them trekked up the narrow stairwell, leaving guards to watch over Alaris's body.

"So the shadow possessing Lady Delimont had latched onto her before its owner died?" Fabian asked.

Darren nodded. "The night we were attacked here several months ago, one of those tenebrae tried to latch onto Relaina before the woman died. If they don't manage to do that before the owner's body dies, the shadow dies with them."

"I see."

Desiree waited at the top of the stairs with more of her city guards, falling in step with Fabian and Darren as they emerged into The Gnarled Root.

"Is Relaina here as well?" Fabian asked.

"She's waiting in the main hall," Desiree said. As much as Fabian had hoped Relaina would rest, he couldn't blame her for coming. His first instinct upon hearing of Kalmali's capture was to travel here alone and throttle the man with his bare hands. But that was neither productive nor his area of expertise.

They stepped into the main room of the inn, a dining area which had been emptied of patrons. The two Shadows that had found Kalmali and Alaris fighting sat silently at a table behind Relaina, who was also garbed in her Shadow attire. She didn't have her mask up, but she did have murder in her eyes. Perhaps that's how Fabian himself looked.

"Where?" Relaina asked, standing.

Desiree looked to Fabian, and he nodded.

"This way," Desiree said, and the three of them followed her to the other end of the room. Two guards stood outside a heavy wooden door, unlocking it at Desiree's request. They stepped into a dingy, unused storeroom with no windows and a single lantern, and a few feet away sat Kalmali, propped against the wall with his hands and feet bound by shackles. His eyes darted to each of them but came to rest on Relaina.

"You've brought the Pretender bitch before me again," he said. Fabian could almost feel the rage teeming from Relaina as she crossed the small room and hauled Kalmali to his feet.

"I'd choose my words more carefully, you slithery fuck."

"You've got your mother's temper, I see." Kalmali smirked. "I suppose Talea didn't live long enough to teach you that threats don't work when your target doesn't fear death."

"Who said anything about letting you die?" Relaina's voice sent a shiver down Fabian's spine, and Kalmali's smirk faded into a scowl. As much as Fabian would like to hand Kalmali over to Relaina and allow her to visit every possible agony upon him, they needed the man coherent. But Kalmali didn't have to know that.

"You'll have to wait, Relaina," Fabian said. "We need to move him."

"Bad business for my brother to disturb his inn patrons with screams," Desiree said. "Darren?"

Darkness appeared along Darren's arms, almost invisible against his black sleeves. Kalmali recoiled.

"You destroy your own and associate with magical bastards," Kalmali spat. "You are a disgrace to Calixtos."

A breeze picked up in the room, darkness nearly blotting out the torchlight before gathering and collapsing toward Relaina. She reeled back and cracked Kalmali across the face with a gloved fist, letting him slump to the ground of the dusty storeroom.

Light returned, and silence grew as Relaina stepped back from Kalmali and turned to Darren, her eyes wide.

"What in Ashima's name just happened?" Desiree asked.

Relaina shook her head. "I...."

"I think...Relaina channeled some of my power," Darren said, flexing one of his hands as the shadows disappeared.

Fabian took a quiet breath as the hairs on his arms stood on end. They needed answers about Relaina and Darren's power, and now Alaris, one of the few people that might have shed more light on it, was dead.

"We need his information, so we must keep him alive," Fabian said as Desiree nudged Kalmali's cheek with her boot. "There's a powerful woman he works for. Jeremiah saw her."

Images of Jeremiah screaming and thrashing in his sleep the night before flashed through Fabian's weary mind. Four times Fabian had pulled him close, drawing him out of some hellish nightmare, and Jeremiah had cried until he'd fallen back asleep.

And the man responsible for Jeremiah's pain lay on the ground a few feet away. Perhaps he ought to leave Kalmali unguarded for a few hours once they moved him to the dungeons, and give Relaina free rein...

But no, as much as Kalmali deserved it, that would not help them get the information they sought. Fabian couldn't allow himself to make decisions based on a reckless desire for revenge.

Desiree motioned for two guards to retrieve Kalmali while Relaina and Darren stood in the corner of the storeroom, speaking softly. They all returned to the well-lit dining hall as Desiree and her guards headed into the streets with their prisoner in tow.

"Fabian," Relaina said, her voice tight. "This woman, Kalmali's master...I have to speak with Jeremiah."

Fabian nodded. "I know. I'll talk to him."

Relaina began to say something else, but merely nodded instead.

"Will you be returning to Seacastle with us?" Darren asked Fabian as Relaina went to speak to the two Shadows several feet away.

"I'll be returning, but I'll take a different route. Please take care as you venture back; my Shadows haven't brought me a report on Quentin Eriver yet."

"Ah." Darren glanced at Relaina before lowering his voice. "I don't think we'll need to worry about him anymore."

"Oh?"

"I paid him a visit earlier today."

Fabian fought a wince. "Is he dead?"

"No. But I think I've frightened him off. And I don't think he's working with Kalmali."

Fabian exhaled. "Well, I'm glad you stayed your hand. I'll still have my Shadows keep watch."

Darren's brow furrowed as Relaina joined them again. "If he's to be believed, he was working with Lord Gerratt to smuggle the explosive crystals into the city and capture Relaina. They promised him safety once Gabriel took over."

"And his purpose in sending his lackeys after Relaina the other day?"

"A leftover grudge, as far as I could tell," Darren said.

"Bastard," Relaina muttered.

"Regardless," Fabian said. "I'll let you both know if my Shadows find out anything more about him. Darren, we'll need to focus on freeing those prisoners tomorrow. Josquin Fontaine and other innkeepers have offered to house a few of them here before their return to Terrana."

"That's very generous of them," Darren said. "We'll see you tomorrow, then."

"Tomorrow," Fabian said with a tired nod.

THE SUN SHONE ON THE HEALERS' sanctuary for the first time in weeks, but Aronn's mood was darker than ever. The frigid panes of glass had warmed beneath his forehead as he stared out the window in the meeting room. Ever since the close call on the outskirts of Parea, he'd been barred from leaving the sanctuary. How they were able to tell him to do anything was a mystery, since according to rank, he should be in charge in Jeremiah's absence. They wouldn't treat Relaina this way, that was for certain.

But Relaina wasn't useless in a fight, and Jeremiah had left Saheer and Misenia in charge. Even when three healers had arrived from Maremer the day prior, they had no message from Jeremiah, nor had they crossed paths with him on their journey. Aronn could at least take solace in the fact that they'd safely delivered Annalise to King Fabian and Relaina's care.

Aronn sighed and stood, heading into the main hall of the healers' sanctuary. It was still strange to know Jeremiah was Relaina's birth father, to know that he, Aronn, was the true firstborn in the Gienty line. But after the events of last autumn, it hardly made a difference. He would always see Relaina as his sister, and she'd relinquished her claim to the Lyneisian throne even before discovering the circumstances of her birth.

Just as Aronn entered the large room, raised voices drew nearer from outside, and three men burst through the doors. The shortest man's brown face and black ponytail came into view as he lowered his snow-dusted hood, talking rapidly to a male healer wearing the veil every healer from this sanctuary wore. Another man covered in snow and travel-worn clothing studied the room with pointed scrutiny, his eyes narrowing as his tawny-brown arms lit up with a healer's light. The veiled healer stopped in his tracks as the short man spoke, his eyes widening in horror.

Dread washed over Aronn. Someone must be dead. Or injured. Or—

"Varun, Shojen!"

Saheer dashed away from a dining table at the far end of the room, greeting the men. Relief lit up Varun's features as she clasped arms with him, but Shojen remained hypervigilant.

"Hello Saheer," Varun said.

"You bring news from Maremer?"

Aronn wanted to get closer, to greet these messengers, but he couldn't make his feet move.

"We do," Varun said, his eyes darting to Aronn, then to the various healers and nobles around the room, whose conversations had quieted in the wake of his arrival. "But we must speak to the healers first."

"What do you mean?" Saheer asked, brow furrowing over her hazel eyes. Shojen held out a hand to her. Puzzled, Saheer placed her hand in the healer's. He stood perfectly still for a moment before nodding to her and Varun.

"What in the name of the gods is going on?" Lady Elke stood from another table and strode toward them, drawing her cloak around her shoulders. Her brother Hektor followed close behind.

"Apologies, Lady Elke," the veiled healer said. "We will return shortly."

The man beckoned to three of his Lyneisian fellows, including the elder, Ericka, and led Varun, Shojen, and Saheer past Aronn into the meeting room. Aronn stared at the closed wooden door. Seconds later, Saheer burst back out of it with alarm in her eyes.

"No one leaves or enters the sanctuary!" she barked, and the healers scurried past her to whisper to others scattered about the room. "Everyone remain where you are!"

Questions and indignant shouts rang out as healers barred each exit. Aronn's heart picked up speed.

"Saheer, what's going on?" he asked. Her eyes barely softened as she looked at him.

"Your uncle was possessed by a tenebrae when he left us," she said, her voice so low only he could hear. Terror gripped

Aronn's insides. That explained his swift and strange departure, the cold exchange he'd had with Aronn. "We must ensure no one else has fallen victim."

"How do we do that?"

Shojen stepped forward, holding out a glowing hand to Aronn.

"A simple test," he said. Tentatively, Aronn placed his hand in the healer's. Soothing warmth spread along Aronn's skin, but nothing more. Shojen nodded and stepped back. "I will assess the others."

While the remaining healers verified each person in the healers' sanctuary, Aronn and Saheer listened intently to the rest of Varun's story. Aronn's stomach lurched when he told them Jeremiah had nearly killed Relaina, the tenebrae evidently unaware of Relaina's ability to sense its presence at the slightest touch.

"She is safe now, I assure you," Varun said, inclining his head to Aronn.

"These gods-damned shadows," Saheer said, nearly smacking a short healer in the face when she flung out an arm in exasperation. "Oh, apologies."

"That's quite all right," the healer said, her voice melodic and her crystalline-blue eyes wide with kindness. Aronn didn't think he'd seen her before, but it was difficult to tell when all the healers here wore the same bone-white tunics and dark blue head scarves and veils. He started to look away when she caught his eye. Did he know her from somewhere?

"And when will Captain Andovier return?" Saheer asked as Aronn blinked and forced his attention away from the healer.

"Soon, we hope," Varun said. "He was recovering when I left but did not seem gravely injured. And now that midwinter has passed, hopefully the trek will be easier."

Saheer sighed. "In the meantime, do we have any instructions?"

"Ensure no one is captured or harmed, continue to gather information on the king and queen's whereabouts as much as you're able. But no breaching city gates."

Aronn avoided Saheer's pointed look. He'd already been chastised enough for his excursion into Parea, and poor Mazin had been given the worst shifts on guard duty. Hektor's punishment had been left to his elder sister, and Lady Elke did little more than briefly chastise him.

"Very well," Saheer said. "Let's ensure no one else is possessed, and then we'll call a meeting."

CHAPTER 20

A PART TO PLAY

Jeremiah gazed at the white curtains by the balcony doors in Fabian's chambers. The glass panes were free of frost. The weather here was so different from Parea, the air more temperate even if the storms were violent. But he wasn't supposed to be here. He was meant to be in Parea, in the cold, leading the Lyneisian loyalists.

"Jeremiah?" Rhea asked. She sat in the chair across from him in Fabian's bedchamber, her eyes patient as she waited for his response. "I asked if you've been eating."

"Some," he said. "But probably not as much as I should."

Rhea nodded. "It will help if you don't skip meals. Are any of your injuries still bothersome?"

Jeremiah shook his head, and the ironclad fist of guilt gripped his lungs; he'd been injured only because he'd attacked Relaina. Rhea stood from her chair.

"May I?"

The healer held out her hands as they lit up, healer markings traveling from her palms to her forearms.

"I've been healed," Jeremiah said.

"True, but this will allow me to better understand how to help."

With a tentative sigh, Jeremiah gave his consent. Rhea placed her hands on either side of his head and closed her eyes. Soothing warmth enveloped him. When the healer stepped back and opened her eyes, they were full of tears. She blinked them away.

"I am so sorry, Jeremiah." The earnest empathy in her voice made it easier for him to breathe for the first time in days. "You have endured much. Your strength was not easily won."

"And yet my strength failed when it was most needed."

Rhea smiled at him sadly. "I don't think you realize how much willpower it took for you to break the tenebrae's hold, even for a moment."

Jeremiah's ever-spiraling shame stopped in its tracks. "What?"

"It's almost unheard of for someone with non-magical blood to be able to fend off a tenebrae's possession. By strength of will alone you saved Relaina's life."

He wanted to believe it. He needed to believe it.

A knock sounded at the door just before Fabian entered, and Rhea bowed.

"Good morning, Rhea," Fabian said. He stood by Jeremiah's chair, taking one of his hands. The king lowered his voice. "Morning, love."

"I was just telling Jeremiah how extraordinary it was that he resisted the tenebrae's possession," Rhea said.

Fabian squeezed his fingers, and another sliver of hope broke through Jeremiah's cloud of despair.

"Even so," Jeremiah said. "How do I cope with these nightmares? I can't sleep without seeing—" It was impossible to say it aloud. His hands around Relaina's throat. Her skull hitting the ground as he aimed a knife at her.

"You may want to drink ulìa tea before bed," Rhea said. "It will help sooth your nerves before you sleep. I'll tell the kitchens."

"Thank you, Rhea," Fabian said, and the healer bowed again before taking her leave. Fabian knelt before Jeremiah. "How are you feeling?"

Jeremiah took a long, shaky breath. "Better. I'll be fine. I can go back to Parea soon."

"Is that what you think I'm concerned about?" Fabian took Jeremiah's face in his hands, his brow furrowing over his lovely eyes. "I am here as the man who loves you, Jeremiah, not your king."

Each word shattered Jeremiah's resolve to suppress the grief, fear, and guilt within. Tears filled his eyes before he could stop them, one escaping down his left cheek. Fabian brushed it away and kissed his forehead.

"I can't sleep...not with the nightmares," Jeremiah said. "I see it all again every time I close my eyes."

"Then perhaps you ought to see Relaina." Fabian ran his fingers through Jeremiah's hair. "So you know for certain that she is well. She wants to see you. She has missed you terribly, and avoiding her will only hurt you both more."

Jeremiah's face scrunched as he fought back more tears. "All right. I'll see her."

THE SHORT MAREMER winter was steadily shifting toward spring. There was still a light chill in the air, but Relaina and the healers had all shed their cloaks after only a few minutes outside, taking advantage of the cloudless morning. The stone table and benches had dried enough after the recent rains that water no longer seeped into their clothing when they sat down.

Relaina tried not to fidget as she sat across from Nehma and the others in the gardens, waiting for their reaction to her theory about the shadowfire scars.

"So you believe these symbols work on light-wielders specifically?" Nehma asked, staring at the book before her with Rhea, Thea, and Catrin looking over her shoulders.

"It's a theory," Relaina said. "It would explain why my scars clash with the light and prevent my own healing magic from spreading in my body."

Catrin swore under her breath while Rhea stepped away, absently twisting the end of her braid.

"We should contact the elders in the Caspian Forest," Thea said. "They might know more about this, about the history of any conflict between the tenebrae and the healers."

"We can't send information like this in a letter," Nehma said.

"One of us could go," Thea said.

"And leave even fewer healers behind to help manage the tenebrae prisoners?"

"Many of them are set to be freed today," Rhea said, turning away from a tree she'd been examining. "And I'm confident after seeing Darren's power that he and the rest of the healers will have a solid handle on the others."

"I agree," Catrin said, flicking her red hair over her shoulder. "I'd be happy to go."

"We can't send you alone, Catrin," Nehma said.

"Then I'll find a guard willing to accompany me. There's a handsome one I've seen by the dungeons a few times."

"And how do you know he'd be willing to go?"

"I've caught him looking at my ass at least twice."

Nehma snorted. "You overestimate the power of your ass."

Someone behind Relaina cleared his throat, and their laughter faded quickly as each of them turned to their unexpected visitor.

"Princess Relaina," the guard said, unamused. "Lord Andovier has requested to meet with you in the portrait gallery."

All humor vacated Relaina's body. She looked to Rhea, who smiled encouragingly.

Relaina's palms grew damp, her heart thundering in her chest as she followed the guard inside the palace. Jeremiah had turned her away two days prior—she would have to make sure he knew she didn't blame him. Knowing him, though, he would blame himself anyway.

Just as the guard reached for the door to the portrait gallery, it opened, and Fabian stepped outside. He placed his hands on Relaina's shoulders.

"Are you all right?" he asked. Relaina nodded. Fabian moved aside to let her through.

Jeremiah stood by a tall window on the left side of the room, turning when Relaina entered. His face crumpled, his upper body shuddering as he took a breath. It was the man she knew, freed from the clutches of the tenebrae, but her heartrate still jumped at the sight of him, her mind calling forth memories of him slamming her against the mosaic tile with his hand around her throat.

The fear was instinctual, and she fought to stay rooted to the spot.

"You don't have to come closer," he said quietly.

Relaina stared at him, torn between the desire to throw her arms around him and flee the room. She took a breath and sat in a chair nearby. Jeremiah did the same with the couch across from her, his movements slow and deliberate. She hated this. Every part of her *hated* that he had to be so careful not to frighten her, hated that now that she saw him, she knew his caution was necessary.

"I'm so sorry, Relaina," he said, his voice breaking. "I'm so sorry."

"I don't blame you." Even as she fought not to tremble, Relaina's voice was firm. "I knew how hard you fought against it. I wasn't going to let that fucker take you from me."

Jeremiah closed his eyes for a moment, as if he were reliving that horrible memory himself. "You're well, then?"

Relaina nodded. "I'm not hurt...well not anymore. The light and dark magic collided again."

Relaina explained the symbol on her back, and what she'd discovered in the book. As they spoke, she watched him carefully, growing calmer each second he appeared more like himself.

"Catrin wants to travel to the Caspian Forest to speak with the elders there," Relaina said. "She thinks they may know more about it."

"Hmm." Jeremiah frowned, his dark brown eyes tired but pensive. "Perhaps she can travel that way with me when I return to Parea."

Relaina's heartbeat quickened. "Has there been any word about my parents?"

"We're confident they're alive, but I was...compromised... before an important mission was supposed to take place. I've sent them word of what happened here and given instructions to keep gathering information in my absence."

Relaina rubbed the glassy stone in the ring Darren had given her. She wanted to insist that she return to Parea with Jeremiah, but it was still too risky.

"When will you leave?" she asked.

"Soon. Within a few days."

The piece of her heart that would follow him when he left cracked.

"I will make sure Christine and Stephan are safe," he said. "I'll do everything I can."

Relaina stood, wrapping her arms around herself. She

approached an old portrait of Fabian's father, King Tristan Thereux.

"What is it?" Jeremiah asked.

Relaina took a moment to respond. "I...gods, Jeremiah, so much has happened here, I don't know where to begin. The Terranian nobles have placed enormous pressure on both Fabian and Darren."

"I'd heard they were here."

"They've been pushing Darren to make a claim to the throne."

Jeremiah's face slackened with shock. "I see. What does he intend to do?"

Relaina looked through the windows at the azure sky peeking through the garden trees.

"I don't know," she said. She turned to face Jeremiah again. "But I think he would make a good king. And I'll stand by him no matter his choice."

Sadness touched Jeremiah's eyes as he smiled. "You truly love him."

"I do." She returned to her seat and reached across the short table between them, offering him her hand. He took it tentatively. "But I love you, too, and I love Aronn and Annalise and my parents, and I want to make sure you're all safe."

Jeremiah shook his head.

"You have always been so clever, Relaina. And so compassionate. I know you have a part to play in bringing Esran toward lasting peace, but even you cannot fix the problems of all three kingdoms."

Relaina sat with that for a moment. He was right.

"So what do I do?" she whispered.

"What you can." Jeremiah squeezed her hands. "Join Darren if that's where you're called. You were born in Terrana. Perhaps you're meant to return there."

Relaina closed her eyes, dropping his hands and leaning back in her chair. "Perhaps I am. But after what has happened recently, I'm not sure how to feel about my birth. About Talea."

Jeremiah frowned. "It seems we both learned more about her recently."

"I don't know what to make of it. An older tenebrae told us about a Seer who worked for Gabriel, and if Gabriel said he knew my mother...I feel like it must have been her."

"That's very possible," Jeremiah said, frown deepening.

Relaina's voice was small as she said, "Right after the explosion on the river, I dreamt of her. I saw her final moments."

Jeremiah's eyes widened. "You had a vision?"

Relaina nodded. "A healers' village in Terrana was on fire, and tenebrae were slaughtering light-wielders. She sacrificed herself to save them."

Relaina hadn't told anyone the details of the dream, but the images of the village had rooted firmly in her mind. Jeremiah rubbed his face.

"Both of us sought solace from our pain, and we found it with each other. She was kind to me for the brief time we were together," he said. "I can't speak to her past, but if she died protecting you and saving healers, that was a noble way to leave the world."

Relaina looked through the windows again, uncertainty raising the hairs on her arms.

"I doubt Kalmali will be forthcoming with information," she said. "But there must be others that knew her, who could provide some answers."

Jeremiah took a moment to respond. "I hope you're right."

CHAPTER 21

THE FREED PRISONERS

Darren glanced at the eastern garden path while he waited at the dungeon entrance, anxious for Relaina to arrive. Fabian stood several feet behind him, speaking softly with Desiree and several guards.

"Kalmali is separate from the others, correct?" Fabian asked.

"He is, Your Majesty. And the healers have him under strict watch."

Voices drifted from the northern path, and the Caspian healers appeared. Thea and Catrin smiled at Darren, and Nehma nodded once.

"Is Relaina not with you?" he asked, and Nehma shook her head.

"Jeremiah asked to speak with her."

"Oh," Darren said. "I hope that went well."

"As do I."

Moments later, Relaina appeared, greeting everyone breathlessly.

"Are we all prepared?" Fabian asked.

Relaina slipped her fingers through Darren's. The warmth of her hand steadied him as they followed the guards, Fabian, and the healers down the staircase into the dungeons.

"Ready?" Darren whispered, leaning close to Relaina's ear. She nodded and kissed his cheek.

"Ready."

The palace guards peeled off to either side of the dungeon as they walked through the first corridor of cells, braced for anything.

Two healers opened the door leading into the next corridor. With a deep breath, Darren released Relaina's hand and summoned part of his darkness. The indistinct tenebrae whispers that entered his mind had become familiar now. When Relaina took his hand again, her power hit him with more force than before as she pushed it toward him. She paused when he started.

What is it? she asked him.

Your power feels stronger.

Relaina was silent—all he could sense was vague surprise. Last night with Kalmali, her darkness had not only joined his, but harnessed it, wielded it. Perhaps she was more capable than she realized.

They stopped before a cell on the left, the one where Mari and Ihara were kept, and a healer opened the door. Both tenebrae stood and bowed as Darren entered the cell. His connection to Relaina remained strong; her presence was like a beacon in the space around him, always within his awareness, always drawing him in.

"Your Highness," Mari said.

"Prince Darren," Ihara said. "We're grateful to you and King Fabian for releasing us."

Darren stepped forward, allowing Fabian room to follow him inside the cell. The two tenebrae bowed again.

"We release you both today as a gesture of earned trust," Fabian said. "We'll have you transported with the other freed prisoners to a local inn." He turned to Ihara. "As for you, Lady Ihara, your wife is waiting for you in the palace."

Ihara dropped to a knee, head lowered. "You have my gratitude, King Fabian."

They released fifteen other tenebrae and six Terranian soldiers who had been thoroughly questioned by Evarian guards. The healers were leery of the shadow people, but Darren trusted the tenebrae more than the others, confident that the way their magic interacted with his had proven their loyalty.

But would their loyalty remain intact if Darren didn't claim the Terranian throne? Was their allegiance to him, or was it to the Heir of Calixtos, as Kalmali had called him?

Once they were above ground, Darren lagged behind the others as they set off with the freed prisoners toward the city. Fabian summoned two other guards to escort Ihara to the palace. Darren hoped their reunion was a joyous one.

"Darren," Fabian said, beckoning. Darren reined his darkness in. Relaina's presence faded from his mind, along with the rest of the voices of the other tenebrae. She glanced back at him with a soft smile before rejoining the conversation with the Caspian healers as they walked. He'd catch up in a moment.

Darren joined Fabian by a large, wintering azalea bush. The sun glinted off the golden circlet that rested on the Evarian king's forehead.

"I felt that went well," Fabian said.

"Agreed. I hope Lady Eyern and her wife find some peace now."

"As do I. And speaking of the Terranian nobles, we are to meet with them again tomorrow."

Darren forced himself to breathe slowly.

"I'll have my answer for them," Darren said. He watched Relaina as she laughed with Nehma and the others, far ahead of him now. He *would* have his answer for the Terranians tomorrow.

He just needed to speak with her first.

CHAPTER 22

THE HEIR'S SERVANT

Fabian watched Darren follow the others for a moment before turning back to the dungeon entrance, where Desiree spoke quietly with a guard and Saheer's healer sister, Nadia. The king approached them, signing as he joined the conversation.

"Are we prepared to question Kalmali?" he asked.

"Yes, Your Majesty," Nadia signed quickly.

"I still don't like this," Desiree signed. Nadia rolled her bright green eyes.

"He's not even tenebrae anymore, Captain Fontaine," she signed. "His tongue is sharp but he can't harm anyone."

"Shall we go, then?" Fabian asked, gesturing to the entrance, and Desiree and Nadia agreed. Fabian would be glad for the day to arrive when he didn't have to venture into these dungeons regularly.

"Do we have a plan for the tenebrae who have proven themselves enemies?" Desiree asked, holding a torch high as she and Fabian descended the steps side by side.

"Darren has stripped them of their power, much like he did Kalmali," Fabian said. "They pose no threat to us now."

"Just mouths to feed, then."

Fabian sighed as they emerged from the stairwell and began the walk to Kalmali's cell. "Indeed. Thank the gods it's not a burden, at least right now."

"I suppose for the short term we must accept that."

"That we must. I do hope that in the next year the whole of Esran will see greater stability take hold."

Desiree sighed as she placed the torch in an iron sconce by the cell they sought, manned by two guards on either side of the door. "I hold the same hope."

Nadia walked on to rejoin her fellow healers by the tenebrae cells further down, and a guard came forward to unlock Kalmali's cell. Fabian and Desiree stepped inside.

Kalmali lifted his chin from his chest, his chestnut hair falling into his hate-filled eyes. But this time, he offered no vitriolic insults. Fabian waited for a guard to bring a chair into the cell and sat slowly, never taking his eyes off the man. Desiree stood beside Fabian with her halberd in hand, the picture of cold intimidation.

"Surely you must realize this is your end," Fabian said.

"You don't know what my lady is capable of," Kalmali said. "She will come for me."

"Perhaps," Fabian said, lacing his fingers together on his lap. "But you underestimated the power of the magic wielders here, and who's to say she won't do the same?"

"How *dare* you—"

"I'd speak more carefully, if I were you," Fabian said, his voice soft as he stared Kalmali down. "You hurt two people I deeply care for. You're lucky I'm not allowing Princess Relaina to peel you apart piece by piece."

"She is an abomination to magic and to the gods," Kalmali spat. "No one is meant to wield both the light and the dark."

"According to whom? Your mistress?"

"According to the very laws of nature."

Fabian almost laughed at him. "You're not the first to claim to speak on behalf of the gods or on behalf of nature. Your arrogance would be astonishing if it weren't so unoriginal."

Kalmali leapt to his feet, chains clinking, and Desiree's halberd was at his throat in an instant.

"Sit. Down," she said. Breathing heavily and staring daggers at Desiree, Kalmali sank to the floor again. Desiree kept the blade close to his jugular. It seemed Kalmali did, in fact, fear death.

"You're powerless here," Fabian said simply. He hadn't moved an inch. Kalmali glared at him. "Except for your power to choose. Share information or rot down here indefinitely."

"You can't torture information out of me," Kalmali growled.

"I'm not going to torture you," Fabian said. "I'm going to talk to you."

Kalmali's brow furrowed, his eyes distrustful. "Why?"

"Because you and the person you work for put my family in danger," Fabian said, standing slowly. "I do not take kindly to threats against those I love, and I will do everything in my considerable power to root out those threats and neutralize them."

Without waiting for a response, Fabian turned and left the cell, Desiree close behind him.

JEREMIAH HAD FELT like this only once before, an unsettled buzzing in his chest and mind that made it difficult to focus fully on the conversation at hand. But he breathed deeply and forced himself to name his surroundings, the way Rhea had taught him. Some of his discomfort waned as he found his way back into his body. He sat at a table to Fabian's right, in the room where Shadow meetings were usually held. This time, though, only two Shadows were present.

"We thoroughly investigated Kalmali and his belongings," one of the Shadows said. "He is not Evarian, as far as we can tell, and his animosity and unwillingness to share information suggests extreme loyalty to whomever this white-haired woman is."

"He's mentioned Relaina's birthmother," Fabian said, one hand propping his chin up, his elbow on the arm of his chair. "So we must assume that Talea, Kalmali, and this woman he follows all knew one another."

"If Talea worked for Gabriel," Desiree said, "does that mean the Tyrant King was also involved somehow?"

Jeremiah closed his eyes. Gabriel, Talea, the prophecy, the white-haired woman...

"They call Relaina 'Pretender,'" Jeremiah said, and the room quieted. "And they knew she was Talea's daughter, but they didn't know I was her father."

"So if she worked for Gabriel, then Gabriel knew Relaina was Talea's?" Desiree asked.

"He knew," Jeremiah said. "He admitted it to Relaina just before she killed him."

"So what is the thread that connects them all?" Fabian stood from his chair and paced. "Gabriel wanted to use Relaina. The white-haired woman and Kalmali call her 'Pretender,' and Kalmali said her magic was an abomination and tried to kill her."

"That wasn't his original intention, though." Jeremiah's voice shook, but he pressed on. "The woman's orders were to gather information. They didn't know Relaina has dark power. He only resorted to murder when she realized what he was."

Desiree sighed and massaged her forehead while Fabian took his seat once again.

"I intend to keep questioning him, but is there anything else the two of you can share that may help us uncover more about this woman and her companions?" Fabian asked.

One of the Shadows reached into their pocket and procured the onyx pendant Kalmali had worn at all times.

"This was around Kalmali's neck. It seems ordinary, but he was furious to learn we'd taken it."

"A sentimental trinket, perhaps," Desiree said, disinterested. "He seems entirely brainwashed by his own fanaticism."

"We will hold on to it," Fabian said. "I want the two of you to continue to watch Kalmali, alongside the healers and guards. See if you can find out anything else."

"Yes, Your Majesty." The two Shadows left promptly. Desiree followed suit after a moment, leaving Fabian and Jeremiah alone.

"Will you attend the meeting tomorrow?" Fabian asked, turning to him.

"I fear it may be too much for me." Jeremiah hated to admit it, but he needed his wits about him if he was going to return to Parea within the next few days. "Do you think Darren will make a claim?"

Fabian inhaled slowly. "I think that depends on whether he has spoken to Relaina about it."

"She believes in him. I've encouraged her to help him, to be with him, if that's what she wants."

Fabian's smile was gentle. "And I've encouraged him to seek her help."

Jeremiah placed his hand on the table, and Fabian took it. "I am both proud and terrified at the prospect of them ruling Terrana together."

"We'll support them at every turn," Fabian said. He paused, then laughed once.

"What?"

"It seems there may soon be an Andovier on the throne of each Esrani nation."

Jeremiah stared at him. "You mean to grant me the crown matrimonial?"

"Why wouldn't I? I trust you, and I need your help in ruling."

Jeremiah leaned out of his chair, pulling Fabian into a firm embrace and burying his face in the king's shoulder.

"Your trust means everything to me," he whispered. "I don't feel like I deserve it."

Fabian's arms tightened around him. "You earn my trust with every breath you take in my presence."

Jeremiah moved his hands to hold Fabian's face, leaning back so he could see the king's eyes. Fabian rested his forehead on Jeremiah's.

"I knew something was wrong," Fabian said, his voice quiet. "When you returned, I knew. I know how you speak to me." The king brushed a thumb along Jeremiah's jaw. "How you kiss me. And that wasn't you."

More guilt throbbed in Jeremiah's veins. "Are you all right after that? Knowing it wasn't me?"

Fabian pulled back. "It was unpleasant to realize, but I'll be fine. Though perhaps you could kiss me again soon and erase it from my mind."

Jeremiah stood, bringing Fabian up with him, holding his hand as he approached the door. Fabian looked at him, perplexed, until Jeremiah turned the lock with his free hand. He brushed his fingers along Fabian's cheekbone, against his smooth, dark brown skin. With one hand on Fabian's neck and the other at his lower back, he pulled the king close.

Jeremiah's back hit the wall as Fabian kissed him back. He indulged in Fabian's touch, in the warmth of his lips and the roaming of his hands, allowing himself to unravel for a moment in the privacy of the meeting room. When Fabian leaned back, running his fingers through his hair, Jeremiah smiled.

"It's been too long since I've seen you smile," Fabian said. He kissed him once more, brief and chaste. "I'm afraid I must go."

"Go," Jeremiah said. "Help establish a new king."

"And perhaps a queen," Fabian reminded him.

Jeremiah groaned as he unlocked the door and held it open for Fabian. "Three Andoviers married to kings. My mother is going to be insufferable."

Fabian stepped into the hallway, his laugh unrestrained. "I look forward to the day she returns to Seacastle."

CHAPTER 23

A CITY SQUARE IN MAREMER

Relaina, Darren, and the healers had spent the day in the city after the freed Terranians settled into the Gnarled Root and another inn called the Merchant's Menace. Getting the Evarian guards to stay behind and not follow Relaina had taken some convincing, but between the four healers and Darren being with her, they'd acquiesced. They ventured to the western part of the city, checking the progress of the new shipwrights and eating at a newly reopened café by the bay. Osha and the others had greeted Relaina warmly, and though they'd been stunned at Darren's introduction, they'd also been kind to him. Relaina watched him closely as he spoke with them about their work. He was more charismatic than he thought, and every bit of it was genuine.

The sun had set by the time they began their trek back to Seacastle, and part of her wished she had taken Amariah instead of walked. She pulled her cloak around her to keep out the night breeze. Beside her, Darren became more unsettled with every step, anxiety radiating off him so potently that Relaina could almost taste it.

While Nehma and the others cackled at Catrin's many

jokes, Darren tugged on Relaina's arm, stopping them in the middle of a narrow street.

"We need to talk," he said. "Alone."

Dread knotted Relaina's stomach. What had happened? The healers had gone silent ahead of them, perplexed as they waited for Relaina and Darren to catch up.

"We'll meet you all back at Seacastle later," Relaina said. Concern flashed in Nehma's eyes, but she nodded and urged the others on. Relaina waited until the only sound was the creaking of hanging lanterns before turning back to Darren.

"Let's walk," she said, brushing her fingers on his lower back. He nodded, and they set off in the opposite direction. Relaina resisted the urge to demand he tell her what troubled him. Their boots thudded dully on the cobblestones as they approached a small, well-lit square. It was empty besides a bubbling fountain in the center. Darren walked ahead of her, leaning over and placing both hands on the fountain's edge.

"Darren, talk to me," Relaina said, standing a few feet behind him. He was gripping the stone so tightly his knuckles were white.

"I have to give the Terranians my answer tomorrow."

Relaina's heart took off. "Your answer about making a claim."

Darren faced her again, his eyes full of uncertainty. "I don't know what to do."

"Do you want to know what I think?"

"Yes."

"I think you would be a king worth following."

She'd thought it, secretly, from the moment they'd begun calling him *King Darren*. She took his face in her hands.

"It won't be easy," she said. "But you could lead Terrana back to what it used to be and help return peace to all of Esran."

His eyes searched hers.

"Will you help me?" His voice was barely above a whisper. A bit of his power appeared at his palms, and everything he hadn't said aloud prodded at her from his vague thoughts. But they couldn't dance around this question, this decision.

"Ask me what you really mean to, Darren."

Where this bravery had come from, Relaina didn't know. Her heart was bound to leap from her chest. Darren covered one of her hands with his and closed his eyes for a moment. Relaina hardly dared to breathe.

"I know this is risky," he said, lacing his fingers through hers. "And I know it's fast. But you were raised to lead, and you spoke out for peace, for *me*, even before you knew me. You're clever and kind and fierce and beautiful, and I can't imagine anyone else by my side."

"So ask me," she whispered.

"It doesn't have to happen soon. We can wait."

"I know. Ask me."

"And we can keep it between us if you want—"

A laugh bubbled from Relaina's lips. "*Ask me*, gods damn it all."

His eyes burned into hers. Emotion built and crashed into her as he said, "Relaina Andovier, will you marry me?"

She'd been raised to expect this question from some noble her entire life, and had wondered who it might be, how she might feel. None of it could have prepared her for Darren LaGuarde standing in a city square in Maremer, laying his heart at her feet.

"Yes." She said it as if breathing the word through time itself, as if she could hear it echo into her future. *Their* future. "Yes, I'll marry you."

Something between a laugh and a cry fell out of him. When his lips found hers, their darkness connected more strongly, but all she could hear of his thoughts was wordless joy and relief. With a wicked grin, Relaina pulled him into a nearby alley. She leaned against the smooth wall, heat flooding her lower abdomen and inner thighs as Darren brushed his thumb along her cheek and gripped her waist. He bent to press his lips to her neck, and his darkness drifted along her skin.

"I want you," Relaina said. Darren laughed softly and leaned back, turning her around and pressing his body into hers. With one hand, he pinned her hands above her head, her palms flat against the smooth stone. With the other, he brushed her hair aside to trail kisses along the back of her neck. Relaina pressed her forehead to the wall and squirmed.

"As tantalizing as you are," he said, his breath tickling her ear, "I'm not going to fuck you in an alleyway, Princess."

Relaina looked over her shoulder, huffing. "That's Queen to you, Darren LaGuarde."

He laughed again and released her. "Not yet. Let's just get back to Seacastle. I want to do this properly."

Relaina fell in step beside him as he stalked away, headed back to the square. "Do what?"

Darren draped an arm over her shoulder and leaned close to her ear. "Touch you in ways that make you forget your name."

RELAINA FLOPPED face-first on the bed the moment they arrived, trying to catch her breath. Darren landed on his back beside her.

"Why is that walk up the cliff so long?" she said breathlessly. Darren wheezed a laugh.

"We'll take a moment. There's no rush."

There *was* a rush, though. She wanted him desperately; she just needed to catch her breath first. After a few more deep inhales, Relaina sidled closer to him and kissed his neck. He closed his eyes and reached around to grip her ass before moving his hand between her thighs.

"Uh, Darren?"

"Hmm?"

"You're just rubbing my inner thigh."

Darren's eyes flew open as he burst out laughing. "Gods, that's embarrassing."

"If you're too tired, we can wait."

"No, no." He brushed her hair away from her face, holding her gaze. "I'm awake. Just missed the mark."

Relaina grinned and leaned forward to kiss him. This time when he reached down, he pressed right where she wanted him to, and Relaina moaned softly into his mouth. Darren got up and pulled his shirt over his head before tossing it to the floor. Relaina marveled at the muscles rippling in his back and arms, at the close-shaven facial hair along his jaw and around his mouth, at his windblown, messy hair. *I'm going to marry him.*

"Take those off, will you?" Darren said, gesturing to Relaina's pants. She kicked off her boots and flung the rest of her clothing away before Darren had discarded his own trousers. He laughed again as he leaned down and placed his hands on either side of her hips, kissing her.

"You." He kissed her jaw.

"Are." Her neck.

"A goddess."

Relaina smiled as he planted kisses along her collarbone and down her chest. She pulled him onto the bed with her as she lay back, and his mouth found her left nipple, teasing it with his tongue and lips.

Relaina's back arched as she closed her eyes, and when Darren's fingers brushed against her clit, her breath caught. He trailed a finger down to her entrance, and Relaina tensed, anticipating it slipping inside her. But he ran it up to that spot again, drawing slow circles that sent waves of smoldering pleasure down her thighs.

"You tease," she breathed, and a low laugh rumbled in his chest. He did the same motion again. The third time, Relaina's hips were lifting of their own volition. "What are you waiting fo—"

She broke off in a gasp as he finally slipped a finger inside her, then another. Between that, the pressure on her clit, and his mouth still working her nipple, Relaina was floating, unaware of anything besides his indulgence of her body. He shifted up, his mouth seeking hers, and she whimpered as his tongue brushed hers.

"Don't hold back, love," he said. Relaina opened her eyes and reached for his erection. He dropped his face into her neck as she stroked him.

"Don't you hold back, either," she said. "I love hearing you moan."

Darren bit her neck lightly. He pushed himself up on his arms and grabbed her legs, tugging her to the edge of the bed. Relaina cried out as he swirled his tongue over her, mirroring the motion he'd done with his fingers. He was single-minded in his aim to pleasure her tonight. Several more slow, indulgent strokes of his tongue, and he sat up once more, gripping Relaina's waist.

"Will you turn over?" he asked. Relaina obliged, getting on her hands and knees. Her entire body sang with anticipation as he climbed onto the bed behind her. He glided his fingers down her back, making her shiver as his power emerged and drifted over her scars. He leaned down, leaving warm kisses on her skin in the wake of the cool shadows.

When he positioned himself, she sucked in a breath. He pushed inside her slowly, until every inch of him was settled, his hip bones pressed against her ass.

All good? he thought to her.

Gods, yes.

He started to move, reaching around her front to work her clit. She gripped the bedcovers as she dropped her head to the mattress, awash in ecstasy as her orgasm approached. Everything was hazy and warm, and *gods*, he felt incredible.

Darren quickened his pace and shifted so his chest was pressed to her back. When her pleasure crested and release flooded through her, he gripped her tightly, his breath ragged in her ear. Relaina turned her head so she could kiss him as he came, his body shuddering on top of hers. Tiredness overtook her as Darren caught his breath.

"Well done," Relaina said. Darren's body shook with laughter.

"How romantic of you."

"Well, I did forget my name for a moment there. Thought you should know you did what you set out to do."

"I'm glad to hear it."

He pulled out of her, rolling over and resting a moment before they both cleaned up in the washroom. Relaina watched the darkness still drifting along his arms in iridescent ribbons. He caught her staring and walked up to her, wrapping his arms around her.

I love you, Relaina thought to him. His brown eyes, especially the one with black around it, were dark in the candlelight.

I love you, he thought back.

Relaina ran her hand through some of the darkness on his upper arm. It floated around her fingers, almost humming at her touch.

"Darren?"

"Hmm?"

"Have you ever dreamt of the gods?"

He didn't answer for a moment, his breathing slow.

"Once. Right after you were taken and I passed out from the smoke. Calixtos appeared to me."

The god of darkness had come to Darren.

"We'd have no stars without the night," Relaina whispered.

"What?"

"Elenia came to me. Before the Winter Festival, before the battle, I dreamt of her in a forest grove. She said, 'Don't fear the dark. We'd have no stars without the night.'"

Darren grew quiet. "Perhaps she knew you would end up with a bit of darkness yourself. Calixtos said something similar to me. 'Don't fear your darkness as I did.' And he told me to find you before it was too late."

"Too late?"

"At the time I thought he meant you ending up in the hands of my father."

Relaina rested her head on his chest. "I wish they'd just tell us about the magic instead of speaking in riddles."

"That would make everything much easier." Darren held her tightly, kissing the top of her head. "If Calixtos appears to me again, I'll tell him my future wife demands answers."

Relaina grinned as he pulled her close again, filled with joy that would not diminish even in her dreams.

CHAPTER 24

BENEATH PAREA

"Prince Aronn."

Aronn jolted awake on the bench in the healers' sanctuary, Saheer's face appearing before him as his eyes adjusted to the dim light.

"Are you ready?" Saheer asked. Aronn stared blankly at her and the team of loyalists gathered behind her before his mind caught up. The underground market. Maurice and Camille. He jumped up.

"Yes, let's go."

He and Misenia had argued for almost an hour before she'd agreed to let him go on this mission, but he'd be damned if he didn't help get Maurice and Camille out of the city after they'd been caught because of him. Mazin was on the team, too, and fell in step beside Aronn as they ventured into the cold night and headed for the stables.

"You think we'll find the king and queen tonight?" Mazin whispered to him. Aronn breathed in deeply, cold air rushing down his throat and into his lungs.

"I hope we do."

SNEAKING into the city was more challenging than last time, but they still managed to leap from the wall at the right place and moment to avoid patrols. Hektor Elke, Saheer, and two healers remained behind this time with a rope ladder ready to help them climb up the icy stone on their return. Mazin had been given command once they were in Parea itself. *A chance to redeem yourself,* Misenia had said. And despite the fact that he'd gone on the unauthorized excursion to the farmer's shop, he had proven himself capable of protecting Aronn.

Aronn walked himself through tonight's plan for the eighth time in five minutes as he, Mazin, a healer, and two loyalist Lynx Guards darted between trees in the outer village. *Get in. Find the false well. Search the south underground. Silence anyone who sees us. Get out.* Aronn told himself it was simple until he almost believed it. Even if it wasn't simple, he had to do it. Maurice and Camille had been imprisoned because of him.

The loyalists trailed after Aronn and Mazin as they darted behind a shed dusted with snow. Ahead, the cluster of outer village houses stood resolute against the cold.

The well they sought was within Parea itself, right past those houses. Aronn was glad Mazin seemed to know where he was going, as the gibbous moon did little to light their way in the dark. Just before they crossed into the city proper, Mazin flung out a hand to stop the rest of them. They crouched behind wiry evergreen bushes. Aronn stopped breathing as a guard strode by.

When the guard was gone, Mazin motioned for them to stay put and darted for the well by a tea shop. He glanced over the edge, checked his surroundings, and leapt inside.

Aronn tried to ignore the cold sweat on his gloved palms as he waited for Mazin's signal. Crunching footsteps sounded from their left, and he ducked down again with his fellows. One of the Lynx Guard gripped a knife at his belt and tensed to spring, but Aronn grabbed his arm, shaking his head. The traitor guard disappeared again.

"We can't have them sounding the alarm yet," Aronn hissed. Seconds later, Mazin's hand appeared above the edge of the well, beckoning. Aronn didn't think—he ran.

He and the healer followed Mazin into the well with no issue, but the two Lynx Guards lagged behind. Perhaps the guard had appeared again. Aronn gazed at the slick, aged stone and the iron rungs that rose above them to the circular opening. It now appeared far smaller.

"Prince Aronn," Mazin said. "Is this the right place?"

He gestured with his boot to a large stone. It stuck out among the others, but only if you knew what to look for. Aronn nodded. Mazin kicked it in, revealing a trapdoor.

"You two go ahead, I'll wait for the others," he said.

The healer ushered Aronn to the trapdoor, which he crawled through gladly, emerging in the stagnant air of the Parean underground. They stood in a dark, narrow offshoot of the main passage.

"What were you thinking?" Mazin's hiss drifted through the trapdoor as the two Lynx Guards climbed through.

"He saw us, we had no choice!" one guard said, straightening.

The second guard, a woman around Aronn's age, held the trapdoor open for Mazin to follow. "We covered the body in snow behind those bushes. No one will find him until sunrise at least."

"We'd better get a fucking move on," Mazin said, ducking through. "Did you leave signs of a struggle?"

"No. No blood."

"Good."

The healer removed his hood but not his veil, lifting his

glowing hand to light their way. They stepped into the empty tunnel, the passage wide enough to comfortably fit two horse-drawn carriages. Horses were never down here, though, and this part of the underground had been abandoned for years. Aronn's spine prickled as they ventured past dusty, rotting stalls and caved-in secret entrances without the light of a torch. The healer's hand was less bright, but also less likely to give them away from afar.

The underground narrowed after they'd walked for several minutes. Aronn felt as though the walls were squeezing his heart, forcing it to beat faster. *It can't be much farther.* Just when Aronn thought his lungs might explode, a pinprick of light appeared in the distance. The healer dimmed his own light further, just enough to prevent them from stumbling over loose stones or a stray piece of wood.

Mazin stopped their progress as they drew nearer to the lit area of the underground. Soft voices drifted from that direction.

"We go dark from here," he said, and the healer extinguished his light. "Remember the areas to check. If we're separated, meet back at the well no later than midnight."

Aronn and the four others nodded. When they began moving again, the slow pace was agonizing against the anticipation in his blood. He lowered into a crouch with the rest of them and hid behind newer stalls. Those had been in use until these bastards had taken over.

More guards patrolled this area than the outer village. It further supported Aronn's theory about his parents' location, but it also filled him with dread.

As another guard passed by the stall Aronn had hidden behind moments before, his palms grew damp again. Why in the name of the gods had he agreed to this? Mazin and the others could have done this without him. But he couldn't sit around waiting for everyone else to do difficult things for him.

Aronn ducked into a gambling den and found it empty. Disappointment sent a pang through Aronn's gut, but he shook his head and kept going, regrouping with the other loyalists.

The black market weapons shop was emptied, and so was another gambling den. Perhaps he'd been completely wrong, and none of these places housed prisoners. He resigned himself to his fate as the hour grew later—they would have to leave soon to ensure they had time to get back to the wall and remain unseen.

With little enthusiasm, Aronn waited until another guard had walked out of earshot before pushing back the curtain to a smoking lounge. His hand flew to his mouth to muffle a curse.

Maurice and Camille were inside, their wrists bound and tied to a wrought-iron room divider. There were dozens of the dividers in the old smoke lounge, separating the plush poufs and blankets formerly used for customers. A guard appeared, and he and Aronn stared at one another for an immeasurable moment.

Mazin leapt from behind Aronn just as the guard reached for his sword. Blood sprayed from the man's throat. Camille gasped, her exhausted eyes widening, and Maurice lifted his head. The farmer's left eye was purple and swollen shut.

"Prince Aronn!" Camille whispered. Aronn crouched next to them while Mazin hauled the guard's body behind another divider.

"We're here to get you out," Aronn said, checking over his shoulder. The Lynx Guard woman stood by the curtain, keeping watch.

"Oh, thank the gods," Camille said. Maurice was dazed beside her. "They planned to kill Maurice tomorrow. A public execution."

Aronn's body went colder than it had been outside in the snow.

"Prince Aronn, we have to *move*," Mazin said. Something inside Aronn's gut hardened.

"Get them to safety," Aronn said. "I'm going to check the fighting ring."

Before Mazin could protest, Aronn peeked outside the curtain and dashed across the wide market. A few more stalls down and he'd be at the entrance.

Aronn stayed hidden behind a stall next to the entryway and listened hard. There was no way for him to enter the fighting ring subtly—if anyone was inside, he'd almost certainly be seen.

"...Don't know how much longer we can keep this up, Archan," a woman said, her voice low and sharp and drawing nearer. "We cannot keep executing citizens who resist our rule if we don't want a full-scale uprising on our hands."

The curtain in the entryway swished, and footsteps sounded on the other side of the stall. Aronn didn't dare breathe.

"I'm aware of the challenges," a second voice said. Aronn knew that one. *Archan Conclave.*

"Then what do you propose we do?" the woman asked. "We haven't heard anything from that white-haired zealot—"

"Do not speak against her," Archan hissed. "She is the reason we've had any victories in this endeavor."

"Then where is she now? We cannot kill the king and queen, we cannot get to the princess, and every day more of us fall to loyalists in the forest. We need something to push the citizens in our favor."

Aronn still didn't breathe as their voices drifted away, straining to hear.

"Perhaps...the eldest...favor..."

Air forced itself from Aronn's lungs, and he crept around the stall, searching his surroundings. He could decipher that conversation later. For now, he needed to peek behind that curtain without being seen. He craned his neck to glance beneath it. No boots, no approaching voices. He shifted closer on silent feet and gently pushed the black material aside, just enough to see with one eye. His heart dropped.

The ring was empty.

Aronn's pulse pounded in his ears. His parents weren't here. He let the curtain fall back in place, his heart wrenching with disappointment as he ducked beneath the stall again. He didn't think, didn't feel as he found his way back to the smoking lounge and crept after Mazin and the others through the market.

When they reached the entrance to the well, Mazin took Aronn by the shoulders.

"What did you see?" Mazin asked, an edge to the calm in his voice.

Aronn forced in another breath as the others filed through the trapdoor, guiding Maurice and Camille into the well.

"Nothing," he said. "My parents weren't there. They could be anywhere."

Mazin nodded. "Then we'll keep searching. But we have to get out of here for now."

Aronn counted his breaths as he ascended the frigid ladder in the well. He just had to follow the others and get back to the sanctuary, then he could fall apart. He'd been right about Maurice and Camille being held prisoner down here, but they were no closer to finding his parents.

Getting Maurice out of the well slowed them down; he was disoriented from his injuries and had difficulty climbing over the edge. By the time Aronn swung his leg over the side of the well, his arms and legs ached with fatigue. But they'd made it—almost.

The journey back to the wall took twice as long with Maurice and Camille. Aronn was sweating while Camille shivered, so he shrugged off his fur-lined jacket and offered it to her.

"Not much farther," Aronn whispered, his breath puffing in front of him as they crept through the outer village.

Urgent shouting echoed in the distance, unintelligible but alarming all the same.

"*Move!*" Mazin hissed over his shoulder. He led them forward faster, the four others nearly carrying Maurice and Camille while Aronn stayed close behind.

"Where the *fuck* is Heron!" a traitor guard shouted.

They were much closer than Aronn thought. He sent up a prayer to the gods. They'd made it this far. *Get to the wall.* The little shed was just ahead. *Get to the wall.*

Aronn could do that. He could get to the wall and ensure the rest of them did too. The guards' angry voices grew more distant.

When they reached the shed, Mazin waited, letting out a low whistle. None of them breathed until another whistle answered. A rope ladder unfurled down the side of the wall. Mazin sent the two holding Maurice ahead to climb first. Aronn's heart beat wildly as he watched their slow progress up and over the wall. They needed to hurry. Camille and the other two loyalists went next.

"Check the perimeter!"

Aronn and Mazin whipped around. Two guards were rapidly heading in their direction, weapons drawn. They hadn't spotted the rest of their party, who was halfway up the ladder now, but—

"*Halt!*"

The guards began running toward the wall, and without thinking, Aronn leapt out from the tree line to draw their attention. Mazin grabbed Aronn by the shoulder of his shirt and hauled him forward, practically throwing him at the ladder. As Aronn started to climb, one of their companions at the top let an arrow fly, taking out one of the guards pursuing them.

"Aronn, *go!*" Mazin shouted from below him. Aronn scrambled up as fast as he could.

Searing pain erupted in Aronn's lower back. He almost lost his grip as he reached the top of the wall, but two sets of strong hands pulled him up and over. He slumped onto the stone and cried out, his hands trembling as he looked down at his abdomen. The tip of an arrow was protruding from his flesh.

The panicked shouts around him faded as quickly as his vision. Soon there was only silence and darkness.

CHAPTER 25

TO BEGIN A REIGN

Darren was up before dawn, pacing their chambers as he fought nerves and nausea. Relaina climbed out of bed after a few minutes, her eyes sleepy as she padded over to him.

"Breathe, love," she said, touching his arm.

"I feel like I may be sick."

Relaina looked at him for a moment. "Do you want me to try and help? With magic, I mean."

"You think that would work?"

Relaina shrugged. "Only one way to find out."

He nodded, and she led him to the couch. He let his darkness free as he held her hand, inhaling slowly when her power joined his and it began to drift around them. Her light appeared, starting in her hands and running up her arms. The markings formed into hydrangeas again. As her healing light spread from her markings and soothed his nausea, he studied her face. A single wrinkle had formed between her dark eyebrows, and her lips were taut with concentration.

"Do you want to get tattoos?" he asked, the pain in his stomach waning. Relaina's eyebrows raised as she let her light fade, and his darkness retreated as well.

"You mean betrothal tattoos?" she asked, one corner of her mouth lifting. Darren nodded. He could still hardly believe last night had been real.

"I know it's more an Evarian custom, but since you're half Evarian..." he trailed off, watching her eyes brighten.

"I...yes, but what would we get?"

Darren lifted her hand to his lips, kissing her palm. "What about hydrangeas?"

Relaina's smile was radiant. "You like them too?"

"It was one of the first times you trusted me," he said. "When you told me how to get into that passage."

"And thank the gods I did."

Darren took her face in his hands, kissing her forehead, then her cheeks, then her lips. Her lush curls shrouded part of her face as she got to her feet and offered him her hand.

"After the meeting today?" he asked, standing.

"Yes."

Darren's heart skipped a beat as he met her fierce gaze. She was going to marry him. He didn't have to be alone as he shouldered the responsibility of ruling his kingdom. A strange, almost savage acceptance burned through him. He'd made his choice, and so had the brilliant woman in front of him. He wrapped his arms around her, burying his face in her hair.

What in the name of the gods had he done to deserve such happiness?

"Let's get you ready," Relaina said. "We don't want to be late."

〜

Darren had known that several of the freed Terranian prisoners would be invited to this meeting, had insisted they be present, even, but it was entirely different seeing the banquet table almost fully occupied when he and Relaina arrived. Lady Eyern looked more at ease than ever sitting beside her wife, who was dressed in a fine gray tunic. Both women inclined their heads as Darren took his seat by the head of the table. He nodded and smiled in return.

Adrenaline rushed through his veins as the doors opened and Fabian arrived. He stopped himself from tugging at the collar of his black tunic.

As the Evarian king sat, the rest of the room did the same, chairs scraping and fabric rustling. Before Fabian spoke, he met Darren's gaze with an almost imperceptible smile.

"Good morning, all," Fabian said, his voice carrying from the head of the table throughout the hall. "I am grateful to each of you for your attendance—"

"King Fabian, may I ask why Terranian *soldiers* are in attendance at this meeting?" Lord Delimont interrupted, his lip curling in disgust.

Darren stared the nobleman down, but Lord Delimont didn't look his way.

"How dare you speak so impertinently to a king," Lord Vontair bellowed, his voice menacing.

"He's not my king," Lord Delimont said, shrugging. Beside him, his wife looked like she wanted to throw herself out the nearby window.

"He is hosting your king and the rest of us!" Ihara Eyern hissed, her eyes going black. The healers in the room tensed.

"I'm not sure I have a king at all."

"This is why Terrana has suffered so greatly for so long. Because rich, pompous pigs like you hold positions of power!" a Terranian soldier snarled, standing from his chair. Darren's skin buzzed with panic. How was this going so poorly already?

"You dishonor us all, Lord Delimont," Lady Tryali said, her eyes narrowed.

"You are nothing but a leftover leech," Ihara said. "The Tyrant King's blood has dried up, and you're sucking at air."

The room erupted into hurled insults and arguing, and despite his efforts to keep a firm hold on his power, darkness pushed toward the surface of Darren's skin. The tenebrae in the room entered his magic's awareness, only adding to his overwhelm.

"Nobles who supported Gabriel should be stripped of titles—!"

"You fought in his army, you snake—!"

"One person from each family that served Gabriel should be executed!"

"*Enough*!" A burst of darkness exploded from Darren as he stood, washing over the room before disappearing. Cold filled his eyes and black vapor crept along his arms. "They are here because *I* asked King Fabian to invite them. I've spoken to everyone in this room, and we all have the same goal in mind. Leave your violent threats out of this. I will not begin a reign with such bloodshed."

Every windblown face in the room stared at him.

Lady Eyern broke the silence. "So you intend to begin a reign?"

The question surprised him so much his magic fell back into him. The faces of the Terranians weren't fearful. They were expectant.

Mustering every ounce of courage he possessed, Darren lifted his chin. "I do."

To his right, Fabian stood, holding out his hand. "I look forward to having a friendly relationship with Terrana with Darren as its king."

Darren clasped Fabian's arm, and they dipped their heads the way sovereigns were supposed to greet one another. Chairs scraped around the room once more as every Terranian stood and laced their fingers together at their hearts before bowing deeply. A memory long forgotten stirred in Darren's mind. The last time he'd witnessed such a show of respect was at his mother's funeral rites. Even Lord Delimont bowed next to his wife, albeit begrudgingly.

Darren and Fabian, along with the rest of the table, returned to their seats, and though Darren had received the room's support, tension still permeated the space. Relaina shifted so her arm brushed against his on the table. He let the smallest bit of darkness drift over her skin, and her magic joined his.

You did it, she thought to him.

Was my outburst painful?

Relaina took a deep breath as Fabian began speaking again. *No. Just a bit startling, but I think that was needed.*

Darren forced himself to focus on the plans and proposals made by the Terranian nobles. Lady Eyern and Lady Tryali spoke through logistics for returning to Terrana, and he started when he realized they intended to do so within the fortnight.

"A fortnight is too soon," Darren said, shaking his head. "There is too much to plan and still much to negotiate with Evaria. Trade, border regulations, the remaining prisoners..."

"Indeed," Fabian said. "We'll send word to every major city in Terrana that Darren has made his claim, and there is no reason negotiations cannot take place here. Terrana will need Evaria's support."

"Still," Lady Eyern said, shifting in her chair. "You should take up residence in the capital sooner rather than later, Your Majesty."

Returning to Lues. Living in the Obsidian Keep again. He would have to face so many memories, so many people from his past.

"I should think no later than spring's end," Lady Tryali said. "That allows more time for negotiations and should be acceptable to the rest of the nobles in Lues."

It was the first suggestion Lady Tryali made that Darren fully agreed with. He nodded.

The rest of the meeting passed quickly, to Darren's relief. Now that he'd given them his answer and there were tentative plans for what came next, all he wanted was to disappear with Relaina into the city so they could get their betrothal tattoos. But as Fabian adjourned the meeting, Darren was approached by each freed prisoner. They all reintroduced themselves, and he tried his best to memorize each name. Once they dispersed, Relaina found him, taking his hand, and they hurried off.

CHAPTER 26

A Form of Seeing

Cold whipped against Relaina's cheeks where she stood on the mountainside, gazing across the black water of Lake Alterna. Stars littered the water's rippling surface.

She breathed deeply, relishing the sharp cold that rushed into her lungs, accompanied by the scent of pine and snow. On the opposite bank, rising high above a sheer cliffside, Parea stood resolute against the Lyneisian mountain winter.

Home. She closed her eyes, and when she opened them, her hands and knees dug into frigid stone as pain ripped into her lower back. She cried out, her bloodied hands trembling as her fingers grazed the arrowhead protruding from her gut.

"Prince Aronn!"

"Oh, gods, he's been shot."

"Get him to a healer, now!"

Relaina shot upright in bed with a cry, panicking even a few moments after she met Darren's eyes in the darkness. He held her face in his hands.

"Hey," he said. Relaina still gasped for air, one hand groping at her abdomen. "It's all right. You're safe."

Relaina shook her head. "Not me. Aronn. Something's happened, he's hurt, I—"

"What? How do you know?"

"I..." How would she make him understand? Aronn was injured, possibly fatally, and she had to help him. She got out of bed, trying to loosen the knot in her throat as she padded along the cool, stone floor. She sucked in a breath, then another.

"Relaina, you're scaring me." Darren's body tensed as he sat on the edge of the bed, watching her every move. "What's going on?"

Breathe. She couldn't help Aronn if she didn't explain, and she couldn't explain anything when she was so panicked.

"I've had visions," she said. "Not just the dreams of Elenia." She did her best to explain what she'd seen of Talea's death, her dream in the library, and what Rhea had shared about Seers. With every passing moment the concern on Darren's face grew more pronounced.

"Wait," he said. "You dreamt of a woman you *thought* was Elenia?"

Relaina nodded.

"And she had white hair?"

"Yes, I—" Relaina stopped, realizing. "You think it's Kalmali's master."

"It would make sense, wouldn't it?"

"None of this makes sense." Relaina pushed her hair back from her forehead. "Why would I be having visions of her?"

"I don't know." Darren stood and approached her. "Do you remember where she was?"

Relaina started, gazing at the new black ink designs across his chest and forgetting all else for a moment. Hydrangeas covered his skin from his shoulders inward, surrounding three circles that contained mountains, seas, and forests.

"Relaina?"

"Sorry." She forced her thoughts back to the white-haired woman from her dream and frowned. "She was in a forest grove, the same I remember from the first dream I had of Elenia. It was winter, but there wasn't snow on the ground."

"So she couldn't be in the Lyneisian mountains."

Relaina wrung her hands as she stepped away. "All I know is that Aronn is hurt, I can't do anything to help him, and I have no way to find out if he's all right."

"Let's send someone, then," Darren said. "We'll find a messenger right now."

They sent a guard for Fabian and Jeremiah and dressed quickly, waiting by the fire in charged silence. As soon as the knock came at their door, Relaina was on her feet.

Jeremiah appeared in the doorway. "Relaina, what—?"

"Aronn is hurt," she said, moving aside to let him and Fabian through. Both of them exchanged a look before standing in front of her. "We need to send someone to Parea."

"Relaina, how did you learn of this?" Fabian asked. She looked to Jeremiah.

"Do you remember that I dreamt of Talea's death?"

Jeremiah nodded.

"Rhea and Thea have visions of one another sometimes, in the present." Relaina winced, remembering all too clearly the pain that had exploded in her back in the dream. Or Aronn's back. "I just dreamt very viscerally that Aronn was attacked, shot with an arrow, and I don't know if he's all right or not."

Her skin buzzed with impatience while Fabian and Jeremiah stared at her, dumbstruck. Darren sat on the arm of a chair behind them.

"I'll return to Parea earlier, then," Jeremiah said. "Day after tomorrow."

Relaina had nearly chewed her lip raw. She pushed her hair out of her face again, breathing deeply.

"I know you want to help him," Jeremiah said to her softly. "I do too. But all we can do right now is take solace in the fact that Aronn is surrounded by dozens of healers."

"You're right," Relaina said, her worry hardly eased.

"I'll be back in Parea soon," Jeremiah said. "And I'll write the moment I arrive."

Fabian and Jeremiah bid them both goodnight and retreated to their own chambers. Relaina returned to bed with Darren, but her eyes remained resolutely open.

"I'm sorry to keep you from sleep again," she whispered as he held her, brushing his fingers along her arm.

"It's not your fault, love. I'm worried for him too."

No matter how hard she tried, she couldn't get the searing pain or panicked voices out of her head. She should take comfort in that, at least; he hadn't been alone when he was shot. But what was he doing that would get him hurt in the first place?

The same thoughts churned in her mind even when she fell into an uneasy sleep, and when she awoke in the morning her eyelids were dry and heavy.

"I have several meetings today," Darren said, approaching the end of the bed and smoothing the fabric of his black shirt sleeve. He was already fully dressed while Relaina had barely sat upright. "But if you need me for anything, come and find me."

The edge of his tattoo peeked through the laces at the top of his shirt, and warmth replaced some of the worry in her chest. She got out of bed and wrapped her arms around him.

"I will. Good luck today."

Darren held her close for a few more moments, one hand on the small of her back and the other in her hair. He kissed her forehead before tucking a few knives away and venturing into the corridor.

"YOU GOT A *TATTOO*?"

Relaina had wanted to avoid calling attention to it until it was inevitable at the banquet that evening, but Annalise's voice carried in the sparring hall. Thea and Nehma's heads whipped around from where they stood at the edge of the training ring, and several guard trainees craned their necks from the archery range. Grimacing, Relaina pulled Annalise through the doors to the gardens. Nehma and Thea followed them.

"Yes, after the meeting yesterday," Relaina said, making for a nearby bench in the gardens. She and Annalise sat as she tugged her black cloak over the fabric of her red shirt, wishing now that she'd worn something with a higher neckline.

"Does that mean what I think it means?" Nehma asked as she and Thea jogged to join them. Relaina looked up at her, then Thea, then back to Annalise. Three pairs of expectant eyes. Fighting the urge to bolt away from them, she nodded.

"You're engaged!" Thea squealed. Annalise squeaked, her gray eyes going wide.

"*Engaged*? Relaina!" Annalise threw her arms around her.

"So am I speaking to the future Queen of Terrana?" Nehma asked, a wry smile on her face. Relaina let out a breathy laugh as Annalise released her.

"I suppose you are."

Thea sat beside her and nudged her arm, raising an eyebrow. "Is something wrong?"

Relaina didn't want to worry Annalise, but she deserved to know. She gestured for Nehma to sit as well, but Nehma merely frowned, crossing her arms where she stood.

"Thea, you and Rhea have visions of one another sometimes, yes?" she asked. The dark-haired healer nodded. "I had a vision of Aronn last night. He's...he's in danger."

Annalise frowned, and Nehma's cool exterior cracked, genuine fear flashing across her face. Thea swore softly.

"What kind of danger? What exactly did you see?" Thea asked. She listened intently as Relaina described as much as she could remember.

"I'm just...I don't know what to do," Relaina said, hating the thickness in her voice. "I'm worried out of my mind for Aronn and our parents and I can't shake this feeling that I—" She stopped herself. She hadn't voiced it aloud, but it was eating at her.

"That you what?" Thea asked, her voice kind.

"That you should be in Parea with the Lyneisian loyalists," Nehma said. Relaina met her eyes and knew she understood.

"And I can't do that," Relaina said. "But having to sit here and *wait* for news of my brother is going to drive me mad."

Annalise had gone quiet next to her, her knuckles white as she gripped her black trousers. Relaina placed a hand on her sister's.

"I know that's probably how you felt for weeks," she said softly. Annalise placed her other hand on top of Relaina's, squeezing.

"I just want it to end," Annalise whispered.

"I think you should go to Parea if that's what you want," Nehma said.

Relaina met her steely gaze. "How? My magic—"

"You got a tattoo," Nehma said, inclining her head. "And an intricate one at that. How did you manage to get a tattoo without your light intervening?"

"Darren and I connected our darkness while the tattoo artisans worked. It's easier for me to control it when the darkness is channeled elsewhere, as you've seen in my training."

"And you held the light at bay for hours while they worked?"

"Yes, then I let it heal me and Darren after they were done."

Nehma and Thea exchanged a look.

"That's progress, Relaina," Thea said. "That level of control for that length of time, even with Darren's help, is significant."

Relaina stared at them, her hand absently reaching for her chest, running over the lines of the flowers. Had her endless frustration in training finally resulted in progress?

"And...you think it's enough that I could go to Parea?"

"It would still be incredibly risky," Nehma said. "An experienced healer should be at your side. But we could make it work."

Hope and dread mingled in Relaina's gut, but before she could decipher either emotion, Annalise sniffed beside her.

"Anna?"

"I don't want to be left behind *again*," Annalise said. "I'm worried for Aronn too. But I don't get a choice to go help. I'll be told I have to stay here."

"Anna, I—"

"I don't want to pretend like I've had it worse than you or Aronn," Annalise said. "I know it's been awful for each of us. I'm just tired of being alone."

"Ah, but you won't be alone," Thea said, holding out her hand, and Annalise took it. "I'll be here still. You and I can come up with all the favors our sisters will owe us upon their return."

"You think Rhea will go?" Relaina asked.

"She was speaking to Jeremiah earlier about going with him anyway," Nehma said. "And I'll go too. Rhea and I can ensure your safety on the journey, and I want to see Aronn for myself."

Without thinking, Relaina stood and drew Nehma into a hug. After a moment of shock, Nehma returned her embrace.

"Can I train with Darren while you're gone?" Annalise asked as Relaina turned back to her and Thea.

"I'll ask him, but I'm sure he'd be happy to," Relaina said. She offered her sister a hand, and with Nehma and Thea, they headed back inside.

CHAPTER 27

───────

SOMETHING TO RETURN FOR

Darren stared at the obsidian crown in the box before him. It was lightweight when he lifted it, carved into crescent moons and four-pointed stars. A cluster of three diamonds was inlaid in the center of each star.

"For tonight," Fabian said. A servant removed the box from the banquet table, and Darren resisted the urge to protest. He turned the crown in the light of the chandeliers, the diamonds glittering.

"How did you have this made so quickly?" Darren asked. He still couldn't bring himself to put it on.

"Ah, it was made over a week ago." Fabian folded his ring-adorned fingers beneath his chin. He wore an ornate crown himself tonight, carved golden vines encasing large rubies.

"You knew I would make a claim?"

"I had a feeling."

Darren took a deep breath before lifting the crown. He carefully avoided the small bun at the crown of his head and let the metal settle on top of his hair. Fabian smiled.

"It suits you."

"Thank you, Fabian. I hadn't thought of needing one."

"Luckily, I always think of everything. Or perhaps that is rather unlucky, for me at least."

Darren laughed. "I'm sure it doesn't help your sleep."

"Indeed it does not."

"I want you to know how grateful I am for your help," Darren said. "Knowing I have your support has made this far less terrifying."

"While I wish you and Relaina nothing but peace and happiness, I cannot pretend I wasn't hoping you would make this decision," Fabian said. "You have the makings of a great leader, Darren. And I'm happy to show support in whatever way I can."

Darren wasn't sure how he'd ever thank Fabian.

A servant came forward again, announcing that Jeremiah was at the door. Fabian nodded, and Jeremiah entered moments later, dressed similarly to both Darren and Fabian in a finely woven shirt layered with a formal jerkin and trousers tucked into boots. He and Fabian both wore the Evarian red and gold, the same way Darren now wore the LaGuarde green and black.

Jeremiah greeted Fabian with a quiet word and a hand on his shoulder before taking his seat across from Darren. Anxiety rippled from him as he hesitantly met Darren's eyes.

"Good evening, Darren," he managed, and Darren offered what he hoped was a kind smile and nod in return. Heat flooded Darren's neck and face a moment later, and he tugged at the front of his shirt, ensuring the tattoo wasn't visible through the laces. He and Relaina hadn't told Jeremiah or Fabian yet that they'd gotten them. He hoped she'd arrive soon —the banquet was supposed to begin at sundown.

When the doors opened and she stepped inside, it wasn't relief that swept through him. She stole the air from his lungs.

Her shadowfire scars and tattoo were displayed above the dark green neckline of her gown, which dipped between her breasts and rested off her shoulders. Black embroidered leaves adorned the center of the bodice and crept elegantly down the chiffon skirts, tapering off before reaching the floor. Her dark, shining curls had been piled atop her head with several ringlets hanging loose. A silver crown, the inverse of Darren's, rested on her forehead as if it was always meant to be there, the shining metal and black diamonds woven among her curls.

She was fucking magnificent.

She somehow wore the LaGuarde green more naturally than he did. Her green eyes, lined in kohl, were even more striking than usual. They remained trained on Darren as she drew closer to the table. He didn't notice that Fabian and Jeremiah's conversation had halted until Relaina was standing beside him, offering a small smile before facing the king and her father.

"We wanted to tell you before the dinner tonight," Relaina said, taking Darren's hand. Thank the gods she was the one speaking. His voice may have failed him. "We're engaged."

Fabian's eyes twinkled as he smiled and stood, taking their free hands in his.

"Congratulations to you both," he said warmly. "It will be a privilege to rule Evaria with you two ruling in Terrana."

Jeremiah stood as Fabian stepped back. He didn't offer a hand or an embrace, but he did smile.

"I wish you both every happiness," he said.

Voices drifted from outside the doors, and Fabian took Jeremiah's hand and kissed his fingers before looking toward the doors.

"It's time."

The doors opened again, and a small group of musicians gathered to play softly at the opposite end of the hall. Terranian nobles arrived shortly thereafter. Ihara Eyern stood out in her all-black attire, less formal than the other nobles. The rest wore gowns or shirts and jerkins in their respective family colors. Each of them bowed to Darren before taking their seats down the table. Evarian nobles trickled in over the next few minutes, adding to the growing sound of chatter and music in the large room.

Fabian stood once everyone had arrived, and the rest of the room followed suit, the music stopping.

"We've gathered tonight in recognition of Darren LaGuarde's claim to the Terranian throne," Fabian said. He inclined his head to Darren. "Your Majesty."

Darren had been nervous to speak before them all, but after seeing Relaina and telling Fabian and Jeremiah about their engagement, he wasn't sure he'd fear anything anymore. He bowed his head to Fabian in turn and faced the room.

"The future is still uncertain," Darren said, his voice stronger than he'd expected, "but I am confident that together we can guide Terrana into an era of peace. I look forward to re-establishing the strong relationship Evaria and Terrana once enjoyed." Darren picked up a freshly poured glass of wine from his place at the table. "To peace and healing for all of Esran."

Echoes of "peace and healing" filled the room as everyone lifted their glass and drank.

"And," Darren continued, taking Relaina's hand in his with a smile. "Princess Relaina will rule at my side as Queen of Terrana."

A beat of silence, then Lady Eyern lifted her glass high again.

"Adtredi!" she cheered in Terranian. *Blessings.* The other Terranians followed suit. Smiles filled the room as everyone raised their glasses in a toast. Darren turned to Relaina, and she brushed her thumb along the back of his hand, smiling at him with pride.

The music began again as everyone took their seats, shortly

followed by the first course of the evening—a thick soup flavored with warm spices.

"I see you've gotten your tattoos," Jeremiah said, gesturing between Relaina and Darren.

"Yesterday," she said. "After the meeting."

"I remember when we got ours," Fabian said quietly, his eyes lingering on Jeremiah for a moment. He glanced behind Darren. "Ah, good evening, Bracken."

"Good evening!"

Bracken leaned down between Relaina and Darren, his hands resting on the backs of their chairs.

"The two of you are *engaged*, and I'd like to air my grievances at being the last bastard to find out," Bracken said. Relaina grinned sheepishly.

"Sorry, Bracken," she said. "It was rather sudden."

"It's fine, I suppose," he said. With a bright smile he nudged Darren. "I'm genuinely happy for you both. Please have a summer wedding so I won't have to travel in the cold."

Darren laughed. "We'll be sure to prioritize that in our plans."

Bracken returned to his seat, and the rest of the meal passed cheerfully, much to Darren's relief. He and Relaina sipped dessert wine side by side as everyone milled about the room. After six nobles had approached them to offer their congratulations, Relaina took his hand.

"Can we step outside?" she asked, gesturing to the open doors at the east end of the room. They led out onto a balcony overlooking the gardens, lit by sparkling lanterns. Offering a smile and nod to nobles as they passed, Darren kept one hand on the small of Relaina's back.

"Relaina, what is it?" he asked once they were outside. The night air had no bite to it this evening, and soft floral smells wafted along the breeze around them. Relaina approached the edge of the balcony, her shoulders tensed as she gripped the railing. He joined her, placing one hand over hers.

"I'm afraid," she said, her voice small.

"Tell me."

She took his hand in both of hers, squeezing it as she met his eyes. "Tonight has been...better than I'd ever imagined. I'm so proud to stand by your side."

Darren took her face in his hands.

"I can't tell you how much that means to me. But what's troubling you? Is it Aronn?"

She closed her eyes as she placed her hands on his chest.

"Yes. I can't shake this worry for him." She looked at him again. "I want to go to Parea."

Oh.

"I've spoken to Nehma and the others about it, and they said my control over the light has improved enough that it wouldn't be as risky," she said quickly. "I can't take not knowing if Aronn is all right and leaving it to others to fight the traitors. I've felt such guilt about not helping them, not helping my people."

Darren's thoughts drifted to Maurice and Camille. He'd worried for them, too, hoped that they hadn't been caught up in the coup or the traitors' plans.

"Parea is your home," Darren said firmly. "We both know the only reason you haven't thrown yourself into helping the loyalists is because of the instability of your magic. If you feel so strongly about going, and if the healers think you'll be safe, then you should go."

Relaina's eyes searched his.

"The prospect of leaving you is more painful than I expected," she said.

Darren brushed her cheek with his thumb. "We'll be all right."

"You've carved your name on my heart, Darren LaGuarde."

Affection and sadness warred within him as he pressed his lips to hers. Music drifted outside, a gentle accompaniment to their slow, indulgent kiss. Relaina pulled back and rested her head on his chest.

"Are you sure you'll be all right without me?"

"I will be completely wrong without you," he said with a humorless laugh. "But we both have important things we must do. I'll be fine to carry out negotiations while you help kick those fuckers out of your home."

"I'll return before the end of spring. I promise."

"I'll pray to every god I know that the loyalists succeed far earlier than that."

They remained outside for a few more minutes, embracing one another in the cool, fragrant night air.

"I suppose we ought to go back inside," Relaina said, sighing.

"They can wait."

Relaina pulled back, smirking. "Already exercising your kingly privileges, I see."

"I'd have said that regardless. They'll see plenty of me over the next few months."

Several nobles had already left the dinner by the time they stepped back inside, and it wasn't long before others did the same. Relaina joined her sister while Darren swiped one of the remaining glasses of dessert wine. Jeremiah stopped beside Darren, holding his own glass of wine.

"Relaina plans to join me in Parea," Jeremiah said.

"She does."

"Tell me truly, do you think she'll be safe?" Though Jeremiah tried to mask it as he took a sip of wine, his eyes betrayed his concern as he looked at Relaina across the room.

"She seems confident that she will be, with the healers'

help," Darren said. "I can't imagine Rhea or Nehma encouraging her to go if the risk was too great."

Some doubt lingered on Jeremiah's face, but he nodded. "Thank you."

"I—for what?"

"For protecting her when I couldn't. And for saving me as well."

Darren's heart swelled and ached at the same time.

"I will always protect her and anyone she loves. And I know she'll do the same for me."

Jeremiah smiled. "And that's why your engagement is a source of comfort and celebration. I'm sorry you must be separated so soon."

Darren breathed deeply as Jeremiah walked off, finishing his wine. Relaina caught his eye from where she stood with Bracken, Annalise, and Thea. She tilted her head toward the door, and he promptly began his final round of farewells for the evening.

RELAINA HAD BARELY SHUT the door behind her when Darren pressed her against it, his mouth seeking hers. She wrapped her arms around his neck as he pulled her lower lip between his teeth, and before she could nip him back he broke away, turning her around.

"You're wasting no time," she said breathlessly, leaning her head to the side as he kissed her neck and unlaced her dress. Her bodice loosened, and Darren slipped a hand beneath its front, brushing his thumb over her nipple. Relaina gasped softly as he kissed her neck just below her ear.

"I have to give you something to return for," he said.

"I'll return for you anyway."

"Even so." He brushed her nipple again as his breath

tickled her ear. "I'm going to memorize every inch of your body to ensure I dream about it each night we're apart."

Relaina shivered as he tugged her earlobe with his teeth. He stepped back just long enough to let her dress fall from her shoulders to the floor in an elegant heap, and Relaina spun around. He kissed her again, his hands cradling her face as she undid the buttons and laces of his attire as quickly as she could. She rubbed the heel of her palm against his erection before unlacing his trousers. He groaned, one hand smacking onto the wall behind her as his body arched into her touch. She smiled against his mouth.

Relaina broke away and stepped around the skirts of her dress, bending to untie the ribbons of the black sandals that wrapped up her calves.

"Wait," Darren said, discarding his shirt next to her dress. "Leave those on."

Relaina straightened, lifting an eyebrow with a smirk. "Anything else, Your Majesty?"

He pinned her against the wall by the door, his eyes studying her face as if he was seeing her for the first time. "The crown stays on too."

She pulled his face back to hers. His mouth tasted like sweet wine, and she was intoxicated. Relaina held her breath as his hand brushed her inner thigh.

"Couch or chair?" he asked.

Relaina's mind was hazy from the anticipation of his touch. "What?"

"Would you rather sit on the couch or one of the chairs while I pleasure you with my mouth?"

Fire shot through Relaina's lower abdomen and spread between her legs. Part of her wanted him to fuck her right there against the wall, but his playful teasing and insistence on drawing this out made every part of her body simmer. Without a word, she walked over to the couch and reclined against it. He grinned at her as she raised her chin, daring him to approach.

"Try not to ruin the upholstery," she said as he knelt before her. With a grin, he grabbed her thighs and yanked her toward him. She yelped a laugh that turned into a moan as he buried his face between her legs.

The orgasm that shuddered through her minutes later had her fingers knotting in his hair and her toes curling in her sandals. She caught her breath for a moment before joining him on the floor and having him lie back, tugging his trousers down and taking him in her mouth. His gasps and moans only emboldened her as she savored the taste of him.

Pulling gently at her hair, he stopped her, and Relaina crawled on top of him, kissing his abdomen, his sternum, his chest. She traced the lines of his tattoo with her finger as she met his eyes.

"Where do you want me?" she asked. He inhaled slowly.

"Is everywhere an option?"

Relaina laughed and kissed him. She adjusted the crown on his head. "Just tell me where to go."

He tucked one of her curls behind her ear and brushed his thumb across her lower lip.

"You pick the first place."

Relaina bit her lip. "Can we go back to the wall?"

Darren sat up with more enthusiasm than she expected, bringing her with him as he stood. She pulled him close as she backed against the wall and hitched one leg around his waist, standing on her toes with the opposite foot. Once he was inside her and began thrusting in earnest, Relaina was so lost in it she almost forgot to hold onto his shoulders so she wouldn't fall. She wrapped her other leg around his waist and threw her head back.

"Ow, fuck." She'd forgotten about the crown until it dug

into her head against the wall. Darren stopped moving, horrified.

"Did I—?"

"No, I just forgot I was wearing this."

"Fuck it." He pulled out of her and set her on the ground, lifting the crown gently from her hair. Relaina discarded the pins holding her curls in a now-lopsided bun while he placed both their crowns on the table by the couch. The relief along her scalp as her hair fell loose was almost as satisfying as Darren's hands running along her skin.

Almost.

"The bed?" he asked, and she nodded. She pulled him after her, wrapping her arms around his neck as they fell back onto the mattress.

He pushed into her slowly, never breaking eye contact, and his shadows appeared at his hands. Relaina's skin smoldered as he circled her clit with his finger and kept his pace slow, drawing every ounce of pleasure from her that he could. A whimper caught in her throat.

Moan for me, love.

Relaina let go, raising her arms above her head as he began moving faster. Every sound he elicited from her made his breathing more uneven, his movements harsher. Relaina's climax loomed as she sensed his pleasure alongside her own through their bond. It built slowly, until she was gripping the bedcovers while her whole body tensed. She came harder than she had before, a high-pitched cry falling from her lips as Darren kept moving. He moaned her name, burying his face in the crook of her neck. She gripped his lower back as his own release overtook him.

Even in their sweaty aftermath, Relaina was reluctant to let him go for even a moment. She would miss this—the weight of him on top of her, his arms holding her close, making her feel desired, safe.

"Can we stay awake tonight?" she asked quietly. Darren propped himself up on his elbows, brushing her hair out of her face.

"Don't you want to rest before traveling?"

"I want to savor every moment with you before I leave."

Darren's smile was tinged with sadness. "All right."

They took their time bathing, and Relaina let herself forget everything but him for a while. Tonight was for soft kisses and whispered jokes. They lay tangled in bed late into the night, talking of dreams for the future and gentle moments of the past.

"My mother had a garden in the Keep," Darren said, tracing soothing patterns on Relaina's bare back. She closed her eyes, resting her head on his chest. "Every color imaginable in flowers and greenery. I loved the orange lilies most."

"Perhaps you can keep your own garden there."

Darren kissed the top of her head. "I would like that."

Despite herself, sleep crept up on Relaina, enticing as she lay in Darren's embrace.

"Relaina?"

"Hm?"

"Promise me you'll be safe."

She opened her eyes and pressed her lips to his inked chest. "I promise."

"I could not bear it if anything happened to you."

Relaina shifted so she could see his face.

"I swear I'll keep myself safe," she said. "And I need you to protect yourself as well. We still don't know if there are others loyal to the white-haired woman, and if anything happens, I want you to write to me immediately."

"I will." Darren kissed her once before she settled down again, tucked into his chest. "I love you, Relaina."

She closed her eyes and smiled. "More than anything."

"More than anyone."

PART TWO

CHAPTER 28

THE SHADOW IN THE INN

Hazy light and warmth greeted Aronn as he awoke. At first, all he could make out was the ceiling of his semi-private quarters, but as the remainder of his senses returned, so did the memory of their mission. He tried to sit up.

"Patience, my prince," a soft, feminine voice said from his left. Firm hands prevented him from rising, pinning his shoulders to the mattress. Aronn breathed a few times and finally focused on the healer beside him. It was that woman from the other day—the one who'd looked at him like she knew him.

"Who are you?" he asked.

Her clear blue eyes squinted above her veil in a smile. "My name is Maya. I've been keeping watch over you after you were injured."

"Maya," Aronn muttered. "Oh, gods in hell, I was shot."

"You were. Three days ago."

"Three days?"

"Indeed. Let's try to sit up, shall we?"

With Maya's help, Aronn propped himself up in bed, his back resting on the wall behind him, and she held a glowing hand to his abdomen. The acute pain from the injury had vanished, but there was a deep soreness in his lower torso that made him wince as he adjusted.

"You were very lucky, my prince," she said. "Your party got you back here before you lost too much blood."

Fear shot up Aronn's throat. "Are the rest of them safe? Maurice and Camille?"

"They are. If I may offer some advice, my prince, I would say you ought not to be so reckless with your own life. You will need level-headed, proper advisors when you're king, not those who allow you to be put in danger."

Aronn bristled. Who was this healer to offer him such advice?

"Danger is inevitable," Aronn said. His face heated as he realized just how exposed he was; he had no shirt or tunic, only undergarments on beneath the bedcovers. He cleared his throat. "And I won't be king for a while yet."

"That is the hope. Still," Maya's hand lingered on Aronn's lower abdomen even after the healing glow subsided, "you will need trusted friends. Allies. Confidants."

Aronn grabbed the woman's wrist and removed her hand from his skin. "I did not ask for advice. I think you ought to leave."

Something akin to wrath flashed in her eyes as she snatched her wrist from his grasp, and Aronn flinched back.

"Prince Aronn?"

Saheer and Misenia entered the room, hardly acknowledging Maya. The healer bowed and left before others appeared in the doorway, their expressions eager. Saheer took Aronn's hand as she sat in the chair by his bed.

"How are you?" she asked, her hazel eyes bright.

More Lyneisian loyalists gathered at the door behind her. Misenia followed Aronn's gaze and barked, "Give him a moment, for Saeva's sake!"

"Thank you," Aronn said as the onlookers dissipated,

mumbling as they went. Should he tell them about Maya? Now that the healer was gone, her behavior seemed uncomfortable but harmless. Plenty of people had attempted to share his bed before, to curry favor with the Prince of Lyneisia. And until recently, he'd reveled in the attention.

"I'm all right," he said. He swallowed against the dryness in his throat. "Was anyone else injured?"

"Mazin was wounded, but it was a shallow slice to the arm," Saheer said. "He's fine now."

Aronn sighed and let his head hit the wall behind him. "Thank the gods for that. Have we gathered any other information since then?"

"Only more evidence that the king and queen are likely in the castle dungeons," Saheer said. "But we still haven't confirmed that."

That would make rescuing them challenging. Aronn knew the layout of the dungeons, but there were four floors of cells and only one contained a secret exit.

"When is the next meeting?" Aronn asked.

"In an hour," Misenia said.

Aronn looked at her again and nodded. "Then I'll be there."

OVER TWENTY YEARS had passed since Jeremiah had been to The Happy Stump inn, and here he was, arriving there for the third time in a matter of months. When he and Aronn had stayed there nearly four weeks past, one of the Evarian escorts had announced Jeremiah as King Fabian's betrothed before he could stop her. Roderick, the old innkeep, had been beside himself with glee.

Tonight, to Jeremiah's dismay, was no different.

"Welcome, welcome, Your Majesty, or Your Future

Majesty or—ah, gods in hell," the innkeep said, bowing clumsily. To Jeremiah's right, Relaina covered her mouth to hide a smile. It was the first time she'd smiled since leaving Maremer two days ago, and it soothed his agitation toward Roderick's simpering.

"Lord Andovier is fine," Jeremiah said. He'd have preferred just his name, but allowing Roderick such familiarity might make the man faint.

"Ah, very well, Lord Andovier, I have all rooms but one available! Not much traveling this time of year, you know, but it's always an honor to host the future consort of the king." Roderick spoke so quickly that it made Jeremiah's head spin. Jeremiah looked to the three healers, the one Evarian guard, and Relaina.

"We'll need rooms enough to sleep six," he said.

Amid Roderick's overattentiveness and the inn workers' curious stares, they settled into rooms on the second floor. Relaina, Nehma, and Rhea took one with three beds while Catrin led the guard to another, and the innkeep shuffled Jeremiah into the room with the nicest view. Despite Jeremiah's insistence that he needed neither two beds nor any view at all, Roderick waved him off, happily taking the coin he offered as payment for both their stay and the inn's discretion. No other guests had been present in the bar downstairs, but paying off Roderick would ensure the presence of their party remained quiet, at least until their departure the next day.

Jeremiah dropped his small travel satchel on the bed he didn't intend to use and sat on the other. His back ached from so much riding. They would push forward as quickly as they could, though—getting back to the healers' sanctuary was the priority.

Being alone for too long still made him uneasy, so he bathed hastily and joined Relaina and the healers downstairs for a meal.

The healers and Catrin's assigned guard chatted as they ate, but Relaina was quiet. Being near her still scared him a little, but she assured him that his presence was a comfort and not just a reminder of—

It wouldn't do any good for him to finish that thought, to spiral into despair and shame in the middle of the inn.

Catrin and her guard disappeared upstairs first, and when Nehma and Rhea retired, Relaina shifted to a chair across from Jeremiah, accepting another cup of wine from one of the barmen. She took a sip and grimaced.

"Bad?" Jeremiah asked.

"Terrible." Yet she still drank.

They sat in silence for a few more minutes, the air stagnant between them.

"Relaina," he said. "What happens if you're hurt?"

She breathed deeply, drumming her fingers on her cup. "I can control the light with minor injuries, just enough to keep it from clashing with my scars. If I sustain more severe injuries I would need help from another healer."

"And if the magics clash?"

Relaina looked away from him. "I'd be in a lot of pain."

Jeremiah suppressed a shudder.

"And you think you can prevent that from happening again?" he asked.

"I think I can prevent it more now than I could a few weeks ago." She met his concerned stare. "And being able to help my family is worth the risk."

Jeremiah didn't like it, but he did understand. He nodded.

"What time shall I wake the others tomorrow?" she asked, standing.

"We ought to leave before first light."

Jeremiah thanked the inn workers they passed as they trudged up the stairs, and before she disappeared into her room, Relaina embraced him. He froze for a moment before wrapping his arms around her.

"Let's make sure Aronn is all right, find my parents, and take back our home," she said.

Jeremiah smiled. "That was precisely my plan."

YOU SHOULDN'T WALK ALONE, Jeremiah Andovier.

Kalmali stood over him, taller than he recalled and silhouetted by black fire. Jeremiah's arms were pinned to his sides on the ground. He tried to scream, but it got caught in his throat, his lips refusing to release the sound. He closed his eyes and squirmed, trying to force them to open again. They finally did, and he was in a dark, quiet room in the inn.

But why couldn't he move? He tried to lift a hand, to even move a finger, but his body did not respond. He couldn't make a sound besides a muffled cry. In the corner of the room, a shadow moved, taking the shape of a man.

No, this couldn't be happening again. Terror sent his heart beating so fast he half expected it to give out. Another tenebrae had possessed him, had taken his control away, and Relaina and the others were in the next room. He hadn't been able to fight it enough to keep Relaina from getting hurt last time. With every ounce of his strength, he fought the shadow holding him down. Tears leaked from his eyes as his breathing turned to labored gasps.

As quickly as it had come, it lifted. He shot upright and clambered out of the bed, curling up on the floor. The shadow was gone.

It took several more long, deep breaths for his heart to slow again. He kept his eyes firmly open, staring at the dust beneath the other bed in his room.

Sleep would be impossible for him now, so he got to his

feet and stumbled into the washroom. A single candle was still burning inside. He lit all the others and peeled off his sweat-damp shirt and trousers before sinking into the bath.

Dawn peeked through the window as he dried himself off and examined his appearance in the old mirror above the water basin. His dark bronze-gray hair had grown long enough to braid now. His fingers remembered the method even after years of keeping it shorter, tying it off at the base of his neck.

He met his own brown-eyed gaze in the mirror. His eyes looked as haunted as he felt. Rage broiled within him. He'd find out what Kalmali and his white-haired mistress had been up to in Lyneisia.

And he'd put an end to it.

CHAPTER 29

THE SUMMONS

"That was much better," Darren said. Annalise straightened, grimacing at the knife in her hand.

"I still can't imagine actually cutting or stabbing someone with this," she said.

"It's not particularly enjoyable. But you'd be surprised what you can do when it's your life or theirs."

Annalise handed him her knife and they started for the sparring hall weaponry, tailed by two Evarian guards and Ihara Eyern. She'd insisted on accompanying him everywhere, saying it was an honor to protect the King of Terrana, and Darren had allowed it. He liked Ihara, and Lucia, for that matter.

Before her departure, Relaina had asked him to keep up Annalise's basic combat training, and he was glad to have a task that felt natural to him. The negotiations weren't going poorly, but the issues facing both Evaria and Terrana were complex and made his head go numb by the end of each meeting. Annalise's presence was refreshing too—she was witty, asked direct questions, and didn't expect anything from him but a listening ear and patience as she struggled to learn fighting skills.

"So," Annalise said as he put away their training knives. "When are you and Relaina getting married?"

Darren laughed. "How long have you been waiting to ask me that?"

"Since she left."

A pang hit him in the chest. Three days had passed since then, and he hadn't expected his magic to sense her growing distance. When he'd used his power, that spark of her presence was now dimmed—where before he could feel what she felt, now it was only a flicker of her emotions before they faded again.

"I'm not sure when it'll be, truthfully," he said, forcing his focus back to the present. "While I wouldn't let the nobles sway my choice of partner, I don't think it's unreasonable for them to expect us to have the ceremony in Terrana."

"I've always been curious about Terrana." Annalise played with the end of her braid absently as they strode back out to the sparring hall and into the corridor beyond, tailed by two guards. "I've read books about the history, the geography. The climate is so different from Lyneisia. I suppose because Terrana has fewer mountains. And tales of the Blackwood Forest have always interested me."

"The Blackwood Forest is beautiful, but dangerous. No one ventures far into it, which is why so few bows are made from its trees."

"Stories say many have entered and never returned."

Darren nodded. "There's no path or road that cuts through it."

"King Darren!"

Darren's head snapped up. A Shadow approached him, huffing through his mask as he held out a sealed envelope. Seeing the symbol in the black wax sent a shiver down Darren's spine.

"It's from—"

"The Terranian Elite," Darren said, taking the letter. "Where did you get this?"

"I was in Ellyr when King Fabian sent word for me to go to Ryos and gather information on the Arteas and the Terranian Elite. The assassins found me tailing them and gave me this for you."

"They let you live?" Darren asked, shocked.

"Most of them have gathered at House Artea, but they said they have no commander and therefore no reason to kill me."

Darren broke the seal and unfolded the letter.

Darren LaGuarde—
If you wish to lead us, you must first prove your strength. We'll await your arrival in Ryos within the fortnight, at the new moon. Be prepared to fight our strongest.

Darren looked to the Shadow and Annalise as if they could offer some advice or guidance on this new development, but neither of them knew anything about the Terranian Elite. He blinked a few times as his head swam.

"My king?"

Ihara approached him for the first time, breaking her usual

silence. Darren had almost forgotten she was there. He handed her the letter. Her eyes flashed across the parchment before she looked up.

"We must tell the others immediately," she said.

"You go tell Lady Eyern now, and I'll ask King Fabian about holding an emergency council," he said. He turned to the Shadow. "Do you know where King Fabian is?"

The Shadow shook his head. "I found you first."

"He is having lunch in his chambers, Your Grace," one of the Evarian guards said, stepping forward with a bow. Darren thanked him, bid farewell to Annalise, and bounded up the nearby stairwell so quickly his assigned Evarian guard nearly lost him.

The guards outside Fabian's chambers stopped him, their faces wary.

"I need to speak with King Fabian immediately," Darren said. The guards exchanged a look before one of them knocked. Darren paced in the corridor.

Fabian's voice called from within seconds later. "You may enter."

Darren forced himself to not push past the guard, heading straight for Fabian's study as soon as the doorway was vacant. Fabian stood from his desk when he saw Darren.

"What's happened?"

"The Terranian Elite have summoned me to Ryos." Darren handed Fabian the letter, which the king read quickly. "They expect me there in a matter of days."

"Is this a custom with which you're familiar?" Fabian asked, stepping around his desk and gesturing toward the chairs by his fireplace. Darren sat, his leg bouncing.

"My father always said the Terranian Elite should only follow the strongest dark magic wielders. At the time, I thought he was discouraging them from following me as I rose the ranks, since I never used magic."

"So you were part of the Terranian Elite yourself?"

"Officially, yes, but my father kept me isolated from them. I was their best fighter when magic wasn't involved. Not all of them were tenebrae, but even those who were never dared use that against me."

"And your father was displeased by this?"

A memory Darren had long suppressed hit him like a blast of icy water. "He always said I was weak for not using magic the way he did. One day, Gabriel came to observe our training and..." Darren exhaled. "During the next spar, he told them they could use magic, and they nearly killed me."

The concern on Fabian's face morphed into disgust. "Gods."

Flashes of that day pressed into Darren's mind. The cold, dark fighting ring. The laughter as three tenebrae assassins attacked him relentlessly, even after he'd yielded the fight. The taste of blood and salty tears and dirt as his father sneered at him.

"Do you think you can beat them?" With Fabian's simple, quiet question, the vortex of despair vanished from Darren's thoughts. Gabriel was dead, and Darren was sitting in a room with a king who had shown him unyielding kindness and grace.

"I don't know," Darren said. "I didn't know how to use my power back then. But I have a grasp on it now."

Fabian nodded. "Very well."

"I know it will halt our efforts with the Terranian nobles here for a few weeks," Darren said. "But I have to try."

"Negotiations can be put on hold in order to secure this asset to your reign," Fabian said. "The fact that the Terranian Elite are not inherently loyal to Gabriel is encouraging. And since we'll need to pause negotiations anyway, I'll join you in Ryos."

Darren gaped at him. "I—are you sure? I wouldn't want to pull you away from your own duties in Maremer."

"Rebuilding efforts are well underway, and Lord Vontair and Desiree are more than capable of managing things for two weeks. Besides," Fabian stood from his chair and returned to his desk, "I've wanted to visit Terrana for many years. I'll draft a note to Jeremiah informing him of our travel plans. If you'd like to write to Relaina, have a servant bring me your letter this evening."

All Darren could do was nod, his gratitude too great to voice.

"I'll need to inform the Terranian nobles today," Darren said. "Can we call a meeting?"

"I'll send for them," Fabian said. "We'll depart tomorrow."

RELAINA HAD SPENT every winter of her twenty-one years in Lyneisia, but as they crossed the Granica and traveled farther into the mountains of her home, the frigid air affected her less than it ever had. While the others shivered or used their light to keep warm, Relaina was comfortable with only her furs. Amariah was at home in the colder air as well. Relaina patted the mare's neck and kissed her nose before leaving her in the hands of the stablewoman at the inn they'd found for the night.

Her conversation with her companions over dinner was subdued; Catrin and her assigned guard, Ivar, had branched off for the Caspian Forest the day before, and the rest of them were exhausted from traveling. Once they ventured farther south, their progress would slow with the snow. Relaina thanked the gods that it was already past midwinter. The weeks following her birthday were usually the coldest and most prone to snowstorms

"Do you and Thea ever have second visions of the same event?" Relaina asked Rhea, after once again voicing concern for Aronn. Rhea shook her head.

"No," Rhea said. "They're rather infrequent, thank the gods. But yours could work differently. Didn't you say you've had a vision of the past?"

"Once," Relaina said. "I saw my birthmother's death in Terrana. A village was on fire."

Nehma set down her fork and stood, leaving the table with a quiet farewell. Relaina looked to Rhea as Nehma disappeared down the hallway toward their rooms.

"All of our parents died in the raids," Rhea said quietly. Relaina's heart fell to her toes.

"Gods. I'm sorry."

Rhea offered an appreciative smile. "We were all too young to truly remember. But it's why there are so many older healers and younger healers in the Caspian Forest. The elders there took in the children that escaped before the tenebrae reached our sanctuaries."

"So you all were born in Terrana?" Jeremiah asked.

"We were." Rhea took another bite of food, brushing one of her signature braids over her shoulder. Heaviness settled on Relaina as she stared down the hallway where Nehma had disappeared. She started to stand, but a tinge of coolness prickled in her chest, followed by short flashes of emotions that left a yearning ache in their wake. *Darren.*

"What is it?" Rhea asked, glancing at Relaina's scars.

"I can still feel it when Darren uses his power. It's faint, but it's there." There was some measure of comfort in that, at least. Relaina finished her ale and stood, bidding Rhea and Jeremiah goodnight.

Nehma was curled up on top of her small bed when Relaina entered their room, her hair wrapped in a dark blue silk scarf. Relaina sat on her own bed and lit a second candle on the table between them.

"When I first sensed Darren's power, I recognized it," Nehma said.

Relaina looked up as she pulled off her boot. Nehma turned over to face her.

"I don't remember the raids or how I escaped as an infant," Nehma said, her voice barely above a whisper. "But my magic remembered the darkness."

Relaina's eyes widened. "That's why you didn't trust him."

"Especially not after seeing your scars. I had never seen anything like them before, but I could sense the dark magic within them."

Though Relaina chafed at the idea of Nehma distrusting Darren so immediately, she could not deny the gratitude that filled her at Nehma's protective instinct. Even before they'd known who she was, the healers had acknowledged her as their own.

"I trust him now, though," Nehma said, sitting up. "And I'm confident you'll only get better at using your magic. Both the light and dark."

Relaina pulled her legs onto the bed, hugging her knees to her chest. "You and the others have treated me as an equal, as a healer, since we met. Your help and friendship have meant so much when I've felt like some kind of fraud or—" *Pretender.* Kalmali had called her that, mocked her as he used her father's hands to try and kill her. "Just...thank you."

Nehma held out both her hands, and Relaina took them in hers.

"You are our sister as much as any other healer. It's not your fault you didn't know about your power, and then it was suppressed by shadowfire. Thea and I meant it when we said you've made progress. And you'll continued to make more."

Relaina squeezed Nehma's hands. "I'm glad to have you as friends. And I hope—no, I know that Terrana will someday be a place where both healers and tenebrae can coexist peacefully."

Nehma released her hands with a smile. "If you and Darren are leading, then I have faith."

After a quick bath and checking on Rhea and Jeremiah in the next room, Relaina settled into bed, blowing out their candles.

"I hope Aronn is all right," she said.

"We'll know soon. Worrying won't help him either way. It will only rob you of needed rest."

She was right. Relaina rolled to her other side, her legs tucked close to her chest. She missed Darren's warm embrace and sleepy kisses. Each morning, she'd awoken with an outstretched hand, only to grasp at an empty place on the bed.

But a new fondness settled alongside the ache of missing him, growing each day she spent with Nehma and Rhea, each magic lesson, each joke they exchanged or fear they shared. These past months had brought pain and betrayal and loss, but they had also brought her joy and real friends. Friends she could trust. *Sisters.*

With a renewed optimism for what they faced, Relaina fell into the waiting arms of sleep.

CHAPTER 30

THE PRINCESS RETURNS

The gods seemed to be on their side for the remainder of their travels to the healers' sanctuary north of Parea. As night fell and they passed by familiar rock formations and ever-thinning pine trees dusted with snow, she spurred Amariah faster. They were close—mere miles away from Aronn and the others.

When the trees parted and the sanctuary's walls loomed ahead, the uncertainty of what awaited her inside turned her stomach. Several figures appeared at the steps leading to the sanctuary entrance, the guards out front shouting something unintelligible. Relaina dismounted Amariah a few feet from the steps, her boots hitting the snow with a light crunch. The guards stared at her. They did not bow.

"Where is my brother?" she asked, starting forward, but two of them blocked her way to the stairs with crossed spears.

"Our deepest apologies, Your Highness," one of them said, not taking his eyes off her as he dipped his head. "But we must examine each of you for dark magic before we allow you entry."

Hooves thundered behind Relaina as the rest of her party

arrived and dismounted. Jeremiah stood by Relaina, lowering the hood of his cloak.

"Captain Andovier!" one of the guards called, but her companion nudged her side and she fell silent once more.

"We're not possessed," Nehma said, stepping forward. She and Rhea summoned their light, placing their hands on Jeremiah and Relaina's shoulders. All six guards visibly relaxed, three of them hurrying forward to greet Jeremiah. Relaina pushed past them and ran up the stairs.

Warmth enveloped her as she stepped inside the sanctuary. Large tables had been erected inside to accommodate dining, and dozens of people milled about. Heads turned in her direction, and silence fell upon the cavernous hall for a heartbeat before the room exploded into yelps of surprise and confusion.

"Princess Relaina!"

"Princess?"

It was all noise, nothing but a hindrance to finding Aronn.

"Where is my brother?" she asked, over and over again, growing more desperate as nobles approached her, inundating her with greetings and questions. She would drown in it all. "*Stop*, please!" Quiet returned, and several Lyneisians took a step back. "Someone tell me where Aronn is."

"Relaina?"

She whipped around. Aronn stood by a doorway at the back of the hall, accompanied by Saheer and Misenia.

"Aronn!" It was a prayer and a sob all at once. She bolted for him and grabbed his shoulders with tears in her eyes. "Are you all right? Are you healed?"

He threw his arms around her with a giddy laugh. "Yes! I mean, well, sort of."

"I saw you were shot and I didn't know if you'd...I've been half-mad with worry, thinking you might be—"

"What do you mean you *saw* I was shot? How did you know that?"

Relaina leaned back, keenly aware of the eyes and ears upon them. "I'll explain later."

The commotion began anew as Jeremiah entered the hall. It took him a few minutes to greet Saheer, Misenia, and the others, and though Relaina desperately wanted a bath and a restful night's sleep, there would be no resting until they met with the nobles and high-ranking members of the Lynx Guard.

But Aronn was alive and mostly healed, and the crushing weight of that particular fear lifted from Relaina's chest.

Nehma and Rhea greeted the Lyneisian healers warmly before following Relaina and Aronn into another room. They all gathered around a long table. Relaina gladly accepted a chair one of the Lynx Guard pulled out for her.

Relaina's sense of relief was short-lived. Across from her, Jeremiah had gone pale, his eyes staring a hole through the maps and papers strewn across its surface. The nobles around him had hardly taken a breath since his arrival. As much as Relaina's body and mind clamored for rest and quiet, he needed her help.

"Enough," she said, and the nobles and Evarians all looked to her. Her back straightened despite her exhaustion. "We all have a great deal to share, it seems."

Jeremiah's eyes focused again as he looked at Relaina. They'd agreed on the journey here that now was not the time to reveal the truth of her parentage, but they would have to explain Relaina's magic, at least vaguely.

After recounting what happened with the fire in the Bay of Trade, Relaina rolled up her sleeve to show them one of her shadowfire scars. The Lyneisian healers in the room recoiled. Lady Justinia Elke spat on the floor.

"Fuck the Terranians," she said.

Relaina's blood ran cold.

"*We* are Terranian by blood," Nehma spoke before she could, her voice sharp and her light pulsing once along her crossed forearms. "Many of the healers from the Caspian Forest are Terranian, and we've protected Lyneisians for years."

Jeremiah nodded and said, "The people who attacked Evaria willingly are either imprisoned or dead now."

"How do we know King Gabriel is really dead?" another noble asked, his teeth bared.

"Because I drove a dagger through his heart and watched the light leave his eyes," Relaina said. The silent stares weighed on her; she'd never spoken so bluntly to the nobles in the room.

Misenia recovered first. "Has anyone claimed the Terranian throne, then?"

Relaina's heartbeat pulsed in her ears. "Darren LaGuarde has made a claim."

"The Tyrant King's own son? Then we're right back where we started," Lady Elke said.

"No, he's—"

"Didn't you free him, Princess Relaina?" Lord Fie asked, looking between her and the others. "Original reports stated that he captured you and fled the city, but then we discovered that you'd willingly relinquished your claim to the Lyneisian throne."

"Here we arrive at the true root of all this." A noble that had largely been silent stood from a chair tucked into a corner, his small frame unimposing but his cold eyes unsettling. This was Lord Tira, if she remembered correctly. "The Prince of Terrana was hiding out in our city weeks before the coup took place. King Stephan never confirmed it was you who helped him, but we all know you disappeared from Parea the same night as the prince. You committed treason, Princess Relaina."

Relaina clenched her fists. "What happened that night is far more complicated than anyone knew. I only did what I thought was right. And I *was* right. Darren LaGuarde is not his father, and he and I have both established trust and a friendly relationship with King Fabian in Evaria. We just want peace in Esran. If you all want to put me on trial for treason after this coup is dismantled, so be it. But first, we must find my parents and root out these usurpers."

Several nobles murmured inaudibly, glancing around the room at one another. Lord Tira sat down again, his pale face disgruntled.

"I can vouch for Darren LaGuarde as well," Jeremiah said. "He fought his father during the Battle of Maremer and has spent weeks questioning prisoners and negotiating policies with Terranian nobles."

Relaina's heart swelled with gratitude for Jeremiah. These nobles trusted him, if no one else.

"Well if he's on our side, then can we request aid from Terrana?" Lord Fie asked.

"The situation in Terrana is too volatile to request aid right now," Relaina said. "I'm not your crown princess anymore, but I am here as an official member of King Fabian's council and as the first diplomatic bridge between Lyneisia and Terrana in decades. I'm here to defend my home."

"A...diplomatic bridge?" Misenia asked.

Relaina mustered her courage. "Darren LaGuarde and I are engaged. I am Terrana's future queen."

She looked to Aronn apologetically, wishing she could have told him in private. His mouth lifted in a lopsided smirk.

"You're engaged to the King of Terrana?" Misenia asked, her voice almost a whisper.

"He has not officially been coronated, but yes."

"Then why *not* send for aid?" Lord Fie said, his mustache bristling. "Surely he would send aid for his intended."

Relaina grimaced. "It's not—"

"You would trust Terranians so easily?" Lady Elke demanded.

"I trust Princess Relaina, and we need help, gods damn it all," Lord Fie said.

"Lady Elke, hold your tongue," Misenia hissed.

"As Relaina said, Darren LaGuarde has not been crowned in any official capacity, and he has not yet set foot on Terranian soil," Jeremiah said, his voice cutting through the muttered conversations around the table. "We cannot rely on anyone but those who are already here."

"Which leads to the news we have yet to share," Misenia said, lifting her chin. "The Pareans we rescued on the night Aronn was shot confirmed they overheard that King Stephan and Queen Christine are in the Castle Alterna dungeons."

Relaina stifled a gasp as it rose in her throat. *They're alive.*

"Have any efforts been made to free them?" Jeremiah asked.

"We decided to wait on your return since Shojen and Varun informed us you would be here in a matter of days, Captain Andovier," Misenia said. "But we have discussed some ideas."

By the time the meeting ended, Relaina was far beyond exhaustion. She wasn't sure she'd even be able to sleep as the healers led her, Nehma, and Rhea toward one of the back halls filled with cots. But she stopped in her tracks at the sight of a couple sitting at a table nearby, sipping tea and speaking quietly. Their faces lit up at her approach.

"Relaina?" Maurice stood, and his wife followed suit.

"Maurice," Relaina said, stumbling into their arms. "Camille."

"It's good to see you again, dear," Camille said.

"How did you get out of Parea?" Relaina asked, pulling up a chair.

"Your brother and several brave young guards and healers rescued us," Maurice said.

Relaina listened to their tale with a growing sense of pride in her brother. He'd never know how much it meant to her that he'd helped get them out of the city.

"I hope it isn't a painful subject," Camille said slowly, her fingers worrying the collar of her shirt. "But how is Darren?"

"Oh!" Relaina extracted a folded piece of parchment from a pocket on her chest. She'd kept it tucked safely there for days, alongside the ring he'd given her. "We weren't sure if I would see you, but he wrote you a letter."

She handed it to them, and they sidled up close to one another to read it, smiling.

"I'm so glad he's safe," Camille said once she'd finished. She looked to Relaina as Maurice folded the letter again. "And I'm glad you've found solace in one another."

Maurice wheezed a quiet laugh. "I told you, Camille."

"Told her what?" Relaina asked.

"That you two were bound to fall in love with one another," Camille said, rolling her eyes as Maurice continued to laugh. Relaina laughed too.

"You ought to get some sleep," Maurice said. "We'll talk more soon."

Relaina nodded, hugging them both again. By the time she reached the cot next to Rhea's, the clamor in her mind had quieted, and she fell face-first into the waiting blankets.

JEREMIAH STRETCHED some of the ache from his back as he sat on the side of his bed and finished tying the laces on his boots. In the only other bed in the room, Aronn remained fast asleep, buried beneath heavy blankets. Despite the late hour they'd all retired, Jeremiah could not sleep much past dawn.

And after his episode several nights prior, he was eager to remain awake whenever possible, anyway. Dream shock, Rhea had called it when he'd described it to her.

The main hall of the sanctuary was quiet in the pre-dawn of the morning, with only a handful of healers and loyalists awake. Guard shifts would be changing soon, and over a dozen of them were already eating breakfast in preparation.

One of the great doors groaned open just after Jeremiah passed it on his way to the small kitchen, a burst of cold air making him shiver.

"Captain Andovier."

He turned to the man that had addressed him.

"A message from Maremer," he said, removing his hood and holding out two letters. "One for you and one for Princess Relaina."

Jeremiah's heart dropped. He took the letters and sent the man off with a healer to get some food. Saheer approached him from the kitchen as he broke the seal of the letter addressed to him and started to read.

"News from Maremer?" Saheer asked. Jeremiah read and reread the letter several times. It was too early to take it all in, but it wasn't bad news, at least.

"King Fabian and Darren are headed to Terrana," he said. "There's some trial of combat Darren must win to gain the loyalty of Gabriel's former assassins."

"Gods in fucking hell," Saheer muttered.

Jeremiah stumbled as a healer bumped into him. The satchel she carried fell to the floor, its contents spilling in every direction. They locked eyes at the same moment, and Jeremiah's blood turned to ice.

"You—!"

Before he could reach for his sword, light blinded him and blasted him and Saheer backward. Air rushed out of his lungs as he hit the stone wall a dozen paces behind him. Pain shot through his back and head. Shouts rang out, accompanied by more blasts of light. Beside him, Saheer was slumped on the floor, unconscious.

Jeremiah tried to reorient himself as Relaina and the other two healers dashed into the main hall.

"It's her," he choked out, shielding his eyes as more light flashed. Relaina, Nehma, and Rhea bolted toward the few healers who were already after the woman. Under their attacks, her healer's scarf had fallen to reveal her snow-white hair. The healer who'd been manning the kitchen rushed to help Jeremiah, but he waved her off, insisting she help Saheer.

Jeremiah had seen the healers fight the tenebrae and Terranian soldiers in battle, but their ferocity in fighting one of their own was less like a spar and more like a dance. Spears of light shot around the room only to be harnessed by another healer and flung at the white-haired woman. When he finally got to his feet, though, everyone had frozen.

The white-haired woman had grabbed Hektor Elke, holding a glowing hand to his neck. His flesh split apart, blood splattering over the woman's face and hair. He screamed, and she threw him to the ground before releasing another explosive burst of light that shattered the nearby stained-glass window. By the time Jeremiah could see again, she had disappeared, and the healers had converged on the bleeding nobleman. Nehma, Rhea, and several others bolted for the doors, shouting for guards to follow the white-haired woman.

At least six healers had gathered around Hektor, including Relaina. She stood as Jeremiah approached, her hands covered in blood and her arms trembling.

"Are you hurt?" Jeremiah asked her. She shook her head, her face stony. Hektor's scarlet blood had pooled around him, and his eyes had gone dim. One by one, the healers' lights receded in defeat.

"What did she do to him?" Relaina whispered.

"Something vile." One of the healer elders, Ericka, appeared, her blue eyes cold. Jeremiah stared at the gaping wound in Hektor's neck as Ericka explained what the white-haired woman had done. It was some kind of corrupt healing, manipulating the flesh and blood to pull apart instead of mend. "It's a forbidden practice that only a few healers have learned."

As the healers prepared to move Hektor's body, Nehma and Rhea returned along with several guards.

"We lost her," Nehma said, breathing heavily.

"What the fuck was she doing here?" Relaina turned away from the dead nobleman, and Jeremiah stepped around the healers to examine the broken glass.

"Perhaps she heard of your imminent arrival," Jeremiah said. His heart had still not slowed its pace. "Kalmali's orders were to observe you before you discovered him. She wants to know more about you for some reason."

"She'll get to know me *very* well if she returns."

"Let's hope she doesn't," Nehma said. "We can't risk you getting hurt again."

A cry rang out, and Lady Elke rushed forward as the healers carried her brother's body toward a back room. Her curses and screams echoed through the sanctuary, casting a shadow of grief over them all. Jeremiah clenched his fists at his side.

"Ericka, gather all of the healers and ensure you recognize them. We'll send out a party to track that woman. Everyone else," he addressed the room at large, "it's time to put an end to these traitors."

CHAPTER 31

THE HEIR OF TERRANA

Fabian felt at home by the water, but boats were not his preferred lodging. They'd been on this vessel for three days now after booking passage in a small Evarian town on the Granica River. The sun glittered on the water on either side of them, warming Fabian's face as he observed what was happening abovedeck.

Darren was sparring with one of the Terranian soldiers that had been freed, his movements fluid and precise. The Terranian nobles, with the exception of a seasick Lady Tryali, stood on the starboard side, their eyes all glued to their declared king. Darren's skill was impressive, but he appeared almost bored with the fight. They'd been at it for an hour, and he looked barely fatigued.

The Terranian avoided Darren's fist just in time, dancing backward.

"You're holding back, Your Grace," Ihara Eyern called. Fabian had spoken to her the least yet trusted her most of all the Terranian nobles thus far. She'd spoken her mind at every chance and passed the test of Darren's magic.

Darren lowered his arms and relaxed his stance. "I don't want to hurt any of you."

Ihara unlaced her cloak and handed it to her wife, gesturing to two other Terranian soldiers nearby. "Then we'll even the odds."

Darren wove through the attacks of all three Terranians, as elusive as the vaporous darkness around him. Ihara and the others' eyes went black as they called upon their tenebrae magic. Fabian had forgotten Thea's presence beside him until she swore softly.

"I've never seen him fight like that," she said. "He and Relaina are ferocious when they spar, but three against one?"

"I am confident he'll be victorious in Ryos," Fabian said. One of the tenebrae hit the deck, and the other hissed as Darren's foot connected with her ribs. Seconds later, Ihara was flat on her back.

"Thea?" Darren called.

"Coming!"

The young healer bounded over to the tenebrae clutching her ribs. The shadow-wielders had been wary of Thea's help at first, but her light only healed them.

The mistrust between light and shadow ran deep, it seemed, but neither harmed the other unless the wielder intended it. Why, then, did the light and dark within Relaina harm her so brutally when they clashed?

Darren offered the tenebrae woman a hand after Thea healed her bruised ribs. She smiled, dipping her head before joining the other Terranians. Fabian's lips twitched into a small smile.

"Do you feel prepared?" Fabian asked as Darren and Thea came to stand beside him.

"As prepared as I can be," Darren said, flexing one of his hands. A small wisp of darkness appeared and then dissipated.

"I'll just need to keep focus while I fight them. Keep control of the magic."

"Your Majesty!" The captain of the ship approached Fabian, bowing. "We're arriving just outside of Ellyr."

Thank the gods. The next two nights would be spent in inns as they finished their journey to Ryos and crossed into Terrana. Highly preferable to the stiff mattress in the captain's quarters he'd slept on. He'd forgone many comforts to which he was accustomed, eating whatever was readily available and wearing only the plainest clothes. Still, Fabian was grateful for the speed of traveling down the river.

The second bridge connecting Lyneisia and Evaria was surrounded by docks and wooden machinery on either side. Fabian had only visited the East Bridge once before, and it had been far livelier in his youth, with workers singing or shouting orders as they transferred goods from one side of the bridge to the other. The arches in the stone below were only tall enough for dinghies and skiffs to pass beneath.

The bridge itself was neutral territory, but they headed for the Evarian side to the north. There were very few merchants and sailors around, and many of the machines used to transfer goods were rotting with age. Terrana hadn't traded with Evaria since Gabriel had taken the crown, so there was almost no reason for merchants and traders to cross the bridge. With a heavy sigh, Fabian added the repair of the East Bridge's docks to his never-ending list of tasks to delegate. It would be far easier once the upheaval in Lyneisia was settled, and once Darren had a foothold in Terrana.

This was the very reason Fabian had agreed to join Darren and the Terranians on this journey—there was much to be done in Maremer, in Evaria, but it would all move with greater speed and success if Evaria had the support of stable neighbors. It had been Gabriel's dream to unite Esran under one oppressive, empirical ruler. But it was Fabian's dream for

Esran to be a mosaic, each piece valuable and vibrant on its own within the larger design.

Although, Fabian couldn't deny he'd wanted to accompany Darren anyway. He was grateful the continent's needs aligned with his desire to support the young king.

Before they disembarked, Fabian and Darren changed into Shadow gear. The former assassin was far better armed than Fabian, but he was also more useful with his weaponry than Fabian could hope to be. It had never been Fabian's duty or preference to become a great fighter.

"Do you think our arrival will cause any issues here?" Darren asked as they headed up the ramp from the docks. Fabian met his distinct eyes.

"It's doubtful," Fabian said. The small town was nearly abandoned. Several buildings were crumbling after the Terranian host had pillaged it on their march to Maremer. Most locals were now housed in Maremer itself or closer by in Rivendya, under the charge of Lord Swanson.

As unsavory as the man was, he was closest to them of any Evarian lords, and had agreed to meet them here with horses for the last part of their journey. Fabian hoped he'd have just sent a delegate to do so, but his hopes were dashed when the lord appeared at the end of the dusty street before them.

"Greetings, Your Majesty," Lord Swanson said, bowing deeply. Several servants held the reins of horses behind him, and a man Fabian didn't recognize stood to his left. Swanson's face pinched as he regarded Darren. "Prince Darren."

"That's *King* Darren," Ihara snapped.

"It's all right, Ihara," Darren said. "He first knew me as a farmer's apprentice, and I'm sure it's very challenging for him to keep up."

Fabian fought a smile. Swanson's thin lips tightened as he bowed again.

"The horses are well rested and fed," Swanson said,

addressing Fabian again. "They should easily be able to get you to Ellyr and then Ryos."

"Thank you," Fabian said, inclining his head. "Are your food stores still sufficient enough to feed the additional residents of Rivendya?"

"They are."

"Excellent. We'll take our leave, then, and I wish you safe travels back home."

"And safe travels to you, Your Majesty." Lord Swanson bowed again, then stalked off with the man beside him, talking to him quietly. The servants helped distribute the horses to their entourage of Terranian nobles, Evarians, and Thea, and they set off across the bridge toward Lyneisia.

DARREN KEPT his guard up as they rode through the streets of Ellyr, a city hardly a fifth of the size of Maremer. Fog drifted through alleys and along the cobblestones as dusk fell, partially obscuring their path to the inn they sought.

Thea led the way, the only one in their group familiar with Ellyr. Stucco buildings passed as they made their way through the foggy evening, and lanterns cast hazy, yellow orbs every few feet. Darren shivered despite the mild air. It was far too quiet for his liking, but no one would choose to be out in this fog if they didn't have to be.

"Here," Thea called over her shoulder, and out of the mist a two-story stucco building appeared. Fog drifted away from the sign above its door just long enough for Darren to read it: *The Lichened Oak.*

While Darren was glad to avoid staying with a noble like Lord Swanson, the inn made him uneasy. Though if he were honest, being around any group of strangers made him uneasy. He'd been able to blend in with the locals wherever he went when he was on the run, but with his blacked-out eye, there was no mistaking him now. It was unusual enough to draw unwanted attention even if they hadn't heard that Darren LaGuarde had one dark eye.

All fourteen of them dismounted in the inn's stables, guided by the stablemaster to the left side of the building. Fabian nodded to Darren as one of the Terranian soldiers helped Lady Tryali from her horse. She'd spent the past three days by the ship's railing, unable to keep anything down. Thea had tried to soothe her nausea as often as she could, but she was the only healer that had accompanied them and needed to preserve her strength. Lady Tryali gratefully accepted the soldier's help as they shuffled out of the stable and headed for the inn's entrance.

The inn itself was furnished with wooden tables, a roaring fireplace, and chairs upholstered in light, earthy green. A painting hung over the fireplace mantel depicting a large, weathered oak tree covered in lichen. Several patrons ate their food while engaging in quiet conversation, while others played strategy games and wagered drinks and coin. Darren kept his hood low as curious eyes followed their group.

Thea approached the bar and quickly dealt with the innkeep, a curvy woman with cool brown skin and thick, black hair. Her red-painted lips turned up in a bright smile as she accepted Thea's payment.

After settling into his surprisingly luxurious room on the second floor, Darren sank into a much-needed bath. Some of the tension he'd harbored since leaving the ship eased. He rested his head on the smooth lip of the bronze bath, staring at the ceiling as he exhaled and released some of his dark power. He closed his eyes and focused, searching for Relaina's dim presence. It wasn't until she'd left Maremer that he'd realized how strange it felt for her to be so far away—his magic's awareness of her proximity had become almost second nature.

This far from her, he only caught those short whispers of her presence, the dim flare of an emotion, but no coherent thoughts.

Still, when that infinitesimal piece of her flickered at the edge of his senses, he thought to her, *I miss you. I love you.* Perhaps she could still feel some part of him too.

Hunger and the cooling bathwater spurred Darren to finish up and make his way downstairs. Fabian and Thea sat at a table with Lady Eyern and Ihara, and Darren joined them, muttering thanks to the barman that placed food in front of him. They ate in relative silence.

"...I'm thinking the Conclaves will be the new royal family!"

Darren stiffened, forcing himself not to turn toward the woman who had spoken at the table behind him. He met Fabian's eyes, and the king shook his head almost imperceptibly.

"Would you *bite your tongue*? Ashima smite you."

"It's been two months! Surely the king and queen are dead by now. They just don't want it to get out."

Thea's fist clenched on the table to Darren's right. Slow footsteps sounded behind them as the patrons around the game table went quiet.

"Get the fuck out of my inn."

Darren couldn't help it—he turned. The innkeep was standing right beside their table in front of the fireplace, holding a sword casually over her shoulders. The loud woman's face had drained of all color, her fair skin sallow. Her four fellows were staring between her and the innkeep.

"A-apologies, madam, I was only—"

"I said," the innkeep said, leaning down. The woman recoiled. "Get the fuck out of my inn. I don't serve traitors."

The woman scrambled to gather her few belongings as a large man approached to escort her out. The innkeep turned to address the room, her sword glinting in the firelight.

"If anyone else here thinks anyone besides a Gienty should be on the Lyneisian throne, you can get the fuck out too."

A cheer rang out around the room. Darren and the others raised their cups.

"It seems we're in good company," Fabian said softly.

"That is the kind of loyalty a ruler should inspire," Ihara said. "Devotion from love and respect instead of fear and intimidation."

Darren knew she meant it to be encouraging, but he wasn't sure how many Terranians would love him. Working as his father's most lethal assassin hadn't given him much time to endear himself to the people.

"Your Majesty," Lady Eyern muttered, looking at Darren.

"No need for titles, Lady Eyern," Darren said. "Especially while we're here."

She smiled. "Very well. Then you may call me Lucia." Darren nodded, waiting for her to continue. She exchanged a glance with Ihara. "Can we speak upstairs with the other nobles?"

Darren wanted nothing more than to fall face-first into the bed in his private room, but he agreed, his chest tightening at the anxiety on Lucia Eyern's face. He bid Fabian and Thea goodnight and followed Lucia and Ihara upstairs to their room, where the Delimonts and Lady Tryali were already waiting. Lady Tryali sat in a wooden chair by a window, still a bit unwell, while the Delimonts had crammed together on a small couch that matched the upholstery from downstairs. The Eyerns sat on their bed while Darren stood before them all, hoping this would be quick.

"We wish to discuss a rather unsavory matter," Lucia Eyern said, folding her hands together on her lap. "We are confident in your ability to achieve victory against the Terranian Elite challengers, but we have not discussed what happens if that is not the case."

Darren raised an eyebrow. "You mean in terms of succession, what would happen if I die?"

Lucia nodded.

"Unless Princess Relaina is with child," Lady Tryali said, and Darren's face flushed, "we have no clear heir after you, and you have not declared one."

Darren swallowed against the dryness in his throat. "I suppose it could go to my mother's parents?"

"Perhaps," Lord Delimont said. "But they are aging, and the Gerratt name has been associated with your little shit of an uncle for too long to garner any real backing from others."

Darren bit back the urge to tell them it wouldn't be his problem if he died. But before him sat five nobles that had sought him out to support his claim. And now that he'd made that claim, they'd each been easier to speak to. *I suppose that's what happens when you give people what they want.*

"Is there a precedent for this?" he asked.

"Not since a LaGuarde has sat on the Terranian throne," Lucia Eyern said, shifting. "There has always been a relative when a direct royal family member died before producing an heir. Always one of the keepers of Calixtos's power."

Darren's head spun. He and Relaina hadn't even discussed wedding plans, let alone heirs. Did she even want children? They would figure out another solution before having a child just for the sake of producing an heir. That very pressure had caused enough strife for Esrani royals.

"Perhaps the way heirs are named should be reexamined," Darren said, mostly to himself.

"I don't disagree," Lady Tryali said. "Handing the crown to the firstborn is how we ended up with the Tyrant King."

"And yet you all say I have the strongest claim," Darren said.

"Because the law says so," Mariana Delimont said, her

voice soft but sure. "But also because you are so unlike Gabriel. Anyone who saw you at court could see that."

Darren held his tongue, clenching his fists. If everyone had seen him and known his suffering, had known he wasn't like his father, how had they simply allowed him to endure it? Darren's magic pulsed beneath his skin.

"A regency rule will be granted to Relaina Andovier," he said. Before the nobles could protest, he spoke over them. "She will work with you and King Fabian to select a new heir." Relaina would help any way she could if he left this request. Slowly, each of the nobles nodded.

Darren would do everything he could to win and avoid this issue altogether. Just the thought of Relaina having to work with the nobles in this room while grieving his death made his chest ache.

"Is that all?" he asked. Lucia Eyern nodded, and he started to leave.

"Darren?" Lucia said. He looked over his shoulder. All the nobles were standing. They laced their hands together the same way they had the day he'd made his claim and bowed.

"Long may you reign."

CHAPTER 32

THE RESCUE

Aronn could only stand back and watch as Relaina armed herself with ruthless efficiency, tucking knives into her armored clothing's various hidden compartments. Rather than the sword he'd come to expect, she sheathed two long, curved daggers at her back. She nodded to him, and he followed her into the meeting room.

Jeremiah spoke quietly with the others around the table, pointing to several places on the map before them. He was dressed similarly to Relaina but armed with a sword on his belt, and to his left were Nehma and Rhea, garbed in their healer armor. Aronn's throat went dry; he was not looking forward to staying behind for the first part of this mission while his family and friends put themselves in danger. But they were doing it to save his parents, and the healers were some of the fiercest warriors he knew.

"Relaina," Jeremiah said. "Aronn."

He beckoned them aside, leaving the healers and the rest of the team to resume conversation by the table.

"Relaina, are you certain about being at the gate?" Jeremiah asked.

Relaina nodded. "I have to do something to help, Jeremiah. And several healers will be there. I'll be fine."

He took a deep breath, but the worry didn't disappear from his eyes. "All right. Just stay safe. Both of you."

Jeremiah headed back to the table, and Aronn lowered his voice. "He seems uneasy."

"Aren't we all?" Relaina muttered. Aronn still didn't fully understand the limitations of whatever magic she wielded, but from what he'd gathered, the scars she'd acquired on that ship created some kind of block with her healing magic.

Even if she wasn't an accomplished healer, he was glad Relaina would be with him tonight. Aronn knew the plan inside and out like the rest of them—they'd at least granted him that courtesy if they weren't allowing him to go with them into the city.

"We will await the breach at midnight," Jeremiah said. "Those on the wall and by the gate do *not* step over the perimeter under any circumstances." The healers, Evarians, and Lyneisians around them agreed, and Jeremiah dismissed everyone. A dozen of them were headed to complete the mission that would free Aronn's parents and allow them to finally make plans to take back Castle Alterna and Parea. Six more, including Aronn and Relaina, would help dismantle the city gate to allow them to escape.

Relaina and Jeremiah embraced as the others filed out, and his uncle whispered something in her ear Aronn couldn't hear. Aronn stood from his chair and headed for the door.

"Aronn."

He turned just as he emerged into the main hall. Nehma's mouth twisted for a moment before she stepped forward and wrapped her arms around him.

"We'll get them back," she said quietly. "Don't get shot again."

Aronn's lungs deflated as she let go, releasing a hollow laugh. "I'll do my best."

"Hmm." Nehma's eyes narrowed, but before she could respond, a call went out for them to depart. Relaina hugged her, too, and clenched her fists as she and Aronn watched them all leave. He exhaled, relieved that being around Nehma hadn't been horribly awkward. He was still deeply fond of her, but amid the struggles in Parea and the need to give all his energy to the reversal of the coup, his romantic affection for her had, blessedly, waned.

Once quiet fell over the sanctuary, Relaina wordlessly turned and stalked into the meeting room they'd just vacated. Aronn found her standing by the window, staring at the reflection of candles in the panes.

"Do you think that white-haired woman is still lurking nearby?" she asked, and Aronn suppressed a shudder.

"Perhaps not nearby," he said. "No one has seen any sign of her since yesterday."

Relaina faced him. She lifted her chin toward the door, and he quickly closed it behind him, joining her as she sat on the couch.

"The tenebrae who possessed Jeremiah serves her," she said quietly, and Aronn felt the blood leave his face. "We don't know who they are or why they're here, but they knew my birthmother, Talea."

"What...what happened when Jeremiah arrived in Maremer?" Aronn asked. He'd been hesitant to bring it up with Jeremiah.

Relaina swallowed hard. "The tenebrae realized I could sense the shadow possessing Jeremiah and tried to kill me."

Aronn swore softly. "What happened to the tenebrae?"

"Darren destroyed it, and then the man, Kalmali, was captured. He's still in the dungeons at Seacastle."

"Clearly that woman isn't terribly concerned about him if

she's still here," Aronn said. "What was her purpose in hiding among us? Do you think she could've been spying for Archan and the others?"

Relaina frowned. "It's possible. But I get the sense they have their own agenda. They...they call me *Pretender*."

"Pretender of what?"

"I'm not sure."

With a sigh, Aronn rested his head on the back of the couch, staring at the ceiling. "I don't understand these magic wielders and their schemes. I just want my family to be safe."

Relaina leaned back beside him and patted his shoulder. "Me too."

"How is Annalise?"

"Upset by our separation, but she's in good company in Maremer," Relaina said. She paused for a long moment. "Though I'm sure Darren and Fabian's departure wasn't easy for her."

"Jeremiah said they're traveling to Terrana."

"Yes."

Aronn was curious to know more, but Relaina didn't seem inclined to elaborate. They fell silent, Relaina closing her eyes and breathing deeply while Aronn continued staring at the ceiling. Images of the Parean underground and the castle dungeons flashed into his mind, and fear and shame spread through him like wildfire.

"I'm not ready to be king," he said, his voice barely above a whisper.

Relaina sat up again, and the concern on her face was more than he could bear.

"I'm so sorry, Relaina," he said. She reached for his clammy hands, squeezing them. "None of this would've happened if I'd hadn't been friends with Zarias and the others."

"No," Relaina said firmly. "Aronn, look at me." He did.

"These nobles had this planned for years. Your friendship with them was calculated on their part, and even if you hadn't been friends, they still would've found a way to do all of this."

The knot in his stomach that had been his constant companion for months finally loosened. "You truly think that?"

"I do. We all make decisions we regret. But that doesn't mean you're responsible for their treason."

Aronn hugged her, and she returned his embrace.

"I've been eaten alive by shame," he said as he leaned back. "Before all of this all I ever did was let other people do difficult things on my behalf. Even when I was awful to you, even when I didn't listen to you about my friends, you still defended me and protected me."

Relaina held out her hand, which he took. "That's my job, little brother. And look what you've done here. You found Camille and Maurice and saved them. You found out where our parents are. And you got shot doing it, for Iros's sake."

"But what if I only did all of that out of guilt?" Aronn asked softly.

"I don't believe you did all of that solely out of guilt for one second," she said, shaking her head. "But even if you had, you still did it. You braved potentially fatal situations for others, and that means something."

Aronn closed his eyes, his mind finally allowing him to believe it—just a little.

"Thank you, Laines."

NEARLY IMMOBILIZING nervousness filled Relaina's body as she waited for midnight to arrive. She, Aronn, Shojen, and a Lyneisian healer were crouched at the tree line by the city gate. The last time Relaina had seen it, she'd been galloping through with an unconscious Darren in tow, fleeing the city she'd always called home.

Gods, she hoped he was safe now. After the white-haired woman's attack, Jeremiah had handed her a letter from him that she'd now read dozens of times, as if perhaps each time there would be something more comforting within its contents. But all she could do was hold on to the knowledge that he was capable of winning the combat trial with the Terranian Elite, and hold on to the final lines he'd written her:

I love you. I'll see you soon.

"You've located the archers?" the Lyneisian healer asked. The healer's breath puffed in the cold night air despite the mask covering her mouth. Half-melted snow crunched beneath her boots as she shifted behind a pine tree. Relaina nodded, her grip tightening on her bow.

A bell tolled in the distance. *Midnight.*

Relaina's nerves quieted, a detached calm overtaking her as she stepped out from behind the tree and took aim. A shocked cry rang out as she took down the first archer, and more panicked voices filled the night as she shot the second, third, fourth. Shojen and the healer sprinted for the gate while Relaina aimed for two guards standing in front of it. Shojen ran through her sightline, and she cursed, lowering her bow.

"No clear shot," she said to Aronn as the Lyneisian healer took down the first guard. The second guard lunged for Shojen, but markings flashed on his hand as he touched the guard's neck, and the man slumped to the ground, unconscious.

It took everything within Relaina to stay put while the two healers scaled the wall and fought off several other traitor guards before they managed to breach the gatehouse. She held her breath after they disappeared. *Please. Please let this work.*

A few heartbeats later, the gate began to lift with a groan.

They'd done it. But it wasn't over until Jeremiah and the others got through.

From where they stood, they had a clear view of the city just inside the gate. The outer village buildings rose around the outermost square, the fountain in the center covered in icicles. Relaina squinted against the cold night air, but there was still no sign of anyone making an escape.

Relaina darted forward, ignoring Aronn's protests. She stopped just before the gate's archway, craning her neck to see further into Parea without crossing into the city. A few flashes of light rebounded off building walls by the square, and seconds later Nehma appeared, yelling something over her shoulder. Lyneisian loyalists and Evarians ran after her, fewer than the number that had left. Jeremiah and Rhea sprinted into view with at least seven guards in pursuit.

Relaina forced herself to stay put. They would make it to the gate—they were faster than the traitors, had enough of a head start.

One of the Lyneisians went down as a knife flew into his back. A cruel, familiar voice echoed through the night, and Zarias appeared on horseback with a horde of other traitors from a side street. Nehma whipped around right as one of the guards reached her, blasting them back with her light. Jeremiah, Rhea, and the other loyalists barreled into the new group of traitors, and shrieks rent the night as blood splattered onto the snow. Zarias cut down another loyalist and wheeled his horse around, preparing to charge at Nehma.

Relaina took aim, anticipating his course, and loosed.

Zarias flew off his horse just as Nehma dove away from the approaching beast. Two other traitors bore down on her. Relaina tossed her bow and arrows back toward the trees and sprinted through the gate.

She reached Nehma first, drawing her blades and taking

down one of the men. Nehma finished off her other attacker and turned to Relaina.

"We have to go, now!"

Relaina looked back at Jeremiah and the others, still engaged in combat with the traitors. Her parents weren't among them. Rhea fought two at once while Jeremiah sent a guard flying into the snow-dusted cobblestones before another was on him. Zarias stumbled to his feet, swearing at the arrow lodged in his shoulder.

"Rel—fuck!" Nehma's curses followed Relaina as she ran toward Zarias.

Zarias screamed as Relaina tackled him to the ground. His body slammed into the cobblestones, and Relaina twisted his arm behind his back, pinning him. He squirmed and shrieked for help as the arrow dug further into his flesh, but his allies were falling around him one by one. Relaina grabbed the knife from his belt that he sought with his free hand and buried it in his outer thigh for good measure. He howled.

"You bitch," he spat. Before he could utter anything else, Relaina hit him over the head with the hilt of her dagger, and he went limp.

Nehma and the loyalist nearby helped her haul Zarias toward the gate as more traitors appeared in the distance, shouting orders and curses at them. They threw Zarias over a horse and sent him and the loyalist off.

"What the *fuck*, Relaina?" Nehma hissed as they hurried to reach their own horses, tethered further back in the woods. Aronn joined them, bewildered and panting, Relaina's discarded bow in his hands.

"Save it until we get back," Relaina said, breathing hard, taking her bow from her brother. Jeremiah and Rhea appeared with the remainder of the loyalists and Evarians.

"Go!" Jeremiah shouted, climbing onto his horse. Relaina loosed the rest of her arrows in quick succession, aiming them over the wall. They were unlikely to hit their pursuers, but perhaps they'd be a deterrent. She vaulted onto Amariah and took off, screams of rage following her into the night.

Relaina's cheeks were numb with cold by the time they arrived. Loyalists came out to greet them, eager to see if their king and queen had been rescued.

The moment Relaina dismounted, Nehma advanced on her.

"What were you thinking?"

"I—"

"We agreed that no one would enter the city, *especially* you, Relaina!" Nehma shouted, her furious expression half-lit by the lanterns at the sanctuary steps.

"You were outnumbered! Did you expect me to just watch?" Relaina snapped, fuming. Amariah huffed and pawed the ground.

"Yes! I expected you to not throw yourself into the middle of a fight where none of us could help if you got seriously injured! You broke from the plan and went after that man without—"

"I *know*!" Relaina yelled, her voice echoing off the sanctuary wall. Several loyalists were staring at them, but she didn't care. "I know. I was stupid and reckless but gods damn it all I couldn't let that little fuck get away again."

She pointed to the healers dragging the still-unconscious Zarias to a nearby storehouse. Nehma's breath puffed in front of her as she sighed and stalked forward, pulling Relaina into an embrace. Relaina returned it, exhaling sharply.

"*Don't* do that again," Nehma said. "But I'm glad we got that prick even if we failed in everything else tonight."

They joined the others inside just as Jeremiah finished relaying what happened to the loyalists in the main hall. Relaina went numb with disappointment as his words fell on her ears.

The king and queen had been moved.

It was a trap.

We lost five.

She'd barely moved from the entrance when everyone dispersed. Jeremiah approached her, and she met his eyes reluctantly. He beckoned her into the meeting room.

"I think Nehma covered my thoughts on this evening."

Relaina shut the door behind her. Jeremiah's stoic disapproval and the flicker of terror that touched his eyes filled her with shame. He dropped into a chair at the table, rubbing his forehead.

"You are more than capable as a fighter," he said. "I pity anyone who finds themselves at the end of your blade or the aim of your bow. But you *must* follow orders here to keep yourself and everyone else safe."

Relaina clenched her jaw. She started to say something several times before deflating and slumping into the chair beside him. "This is so unfair."

"I know."

"I'm sorry."

"I know. I'm glad we captured Zarias so we have another potential source of information, but from now on, promise me you'll follow orders."

Relaina studied him for a moment, then sighed.

"I promise," she said.

CHAPTER 33

THE EXCHANGE

Relaina left her weapons by her cot before she ventured into the early morning. There was still a stark chill in the air of the Lyneisian mountains, but the snows had passed for the season. Spring had always been her favorite in Parea. The pine trees remained resolutely dark green, but the trees that went dormant in winter began to bud and bloom. Flowers appeared on mountainsides and riverbanks and even in the cracks of cobblestones in the city. And the air itself sighed into gentleness, leaving its sting behind until winter came again.

Yet as Relaina marched through the slowly melting snow on the ground toward the small storehouse by the sanctuary, there was no gentleness in her heart.

Two guards bowed and opened the wooden door for her, and she stepped inside, joining Jeremiah, Saheer, and Ericka. The light of the dawn shone through the single dirty window to her left, and at the back of the room in a heap lay Zarias, his wrists and ankles bound by thick rope. Relaina's eyes narrowed.

"Wake him," Jeremiah said. Ericka glanced at Relaina before sighing and approaching Zarias. Her hand lit up with markings as she touched his head, and an instant later he gasped awake, nearly smacking into the stone wall behind him. Relaina and the others waited as he spewed curses and struggled before noticing his bindings. He sat up, his chest heaving with panicked breaths as his gaze shifted from Ericka to Jeremiah, and finally settled on Relaina. He froze.

"You Terranian-fucking *bitch*," he spat. Ericka flicked his nose, a bit of light bursting from her fingers, and he yelped.

"That was rude," she said softly. She stood, rejoining Relaina and the others by the storehouse entrance. Zarias's eyes watered as his nose crinkled.

"You're right," he said, hanging his head, and Relaina raised an eyebrow. "You're right, I forgot myself." He looked up again at Relaina. "You can stop all of this, you know."

"I fully intend to," Relaina said.

"But you can't now, not your way. You don't know where your mother and father are."

Jeremiah's fist clenched around the hilt of his sword. Relaina exchanged a glance with him, and knew the same thought had occurred to them both—keep Zarias talking, however revolting he was.

"I'm listening," she said. Zarias smirked.

"Marry me—"

"Not fucking this again."

"Do you want your parents to live or not?"

Relaina's hand twitched toward the phantom weapons at her waist. This was why she'd left them behind. Not that she needed them.

Zarias took a deep breath and continued. "Marry me, and all of this resolves in an instant. Your parents live, and our forces don't obliterate your little sanctuary here when spring arrives."

Relaina's companions shifted around her, and Zarias raised his eyebrows with a smile.

"Oh, yes, I suppose I let our intentions slip. But now that a Gienty princess has returned...all you have to do is say yes."

For a moment, Relaina imagined how this conversation would go if Darren was here. A smile crept onto her face.

"Are you seeing the truth now?" Zarias asked, his eyes flashing. Relaina approached with steady steps and crouched down in front of him. The healers had mended the stab wound in his thigh as well as the arrow wound, but they'd left the bruises and scrapes on his face. Relaina stared into Zarias's gray eyes.

"You remember what I said about marrying you at the Harvest Festival?" she asked.

"We all say things we regret."

"That wasn't one for me. And I've already said yes to someone else."

Zarias's face soured. "You'd bind yourself to an exiled prince?"

"No," Relaina said, her voice low. "To the King of Terrana."

All color drained from Zarias's cheeks. "He's no king. There's been no coronation, no announcement—"

"He's made an official claim and has the full backing of Terranian nobles and the loyalty of the realm's most lethal assassins." He would soon enough, anyway. Relaina hoped Jeremiah's face betrayed nothing as she continued, weaving fear into Zarias with every word. "So here's what's going to happen: You're going to tell me where my parents are, and once they're freed I'll hand you back over to your cousin and the rest of the usurpers in Parea. You will all surrender gracefully if you hope to live."

Relaina grabbed Zarias's collar, squeezing until he grimaced. "But if any harm comes to my parents or anyone here, I will bring the full wrath of the Terranian Elite and the tenebrae down upon you all. I will burn Castle Alterna to the fucking ground if I have to. And if any of you escape, Darren LaGuarde and I will hunt you to the farthest reaches of the continent."

Zarias's face twisted, his handsome features tarnished by the furious desperation in his eyes.

"Mention marrying you again and I swear to the gods I will kill you right now," Relaina said.

"You won't kill me," he growled. "You need my information."

"We both know my temper can get the best of me, Zarias." Relaina's grip tightened on his collar. "So what will it be?"

Relaina's companions didn't dare to breathe behind her as they waited for Zarias's response.

"The fifth floor of the castle," Zarias said, his eyes blazing. "In one of the guest chambers."

Relaina started to ask him for specifics, but a knock rapped on the door to the storehouse, and Jeremiah strode to answer it. A healer appeared and whispered something to him. He nodded and sent them off.

"Ericka, if you would sedate him again," he said, and Relaina stood back. Zarias fell limp at the healer's glowing touch, a protest dying on his lips.

"There's a messenger here from Archan," Jeremiah explained. Relaina tensed. She, Jeremiah, and Saheer stepped outside, leaving Ericka with Zarias to keep him quiet if he should wake again.

Four loyalist guards stood in a circle by the road ahead, swords drawn and pointed at Archan's messenger. Aronn and Misenia stood several feet back from them, waiting. The messenger had his hands raised by his shoulders.

"What message do you bring?" Jeremiah asked, crossing his arms as he came to a halt between two guards.

"Archan Conclave wishes to propose an exchange of prisoners," the man said. "The King and Queen for his cousin."

Absolute silence met the messenger's proposal. Relaina could only stare at him. The most valuable people in the entire kingdom...for Zarias?

"You can't be serious," Jeremiah said.

"I am," the messenger said. He slowly reached into his cloak to extract a piece of parchment. "I have a letter with Archan's signature on it here."

Jeremiah nodded to one of the guards, and the woman stepped forward to retrieve the letter for him. The messenger stood in silence as Jeremiah unfolded it and read quickly. He turned to Relaina and the others once he'd finished, fixing them all with a hard look. Relaina kept her face impassive.

"We accept," Jeremiah said.

A LANTERN BOBBED in the darkness of the trees beyond the clearing where they waited, and Relaina stood silently as Archan Conclave, Lord Norhen, Lady Tarod, and a slew of traitorous guards emerged from the forest path. A wooden carriage with bars on each of the two small windows trundled behind them. Relaina quieted the fire that ignited in her chest.

Nehma and Rhea stood to her left, shifting, while Jeremiah stood to her right. She forced herself not to look at him as the traitors drew near. Her hands itched to draw her blades. If anything went wrong, they weren't far from the sanctuary. *Stay calm.*

"Greetings, Captain Andovier," Archan said, inclining his head. "Princess Relaina."

One fluid movement and her dagger would be in his chest. But she had to play along. She would engage in this excruciating game for her parents.

"Hello Archan," she said, flashing him a smile. Several guards around him recoiled. "Where the fuck are my parents?"

He shrugged, gesturing toward the carriage. "We won't risk losing them until we know you have my cousin alive."

Vindicated rage simmered in Relaina's bones. Her parents weren't here. She knew they'd do this—Jeremiah had known too, and they'd planned for it. Noble or not, these Lyneisians weren't foolish enough to trade a king and queen for Zarias. No, they were here for some other reason. But none of it mattered as long as they wasted as much time as possible.

With as much composure as she could muster, Relaina looked to Jeremiah. He nodded, and she held up her left hand, signaling the loyalists to bring Zarias out. His hands were bound by shackles behind him as they walked him forward from the tree line, but he was in perfectly good health. A healer held a torch close to his face so the traitors could see him clearly.

Jeremiah stepped forward. "Now we need to see the king and queen."

Archan frowned, his face one of few lit by torchlight. "How do I know you won't have all of us shot as soon as you see them?"

"We'd never do something so dishonorable," Relaina said, her boots squelching in the muddy earth as she sauntered over to Zarias. The two Lynx Guard holding him tightened their grip. "We're offering you peace, Archan."

Relaina reached for one of the daggers at her back slowly, unsheathing it for all to see. She turned, holding it to Zarias's throat, and her mouth twitched at the nervous movements of the nobles several yards away.

"You have thirty seconds to produce my parents, or I resort to violence," she said, staring right at Archan. His dark eyes scanned the trees behind the loyalists, and the hair on the back of Relaina's neck stood on end.

"Archan, enough of this!" Zarias blurted, and Relaina froze. "They know where the king and queen are!"

Muttering broke out among the traitors, but Archan silenced them.

"They will destroy us, Archan," Zarias called, his throat bobbing against Relaina's dagger. She stayed her hand; perhaps his outburst would continue to buy them time. "They have healers and tenebrae. Without Acantha, we cannot stand against them!"

Relaina's thundering heart nearly stopped. *Acantha*. She committed the name to memory.

Archan studied his cousin, then looked at the loyalists. He sighed.

"You've lost faith, Zarias," he said, shaking his head.

Archan raised his right hand. Before Relaina could take another breath, an arrow flew from the trees behind him and lodged itself in Zarias's left eye. Another landed inches from her foot, and she leapt back.

Jeremiah bellowed orders nearby, but Relaina barely registered the scrambling that had broken out until someone grabbed her arm. She only realized it wasn't a loyalist when the cold metal of a blade touched her throat.

"You're coming with me, Princess—"

Relaina rallied her senses and shoved a dagger into the man's gut. His knife grazed her neck as he slumped over, the pain sharp as it slashed her skin. Screams and clanging metal pressed on her ears as she faced the bloodbath that had erupted in the clearing. Two more traitor guards ran at her, and a loyalist archer shot one while Relaina met the other with crossed blades. The woman jumped back, flipping her sword before attacking again. Relaina rolled out of the way, slicing her dagger up the woman's calf as she came up. With a roar, the woman crumpled.

"Get Relaina out of here, *now*!" Jeremiah shouted,

yanking a bloodied sword out of a man's stomach. Two nearby loyalists converged on Relaina, guiding her toward the safety of the trees. Another arrow flew from the direction they were headed, taking out the woman on Relaina's left. She and the other loyalist dove to the cold, muddy ground. They were still several paces from the relative safety of the woods.

Relaina peeled herself from the ground, crouching low and searching the trees for any hidden archers. A gauntlet glinted between two pines, and she threw herself down again, taking the loyalist guard with her.

"Princess—"

"Let's *move,*" she growled, and the woman nodded. They made it to the trees just as warmth began to bloom in Relaina's chest. *Not now, please, not now.* She whipped around to face the clearing again—the healers that had come with them were visible in the darkness by the markings along their arms and the flashes of their light as they fought. Every one of them was engaged in combat, unable to help her.

While Relaina was distracted, her companion took down a traitor archer nearby. Relaina darted behind a tree, slowing her breath, but it was almost impossible to focus with the cacophony of shouts and metal in the clearing. The loyalist guard hid behind a tree beside her.

"Princess, please, we must return to the sanctuary!" the guard said, her green eyes wild with urgency. Relaina nodded, and they took off through the trees. As her fear rose, her grip on the light faltered, and Relaina gritted her teeth.

She sprinted through the dark woods with the guard on her heels, careful to not catch her boot on a loose branch or rock. A pinprick of cold shock and alarm plucked at the edge of her mind, and the darkness along her scars rippled. It was too much—the light, the darkness, the pain in her neck, the fighting echoing from the clearing, and now Darren's emotions, however faint, adding to her own...

Breathe. If she lost all control, the light and darkness would clash faster. More screams and curses rang out from behind them. *Focus.* The warmth had spread, nearly reaching one of her scars. She grabbed hold of it with everything she had and held on, employing all Nehma and the other healers had taught her. Its spread slowed but did not stop. Relaina swore as she stumbled, but regained her footing and kept running.

Jeremiah and the others would be fine. She repeated that in her head over and over, keeping as firm a grip on her inner light as possible. There was no moon to light their way through the needle-strewn forest, but somehow it was only minutes before they burst into the large clearing where the healers' sanctuary stood tall. Relaina bounded up the steps and flew through the doors.

"Ericka!" It didn't matter which healer came for her, but it was the only name she could remember right now. Relaina's light continued to grow, pushing against her hold on it, and she sank to her knees. Controlling it without Darren around to channel the darkness was infinitely harder, like trying to grasp a heavy stone covered in river moss. She clutched at her center, willing the light to halt, her eyes squeezing shut. Footsteps hurried toward her as she curled in on herself and dug her fingers into her chest. A gentle hand touched her shoulder. She couldn't speak, couldn't focus on anything but holding the light at bay—

"Breathe," Ericka said softly, and Relaina forced herself to exhale. Ericka touched Relaina's neck, warm light spreading over her wound. The pain faded after only a few moments, and Relaina's own inner light began to wane.

"What happened?" Aronn appeared, his hair disheveled, dark circles beneath his eyes.

"They killed Zarias," she managed, taking Ericka's hand

and standing. "And tried to take me. The others were still fighting when I left."

When I left. She hated saying it, but she'd promised Jeremiah she'd follow orders.

"How many?" Aronn asked.

"A dozen or so," Relaina said, and the guard that had rushed back with her confirmed with a nod. "And some archers in the trees."

"Gods in hell," Aronn whispered.

Relaina forced herself to keep breathing. Archan and his traitorous snakes didn't stand a chance against fighters like Nehma and Rhea, surely. She had to hope they would be all right.

"They're back!" The call resounded through the hall from a guard outside. Relaina turned to the still-open doors behind her, and all other thoughts vacated her mind. It wasn't Jeremiah and the others who had returned.

Several yards from the base of the stairs was the small team they'd sent into Parea while the rest of them distracted Archan in that clearing. The loyalists helped two figures dismount from horses. Strands of golden hair fluttered past the hood of one of them, catching the light from the lanterns.

Relaina's knees began to shake, her chest hollow as she stumbled through the door.

"Mother," she said, but it barely came out. She tried again. "*Mother!*"

Halfway to the stairs, Christine looked up, her eyes widening as Relaina closed the distance between them. The queen picked up her tattered skirts and hurried forward, ignoring a loyalist guard that tried to help her.

Warmth enveloped Relaina wholly as her mother pulled her into an embrace, and the two of them sank to the ground. Relaina sobbed into Christine's shoulder. She didn't care that

Lyneisians and Evarians had emerged from the sanctuary and were watching them—her mother was holding her. Her parents were alive, and they were here.

It was over.

CHAPTER 34

A PIECE OF POWER

With a quick glance at the sliver of moon high above, Darren stepped into the streets of Ryos, disappearing into the shadow of the inn. His boots made no sound on the cobblestones, which had been well-maintained throughout the city. The Arteas had certainly put money and effort into the city's infrastructure despite Gabriel's years of neglect. Darren was glad for the citizens of the small, beautiful river city, but if the Arteas were to contest his claim to the throne, what reason would the Terranians have for supporting Darren? Winning the combat trials against the Terranian Elite tomorrow would be the first step.

He steeled himself as he darted through the streets, recalling the route they'd taken earlier to the fighting arena. It was slightly larger than the ring in the Parean underground, and located south of the Artea estate. It was also, unlike the Parean ring, fully legal and regulated by city guards employed by the Arteas. According to Ihara, much of the Arteas' growth in wealth stemmed from profits made off matches in the arena, which were well-attended.

After avoiding patrolling guards and scaling the side of the cylindrical building, Darren climbed through one of the intermittent openings in the stone, landing on the last row of the arena benches. His eyes adjusted quickly to the darkness, and he sat on the stone bench, catching his breath. The arena would be well-lit by sunlight and lanterns in the morning, and he'd be there to fight the Terranian Elite in whatever combat trials they wanted.

He would win. He had to.

And he'd bring Relaina back here someday. His heart ached, and he called upon the darkness, letting it spread in front and around him along the rows, descending toward the ring in the center.

He'd felt Relaina more clearly last night than he did now, just for a moment. Rage had danced at the edge of his senses. Gods, he hoped she was all right. He hadn't prayed to any of the gods in a while, but now he sent a prayer to Calixtos in particular.

If you chose me…lend me strength tomorrow. And lend Relaina strength, too.

It should be impossible that Relaina wielded Calixtos's power, that anyone besides a LaGuarde could, but that had to be the reason they were so connected. Whatever had happened when she'd touched him during the battle had transferred a part of it to her.

As if his thoughts summoned her, her presence grew stronger, and Darren held his breath. The terror she felt crept into his veins, mixing with anger and desperation. The last time he'd felt her like this was when the tenebrae had attacked her at Seacastle.

But he wasn't there to help her this time, to hold the darkness for her so her light could manifest freely. He reined in his own fear as best he could—he would only add to the turbulence in her mind. An eternity passed as he closed his eyes and forced himself to detach from the worry that gripped his insides, and Relaina's terror changed to desperation, then focus, and finally calm. Relief made his own magic shudder and drift more slowly around him. If her magics had collided, surely he would have felt her emotions disappear altogether as they had in the Seacastle gardens. He had to trust that she would be all right.

Another entity entered his magic's awareness, far stronger and closer than Relaina's dim presence, and he crouched, scanning the dark room. A figure appeared five rows down, emerging from a door in the stands.

"Forgive me, Your Highness." The man's voice was low but clear. His steps echoed throughout the room as he approached, his posture relaxed, but Darren remained alert. The man bowed as Darren pulled his darkness back to himself. "I didn't mean to startle you."

"Who are you?" Darren asked.

The man sighed. "I suppose it is rather dark in here. And it has been quite a few years." The man removed his hood, revealing pale skin and short hair, and ascended until he was on the same row as Darren, his face still obscured in shadows. He held out a hand, which Darren took after a moment. The tenebrae's shadows were gentle, cool. The feeling of darkness that melded with Darren's, confirmed allegiance.

"I know you could not feel it when you were younger, since you weren't connected to the darkness yet," the man said. "But I have always been loyal to you, Darren."

Darren's brow furrowed as he pieced it together. "Captain Vrana?"

"It's good to see you, Princeling."

Darren yanked his hand back, his darkness flaring in warning. Captain Vrana held out his hands and backed away.

"I know you must have questions," Vrana said. "My leadership during your training—"

"You almost killed me," Darren choked out. "You and two others, that day my father..."

"You know how your father was," Vrana said, dropping his hands to his sides. "My priority was my own survival. But you survived him, too, and now look at you. The level of control you have with that much power—"

"Credit my father with any part of my survival or strength, and I will end you right here." Darren clenched his fists to keep them from shaking.

"On the contrary, it is entirely your own strength that led you here. It's why I convinced the Elite to send you the summons."

Darren's eyes narrowed. "Am I supposed to be grateful for that?"

"Do you want to rule or not?" Vrana asked, stepping closer again. Darren didn't respond—there wasn't an easy answer to that question. "If I hadn't stepped in and insisted we honor the Terranian Elite's code, many of them likely would have pledged themselves to the Arteas."

"Perhaps that's how it should have been," Darren muttered. "How can I trust them if they've only agreed to this because you asked them to?"

"Because you have a chance to win them over." Vrana pointed to the ring below. "They won't hold back tomorrow, and if you beat them...you remember how it was. They respect strength more than anything else. You'll have them until your dying breath."

The weight of that knowledge settled on Darren fully as he stared at the ring. Dozens of Esran's most lethal assassins loyal to him. How many lives he could save. How much widespread violence could be avoided. He could dismantle the corruption his father had put in place right from the rotten belly of it all.

"How many will I have to fight?" he asked.

"Two single-combat fights against our two strongest," Vrana said. "And one against three of us."

"Will I have to kill them all?"

"If you can keep them down without killing them, I will be surprised."

Darren breathed deeply, then nodded. "Then I will see you in the morning, Captain Vrana."

Vrana bowed again. "I can sense how much darkness you wield. Your father never knew such power. Tomorrow, show them what you can do with it."

Turning on his heel, Captain Vrana left the same way he'd come, and Darren was alone in the darkness once more. He *would* show them. For the fifteen-year-old boy that had only wanted his father's approval and the respect of his people. For future Terranian soldiers and tenebrae.

Calixtos, may it be so.

CHAPTER 35

THE TERRANIAN ELITE

An endless pool of stars stretched in every direction from where Darren stood. *No.* He couldn't be back here, he hadn't even fought the Terranian Elite yet—

Calm yourself, Prince.

Darren whipped around, the deep voice of the god of death resonating in his bones. Calixtos stood a few feet away, almost blending in with their surroundings, but the hazy glow emanating from each tiny prick of light in his indigo-onyx skin made his silhouette discernible. His long, braided hair matched the deep black color of his elegant robes.

I'm not just the god of death, you know.

Darren stared at Calixtos.

I am frequently exasperated by how often mortals misunderstand the gods.

The god offered him a bemused smile, teeth white as starlight, and Darren tried to speak.

No need to speak as you normally would. Though I expect you're used to this type of communication with your calirhán.

Darren blinked at the god. *My what?*

Calixtos frowned as he glided closer. *Your calirhán. Your chosen bonded. You gave her some of my power, no?*

I…I was supposed to do that?

Calixtos's starry brow furrowed as he folded his hands behind his back. *It is a small mercy bestowed upon the keepers of my power, to lighten their own burden by sharing some of the shadows with the person they choose. It does not matter who, so long as the connection is deep and steadfast.*

Darren's mind flooded with questions, and Calixtos grimaced.

Your family line has failed you, I see. He sighed. *I should have known—*

Can I take the power back? If he could take the shadows from Relaina, perhaps it would allow her light to manifest freely. Calixtos studied him as his mind raced.

No. But why would you wish to revoke it?

The memory of Relaina's agonized screams made him wince. *She is a light-wielder, and the shadows inflict immeasurable pain.*

Calixtos's eyes flashed with an age-old grief, and shadows pulsed around him briefly. As they drifted over Darren's skin, he felt the god's regret and sadness as if it were his own.

I am sorry for her pain.

Darren's shoulders sagged, his hope deflated. *Why have you brought me here? We've never spoken this long.*

And we don't have much longer. But I did not summon you —you summoned me.

I did?

Calixtos nodded. *Something within you called to me.*

Looking around at the sea of night, Darren tried to recall why he might have done so. It was on the edge of his memory, just out of reach.

Just know, Calixtos said, his voice and form beginning to fade, *whatever you face, my power is with you.*

The night disappeared with Calixtos's presence, and Darren inhaled deeply. His eyes fluttered open, revealing the carved ceiling of the inn in Ryos.

He flew out of bed and approached the window. Dawn had broken. He'd wanted to be up earlier, to get a few more drills in before the fight, but instead he'd—

He looked down at his hands. Small wisps of shadows coiled around his fingers. *My power is with you.*

He'd spoken with Calixtos, called him to his dreams without knowing how. He ached for more answers about his power, about Relaina's, but right now, he had a more pressing task at hand.

DARREN HAD EXPECTED spectators at the arena, but he hadn't been prepared for the sheer number of Terranians that lined the stands rising from the pit in every direction. He tuned them out as he faced Fabian in the short tunnel leading into the pit. The Evarian king wore Shadow armor, while Darren was dressed in only the lighter layers of the gear. Armored clothing wasn't allowed for this trial, but the black form-fitted shirt and pants allowed him the most freedom of movement of any attire he'd brought. He'd worn the boots too.

Thara and Thea stood by the narrow stairwell that led to the stands, watching their surroundings carefully.

"How are you feeling?" Fabian asked.

"Calm," Darren said, glancing to the opposite end of the ring, where a second tunnel held the assassins he would fight.

Fabian nodded. "I have every faith in you. You said you will face five of them?"

"Two single fights, and a third against three."

"And death decides the winner?"

Darren grimaced. "Being unable to rise decides the winner. But Terranian Elite are trained to rise unless they're dead."

"Then may Calixtos have mercy on them all."

Darren looked back to Fabian. The king pinned him with the same look he'd given Darren many times, one that never failed to shore up his confidence. Before Fabian could bid him farewell, Darren held out a tentative hand. Fabian smiled and drew Darren into a fierce hug.

"Every faith in you," Fabian repeated. A piece of Darren's battered heart mended as the King of Evaria embraced him the way he'd always imagined a father should.

As Fabian released him and left for the stands with Thea, Darren held on to the knowledge that Fabian believed in him. Relaina believed in him too.

Gods, he wished he could talk to her. He smiled as he checked his weapons for the third time since arriving, imagining what she might say if she were here.

"Are you ready, Your Majesty?" Ihara asked. Darren took a deep breath.

"I am."

Ihara bowed. "My strength is yours, King Darren."

She remained in the tunnel beside him until a short man approached. His black hair was long and pulled back with a ribbon at the base of his neck. He extended his hand to Darren.

"I am Lord Gio Artea, Your Highness," the man said with a small bow as Darren took his hand. He didn't hold Lord Artea's grasp for long; he had no desire to interact with a man seeking to seize the Terranian throne for himself. Darren had never felt particularly protective over or entitled to his birthright, but now that his father was dead, now that he'd made the claim and envisioned a better future for Terrana, things were different.

The crown and all that it represented was his, and he would fight for it. But he couldn't afford to make an enemy of Lord Artea. Trying his best to do what he'd seen Relaina do many times now, he inclined his head.

"This place is impressive," Darren said. "I'd like to learn more about how you utilize its funds to support the city."

Lord Artea raised his eyebrows, the corners of his mouth lifting slightly. "Then you would do well to win this trial today, Prince Darren. Your first opponent is ready when you are."

Darren rolled his shoulders and flexed his hands.

"I'm ready."

Lord Artea led him into the ring, and the loud hum of the crowd became a roar. He gazed around at the hundreds of figures, awestruck as he realized that this was the first time many of them had ever seen him.

Would they love him or hate him?

It doesn't matter. Not right now. From the other tunnel, Captain Vrana emerged, a knowing smirk on his face. He stopped a foot away from Darren, and another Terranian Elite joined them as Lord Artea took his leave. She was tall and muscular, and when she spoke, Darren forced himself not to wince at the thunderous volume of her voice.

"We've gathered in witness to this sacred trial!" The crowd quieted as she addressed the arena. Over Vrana's shoulder, dozens of Terranian Elite sat in the lower stands above the tunnel entrance. To the right, in the first few rows, Darren could just make out Fabian, Thea, and the rest of the nobles that had accompanied him on this journey. "Today Darren LaGuarde challenges our five strongest. Should he be victorious, the Terranian Elite will pledge our loyalty and our lives to him."

The crowd cheered again, and Darren didn't allow himself to dwell on the hope that they might want him to succeed.

The only thing that mattered for the next hour or so was winning.

The tall woman silenced the crowd again. "On my signal, you may begin."

Darren's heart throbbed in his ears with each step she took toward the tunnel.

"I'll try not to kill you," Darren told Vrana. The captain huffed.

"That will be deeply unpleasant for me."

The assassin woman stepped into the tunnel, and bars fell into place at each tunnel opening. Darren glanced over his shoulder, caught sight of Ihara as she nodded to him, and faced Vrana once more.

A horn sounded, and Darren moved.

Vrana matched Darren's pace, the swipe of his blades swift, his dodges precise. Darren fell into the rhythm of the fight with ease. Training with Relaina at Seacastle had kept his skills honed better than anything in recent years.

Vrana avoided Darren's left dagger a moment too late—it sliced through his clothing, leaving a deep cut in his upper arm. Darren didn't relent. He took advantage of Vrana's destabilized stance and delivered a kick to his knee, sending him to the dusty ground. With bared teeth, Vrana rolled out of the way before Darren buried his blade in his shoulder. The captain's eyes filled with darkness. Darren's power thrummed in his veins, but he kept it tightly leashed. Not yet. Not until he needed it.

Vrana swiped at him again, the blade barely missing Darren's chest. He threw a small knife from the sleeve of his shirt. Vrana dodged, ducking down. Stinging pain in his calf made Darren dance backward—Vrana had thrown his own small knife, and it had found its mark.

"Use your power, Princeling," Vrana hissed. "Save your energy for the fucks who truly want to kill you today."

He had a point. *No hesitation. No mercy.*

Darren's darkness leapt at his command, appearing all the way up his forearms. The presence of dozens of tenebrae entered his mind, incoherent whispers of emotion. Vrana lunged at him, and Darren sidestepped, the darkness reaching to coil around the captain's wrist. Darren squeezed his fist shut, and Vrana yelped, the dagger falling from his hand.

Calling upon his own dark power, Vrana twisted out of Darren's shadowy grasp, but a moment too late—Darren landed a kick to the back of his legs, and he went down face-first. Before Vrana could rise, Darren drove his daggers into the captain's upper arms, pinning him to the ground. Vrana howled.

Even with the added strength of his shadow, Vrana could not maneuver to remove the daggers. A horn sounded, and the crowd roared again.

"The others won't be so easy," Vrana growled as Darren removed the daggers, pulling the shadows back to himself. The captain swore again as another Terranian Elite helped him up.

Darren returned to his tunnel as the next assassin prepared to fight. Thea appeared next to Ihara, her eyes darting to the cut on his leg.

"I'm fine," he said, sitting on an old bench and turning his leg in the dim light. It was a shallow, clean cut. He'd simply have to ignore it. Thea sat next to him and patted him on the shoulder.

"I still don't think it's fair you can't be healed between fights," Ihara said. Darren sighed, gladly accepting the canteen of water she offered him.

"One down," Thea said, her smile hopeful.

Four left.

~

THE SECOND ASSASSIN was smaller than Vrana, his entire body vibrating with energy and bloodlust. Just looking into the man's eyes before the horn sounded, Darren knew. This tenebrae fully intended to kill him.

Darren narrowly avoided a knife to the chest the moment the fight began, nearly losing his balance as he ducked left. He sliced at the man's exposed right torso, only for him to dodge and grab Darren's forearm, knocking the blade from his hand.

Reset. Darren twisted his arm from the assassin's grasp and backed away a few paces, but the man didn't allow him even a moment. His voidlike eyes and snarling mouth sought murder.

He was faster than anyone Darren had fought before, even Relaina. A thrown knife slashed through the fabric at Darren's arm, leaving a shallow cut. A heartbeat later, the man was on him, a dagger swiping at Darren's neck. He avoided that blow only for pain to erupt in his left hand where the man grabbed his wrist and shoved a knife through it, forcing him to drop his other blade.

Use your power, Princeling.

The tenebrae was poised to drive a dagger through his heart. Darren threw up his hands at the last moment despite his lack of blades.

The assassin's dagger missed its mark, only digging into Darren's shoulder, redirected by two blades made of solidified shadows. Darren didn't have time to wonder at how he'd managed to form them—he kicked the man squarely in the chest, sending him flying backwards. The dagger fell from his shoulder, having only breached an inch into his flesh. It hurt like hell, alongside the wound in his blood-soaked hand, but it wouldn't kill him.

More darkness gathered around him, bolstering him enough to ignore his injuries as he fought the assassin. He and Darren were a whirlwind of movement in the wake of

Darren's power. At last, Darren got close enough to tackle him to the ground, driving his magic-honed blade into the assassin's heart.

As the man's life slipped away, his shadow began to emerge, and Darren prepared himself to destroy the tenebrae. But it shrieked and collapsed into the blade shoved into the man's chest. When Darren recalled his power, both the daggers and the tenebrae vanished.

Gasps from the crowd rang dully in his ears as he stood and backed away, watching blood pool beneath the assassin's body. Pain twinged in his side; the hilt of a knife stuck out from his ribs. How had he not noticed he'd been stabbed? He removed it as the crowd cheered. *Fuck*, it hurt.

"Are you all right, Your Majesty?" Ihara asked the moment Darren walked, wincing, into the tunnel. He slumped onto the bench and watched the Terranian Elite retrieve their second assassin's body.

"I'm getting bandages, gods damn it," Thea said. "They can't expect you to fight with freely bleeding stab wounds."

Darren nodded, and Thea hurried off. Ihara's eyes sparkled with worry.

"I'll be okay, Ihara," he said. "One more fight and then Thea can heal me."

Thea returned moments later, bandages and a salve in tow. "I asked, and non-magical healing practices are allowed," she said. Darren nodded, hissing as pain shot through his right side.

Thea wrapped the wound on Darren's hand first, then his side and shoulder. He watched with a frown as arena workers raked the top layer of dirt away that had been saturated with blood.

"I've heard stories of that one," Ihara said, her voice hard. "None will mourn his death."

"Who was he?" Darren asked, wincing as Thea tied off the

last bandage. The salve had slowed the bleeding, thank the gods. "I didn't recognize him."

"He only joined the ranks two years ago, but it's said he was vicious. The way he killed... All I'll say is his victims suffered greatly."

Darren frowned again. Even if he won today, there would be others like that assassin among the Terranian Elite, oath of loyalty or not.

"After this, I'll ensure no man like that is part of the Terranian Elite."

Ihara's gaze softened as Thea stepped away, looking out at the ring. "Then let's make sure you survive this, yes?"

Darren took her hand gratefully and stood. Thea looked back at Darren and nodded toward the ring. It was time.

"Thank you both," Darren said. His wounds throbbed, but once he called upon the shadows it would dull. He just had to get through this next fight. He scanned the crowd and found Fabian and the Terranian nobles looking his way. He gave them a confident nod before stepping out of the tunnel once more.

The three assassins that entered the ring were clad in black like the others, faces hidden and hands itching to draw their weapons. Darren ran through strategies in his mind as the Terranian Elite facilitator spoke to the crowd. He vaguely recognized the tall man with scars all over his hands even if he didn't remember his name, but not the two smaller assassins that appeared to be twins. One had cropped, dark hair, and the other had theirs in a braid that reminded him of Relaina. His chest ached.

Don't get distracted.

Darren settled into his stance as the facilitator left the ring and the gates thudded into place over the tunnels. The horn wailed.

Darkness poured from Darren's hands as he ducked and

dodged a flurry of blows. These three were neither mildly reluctant like Vrana nor wild like the second assassin—they were cold and calculated. They were lethal.

Just when he thought he'd never find an opening, the tall man lunged at him. Darren pivoted and grabbed his upper arm, using the man's momentum to flip him into the dirt. Before the man could gasp for the air that had been knocked from his lungs, Darren buried a dagger in his heart. He went still, and the feeling of death snapped free in Darren's chest. *Not tenebrae.*

Darren leapt to his feet just in time to avoid getting his throat slit by the short-haired twin. The one with the braid barreled into him a second later. They hit the ground hard, Darren taking the brunt of it on his side, but he managed to prevent his head from hitting the dirt. He grabbed the assassin's wrist before her dagger could pierce his neck. She was strong, and the wounds in his shoulder and hand protested painfully as he attempted to maneuver her arm. He pulled more of his power to the surface and threw her off, wresting the dagger from her grip and tossing it to the side.

Darren got to his feet again, his body tensed to block another attack, but the twins had retreated, standing close to one another. Something ignited on the edge of his senses, cold and menacing. When they separated, circling him, they were holding knives with blades swathed in black fire.

Flashing memories of hooded figures and searing pain made Darren nearly crumple where he stood. His power pulsed and dimmed. Much of the crowd continued to cheer, but there were pockets of disapproving shouts.

The short-haired twin sprang. Darren avoided a fatal blow, but fiery pain burst from where it grazed his shoulder. It had burned through his shirt in an instant. The second twin's attack was more effective, leaving a nasty gash on his left side that had him on his hands and knees. The shadowfire burned through logical thought, disorienting him.

You are still too soft.

Father, please—

More pain, more burning, and this time it didn't stop. His entire body was on fire, the source a knife shoved into his upper back.

You will do as I command from now on—

"NO!"

Darkness erupted from within him, soothing the icy heat of the shadowfire instantly. Reaching over his shoulder, Darren gripped the hilt of the shadowfire blade and yanked it out of his flesh. The twins had been thrown back against the stone walls of the enclosure. The one with the braid got shakily to her feet while the other remained listless on the ground. Wind and shadows rushed around them in the ring, a storm of darkness, and Darren prepared for the remaining assassin to attack. Blades made of pure darkness appeared in his hands again.

But the twins didn't advance. The short-haired one stirred, sitting up, and looked at Darren from where he stood several yards away. Her eyes, no longer black, filled with awe. She scrambled into a bow, her forehead touching the dirt of the ring. The other one threw her blade down and did the same.

The horn sounded. It was over.

Darren gritted his teeth with the effort of reining his power back in, pulling it bit by bit until finally it conceded and settled within him. The pain of his wounds returned with a vengeance.

The crowd's cheers built in volume until his ears rang. Relief bloomed in his chest as he glanced back at the tunnel and found Ihara and Thea cheering with the rest of them. As soon as the gates lifted, Thea rushed out to greet him, grabbing his face and grinning. A smile split his face. He'd done it. The Terranian Elite were his to command.

Darren surveyed the crowd in a daze, his disbelief dulling everything around him. He stumbled backwards, slow to realize the blow to his shoulder wasn't another body bumping into him. Pain tugged at him, and he reached for its source, the soft place on his left shoulder just below his collarbone. His fingers brushed something hard, and its movement brought him violently back to his senses.

A crossbow bolt was lodged deep in his muscle. The fletching on the end was as white as the shaft.

The crowd's roaring transformed in a wave of horror to screams, and the assassins around him began dropping, blood painting the dirt of the ring. Darren summoned his power, but it remained resolutely dormant beneath his skin. No coolness, no sense of the tenebrae around him, even as they used their magic to fight the hooded assailants that had inexplicably appeared all around the stands. Beside him, Thea's markings illuminated her arms and hands.

"What the fuck is happening?" she yelled above the crushing noise. A dozen hooded figures dropped from the stands into the pit and advanced on Darren and Thea. Trying his best to ignore the pain from his wounds and the warm blood leaking from them, Darren grabbed his daggers and fought off one, two, before another grabbed the shaft of the bolt in his shoulder and shoved. He screamed, black spots clouding his vision as he sank to his knees. A strong hand forced him to the ground, the side of his face pressed to the dirt as they pinned his arm behind his back. The bolt dug deeper into his flesh, and he strained to stay conscious.

A few feet away, Thea fought off two hooded attackers and straddled a third with a knife in hand before a black bolt hit her between her shoulders. Her light vanished. She looked to Darren in horror a split second before one of the figures grabbed her by the hair and opened her throat with a knife.

"*Thea*!" The cry tore through his lips as Thea slumped to the ground, her eyes wide, her lifeblood spilling beneath her. Rage and fear and grief wrestled inside him as Darren fought to free himself. His power stayed silent, unreachable.

A pair of boots appeared in front of him, one foot reeling back.

"N—!" His shout cut off as oblivion took him.

CHAPTER 36

A VISION OF DEATH

F abian's head throbbed as he woke, his eyes adjusting to the light in the arena. The screams had stopped, the mad scrambling over, leaving behind dozens of bodies and several Terranians stumbling around, calling for loved ones. As carefully as he could, he sat up, placing a hand to his head. Half-dried blood coated his fingertips from a cut along his forehead. Around him, bodies were slumped at odd angles. He blinked and forced himself to look at their faces. Nausea roiled through him as he recognized Lady Tryali, the Delimonts, and each Evarian who had come with him.

Darren. He looked into the ring, but the collection of bodies was indistinguishable. He crouched low and headed for the tunnel.

It had been chaos. Darren's dark power had receded, victory had been achieved, and out of the crowd a group of hooded figures began shooting into the ring and murdering surrounding bystanders. Fabian didn't recall how he'd gotten injured.

Quiet voices echoed up the short stairwell to the tunnel, and Fabian held his breath as he crept down. Opposite the bench, Lady Eyern was crouched with her wife's head in her lap.

"Lady Eyern," Fabian called softly. She whipped around, brandishing a knife, but her arm fell at Fabian's approach. He hurried forward, looking down at Ihara. Her breathing was labored, her eyes half-open, and blood seeped from a wound in her abdomen. A white crossbow bolt was stained scarlet where it had lodged into her flesh.

"She says they did something to her power," Lucia choked out. "She cannot access the darkness, and she was cut off from Darren before...before they—"

Fear ripped through Fabian's mind. He'd seen Darren get shot by that bolt. "Did they kill him?"

Lucia shook her head. "They took him. I didn't see where, and neither did she."

Hope and grief mingled within Fabian. Darren was alive but captive to some violent, mysterious group.

"Fuck," he whispered. It had all gone so, so wrong.

Carefully, Fabian stepped into the ring, examining the bodies strewn around the dirt. At the sight of Thea's slashed throat and widened eyes, he fought the urge to vomit before dropping to his knees before her. Tears leaked down his cheeks as he closed her eyes. A bolt like the one in Ihara jutted out from between her shoulder blades. With a ragged sob, he broke off the fletching and pushed it through, removing it with as much care as he could. The point was wickedly sharp and, beneath the blood, black as obsidian.

He shifted Thea onto her back and placed her hands on her chest. He bowed his head, muttering a quick prayer, and rejoined Lucia and Ihara. Lucia whispered soft assurances to Ihara despite the tenebrae's delirium. Fabian's eyes fell back to Ihara's wound, to the white bolt below her ribcage. Fabian's breath halted.

"Does her power offer any measure of healing or support to her body?" he asked.

"Not like that of a healer, but it can help." Lucia sniffled, brushing away a rogue tear.

"We should remove the bolt."

She blinked up at him. "What? She'll bleed out."

"It may be what's preventing her magic from working."

Lucia looked down at Ihara, who took another shaky breath.

Swallowing against the bile rising in his throat, Fabian helped Lucia lift Ihara upright before quickly breaking off the fletching the same way he had with Thea. Lucia handed Ihara her knife to bite down on as Fabian shoved the bolt through. Ihara's scream was muffled around the blade's handle. Moments later, her eyes filled with darkness, and her body relaxed somewhat, the bleeding slowing. Lucia took the knife and cut through the thick fabric of her skirt. With Fabian's help, she wrapped Ihara's wound as best she could.

"We need to leave," Fabian said, helping Lucia get Ihara to her feet. "Find someone in the city who can help us."

"Where are the others?"

Fabian stared ahead as they started up the steps. "Dead."

RELAINA STOOD outside the door to the meeting room in the healers' sanctuary, fidgeting with the fabric of her crimson shirt sleeve. She sighed and knocked. Putting off this conversation would do nothing but waste precious time.

Jeremiah answered promptly, and she stepped inside. Christine and Stephan were seated at the large table beside one another, with Aronn on the king's right side. Her brother spoke softly with Stephan, his expression more relaxed than

Relaina had seen since her arrival. Jeremiah took a seat across from them, and Relaina joined him.

Her parents were alive, and despite their clear exhaustion, were relatively healthy. Stephan's graying hair lacked luster, but his auburn beard was still full, and his gray eyes looked brighter this morning. Relaina had spent hours the night before speaking with her mother about Seacastle, Annalise, and anything else they'd missed the past two months as she detangled Christine's hair with the aid of soaps and oils provided by the healers. Now it was neatly braided, the golden strands catching the light from the window. Both the king and queen carried more color in their fair cheeks than they had just yesterday.

Jeremiah and the others had escaped the scrimmage with two additional noble hostages, guaranteeing their success in gaining the upper hand and quashing the coup. Archan was losing, even if he still believed Acantha was on his side.

Acantha. Her name made Relaina shiver. If she'd been involved in the coup and tried to have Kalmali spy on Relaina, where else had she sown unrest in Esran?

The distant pull of cool, dark magic within her halted her musing instantly. Darren was focused and detached. Relaina's hand gripped the table. Today was the new moon, which meant he was fighting the Terranian Elite at that very moment.

Relaina inhaled slowly, calming her racing heart. Despite their distance, the connection had grown stronger again over the past few days. If he sensed her emotions the same way she sensed his, she didn't want to be a distraction for him. The darkness waned, her awareness of him dimming again.

Across the table, Christine nudged Stephan with her elbow, and he cleared his throat.

"Before we say anything, I owe you an apology, Relaina,"

he said. She met her father's eyes and forced herself not to look away. "Well, a thousand apologies."

Relaina clenched her fists. It was a bad time for this; she wanted to tell him everything, to make it clear how much he'd hurt her. But she also wanted to throw her arms around him and cry the way she had with her mother, and she had no idea how to handle both of those impulses at the same time.

"You can save them for another time, Father," Relaina said. "There is much else to discuss."

Stephan deflated but nodded. He and her mother listened intently as Relaina began her tale, explaining their arrival in Maremer last autumn, the tenebrae attack in the inn, and Fabian finding them.

"I was no longer an heir, but I still wanted to do what I could to serve the realm," Relaina said. "Fabian's network of Shadows seemed like the best way to utilize my skills. And then Jeremiah arrived, and we began preparing for battle."

A lump formed in Relaina's throat as she recounted the night of the Winter Festival and her capture. She hadn't told anyone but Darren exactly what had happened to her on that ship, and she gave only vague details to her parents. With a shaky breath, she rolled up her sleeve and gestured to her neck.

"They contain some dark power," she said. "We don't fully understand it yet."

Silent tears rolled down Christine's cheeks. "Saeva have mercy," she whispered.

Relaina took a deep breath, willing tears away, and continued. When she told them how she and Darren had defeated Gabriel, how she'd killed him with the healers' help, they stared at her, unblinking.

"So who now rules Terrana?" Stephan asked quietly.

Relaina straightened in her chair before meeting his eyes. "Darren has made a claim, and I'm to rule at his side as queen."

Their eyes grew wider. They looked at each other, then to Jeremiah, then back to Relaina. She shifted the collar of her shirt slightly so they could see the edge of her betrothal tattoo.

"We haven't married yet, but we will after we arrive at the Terranian capital."

Christine's eyes welled with tears again. Stephan didn't say a word.

"Are you happy?" Christine asked, reaching her hand across the table. Relaina took it and squeezed.

"I am, with him," she assured her mother. "I cannot imagine anyone better than Darren to lead Terrana into an era of peace."

If her father had an opinion on the matter, he did not voice it.

"And speaking of engagements," Jeremiah said, clearing his throat, "we'll need to discuss a replacement for me as captain of the Lynx Guard."

Christine's entire face lit up. "You and Fabian?"

The smile that tugged at Jeremiah's mouth made the entire room brighter. Some of the heaviness in Relaina's soul lifted as he nodded and Christine let out a laugh that was very unlike her. She reached for his hands, too, her smile bright. The room filled with laughter, and for a moment, Relaina could see it all before her—a future with her family, and Esran itself, at peace.

After making plans to meet with the loyalists later that day, Relaina and Aronn headed for the door, leaving Jeremiah and her parents to continue discussion. They lingered in the doorway as Jeremiah laughed at something Christine said. More darkness tugged at Relaina, and she kept as calm as possible, even as fear crept into her mind. It wasn't long before it faded again, and she exhaled.

"Queen of Terrana," Aronn said, leaning against the door-frame. "You'll wear the crown well."

Relaina smirked as she watched the healers and loyalists shuffle around, a few grabbing a late breakfast.

A strange emptiness spread within her in an instant, leaving her chest feeling uncomfortably light. She looked down at the scar on her forearm, brushing her fingers over it. She hadn't realized how constant Darren's presence was, even when it was dim, until now.

She couldn't feel him at all.

"Something is wrong," she said, dread settling in her chest.

"What do you mean?"

An earsplitting, agonized scream tore through the air, echoing off every surface of the cavernous main hall. Everyone jumped or froze, several people covering their ears. Relaina sprinted for its source and came to an abrupt halt by one of the large windows.

Rhea was kneeling on the floor, her arms wrapped around her middle as her body convulsed with sobs. Relaina knelt before her, barely pushing her rising panic down as she drew Rhea into her arms.

"*Thea*," she sobbed, grasping Relaina's shoulder as if it was the only thing preventing her from tumbling into an abyss. Relaina's eyes were wide with fear as she looked at the shocked faces of healers around them. Jeremiah appeared, his face hardening as he approached and crouched by Relaina and Rhea. Rhea trembled as Relaina cradled her friend's head against her chest and turned to Jeremiah.

"Something is *wrong*," she whispered.

Chapter 37

Heart and Mind

A chill wind blew through the stables as Relaina packed the last of her supplies and prepared to saddle Amariah. The black mare shifted in her stall, as restless as her person. Relaina rested her forehead on Amariah's and brushed her hand down the horse's neck.

"I know, beauty," she murmured. "I'm worried too."

"Relaina."

She turned. Jeremiah stood at the stable entrance, his expression blank. He'd hardly shown a glimmer of emotion since last night. Thea's death weighed heavily on them all, and both Jeremiah and Relaina knew what it could mean for the others who'd been with her.

Through broken sobs and hiccups, Rhea had told them what she'd Seen. An arena in chaos, hooded figures attacking, pain as something hit her back, a knife slicing into her neck, and then—nothing.

"I have to go," Relaina told Jeremiah. He merely nodded.

"I know. I won't stop you."

"Are the others ready?"

"They are."

Relaina finished saddling Amariah in silence and followed Jeremiah back outside toward the sanctuary entrance. Her family waited at the bottom of the steps, wrapped in cloaks to ward off the early morning chill. She approached Christine and hugged her.

"I'm sorry to leave so soon," Relaina said quietly, and her mother squeezed her.

"Please be safe, my love," she said.

Relaina stepped back and looked to Stephan, who appeared more unsure than she'd ever seen him. She wrapped her arms around him, too, and he held her tightly.

"We'll talk soon," she said. When she pulled away, he nodded. Aronn stood to his right, his lips pressed together in a hard line. Relaina embraced him next. "I'm proud of you, little brother."

Aronn huffed a breath. "Don't get yourself killed, Laines."

Before she could respond, the doors at the top of the healers' sanctuary steps opened, and Rhea and Nehma stepped outside. They walked down the stairs and stopped a few feet from Relaina and her family, Nehma looking her way expectantly. Rhea stared ahead, her eyes deadened, a pack on her back and weapons fastened to her waist. Nehma was outfitted similarly.

With one last goodbye to her parents and Aronn, Relaina led the way to the stables. She paused at the entrance and turned to Jeremiah.

"We'll find them," she said, but still, not a flicker of emotion crossed his face. She understood—if she let her own fear take hold, she might fall apart. Even so, Jeremiah's embrace was fierce as Relaina stepped into his arms.

"Find them," he said. "But don't lose yourself along the way."

Relaina gritted her teeth as she let him go. *No falling apart.*

She returned to Amariah and mounted up. The crisp morning air bit at her cheeks as she rode out of the stables with Nehma and Rhea just behind her. She donned her hood and mask, and after a final glance at her family, she took off down the northern road.

~

"Captain Andovier?"

Jeremiah blinked himself back to the present, his mind and heart miles away. While he was beside himself with worry for Relaina, he couldn't help but feel relieved that someone was going to find Darren and the Evarians that had gone with him—Fabian included.

The Lyneisian nobles and Evarians around the table stared at him with varying degrees of worry and impatience.

"Apologies," he said.

"Lady Elke asked if you think the guards should be executed alongside the traitor nobles," Saheer said.

"No," he said. "I believe that would only fan the flames of what caused the coup in the first place. We don't know how deep the discord runs, what those four noble families have been saying to them for years."

"I agree," Christine said. "I say we imprison them for now and find out more about this Acantha and her followers."

The meeting dragged on for another hour as they discussed the stabilization of Parea following the coup. It was fortunate that the winter had halted any expansion the traitors may have sought; the Gientys would need to conduct thorough searches of each traitor noble's property and records, but at least the majority of their power had been in Parea alone.

As the nobles filed out, Jeremiah remained in his chair, staring out the window, his mind drifting to the northern road now that his focus wasn't required.

"Jeremiah." Christine sat in the chair beside him and placed her hand on his. "If you want to follow them, you should."

He met his sister's eyes. "My duty is here."

"For Iros's sake," Christine said, shaking her head. "You've denied your heart for twenty years in order to keep Relaina safe, and now both she and Fabian need your help. *Go.* Stephan and I will be perfectly fine here."

Jeremiah looked from her to Stephan. The Lyneisian king sighed.

"She's right. Go. We'll send word of our developments here."

Jeremiah pulled Christine close. "I love you, Christine."

"I love you, too, Jeremiah. I expect a wedding invitation very soon."

He laughed, energy beginning to buzz in his veins. He bowed to Stephan quickly and headed for his rooms.

Less than an hour later, he was mounted on a horse in the midday sunshine, waiting for Saheer. The other Evarians had agreed to remain behind.

"Ready?" Saheer asked, her snow-white stallion flicking his tail as they approached.

"Ready."

They galloped off, and Jeremiah glanced back at Christine and Stephan, grateful that this time, he wasn't abandoning them to danger.

CHAPTER 38

THE ORDER OF THE ETERNAL FLAME

Darren inhaled sharply as he awoke, leaning into the plush upholstery beneath him. He stretched, and his eyes shot open as pain snarled through his shoulder. He sat up, wincing at the metal digging into his wrists. His hands were shackled behind his back, and his ankles, too, his boots removed.

Disoriented, he took in his surroundings. The room was decorated in earthy oranges and yellows, with curtains hanging by a small window behind a decorative table. A large brown rug centered the short, rectangular table before him, and two plush chairs stood on the other side of it. A polished wood door stood at the far corner to his left. He had to be in some noble's dwelling.

His breath came in gasps before he could quell the rising panic.

Thea was dead. He had no idea what had happened to Fabian and the others. He was someone's prisoner.

He was alone.

My power is with you, Calixtos had said.

But it wasn't. Darren couldn't feel the darkness rippling

beneath his skin. The comforting presence of its coolness was absent. His sense of Relaina, however hazy it had been, had vanished entirely.

He looked down at his shoulder. The white bolt protruded through a large tear in an old brown shirt, right where one of the hydrangea leaves was inked onto his skin. It appeared someone had cleaned around it, even healed part of the wound. The stab wounds and other cuts he'd sustained during the trials were gone. His face heated at the realization that someone had changed his shirt for him.

The wooden door creaked open, and two figures stepped inside. A short woman with light blonde hair remained by the door. The other, a willowy woman with ivory skin and dark hair pulled into a bun, approached Darren. He pushed himself as far back on the couch as he could. She sat across from him in one of the chairs, folding her hands in her lap.

"Hello, Darren," she said, her voice low and soothing. "I'm Hedda. It is my honor to meet and serve the Heir of Calixtos."

Darren stared at her, silent. *The Heir of Calixtos.* She must be part of the same group Kalmali belonged to.

"You must have questions," Hedda said, her brown eyes placid as she smiled. "I am happy to answer them."

He didn't know much about these people, but he did know they'd targeted Relaina and had killed dozens in the arena, including Thea. Fabian could be dead, too, for all he knew. He needed to tread carefully.

"Can you remove this bolt?" he asked. Hedda's eyes flashed.

"I'm afraid you will need to wait a bit longer. We cannot remove it unless we're assured of your sympathy to our cause. The suppression of your magic is necessary for now."

Suppression of his magic. Thea had been shot by one, too, her magic extinguishing the moment it pierced her back.

"You killed my friend," Darren said. "And dozens of others. Whatever your cause is, I want no part of it."

Hedda frowned. "An unfortunate, but necessary incident. Surely you're familiar with the concept of collateral deaths. You've taken many lives, too, from what I hear."

"That's not the same."

"Isn't it?" Hedda stood, clasping her arms behind her back as she sauntered to the window. "You killed for your father, in the name of a higher cause, but you took no pleasure in it. The Order of the Eternal Flame does the same."

The Order of the Eternal Flame. The name rang a distant memory, but he couldn't place it. He shook his head. "Then you are as deceived and manipulated as I was."

"Acantha does not deceive us," Hedda said, returning to the center of the room, looking down at Darren with her lip curled. "She offers us freedom and peace. She is bringing forth the will of the gods."

I am frequently exasperated by how often mortals misunderstand the gods. "The slaughter of innocents isn't the will of the gods."

Hedda's frown deepened. "I told Acantha you would be difficult. The Pretender has her claws in you."

Darren swallowed the threats of violence that danced on his tongue. This was a game, like the politics with the nobles in Evaria and Terrana. He just needed to play it long enough to figure out an escape.

"What is it you want with her? With me?"

Hedda took a seat again, the skin of her brow smoothing out, her eyes brightening.

"You are the Heir of Calixtos," she said. "The keeper of his power. The LaGuardes have long been the wardens of darkness, but you are the first to wield it all. You are destined to join the Heir of Elenia. In accordance with the will of the gods, you are destined to lead Esran."

Darren tried his best not to grimace. "And you think Acantha is the Heir of Elenia?"

"She *is* the Heir of Elenia. It was foretold, and she is the most powerful light-wielder in all of Esran. She has abilities few even seek to attempt." Anger flashed in Hedda's eyes as she met Darren's gaze. "Talea sought to take power for herself, claiming that her daughter was the true heir."

Darren could not hide the skepticism on his face. "We don't know about any of this. Relaina and I want no part of it."

Hedda stood, and a tendril of light shot out from her hand, wrapping around Darren's neck and yanking him forward. He gritted his teeth against the pain in his shoulder and now his neck.

"You will not speak her name here," she snarled. She released him, and Darren nearly fell to the floor, gasping for air. Hedda smoothed out her tunic and smiled curtly. "It will displease Acantha. It's bad enough you've marred your body with that heretical ink."

Darren coughed before responding. "If you think I'm going to abandon the life I've begun to build to join a delusional zealot, you're deeply mistaken."

Hedda shoved the table out of the way and backhanded him so hard he hit the floor. He growled through the pain in his shoulder as he rolled onto his back and thrust both feet at Hedda's right knee. She went down with a howl, and before the other woman could reach them he tucked his legs to his chest, maneuvering his shackled hands in front of him. He grabbed the end of the bolt in his shoulder, hoping to the gods it wasn't barbed, and wrenched it from his flesh.

His power exploded, blowing out the window nearby and throwing them all into darkness. It was nearly as untamed as the moment he'd jumped in front of Relaina during the battle in Maremer. The realm of Calixtos called to him, but a light blazing with panic and fury brought him back from the edge of the abyss. *Relaina.* He got clumsily to his shackled feet.

"Stop him!" Hedda screamed.

Darren dove for the floor beneath the window, scraping his upper arm as he hit the stone. He grabbed for the windowsill and hauled himself up.

It was too high to jump, but he knew where he was now. Four stories below was a sprawling garden, and for miles ahead he could see all of Ryos and the fields and river beyond. The fighting arena was just south of here. *The Artea estate.*

He yelped as pain lanced through his lower back, and the darkness around him vanished, along with Relaina. Two others he hadn't seen before grabbed his upper arms, turning him around and forcing him to his knees. The small blonde woman helped Hedda to her feet. Her light had begun to heal her leg, but she still placed all her weight on the opposite foot.

"You will answer for that," she hissed. Darren recalled the shock and determined rage that had flooded him when his power manifested, and it hadn't been his own. He huffed, halfway between a laugh and a grunt of pain.

"And you will answer to Relaina Andovier," he said.

RELAINA WONDERED if she'd ever travel without the fierce desire to fly out of her own skin. Even taking short breaks to rest ate at her, but Nehma reminded her they'd be useless if they arrived in Ryos and couldn't function.

It would seem Nehma was the voice of cool reason for this journey. Rhea hardly spoke, and Relaina was ready to rip branches from trees with her bare hands.

Stop him!

Relaina stumbled, nearly landing in the creek by Amariah.

Images flashed and swirled before her eyes, and the forest, the creek, her companions all disappeared.

Darkness rushed around her, making it hard to discern the scene, but she caught glimpses of furniture; a wooden table, a chair, a woman bellowing orders nearby.

Shoot him, gods damn it all!

Darren. His racing thoughts became hers, his defiance and fear. She forced herself to pay attention, to reach for him so he knew she was there. He dove for a nearby window, grasping at its edge to peer outside. A city lay below, clay roofs and gardens built around winding channels fed by a river in the distance.

Ryos. Noble house. Artea.

Pain began and ended in the same instant in her lower back, and she yelped, pine needles appearing beneath her hands, birdsongs filling the air, mocking her with their cheeriness. Rhea and Nehma crouched beside her.

"What did you see?" Nehma asked, one hand on Relaina's shoulder.

"Darren," Relaina said, brushing off her hands and sitting upright. She leaned forward, holding her head as she closed her eyes. "He's still in Ryos. They've taken him to the Artea estate."

"Who took him?" Nehma asked. Relaina shook her head as she trembled with rage.

"I'm not certain, but I have my suspicions. I think something they've done to him has blocked our connection. But he broke through it for a few moments."

"Do you think that's why you lost the connection the first time?" Nehma asked.

"It must be. But that...that wasn't just our connection through the darkness this time. It was a vision."

"Whatever it is, I bet they did it to Thea too," Rhea said,

her voice hard. "It triggered my vision of her. We have to find him. And find the people who did this."

Nehma stood, offering Relaina a hand. "We will."

"Then let's keep going," Relaina said, standing. "We'll need to find a ship on the Granica River. How much farther to the nearest port town?"

"Another day," Nehma said as they led their horses back to the path. Relaina stepped into Amariah's stirrup and swung her leg over the saddle, trying not to anguish over how long it would take to get to Ryos.

Hold on, Darren. She knew he couldn't hear her, but she said it anyway, like a prayer, like an oath to the wind. *I'm coming for you.*

Chapter 39

The Shadow and the Cat

Fabian's footsteps felt entirely too loud on the cobblestones as he adjusted the cloak given to him by Lucia Eyern's friend. They'd found their way through the nearly empty streets of Ryos the day before, mostly thanks to Ihara's ability to project her shadow ahead and ensure their path was clear. Lucia's friend had graciously taken them into his home without asking many questions. Fabian had the distinct sense that the man suspected who he was, but he'd held his tongue, and Fabian was grateful.

The streets were dark and still eerily quiet now, the population terrified after the attack at the arena. City guards were scattered everywhere, but there were not nearly enough to keep a watchful eye on all of Ryos at once. Fabian was grateful for that, too—his height didn't make it easy to walk around unnoticed, but he had to find the Shadow stationed here.

His distress had subsided somewhat now that the Eyerns were in the care of a trusted friend, and especially since he'd had a chance to send messages to Desiree and Jeremiah. If the gods were with him tonight, he would find his Shadow and decide how best to move forward. Each time he recalled that bolt hitting Darren's shoulder and Thea's blood-soaked body, despair threatened to overtake him.

But despair wouldn't save Darren and it wouldn't bring Thea back.

He inhaled and glanced at the lanterns lining his route. The pub where his Shadow was stationed would be several blocks down, right by the water. The street curved south by one of the channels that wound through the city, and around the bend the glow of a lantern or torch grew brighter. Fabian stole into an alley on his right, pressing his back against the slick stone. Voice drifted from the street, the hazy light illuminating two guards as they passed by without so much as a glance in his direction. Fabian's heart thudded in his ears as he exhaled.

A pitiful sound by his feet froze him in place. He crouched, and beneath a discarded wooden crate, two eyes stared up at him, catching the light of the street lanterns. The kitten mewed again.

"Hello, little creature," he whispered, holding out his hand. The kitten popped its head out, sniffing, and Fabian waited patiently for more of its fluffy, black body to appear. After nearly touching its nose to his fingers, it backed away again, uncertain. He sighed. "Understandable. I don't like strangers much, either."

He stood and began his journey once more. Only two more blocks before he reached the pub, if the directions he'd memorized were indeed correct. Each time he passed another street or alley he checked his surroundings for guards or more nefarious shadows. His heart jumped into his throat as a small figure skittered closer to him before he realized what it was. Despite himself, he smiled and let out a chuckle.

"Change your mind, did you?"

The black kitten mewed at Fabian again. He bent down and offered his hand once more, and this time its nose touched his fingers before it began rubbing its face against his hand in earnest. *Gods in hell.* Fabian gathered the excess fabric of his cloak and lifted the kitten carefully. It mewed yet again as he swaddled it and held the bundle close to his chest.

"You were not part of my plans this evening, little creature," he said as he set off, scratching its small head. It might garner him some curious looks, but surely there were far stranger patrons in a pub as quiet as the one he approached.

A faded, nearly illegible sign creaked above the steps leading into the establishment, reading *Channel Spirits.* Bracing himself, Fabian secured his grip on the kitten wrapped in his cloak and opened the door.

The pub was small, narrow, and dimly lit, its dark wood chairs and tables empty. At the back, two people lounged behind the bar, both with deep brown skin and black hair. The woman's laugh echoed around the empty room until she caught sight of Fabian and nodded to her partner. A man with locs similar to Fabian's glanced his way, his smile vanishing.

"Your Majesty!" he exclaimed, slipping and spilling his drink all over the woman.

"Gods damn it, Heris!" she hissed.

The Shadow and his companion bickered for a moment in Terranian before he shunted her out of the room and approached Fabian, bowing low.

"I am grateful you are safe, Your Majesty," he said.

"Rise, please," Fabian said. The kitten in his arm chirped, and Heris's brown eyes darted to the bundle, eyebrows lifting. "An unexpected companion that joined me on my journey."

"Of course," Heris said, bowing his head again. "How may I serve you, my King?"

"I sent word earlier to Captain Fontaine and Jeremiah Andovier, but they likely won't arrive for at least a week. In the meantime, I'd like to find out as much as I can about the city and this group that attacked the arena."

Heris gestured for Fabian to sit at a nearby table before retrieving tea and bread. He placed a small saucer of water and a bit of fish on the floor for the kitten.

"I've discovered very little about this group, but I know they call themselves the Order of the Eternal Flame," Heris said. "I believe the man you have imprisoned in Maremer is one of them."

"So this Order is behind Jeremiah's possession," Fabian muttered. He took a sip of tea. "And the white-haired woman, has she been seen here?"

"Not to my knowledge. All I know is their name and that they are made up of both light and shadow-wielders."

Fabian reached into a pouch at his side and retrieved the two broken bolts he'd removed from Thea and Ihara. He placed them on the table. "Have you seen anything like these before?"

Heris leaned forward in his chair, his brow furrowing as he studied the bolts. They'd been cleaned, but the shaft of the pure white one still held light pink stains from Ihara's wound. The sharp tips gleamed in the dim light of the pub.

"No, Your Majesty." He shook his head. "I'd heard that they shot people with crossbow bolts, but have not seen the weapons up close."

Fabian frowned, putting the bolts back in his pouch. He'd have to discuss his theory with others when they arrived, and the potential risks; he could not very well send healers into a place where their magic could be rendered useless. If that was, in fact, what these bolts did.

"Tell me what you know of the Arteas," Fabian said. "They own the arena where the attack took place. Are they connected to this Order?"

Heris launched into descriptions and details that Fabian silently committed to memory. The Arteas were a well-respected Terranian noble family with a daughter close to

Relaina's age—details Fabian already knew. But it seemed very possible they were connected to the Order of the Eternal Flame.

"Are you able to keep watch near the Artea estate?" Fabian asked. "Or do you know someone who can?"

Heris bit his lip as he considered, his brow furrowing.

"I know a woman who delivers shipments of food and drink there," he said, his eyes brightening. "Perhaps she can provide some information."

"Please contact her." Fabian got up to retrieve the kitten, which had ventured to another table and was batting the chair legs.

"Would you like an escort back to the inn?" Heris asked.

"I'm staying elsewhere, now," Fabian said as the kitten curled up in the crook of his arm. He winced as its tiny claws dug into his skin. "I'll return here tomorrow evening."

Before venturing outside once more, Fabian turned back to his Shadow.

"Time is short," he said. "This may be the most important mission I ever give you."

Heris bowed deeply again.

"I won't let you down, Your Majesty."

CHAPTER 40

IN DREAMS AND DARKNESS

Pain throbbed through Darren's back and shoulder as he drifted back toward consciousness. His eyes opened slowly, revealing faint lighting and a low wood ceiling. He tried to sit up, but the rope around his wrists and ankles held him firmly down on a stone table in the center of this windowless room. *No.* His heart took off, his breathing erratic. Had they somehow removed the air from the room?

He strained against the bindings, crying out as the bolt in his shoulder shifted. They'd driven it right back through the place where he'd removed it. A door opened at the top of a short staircase across the room, casting more light inside and throwing dusty, empty shelves into relief. The figure that entered was cloaked, their face obscured, and Darren squeezed his eyes shut. *I'm not there. I'm not there. I'm not there—*

To think that my own son has betrayed me...

He's dead, he's dead, he's dead...

...You will do as I command from now on, or live out each day like this.

"Darren."

The voice broke through his panic, but when he opened

his eyes, the concerned expression above him didn't belong to anyone he wanted to see. Hedda's hand lit up with healer's markings as she placed it on his face. He flinched back.

"Come now," she said. "I'm trying to help."

Amid the warm glow of her magic, Darren's heart slowed, his insides unclenching.

"What are you doing?" he asked.

Hedda pursed her lips. "Healing magic isn't simply mending wounds. It manipulates the body and each of its smallest functions. I can't have you frenzied with panic when I need our conversations here to make a difference."

With a flash of horror, Darren recalled how the priests of Calixtos used to keep him conscious even when he was sure he'd faint from the pain they inflicted. Did the tenebrae have an ability similar to what Hedda described?

"Conversations," Darren spat, turning away from her as much as his bindings would allow. "You have me tied down to a table in a cellar."

"Only because you have refused to cooperate." Hedda walked over to a shelf, running her finger through the layer of dust and making a face. "It took me two days to fully heal my knee. That was quite vicious of you."

Two days. I've been here two days. At least. How long had it been since the attack on the arena? Darren swallowed against the dryness in his throat. "I'm not going to feel guilty about that, if that's what you're trying to do."

"What I'm *trying* to do is reason with you, Darren." Hedda returned to the table, leaning on the side as she crossed her arms. "Don't you want peace in Esran? Don't you want to heal the wounds your father left behind?"

"How dare you pretend you aren't *exactly* like him," Darren said, turning his head toward her again. "He wanted to conquer all of Esran and rule over everyone with magic. How are you any different?"

"He wanted to rule over everyone with only darkness, and sought to destroy light-wielders the moment he found out one of us would end him," Hedda snarled. "He was a disgrace to the Order."

Darren stopped breathing. "He was one of you?"

"Until Talea betrayed us all and told him of her vision. She is as much to blame for the mass murder of healers in Terrana as the Tyrant King."

They'd suspected it weeks ago, but for Relaina's mother's connection to his father to be confirmed—it was all connected. Talea, Gabriel, Kalmali, all of it.

"She was that loyal to my father?" Darren asked.

"She was that *selfish*," Hedda said, disgust plain on her face. "And when she realized it was *her* child who would destroy Gabriel, she abandoned the king, too."

Darren said nothing. Hedda leaned down and he tried not to recoil.

"You see? The Pretender is the child of deception and greed. Her magic is stunted from lack of use, her power tainted by her mother's misdeeds."

"And what of my father's misdeeds? You see no fault with me, with my power?"

"That is different. You are the true Heir of Calixtos, and you wield all of his power. Acantha is your true match. The Pretender is nothing but a half-breed fraud—"

"You know *nothing* of what she is," Darren growled. Hedda gripped his face in one glowing hand, and pain shot through his left cheek as if someone had sliced it with a knife. He gritted his teeth even as tears formed in his eyes.

"You think she'll come for you?" Hedda hissed. The skin on Darren's face split further, and he couldn't contain the cry that escaped him. "She left you. She's as self-serving and disloyal as her snake of a mother."

Hedda's magic grew brighter, and the pain subsided as Darren's cheek mended.

"I will make you see the truth of things," Hedda said, her voice calm again. "You will see her clearly." She barked an order, and the door opened again. Four others filed inside, each wearing flowing white robes.

"These are the Flameguards," Hedda said, and the four figures bowed. "They are here to serve and aid the Heir of Calixtos."

"Excellent," Darren said, his face scrunching as he caught his breath. "They can serve and aid me by releasing me."

"Such *insolence*, Hedda!" one of the figures hissed, her blue eyes widening.

"As I told you," Hedda said. "He needs our help."

As they gathered around the table, Darren braced himself. He'd survived the priests of Calixtos torturing him, cutting into him with shadowfire. He could survive whatever this would be.

"Sleep now, Heir of Calixtos."

One of them placed a hand on his head, and his vision went black.

I'm coming for you.

His magic was dormant, but her voice was clear in his head, and Darren fought against the pressure in his skull trying to muddle his thoughts. Relaina. *Relaina.*

"Wake him, now!"

The dark cellar appeared once more as Darren awoke, Relaina's name still on his lips. Each of the four Flameguards gripped one of his arms and legs, and an instant later, his skin was burning or splitting at their touch. He screamed, disoriented and still half caught in dreams.

"She's invaded your dreams, Darren," Hedda said into his ear. The Flameguards stopped their progress, leaving the wounds to sting and burn in the dank air. "We will make sure you're safe and fulfilling your true purpose. Acantha will be here soon, and all will be well."

The pain of the wounds began to fade as the Flameguards healed them. He says Relaina's name, they hurt him; Hedda mentions Acantha, they heal him. He knew what they were trying to do, and it wouldn't work.

"Fuck you," Darren coughed. "And fuck Acantha."

Rage filled Hedda's eyes. "Again."

～

"LET ME TELL YOU A STORY, Heir of Calixtos."

Darren's chest rose and fell rapidly as Hedda traced a glowing finger along his arm, healing the most recent gash the Flameguards had inflicted. The robed figures stood back several feet, awaiting their next instructions.

"The tale begins in a forest grove," Hedda said quietly, "around the sacred flame, the fire lit by Caliena, the first queen of the gods. You see, Esran was dying, so Caliena knelt, placed her hand to the soil, and imbued it with her divine spirit."

Hedda moved to his left leg, healing the burns there.

"Her sacrifice brought new power to the gods, life to the land, and a new queen was named. Elenia, goddess of sky and sea, became our new goddess of light. And Iros, on her behalf, granted mortals the power to wield that light and heal. Mortals he deemed worthy, that is."

Darren didn't understand why Hedda was telling him all this, but he tried his best to listen. Anything she said might help him figure out a way to escape.

"And Calixtos, the Death-bringer," Hedda continued, "soul-taker." She began healing Darren's other leg. "Griefgiver, god of darkness and death. Calixtos's power was too much for him, so he gave part of his power to mortals as well, and exiled himself to another realm."

Hedda approached Darren's other arm, looking down at him with reverence.

"You see," she breathed. "It is your duty and your destiny to control the darkness. And it is Acantha's duty to bring light to Esran. You must work together. You are meant for one another."

Darren tensed when Hedda placed a hand on his upper arm. She healed the cut there too and stared at him for a long moment.

"But the Pretender," she said, and she tore open the flesh she'd just healed. Darren cried out as it traveled down his entire arm and stopped at his wrist, right above the rope binding him to the table. "She won't bring light. She will only bring tainted magic and endless chaos."

Hedda removed her hand, and the wound in his arm throbbed, warm blood running down his skin. She leaned down close to his ear.

"Do you understand your destiny, Heir of Calixtos?" she asked softly. Darren didn't speak. He turned his head away from her and closed his eyes. Hedda sighed, footsteps approached, and blackness swept over him again.

DARREN no longer had the strength to conceal the pain they caused him. He'd lost count of how many times they'd repeated the same technique: heal him, force him to sleep, then wake him as his thoughts drifted to more pleasant places, only to inflict their corrupt healing magic upon him. Tears streamed down his face as the Flameguards ripped his flesh open and mended it again and again.

"It's been weeks," Hedda said softly in his ear as the Flameguards healed him. "The Pretender hasn't come. All you must do is accept us, and we'll treat you like the king you truly are. We won't let her hurt you anymore."

"*You*...are hurting me...you fucking sadist," Darren choked out.

Hedda grabbed Darren's chin, forcing him to look at her.

"We will protect you from her, no matter the cost. If we ever find her, the Flameguards and I will handle her."

No. He couldn't let them do this, or worse, to Relaina. Even if it had been weeks and she hadn't come for him. *I'm coming for you.* How long ago had he heard her voice? Perhaps he'd just imagined it. Perhaps no one would come for him. He would have to do what he'd done in the catacombs of the Obsidian Keep and get himself out.

"It's been weeks?" he whispered.

"Weeks," Hedda confirmed, releasing his face. "And it can all end now. It's up to you."

Darren took a long, shuddering breath. "I want to speak to Acantha."

Hedda exchanged a glance with the Flameguards.

"She has been delayed," she said. "A few more days, and she'll be here. We'd like for you to be presentable by then."

Darren nodded. "All right."

"We will not remove the bolt," Hedda warned. "Only Acantha will decide upon your loyalty."

Darren agreed. Anything to placate her. He couldn't form a plan if all they did was pull him in and out of sleep to torture him into hating Relaina. He kept his breathing even as they untied one binding at a time only to replace them with shackles, his eye catching the knife at Hedda's hip. Bolt or no bolt, he could figure something out. He didn't need magic to kill.

They guided him upright slowly, and his head swam. He was in no condition to fight, but it seemed they'd maintained his weight and proper body functions since bringing him down here. Darren shuddered; somehow that was more violating than the torture itself. With careful hands, the Flameguards helped him off the table. He collapsed to the ground.

"I told you all to maintain his strength when you healed him," Hedda hissed, crouching by another Flameguard. They hauled him back to his feet, but not before he swiped the knife from Hedda's belt and tucked it behind his shackled wrist.

He continued to feign weakness as they chauffeured him toward the steps of the cellar. He winced at the continued throbbing in his shoulder and forced himself to breathe. *Just a few more steps.*

They entered a narrow hallway covered in thick purple carpet, with several doors lining the walls on either side. Light streamed through an open door several feet away.

"I'm pleased you've come to your senses," Hedda said, a few steps behind him. "I'm sure you still have doubts, but I can assure you those will be put to rest soon."

"You seem very self-assured," Darren said carefully.

"Indeed," Hedda said. "And I'll ensure you see the light fully. That Pretender bitch will shatter like a fragile glass when she faces Acantha. You'll see."

Hedda prattled on about Acantha as they drew near the open door. Darren folded his fingers over his other hand and threw all of his strength into wrenching his arm free of one of the Flameguards. The other released him in shock, and he drove the knife into her chest.

They were on him instantly, but he ducked and rolled forward out of their grasp. Another leapt at him and he stabbed her in the neck. She writhed on the ground as he dug his heels into the carpet and pushed himself closer to the open door. Hedda struck at him with a whip of light, and he rolled out of the way just in time.

"You still don't see!" she screamed at him. Darren didn't think—he lunged, throwing his body closer to the door, but Hedda's magic caught him at the ankle. She and the two remaining Flameguards overpowered him, but he burned the image of his surroundings into his mind. Hedda gripped his hair and yanked his face back as the others held him in place.

"I lied to spare you suffering until you see the light, Heir of Calixtos, but no more. The Pretender *is* on her way here now, and we'll use you to lure her to her destruction."

Fear greater than anything he'd yet felt seized him by the throat. *No...*

A moment later, Hedda forced him into a terror-filled sleep once more.

CHAPTER 41

THE RUSE

Relaina couldn't deny that Ryos was beautiful, but the persistent ache of fear in her chest made it difficult to appreciate the pinks and purples of the dawn shimmering in the channels that ran through its cobbled streets. It had been five days since her vision of Darren, and she hadn't felt even a whisper of him. A cool breeze brushed a loose curl against her cheek, carrying with it the scent of early spring.

Every part of her raged against the serenity of their surroundings.

"How in hell are we supposed to find this estate?" Nehma asked, squatting by Relaina and Rhea behind a merchant stall. The channel-side market was empty save for the occasional passing city guard.

"All I know is that it's east of where we entered the city," Relaina said. "And that it was taller than most surrounding buildings."

"We need to get to higher ground," Nehma said, peeking over the counter of the stall. She ducked down again quickly. "I see more guards."

"The Arteas are the highest-ranking nobles in this city," Relaina said. "The city guard must work for them."

"What's their sigil?" Nehma asked.

"Fuck if I know."

"Well, the guards have a fox on their uniforms."

"We should capture one and question them," Rhea said, speaking for the first time since yesterday. Relaina and Nehma needed no further convincing.

After ensuring there were no additional guards around, Nehma and Rhea darted out from the stall to pursue two headed west. Relaina ground her teeth as she waited for them to subdue the guards, vigilant as the minutes dragged past.

A body slumped by her feet, and she shifted aside to make more room. Nehma and Rhea dragged the unconscious guard closer to the stall and hunkered down again. With a hard expression, Rhea's light pulsed on her hand briefly, and she woke the guard.

"Make a sound, and you're finished," Nehma said. The man recoiled, nodding.

Relaina moved closer to him, lifting his head by the roots of his black, curly hair. His brown eyes were almost the same shade as Darren's. Relaina pushed the thought away and drew a knife.

"Do you work for the Arteas?" she asked.

"Yes, they've had us patrolling since the attack in the arena," the man spoke so fast Relaina barely understood him. "Please, I'm just doing my job! I didn't know the Arteas planned to betray the Order!"

"The Order?" Relaina asked. The guard's eyes darted between Relaina, Nehma, and Rhea.

"You...you aren't with the Order of the Eternal Flame?"

"What in Saeva's name is that?" Nehma muttered. The guard visibly relaxed, panic melting away from his eyes.

"Oh, thank the gods," he said. "Then are you here to fight against them?"

"We're asking the questions," Relaina said. "Tell us about this Order and how they're connected to the Arteas."

"They've been working together for months, ever since King Gabriel marched on Maremer," the guard said. "I don't know all the details, but I know their leader and Lord Artea had an agreement to place him on the Terranian throne. The Flameguards have slowly joined the ranks of the city guard, they told us it was for extra security and safety in Ryos, but all of it went horribly wrong at the arena last week. Prince Darren challenged the Terranian Elite and won, but after that..."

The guard swallowed, shuddering.

"Go on," Relaina said, her heart thundering.

"After that, at least a dozen of them appeared in the stands and started shooting people with crossbows. I've never seen anything like it. The Arteas escaped that day and told us they didn't approve of the violence and wanted out of their alliance."

"What of King Fabian?" Relaina asked.

"No one has seen him."

Relaina swallowed that as best she could. *It doesn't mean he's dead.*

"Where are the Arteas now?" she asked.

"We haven't received any orders in two days," the guard squeaked. "We don't know if the Order has killed them or imprisoned them. I saw your light and I thought—"

"Are Flameguards all healers?" Nehma asked. The guard nodded.

"But they don't heal," he whispered.

A beat of silence passed before Relaina asked, "Where is the Artea estate?"

"About ten blocks east of here, then three blocks south."

"And what is the best way to get inside unnoticed?"

"There's a servants' entrance by the south stables. I haven't seen any of them go in or out in over a week."

"Thank you," Relaina said, and she meant it. "Nehma?"

With a gentle glowing hand, Nehma knocked the guard out. He slumped to the ground.

"How widespread *are* these fanatics?" Nehma asked as they sprinted across the street and ducked into an alley. Relaina had no answer. All she had was rage, and fear, and desperation to find Darren and get him away from them. After avoiding several other guards and making it five more blocks, the three women stopped behind a stack of crates holding a variety of fruit.

"I'm going into that estate," Relaina said. "If all goes well, we won't even need to fight."

"That's unlikely," Nehma said.

"Then I'm asking you to cover me." Relaina glanced around the crates and watched two city dwellers quickly step into a shop. "If I have a vision again, I need to be able to tell you both where to go."

Nehma and Rhea studied her for a moment before they both nodded.

"We stay together," Rhea said.

"We'll get inside and find that room I saw," Relaina said. "I'll raze that gods-damned house to the ground to find him if I have to."

Nehma held out her hand, which Relaina took.

"To the estate, then."

EVEN IF THAT guard hadn't told them servants hadn't been around the estate in days, it was apparent by the filth emanating from the stables. The stench assaulted Relaina's nostrils even by the back entrance of the estate, and she was glad they'd left Amariah and their other horses at a stable in the city's outskirts.

"I'll stay here," Rhea said. "I'll give you both an hour before I come in after you."

Relaina and Nehma nodded before dashing to the door. Relaina turned the knob, not truly expecting it to give way, but it was unlocked. They stole inside and shut it behind them, listening hard for any sign that they'd been seen. Floorboards creaked above the narrow hallway they'd entered, accompanied by muffled voices. They'd need to avoid that area as they made their way up.

Stairs. Just ahead. Nehma stayed on her heels as she climbed the stairs silently, grateful for the carpet beneath their feet. They emerged into a hallway with more natural light, the stone walls painted a burnt orange color. A man in white robes walked out of a nearby room. Before he could look up Relaina leapt at him, clapping a hand over his mouth. Nehma silenced him with a touch.

"I can't do that much more," Nehma said. "I need to conserve my magic."

"Let's try to avoid anyone else," Relaina said. And if they didn't, she'd take care of them herself. She could deal with the repercussions of taking more lives later. All that mattered was getting Darren out, and hopefully finding out where Fabian was too.

They located the main staircase down the hall, glancing over the railing before racing to the fourth floor. The room she'd Seen had been up this high—Darren had to be up here somewhere, unless they'd moved him. Relaina wiped her sweaty palms on her pants before reaching for the first doorknob. At least they'd have a place to start.

Relaina began with the first room on the left. It was an empty bedroom, with a rusty orange color accenting the bedcovers and draping. Nehma followed her down to the next room. Another empty bedroom. And why were all these doors left unlocked?

Only two rooms remained on the hall. Relaina reached for the next doorknob as Nehma kept watch down the hall.

Locked. Her heart took off. Nehma hurried forward and knelt, retrieving a small pin from her pocket while Relaina listened for any approaching footsteps. Though it only took a few seconds, it seemed like hours before the lock clicked and the door swung open.

Inside were three prisoners bound and gagged, but none of them were Darren. Relaina met their terrified eyes, trying to parse who they could be when something sharp pierced her upper back, the force of it sending her to her knees. Nehma hit the ground to her right. Relaina lunged forward with a cry, nearly crashing into one of the other prisoners before their assailants grabbed her and yanked her back. Three other white-robed figures began binding Nehma's hands. She was unconscious.

Relaina swore. She tried to wrench her arms out of her attackers' grasps as they dragged her from the room. With a flash of horror, Relaina caught sight of two more white-clad figures dragging a dark-haired woman down the hall. How had they found *Rhea*? Relaina struggled against her captors again to no avail, and growled as pain shot through her back again.

Foolish. She'd been so foolish to think they could do this.

They'd shot her. She was hurt, and Nehma and Rhea were out cold. It was only a matter of time before her insides were on fire with pain.

They opened a door across the hall, throwing her to the floor of the new room. With a whimper, she lifted herself, gritting her teeth through the pain in her back.

She forgot all of it at the sight of the man lying on the ground before her, his hands bound behind him, his brown shirt tattered and ill-fitting. She scrambled forward, taking his pale face in her hands.

"Darren," she croaked. He didn't stir. "Darren!"

She searched him frantically for injuries, for any reason he wouldn't wake, but before she could find anything their robed assailants pulled her away from him and forced her to her knees. Two others hauled Darren upright. A white crossbow bolt was jutting out of his left shoulder.

"Don't touch him!" Relaina snarled, but their arms lit up as they gripped his arms, and Darren's eyes fluttered open and then widened.

"No," he whispered, the pain in his expression worse than the bolt in her back. "Relaina—"

Two tendrils of light wrapped around Darren's upper arms and held him in place as one of the robed figures forced a rope between his teeth. Relaina threw herself forward, trying to break her captors' hold, but one of them gripped the bolt in her back and shoved. She screamed.

"Thank you, Zara," a cool treble voice said. Relaina forced her eyes back open, breathing through the pain. A tall, thin woman with dark hair crouched before her, blocking her view of Darren. Her brown eyes were anything but kind.

"Hello, Pretender."

CHAPTER 42

THE PRETENDER

Relaina scowled at the woman in front of her. *Pretender.* That's what Kalmali had called her.

"My name is Hedda," the woman said. "The Heir of Elenia's right hand, most faithful servant to Acantha. And I'm going to destroy you."

Darren shifted behind Hedda, uttering what were surely curses muffled by the gag in his mouth.

"A man said that to me months ago," Relaina said, her voice steady. "He's dead now."

"You are no match for me, Pretender," Hedda sneered. "The Heir of Calixtos will be free of you."

Before Relaina could reply, Hedda motioned to her robed comrades and stepped away. Warm light glowed for a moment, then pain raced up Relaina's arms as though someone had dragged knives along her skin. She jerked back, but they held fast, their magic tearing her apart. Blood seeped through the black sleeves of her Shadow gear. She gritted her teeth hard against a scream.

"Don't you see?" Hedda's voice drifted to where Relaina knelt as they ceased their corrupt healing. Relaina looked up, locking eyes with Darren. Hedda grabbed his chin. "She is *nothing.*"

Darren jerked his chin out of her grasp.

"Darren—" Relaina cut off with a cry as the light-wielders began ripping open her flesh anew. This time one of them tore at her ribcage. She fought to pull away from them again, her movements erratic, desperate. She was losing so much blood.

"I'll take it from here," Hedda said.

The light-wielders dropped Relaina to the floor. Every breath was agony as her ribs moved against the wound in her side. Hedda's boot slammed into Relaina's stomach. Tears leaked from her eyes as she let out a ragged sob.

"She is weak and unworthy," Hedda said. Relaina's vision went black as Hedda grabbed the bolt and drove it even deeper into her back. She eagerly fell toward the waiting relief unconsciousness offered, but a blinding light brought her back to reality a moment later. Her heart shattered at the look on Darren's face, at the tears streaming down his cheeks as he struggled against those holding him. Their hands still glowed where they held him firmly in place.

"I'll fucking kill you," Relaina said softly, her throat raw. Hedda grabbed Relaina by the neck, her face inches away.

"What was that?"

"I'll fucking *kill you,*" Relaina said, her voice menacing even as it broke. Hedda's arms lit up as she lifted Relaina from the floor, her light tearing into Relaina's neck. This was it— she was going to end up just like Hektor Elke, his throat torn open by vile magic.

But Hedda threw her to the ground again. "Hold her down."

Even if she'd had the strength to fight back, the robed figures moved too quickly. They pinned her facedown to the floor, her arms immobilized on either side of her. Hedda ripped through the fastenings of her Shadow armor with a knife and opened it at the back, exposing her bare skin. Relaina flinched violently. Suddenly she was on that ship again, chained to the mast.

Daughter of Iros, I will destroy *you.*

She'd survived Tridset, but how would she survive this?

"What...what is *that*?" One of the robed figures spoke for the first time, horrified.

"She has been marred by shadowfire," Hedda said breathlessly. She let out a derisive laugh. Relaina tuned her out as best she could. Hedda's hand touched her back, and her skin began to split apart. She fought to force down her screams for Darren's sake, but it was too much, the pain too overwhelming. Each time she thought she'd black out, one of the light-wielders drew her back to alertness.

Hedda removed her hand, giving Relaina a moment of respite. For what reason, Relaina didn't care. A tear fell over the bridge of her nose as sunlight from the nearby window warmed her face. She could almost pretend it was the warmth of a healer, the warmth of her own inner light.

Her inner light that was now absent.

How long had it been since they'd shot her? Her light had not materialized, had not raged against her shadowfire scars in an attempt to heal her. Holding her breath as Hedda reached for her back, ready to tear into her skin once more, Relaina silently grasped for her other magic, the darkness waiting in her scars, in her blood.

But Hedda didn't inflict more wounds; instead, she ordered the healers away before grabbing Relaina by the roots of her hair and yanking her upright. Her blood smeared on the stone floor. Relaina's grip on the darkness snapped, her mind focused only on the pain from her wounds. Her stomach lurched at the sight of the deep gashes in her legs.

"You must see." Hedda took another fistful of Relaina's hair and yanked her head back. She couldn't feel Darren's horror and rage, but she could see it on his tearstained face, in his eyes. "I won't give her to Acantha."

Darren stopped struggling, his eyes flicking to Hedda, his chest heaving. Relaina remained limp as she began reaching for the darkness again. Hedda unsheathed a long knife and held it to Relaina's throat. Out of instinct, Relaina grabbed at Hedda's forearm with a bloodied hand, but the healer didn't react.

"She's not even worthy of facing Acantha," Hedda said. "She's so weak, she'll fall to me."

Darren's agonized eyes locked with Relaina's.

"P-please," Relaina croaked, and Hedda pressed the knife into her flesh, drawing blood.

"Begging will do nothing, Pretender. Prepare to face Calixtos."

Relaina reached further within, dredging up whatever power she could grasp. It was cold where her light was warm, especially concentrated in the shadowfire scars. She could sense it so *clearly* now. She gripped Hedda's arm and shoved every bit of the magic funneling in her veins toward her hand.

The healer shrieked and dropped the knife, releasing Relaina's hair as an arc of iridescent darkness crashed into her and the other light-wielders, forcing them backward, forcing the ones holding Darren to release him. Relaina half-fell, half-lunged for him, gripping the bolt in his shoulder and ripping it out.

Darkness consumed them all.

DARREN'S DARKNESS had never raged like this before, had never plunged everything around him into utter obscurity. He might as well have already dived headfirst into the realm of Calixtos.

Darren!

Shadows swirled around Relaina's bloody, tearstained face, her eyes wide and bloodshot. Using the knife Hedda had dropped, she cut through the ropes binding his wrists and removed his gag. He lifted her to her feet and ran, his power beginning to push against pockets of thrashing light around the room. He drew it back to himself as they burst into the hallway.

Nehma and Rhea! Relaina pulled him into the room across the hall. Two Flameguards stood watch by the bound healers. Darren formed his darkness into two daggers and sent them flying into the Flameguards' chests. They dropped, and the daggers vanished. Relaina cut through the healers' bindings and pulled the bolts out of their backs. They yelped and swore.

"Fabian?" Relaina asked, looking to Darren.

"I don't know," Darren said, his voice rough. "I haven't seen him." The healers' bodies illuminated with their markings.

"We have to *go*," Nehma said. She and Rhea followed Relaina and Darren back into the hallway, dodging flashes of light hurled at them from the other room.

"Stop them!" Hedda roared.

Darren pulled his darkness to his center before turning and releasing it all toward their pursuers, filling the hallway with black shimmering wind. They flew down the stairs, skipping several at a time, and Relaina stumbled into Darren on the second-floor landing, her breathing labored. She was still bleeding profusely.

"Have to keep going," she mumbled as he steadied her. A Flameguard appeared down the hallway. Nehma caught the slash of light sent their way and hurled it back at the Flameguard, flinging her to the ground and silencing her.

"This way," Rhea said. She led them down the short hallway, leaping over the dead Flameguard and racing for the stairs. Relaina grew slower with every step. "You two go first. We're right behind you."

Darren's magic sang as he summoned more of it, as it connected with Relaina's. He lifted her into his arms and shuffled down the stairs, shoving the door at the base open with his back. He set Relaina back on her feet once they were several yards clear of the door, but kept one arm firmly around her waist. Nehma and Rhea burst through the door, swearing as beams of light flew past them.

"Nehma!" Rhea growled, almost an order. Nehma stopped and turned a few feet away from the door. She bent low, her thighs almost parallel with the ground, her hands forming a ball of light at her abdomen. It grew for a moment, and she thrust her hands out from her chest. It shot toward the door, exploding when it hit the wood. A crack formed and skittered up the side of the clay building.

"Go!" Nehma yelled, and they all took off again as more cracks formed, and the building's south wall began to collapse.

Darren barely heard the Flameguards' screams that followed—Relaina stumbled, her hand nearly slipping out of his, and he pulled her onto a side street. Rhea and Nehma followed.

"I'll be fine," Relaina said, her voice a rasp.

"Gods in fucking hell, Relaina," Nehma said, her voice hardly more than a whisper. "Sit and let me heal you a moment."

"We need to keep going—" Relaina started.

"*Sit*, gods damn it," Nehma said, and Relaina obliged. Rhea and Darren kept watch as Nehma tended to Relaina's more serious wounds. Darren tried not to look at the gashes and burns covering her body, the ones he'd watched form at Hedda and the Flameguards' hands. When Nehma started to remove the bolt from Relaina's back, she protested.

"Unless you plan to fully heal me right now, leave that in," she said. Nehma retracted her hand and nodded.

"How the fuck are we going to get out of this city without them seeing us?" Rhea asked.

Darren offered Relaina a hand and pulled her to her feet. She was more stable, no longer at risk of bleeding out, but she was nowhere near healed.

A figure appeared at the other end of the side street and began running at them. Darren and the others tensed, their magic bursting to life in their hands.

"Wait! Wait, please," the man said, stopping halfway down the street with his hands raised. "I'm with King Fabian. I can take you to him."

CHAPTER 43

A PLACE TO HIDE

"Who would've thought you'd find such an endearing creature amid all this?" Lucia huffed a good-natured laugh at Ihara as Fabian's kitten pounced on a string she'd been waving around. The woman's relief was palpable as she smiled at her wife, who was now close to full health after they'd finally located a healer.

Fabian had led them to the Channel Spirits pub that morning for his second meeting with Heris. His Shadow had updated them on what he'd witnessed surrounding the Artea estate before setting out to do additional reconnaissance. The Arteas hadn't been seen in days, and their guards were taking orders from light-wielders dressed in white robes.

"Have you thought of a name yet, Your Majesty?" Ihara asked, her eyes bright as she sat on the floor. She cast a small piece of her tenebrae shadow from her hand, enticing the kitten to stalk it.

"I was thinking Ash," Fabian said, chuckling as she crouched, wiggling before pouncing on Ihara's shadow.

Shouts from the street pulled their attention to the door, and Ihara scooped Ash from the floor as they all turned. Heris flung the door open, and Fabian squinted in the morning sunlight as four others tumbled into the pub after him. Heris slammed the door, latching it. Nehma and Rhea pressed their hands to the wall on either side of the door. Their light spread across it until it formed a glowing seal.

"We can't hold this for long," Nehma panted. "They're right on our heels."

Fabian rushed forward for the two figures on the floor behind her, kneeling beside them. "Darren!"

"Fabian," Darren said, the break in his voice shattering Fabian's relief. Relaina's eyes were closed where she lay in Darren's arms, her armor in tatters, her face and neck covered in half-dried blood. For a moment, he feared the worst, but her chest rose and fell, even if her breathing was ragged. Her eyes opened halfway.

"Fabian," she said, her voice hoarse as she reached for his hand. "Thank the gods."

"What happened? How did you get here so quickly?" Fabian asked.

The wall by the door shuddered as something crashed into it. Nehma swore, and Rhea stumbled back from the wall before pressing into it again, her light pulsing brighter. "They're here."

"Visions," Relaina muttered. She lost consciousness a moment later.

"Nehma!" Darren called, his panic scarcely concealed. Desiree's niece glanced over her shoulder as the wall shuddered again.

"Fuck!" she yelled. "Rhea?"

"I'll be quick," Rhea said through gritted teeth.

Fabian stood back as Rhea approached to heal Relaina. Ihara stepped around them.

"Are they all light-wielders?" she asked Nehma. Sweat beaded on Nehma's forehead, her arms trembling where she held them pressed to the shield she and Rhea had made for the wall.

"No," she spat out. Ihara nodded.

"Drop the shield for a moment," she said. Nehma released the wall, gasping, and Ihara's eyes filled with darkness. Her shadow swept from her body, slithering under the door. With a growl, Nehma formed the shield again, but it wobbled and spread thinner than it had before.

And yet, the blows to the door and wall subsided, replaced by shrieks of fear.

"Four light-wielders, two guards," Ihara said, her eyes black. Another beam of light crashed into the door.

"Fuck this," Nehma said. She dropped the shield again. "Let's take them out."

Rhea and Darren transferred a still-unconscious Relaina to Fabian's care before rushing to join Nehma and Ihara. He tried to keep her somewhat upright to avoid driving the black bolt deeper into her back. Why hadn't they removed it yet? He didn't have time to ask before the four magic wielders kicked down the door and rushed outside to face their attackers. Heris and Lucia were frozen where they stood. Ash wiggled in Lucia's arms.

More light flashed outside, followed by yelps of surprise and curses. The door burst open again, and a man in white robes raised a glowing hand in Relaina's direction. Fabian hauled her out of the way just in time. He scrambled backwards on the floor, pulling Relaina along as the man stalked toward them, raising his hand again. Fabian's back hit the bar, and he wrapped his arms around Relaina's chest, tucking his head to shield her from the blow—

"Urgk!"

Fabian looked up. The light-wielder's white robes bloomed with crimson at his chest, a blade jutting out from the fabric. The face of the man behind him was the last one Fabian expected to see, but the one he most longed to.

"Jeremiah." It came out like a sob. Jeremiah sheathed his sword and rushed forward, one hand on Relaina's face and one on Fabian's.

"Is she—"

"She's alive," Fabian said. "But she's badly hurt."

Footsteps thundered back into the pub, and Fabian tensed as Jeremiah twisted around, a knife in hand. But it was their allies, all of them alive, if not a bit bloody and haggard. Fabian's heart lifted at the sight of Saheer among them, her lip curled in disgust as she prodded the dead light-wielder with her foot.

Fabian looked back to Jeremiah. "How did you—?"

"I'll explain later," Jeremiah said, sheathing his knife and reaching to help Fabian lift Relaina off the ground. "We have to get out of this city before more of these zealots show up."

Darren came forward, shadows still dancing around his arms and hands. Both of his eyes flashed black, and cold pulsed around him.

"I'll take her," he said. With the added strength of his magic, Relaina's weight hardly appeared to affect him. Her injuries were no longer bleeding freely, but that bolt was still in her upper back, black as obsidian. "Do any of you have horses nearby?"

"We left ours at a stable on the west side," Nehma said. "But there are only three."

"Saheer and I left ours just north of here," Jeremiah said. "Darren, you can take mine and get Relaina out of here."

Darren nodded, and Fabian frowned, looking at the faces around him. "But what about—"

"Ihara and I will remain here," Lucia said, silencing the room. She handed Ash to Fabian; somehow the kitten hadn't fled the scene in the chaos. "King Darren will need allies inside Ryos if we are to take it back from these religious insurgents."

"I'm not leaving until I recover Thea's body," Rhea said, her voice icy. "One of you can take my horse."

Fabian turned to Jeremiah and Saheer.

"Saheer, you go with Relaina and Darren," he said. "We'll regroup at the village we passed on the way here, several miles east. Darren knows it."

When both Jeremiah and Saheer started to protest, Fabian held up his free hand. Ash mewed, and they both stared at the kitten in his arm.

"A new friend of mine," Fabian said quickly. "Saheer, you will have better protection from these fanatics if you go with Darren."

"And I'll join you, King Fabian," Nehma said, though she didn't look happy about leaving Rhea. Fabian thanked Heris, and Rhea promised Nehma that she would try to meet them in the village as soon as possible.

"If the weather holds, Desiree should arrive in Ellyr within the week," Fabian said to Rhea. "We will remain in the village until that time."

Rhea nodded.

"She is in the arena," Fabian told her. "Southeast of here in a large circular building. I...I said a prayer for her, but it was all I could do. Just...be prepared for what you will see."

Rhea took a shuddering breath. "Thank you, King Fabian."

"We need to go now," Nehma said, glancing outside. "I can hear shouts."

Fabian nodded, and they set off.

∾

As Saheer helped Darren haul Relaina onto Jeremiah's horse, he grimaced at the black bolt still lodged into her upper back. He had no way of knowing if Nehma's healing had done enough that Relaina's own magic could heal her fully when connected to his. It was best to leave it in place for now. *Just get her out.*

Jeremiah's horse was not as fast as Amariah, nor as strong, but their progress was still swift. They by passed shops and residences in a blur, the streets nearly devoid of people. Darren pushed away the guilt at leaving the citizens of Ryos at the mercy of the Order of the Eternal Flame. He could do nothing to help them if he got captured again.

The north city gate came into view, and Darren breathed in relief. A few more blocks and they were free—

A flash of light nearly blinded them. Darren and Saheer's horses reared, and he held fast to Relaina, his shadows rushing out to break their fall to the cobblestones. The force of his back hitting the stones still knocked the wind out of him. To his right, Saheer managed to stay mounted on her own horse.

"Are you all right?" she called. Darren gasped for breath as the culprits appeared, two Flameguards and three others dressed in black robes. The knives in their hands ignited with black fire. *Priests of Calixtos.*

Relaina coughed and groaned in his arms, her legs entangled with his on the ground. The moment she was conscious again, her power started to connect with Darren's, bolstering his and making it easier for him to catch his breath.

What's happening? she thought to him. He sat up and helped her to her feet, both of them tensing to fight.

More Order members.

"King Darren," one of the priests called as the others closed in on them. Saheer drew a shortsword and guided her horse close to Relaina and Darren. "Heir of Calixtos, please. We only wish to serve you and guide you to the Path."

Darren gritted his teeth as his magic flared again, his voice guttural and menacing as he spat, "You've lost any chance of peace with me."

Take it out.

Relaina still leaned on him for support, but when he glanced at her face, her gaze burned with resolve.

But your magic—

Do it.

The Order members were drawing closer, their shadowfire blades and glowing arms poised to attack. Darren gripped the bolt in Relaina's back. *I'm sorry.*

Her scream echoed around the street as Darren broke the fletching off and shoved it through her. She grabbed the front end of it and hurled it to the ground. Her body lit up with her healer markings an instant later, and the injuries Darren had sustained began to mend alongside hers. Relaina's back and arms glowed as shadowy vapor raced up her arms, her left eye glowing white while her right held their iridescent darkness.

Both. She was using both.

CHAPTER 44

THE ANSWER

Warmth built within Relaina from her chest outward as her light healed her, and coolness pressed against it from the shadows now floating along the surface of her skin. But with the shadows outside of her, the light and dark did not clash. They danced.

She dove for one of the tenebrae wielding a shadowfire blade, knocking it from his hands. Their dark magic collided as Relaina gripped his wrist, flowing coolness against unyielding ice, but the tenebrae crumpled when Relaina's light pulsed. Darren felled the two light-wielders with his shadow daggers, and Saheer narrowly avoided the slice of a shadowfire knife before driving her sword into a tenebrae's abdomen. Darren's darkness enveloped the shadow as it roared out of the man, swallowing it. The remaining priest turned and ran.

Saheer prepared to throw a knife at the retreating woman, but before the priest made it three steps, light caught her across the face. She went down, screaming. Relaina searched wildly for Nehma or Rhea, but it wasn't her friends who appeared from an alley.

Hedda stalked forward and grabbed the priest by her neck.

Blood flowed down her body as her skin split open and Hedda dropped her back to the ground.

"I do not abide cowards or traitors," Hedda snarled. "And I do not abide abominations to the gods. You won't leave this city alive, Pretender."

Relaina could almost taste Darren's rage as it barreled through her mind, wordless and raw. She was ready to rip Hedda's throat out herself, but a small clicking sound behind them made her grab Darren and shove him down. The bolt narrowly missed his back. Relaina scoured the street behind them for the source of the shooter but found nothing.

Where are these crossbow-wielding fucks?

Darren didn't answer her; his mind was consumed by rage and pain. Another bolt barely missed Saheer.

"Saheer!" Relaina barked. "We'll meet you at the gate!"

With a nod, Saheer took off, ducking another bolt, and Relaina traced the trajectory to a nearby shop. She raced for the door while Darren covered her, blocking Hedda's attacks with those menacing blades he'd made of pure darkness.

Relaina hardly saw the startled people cowering behind the counter inside the tea shop—she headed straight for the stairs and flew up them as fast as she could. The second floor was a single room filled with crates and shelves of tea. *Where are you?*

A man darted out from behind a shelf, and Relaina ducked and threw out a leg, sweeping his from under him. He hit the floorboards with a solid *thud.* Relaina grabbed for the crossbow in his hands, shoving it back as he aimed at her. An instant later, the trigger clicked again, and a black bolt lodged itself beneath the man's chin. He went limp. Relaina climbed off him, her light quickly healing the small bruises and cuts she'd sustained in the scuffle.

She rushed back down the steps and out of the shop.

Darren and Hedda fought ferociously in the street, darkness and light colliding and crashing into the sides of buildings.

"You don't know what you're doing!" Hedda shrieked. "You betray the god whose power you wield!"

Relaina was going to end her.

"You're as corrupt as your father!" Hedda screamed, landing a blow on Darren's right arm. He stumbled back. Relaina ran for him as the fury within him fueled his darkness. It would soon build to the same peak it had reached during the battle. She couldn't lose him to the realm of Calixtos again —not knowing when, or if, he would find his way back.

Darren!

He still didn't respond to her, his mind a raging sea. Shadows burst out of him the way they had nearly two months ago, creating a fierce wind that shrouded the entire street. Hedda's light flared as Darren sliced her arm with one of his blades, and she shrieked, leaping backwards. She disappeared a moment later. Relaina squinted her eyes as she drew closer to Darren, reaching for him.

Pain flooded her upper arm and her light winked out, the warmth gone in an instant as she stumbled forward. But her darkness remained, rushing around her in swirling shadows, the same way she'd seen Darren use his so many times now.

Before she could get the bolt out, a white-robed figure leapt at her, and they tumbled to the ground. Kneeling, the Flameguard plunged a knife toward her chest, and Relaina caught the man's wrist, her arms trembling. Relaina's shadows faltered around her. The darkness bolstered her, but the light was gone again with that bolt in her arm, and her strength was waning. The Flameguard drove the blade downward another inch. Relaina gritted her teeth and snarled as her arms continued to shake.

Relaina.

Darren's darkness slowed around them, and a moment

later the Flameguard's body lurched as the blade of a shadowy dagger sank deep into his neck. The knife aimed at Relaina's heart fell from his hands, and Relaina heaved him off of her with a roar.

The all-consuming rage in Darren's mind dissipated as he ran for her, abandoning his pursuit of a retreating Hedda. He helped Relaina to her feet as night-dark wind whipped around them once more.

Before another bolt could hit either of them, they raced for the north gate.

~

JEREMIAH HAD THOUGHT their escape from Ryos had been slow, but they'd arrived in the little village nearly an hour before, and Relaina, Darren, and Saheer had not appeared.

He sat on the steps of an inn beside Fabian, trying to stave off the growing urge to grab Relaina's horse and ride back into Ryos to find them. The small kitten Fabian had brought along had been surprisingly quiet and docile throughout their journey, settled into the cloak Fabian had slung across his chest. Fabian now scratched her small head absently while they waited.

"I hope they're all right," Jeremiah whispered. Fabian turned, but Jeremiah couldn't look away from the path that led out of the village, to the road toward Ryos.

"We'll give them until nightfall," Fabian said, placing one hand on Jeremiah's knee. Jeremiah gripped Fabian's fingers. The kitten mewed, and Jeremiah finally met Fabian's gaze. The king's eyes shone in the setting sun.

"Have you given her a name?" Jeremiah asked, watching the kitten as Fabian set her down on the ground.

"Ash."

Jeremiah reached down to let her sniff his fingers. She

rubbed her face on them, and he scratched her chin. "She's very cute."

Surprise painted Fabian's face. "I wasn't sure you'd approve."

Jeremiah lifted Ash into his lap, and she closed her eyes contentedly as he continued scratching her chin. "How could I disapprove of something so charming?"

To their left, Amariah began stamping the ground, shifting where she was tethered by the other horses. Jeremiah handed Ash back to Fabian and stood, stepping onto the path and peering toward the village entrance. Three figures and a horse slowly emerged from the woods. Jeremiah took off running as Fabian called for Nehma.

Relaina was conscious, walking beside Darren and Saheer, who led her horse instead of riding it. The horse Jeremiah had brought along was nowhere in sight. He slowed his pace as he drew nearer, and Relaina's exhausted, bloodstained face lit up at the sight of him. She stumbled into his waiting arms.

"Nehma and Fabian?" she asked.

"Both fine," Jeremiah said.

"Relaina!"

Jeremiah stepped aside so Nehma could embrace her.

"What happened?" Nehma asked as they all began walking together. "You're mostly healed, but you lost a horse?"

"Those zealots found us close to the city's northern gate," Relaina said. "I had Darren remove the bolt and we managed to escape, but our horse had run off."

"What the fuck were those bolts they shot us with?" Nehma asked.

Jeremiah frowned as Relaina explained how a black bolt had blocked her light magic, but not the shadow magic. Fabian had told him about the bolts, even shown him the two that he'd removed from Ihara and Thea. They were made of white and black onyx on the ends.

"They knew about me," Relaina said. "But they didn't know I had dark magic."

They reached the little inn, and Fabian came out to greet them with the innkeeper. The woman gaped at Darren when he approached, immediately dipping into a low bow.

"It's my honor to host you, King Darren," she said.

"You have my gratitude," Darren said, but his eyes did not convey it. Jeremiah suppressed a shudder. What had he been through between the time of Thea's death and his escape?

"Would you all like to eat something?" Fabian asked as they all stepped into the inn. The main floor boasted a small but clean dining room. All bedrooms were on the floor above.

"I think," Relaina said, taking Darren's hand and swaying slightly. "I just need to bathe and sleep a while."

"As do I," Nehma said.

"Then sleep," Fabian said, gesturing toward the staircase. "We'll keep watch."

As Relaina, Darren, and Nehma followed the innkeeper up the stairs, Jeremiah took Fabian's hand. They *would* keep watch.

They always would.

CHAPTER 45

THE NEW HEIR

A small fire crackled in the room Darren and Relaina had been given, offering welcome warmth and light as the night wore on. Despite his utter exhaustion, Darren fought it with everything he could, sitting on the floor at the foot of the bed while Relaina slept. She'd fallen asleep hours ago in his arms. He didn't want to let her go, but if he remained in bed sleep would have taken him, too, and he couldn't bear it.

Relaina stirred behind him, startling him for an instant before he realized it was just her shifting in bed. One of her hands groped the empty space beside her. Guilt settled in Darren's chest alongside the other unpleasant emotions that fought for his focus. He got up and climbed back in bed as Relaina's eyes drifted open. She tucked her head under his chin as he pulled her close, wrapping her arms around his middle.

"Have you slept at all?" she asked quietly. Darren stared at the reflection of the fire in their window.

"No," he said. "I can't, I—"

It all flooded him at once, his heart cracking open. He clutched Relaina to his chest.

"I'm terrified that I'll wake up and find myself back there," he said, his voice strained. "They forced me to sleep and wake for weeks."

"Weeks..." Relaina whispered. She leaned back and brushed his hair away from his forehead. "Love...it's only been six days."

Six days. "What?"

"We left Parea the day after Thea died," she said. "Rhea... Rhea sensed Thea's death immediately."

It's been weeks. Of course Hedda had lied. She'd tried everything in her power to poison him against Relaina.

And Relaina had come for him the moment she'd known something had gone wrong.

"I'm sorry," he whispered, closing his eyes.

"Darren."

He didn't open his eyes until she pressed her lips to his furrowed brow. Dim firelight danced in the green of her irises.

"None of this is your fault," she said. "I...*I'm* sorry I wasn't more careful in that house. I'm sorry you had to see what they did."

What they did. The way she'd screamed when they'd ripped open her skin, the pain and despair in her eyes while he'd been forced to watch, unable to stop it. It would haunt him forever.

"Are you all right?" he asked, his voice small.

Her face crumpled as she shook her head. "No. But I will be. We will be."

"How can you be so sure?" His chest felt like it might collapse. "How am I supposed to mend a nation when I'm so broken myself?"

Relaina traced his face with her fingertips.

"I'm sure because I believe in you," she said. "We have each other and our friends to help carry the broken bits of us while we press forward."

Darren pulled her close again, lacing his fingers through her hair. "You will always have me. Always."

"And you, me." Relaina ran her fingers up his chest and along his neck. His eyes drifted shut.

"I have to tell you what I found out," he murmured, even as his mind began to drift.

"Tell me in the morning, love. Please sleep."

Relaina began humming the same song she's sung to him weeks before. *If ever you know anything, know the depth of my love for you.* Mercifully, blissfully, Darren fell into a dreamless sleep.

THE AFTERNOON BREEZE in the small Terranian village carried the promise of spring with it as Fabian walked along the central road with Jeremiah at his side. Relaina, Darren, and Nehma had spent the majority of the past three days resting and regaining their strength. There was very little lightness within any of them since their escape from Ryos and since Rhea had not appeared, but Ash had provided needed distraction and enchanting entertainment.

Fabian's head still swam with everything they'd discovered since arriving in Ryos: the Order of the Eternal Flame, their hatred for Relaina that was apparently tied to her birthmother, Gabriel's involvement in it all.

He'd known Gabriel was a merciless tyrant, but to discover that he'd been involved in this Order for the gods knew how long, and that Talea had been part of it too... It explained much, but it also raised more questions. If they wanted to stabilize Terrana and Lyneisia and ensure Evaria was protected, they would need strong leadership in each kingdom, and soon.

Fabian stopped at the edge of the village, staring at the wooded path ahead of them.

"Jeremiah," he said, his voice soft. Jeremiah's dark brown eyes met his, patient and lovely as always. "I think we should get married as soon as Desiree and the Evarians arrive."

Jeremiah's brow furrowed. "I'm eager to marry you, too, but why the sudden rush?"

Fabian hadn't let himself dwell on it too much, hadn't truly felt the weight of the guilt and shame over Thea's death and Darren's capture, the fear of how close he'd come to death himself. He swallowed against the lump in his throat.

"I could have died," he said, his voice measured despite his distress. "And Evaria would have been left without a leader. I've worked too hard for what my nation has become to have been so careless with her succession."

"Who did you name before fighting Gabriel?"

Fabian huffed a humorless laugh. "It made sense at the time, but she can no longer accept the role."

Jeremiah's eyes grew wide. "Relaina."

Fabian nodded. "An Evarian noble by blood, a fierce warrior that had been raised with the skills to rule a kingdom. And your daughter."

After a moment of stunned silence, Jeremiah said, "Did you ever tell her?"

"No. And it's pointless now that Gabriel is dead and she's to marry Darren. I will be equally as glad to have them as neighboring rulers."

"So who will you name now?" Jeremiah smirked. "The cat?"

Fabian laughed, lifting Jeremiah's hand to his mouth to kiss his fingers.

"For now, I want to marry you to ensure someone is there if I should die."

"Fabian—"

"Let me finish, love."

Jeremiah pressed his lips together and nodded.

"That is what's needed for now, but I do have a successor in mind," he said, glancing back the way they'd come. Nehma trailed behind them, out of earshot but ever watchful. "Did you know the Fontaines have noble blood?"

Jeremiah followed Fabian's gaze, studying the young healer for a moment.

"The Fontaines were nobility?"

"Records show they were until my grandfather's reign. I'm not entirely sure what happened, and Desiree was apathetic when I told her what I'd found."

"Why not name Desiree?"

Fabian laughed again. "Desiree would have my head if I named her my heir. And I do think it wise to choose someone younger than we are."

Jeremiah sighed. "I suppose you're right." He lowered his voice more. "So what brought you to Nehma as a choice?"

"Being an Evarian noble by blood will strengthen her position in the eyes of the other nobles," Fabian said. "But I see such potential in her that goes far beyond that. She's a warrior who saved many Evarian lives during the Battle of Maremer. A healer who set aside years of mistrust and fear of dark magic so she could help her friend and Esran as a whole. And after getting to know her better these past months, I can see she has the temperament for it. Perhaps even more so than Relaina, if I may."

Jeremiah laughed softly. "Relaina is well aware of her own disposition. She'd likely agree with you."

"Relaina will help Darren hold his ground in Terrana," Fabian said. "And in Evaria—"

Before Fabian could finish, Nehma jogged over to them, her eyes bright as she gazed down the wooded path.

"Rhea," she said. "Rhea's coming."

Sure enough, an exceptionally tall woman with dark brown hair appeared around the bend in the path, her arms glowing dimly where she held a figure in a black shroud. *Thea.*

But Rhea wasn't alone; traipsing behind her were a dozen figures clad in black and armed to the teeth. Several of them walked with apparent injuries. Even Nehma hesitated to run to her, though Fabian could practically feel her longing to do so. As they drew nearer, Fabian recognized two of them with a jolt.

The two women Darren had fought in the arena.

"The Terranian Elite," Fabian said softly.

Relaina's jaw clenched as she concentrated on trying to project her light magic outward, the healer markings on her arms mocking her.

Breathe, Darren thought to her, and Relaina did, allowing air to rush into her lungs. He sat across from her on the floor by their fireplace, his shadows gently drifting around them. After another few moments of fruitless trying, Relaina huffed, and her light disappeared, her own shadows falling back into her. Darren's magic receded, too.

"It still won't do anything but heal me, and it won't even do that unless my shadows are connected to yours," Relaina said, rubbing her face in frustration. "Even if I can use the darkness outside of myself now, if I can't keep the light from clashing with it when I get injured, then I'm just as stuck as before."

Darren reached for her hand, and she met his eyes.

"We'll find answers," he said. Relaina stared at him, her mind replaying the events of the day in Ryos, how she'd been able to use the shadows the same way Darren could when the light had been blocked.

"The bolt," she said quietly. "I was able to use the shadows the way you can. And without fear of my light clashing with them."

Darren grimaced. "But it still hurt you. There has to be another way to achieve that same end that doesn't require you getting shot or stabbed."

A knock sounded before Relaina could reply, and Jeremiah appeared at their door.

"It's Rhea," he said. "And the Terranian Elite are with her."

Relaina blinked. The Terranian Elite had survived the Order's attack.

They rushed through the village after Jeremiah, hands clasped. Darren had hardly let go of her the past few days. He needed a physical reminder that she was safe, and she did not begrudge him that comfort as they both recovered.

At the entrance to the village, Rhea and Nehma stood together with glowing arms holding a body in a black shroud. Grief squeezed Relaina's heart. To the left, a group of black-clad, heavily armed Terranians stood gathered, their eyes trained on Darren. Fabian stepped aside as Darren came forward. Relaina squeezed his hand before joining Nehma and Rhea.

"King Darren," one of the Terranian Elite said, his voice coarse and low. The rest of them knelt behind him, their heads bowed. "You answered our summons and completed our sacred trial. We pledge to you our loyalty."

The man knelt by his fellows.

"How do I know I can trust all of you, Captain Vrana?" Darren asked, his voice quiet but menacing.

"They helped me," Rhea said, and every head turned in her direction. "When I went to retrieve Thea, they helped me with her body, and they hid me until we could all escape the city. The Order now controls Ryos."

"We've dealt with this group before," Captain Vrana said.

"King Gabriel formed the Terranian Elite after leaving the Order, but there were attacks over a decade ago where several of their Flameguards came for us. They tried to recruit the tenebrae and kill the non-magic wielders."

"How many Terranian Elite are left?" Darren asked.

"Those you see before you," Captain Vrana said, bowing his head again. "It will be our honor to serve you, King Darren, and to root these zealots out of our land."

Darren stepped closer to the kneeling assassins, then held out his hand to Vrana. Relaina's chest filled with the fiery warmth of pride.

"We'll make sure they are defeated," Darren said as Vrana took his hand and stood. "We'll give them what they deserve for what they've done. No hesitation."

"No mercy," the assassins responded as one.

CHAPTER 46

BENEATH THE SUN AND STARS

The cool Ellyr morning was heavy with fog and grief. Relaina had been to several nobles' funerals over the years, but this weight on her heart was new to her. With Rhea and Nehma, she had risen before dawn to prepare for Thea's rites, and soon a whole host of Evarians, Lyneisians, and Terranians would gather by the Granica River to honor her.

Desiree had arrived the previous day with ten Evarian guards to escort them out of Terrana, and Relaina had nearly fallen apart at the sight of Bracken among them. After sailing up the river they'd taken up rooms at the Lichened Oak inn in Ellyr. Now, though, Relaina and her healer sisters stood around a table in a local apothecary. The closest healers' sanctuary to Ellyr was the Caspian Forest, so this would have to do for Thea.

Rhea had already healed Thea's wounds, including the hole in her back from the bolt. They were made of either white or black onyx, according to Fabian, who'd studied two in the days following the Order's attack on the arena. The black bolt had been Thea's downfall. But for Relaina?

Perhaps for her it was the answer. She couldn't very well

walk around with a crossbow bolt shoved into her flesh at all times, but what if there was another way to utilize the onyx to work in her favor?

"Ready?" Nehma asked, drawing Relaina out of her ruminations. Rhea nodded, and Relaina stepped back so they could complete the preparations. She watched in somber awe as Nehma began to sing, and they both held glowing hands over Thea's chest.

> *The bark of an oak tree,*
> *The soil from the ground,*
> *The singing of the western wind,*
> *And a star, plucked from the sky...*

The insignia Relaina had seen on the healers' garb in Lyneisia appeared on Thea's skin—a glowing island lily. Relaina stifled a sob.

> *Rest now, in dreams,*
> *And gaze upon the fire.*
> *Forest groves and gentle breezes*
> *'Til we meet again.*

Nehma and Relaina left the room after that, allowing Rhea several minutes of privacy with her sister. The apothecary's storefront faced the tall grasses that led to the river's edge.

"How are you?" Nehma asked quietly, sitting beside Relaina on the stone steps.

Relaina shook her head. "Today isn't about me."

"Maybe not. But I'm still asking."

Relaina squinted at the wispy clouds above, pink and purple in the early morning sunlight. Her hands trembled in her lap, and she clenched her fists. "I'm fine. I'm more worried about Rhea and Darren."

Nehma placed her hand on top of Relaina's clenched fingers. "You lost Thea too. And what they did to you in that house..."

"I..." Relaina cleared her throat. "I can't talk about that right now."

Nehma withdrew her hand and sighed. "Well if that changes, I'm here for you."

After a moment, Relaina reached for Nehma's hand. She couldn't speak past the lump in her throat, now, but until Rhea emerged, they sat in silence, hands clasped, and Relaina believed her own words a little bit more. *We have each other and our friends and allies to help carry the broken bits of us while we press forward.*

They both stood and embraced Rhea as she wiped her eyes. It was time.

They carried Thea's shrouded body to the northern edge of Ellyr, toward a funeral pyre surrounded by small, colorful stones by the Granica River. The lily on Thea's chest steadily glowed through the thin black shroud.

Everyone had gathered by the pyre—even the Terranian Elite stood behind Darren on the left side of the stones. As they placed Thea on the pyre, Darren came forward with a blackwood arrow. He held it out to Rhea with both hands, bowing.

"I know you have your own rites," he said. "But I wanted to honor her. Terranian warriors are laid to rest with blackwood arrows."

Rhea bowed to him. "She would be deeply moved, Darren."

He placed the arrow on Thea's chest, right over the glowing lily. He started to rejoin the gathered crowd, but Rhea took his hand.

"Please," she said. "I want you and Relaina to help with the circle."

Darren's eyes flicked to Relaina's for a moment before he nodded.

Rhea and Nehma stepped outside the circle of stones, and Relaina took a deep breath after joining them with Darren. Rhea stood back while the three of them knelt on the grassy earth. Relaina inhaled, reaching for Darren's hand. When their darkness connected, it appeared around her again. She held up her hand as shadowy vapor drifted along her palm and fingers, then pressed it to the stones. A moment later, Darren followed her lead.

Darkness and light wove between the stones as Nehma, Relaina, and Darren pushed their magic into them, the circle shimmering with iridescent blues, greens, and purples. She'd never attended the funeral of a magic wielder, and this particular ritual of stones infused with magic was foreign but beautiful. Thea deserved it all.

To the right of the circle, Rhea took the bow offered by Desiree, and Fabian held the torch to light the tip. Rhea took aim, a tear cascading down her cheek as she loosed the flaming arrow. They all stood, stepping back as the kindling caught fire beneath Thea's body. Relaina watched embers float toward the overcast sky and said a prayer to the gods.

WHEN THEY'D APPROACHED the owner of the Lichened Oak about hosting a small wedding ceremony, Jeremiah hadn't expected, well, *this.*

The inn workers had woven flowers around a wooden arch in the square outside and dragged tables and chairs into the street. Candles were placed on each one alongside a small vase of flowers. The citizens of Ellyr brought baskets of food and wine, eager to contribute to the wedding of a king. Fabian had spent most of the day throwing Jeremiah apologetic looks, and the king now settled into a large bath after a local spa owner had treated his hair with oil. The scent was distinctly Fabian's, rich and warm with hints of vanilla.

"I didn't mean for it to get so...lively," Fabian said, while Jeremiah sat with his back against the tub, tossing the strip of fabric he'd been teasing Ash with several feet away. The kitten pounced on it as Jeremiah looked over his shoulder at Fabian's pensive face.

"Stop apologizing," he said. "They want to be part of the celebration. Let them have this joy, and we'll have ours."

Fabian smiled, his expression softening. "I love you."

"I love you."

A soft knock interrupted their easy silence minutes later, and Jeremiah kissed Fabian before venturing out of the washroom, shutting the door behind him. He crossed their shared bedroom in just three strides and stepped into the hallway, greeting Relaina. She'd come to join him in town as they searched for a wedding scarf, a detail he'd forgotten in the haste to hold the ceremony.

"I know you'll have the large celebration back in Maremer," she said as they traipsed down the stairs of the inn. "But you should still have everything for the actual wedding."

"I agree," Jeremiah said. They stepped into the midday light, squinting against the sun that warmed their faces. "And truthfully...I think I'll remember this smaller affair most fondly."

Relaina's smile was still tinged with sadness, but he cherished it; her smiles were few and far between these days. His chest ached when he thought about everything she'd been through.

They entered a tailor shop down the street, the only one in Ellyr, and rifled through their selection of silk wedding scarves piled in two large barrels. Relaina found several in Evarian red with lovely embroidery, but Jeremiah didn't feel drawn to any of them. As he reached nearly to the bottom, overturning a sea of smooth fabric, he extracted a scarf made of shimmering gold and bronze. It reminded him of Fabian's eyes in the sunlight.

"This one," he said.

The shop owner gratefully took their payment and folded the scarf carefully, ensuring it was undamaged. When they exited the shop, Relaina lingered by the front steps, looking across the way at a jeweler's shop.

"Do you mind if I meet you later?" she asked. Despite the fact that Evarian guards and Terranian assassins were stationed all over Ellyr, Jeremiah glanced around, his skin prickling with nerves. But he'd have to get used to not being around Relaina to protect her—they were all leaving the day after tomorrow, and Relaina wouldn't be returning to Maremer.

"All right," he said. "But don't be gone too long."

Relaina smirked. "Don't worry, I won't leave you to braid your own hair for your wedding, Father."

It pulled a laugh from him, and the glow of happiness within him grew brighter, as it always did when she called him that. *Father.*

He'd made many mistakes in his life, but his daughter wasn't one of them.

FABIAN STOOD before the mirror in his and Jeremiah's room, fidgeting with the sleeve of his shirt. Their attire would be far grander under normal circumstances, but something about the billowy red fabric and neatly tied laces felt more authentic anyway. Simple gold stitching ensured that he wore his royal colors, but otherwise he wore plain brown trousers tucked into leather boots. He felt exposed, in a way, and it was both terrifying and exciting. He would marry Jeremiah today without the extravagance and pressure of a royal wedding held at Seacastle. He would marry Jeremiah simply as a man who loved him.

Someone knocked, and Fabian answered the door to let Desiree and Saheer inside.

"How are you feeling?" Desiree asked. She'd shaved her head recently, and it suited her. Saheer's long, raven hair was pinned into a bun at the nape of her neck.

"Nervous," Fabian admitted. "But content."

Fabian sat on the bed while Saheer handed Desiree a kohl pencil infused with gold. Fabian hadn't worn kohl in quite some time—not since his coronation—and it felt heavy around his eyes. But when he saw his reflection in the mirror, he couldn't help but smile.

His eyes shine golden in the sun. They did shine now, accented by the golden kohl and the deep joy within.

"Thank you, Desiree," Fabian said.

"Fabian, I think they've got—"

Jeremiah appeared in the doorway of their room, his face going utterly blank as he locked eyes with Fabian. His bronze-gray hair had been braided on either side of his head into a bun at the back, with deep purple flowers woven throughout. His white shirt was simple like Fabian's, and his beard had been trimmed close to his face.

"We'll be downstairs," Saheer said, taking Desiree's hand with a wry smile and leading her from the room. Jeremiah broke out of his stupor as they passed, nodding before stepping inside and shutting the door behind him. Fabian stood as he approached.

"Gods," Jeremiah said, stopping in front of him. He put one hand on Fabian's neck, brushing his thumb lightly along his jaw. His eyes welled with tears.

"Jeremiah, if you make me cry right now—"

Jeremiah cut him off with a kiss, his other hand joining the first to hold Fabian's face. His touch was impossibly firm and gentle at the same time. Desire shuddered through Fabian as Jeremiah kissed down his jaw and neck, his facial hair pleasantly coarse against Fabian's skin, and he tugged Jeremiah closer by the small of his back.

"You're beautiful," Jeremiah whispered in his ear, and Fabian's insides became molten. His fingers dug into Jeremiah's back.

"Careful," Fabian said. "I may ruin your hair if you don't stop."

Jeremiah huffed a laugh and leaned back, his eyes scanning Fabian's face. "Well, we can't have that."

"Not until after the ceremony, at least."

The light joy in Jeremiah's eyes shifted to twinkling mischief. He traced Fabian's lower lip with his thumb.

"I have over twenty years' worth of nights with you to make up for," he said, his voice nearly collapsing Fabian's knees. He dipped his head, planting a kiss just below Fabian's ear. "I intend to begin that penance tonight."

"Gods in hell, Jeremiah," Fabian whispered, closing his eyes. With a laugh, Jeremiah backed away, and Fabian mastered himself, shaking his head.

"Shall we go, then?" Jeremiah asked, holding out his hand as he stood by the door. Fabian inhaled slowly and joined him, taking his hand.

THERE WAS a strange edge to Relaina's happiness as her father and Fabian stood before the crowd of Evarians, Terranians, and Lyneisians, their hands clasped while Desiree led the ceremony. King Gabriel, the Order of the Eternal Flame, and anyone else that had tried to hurt her could not steal this day, could not poison her heart against joy.

Relaina stood off to the side and came forward when Desiree requested the wedding scarf, handing her the golden fabric. She backed away again as Desiree wrapped Fabian and Jeremiah's clasped hands together and spoke the binding words.

Rooted in the earth, I bind your hands,
Across the deepest seas, I bind your hearts,
Beneath the sun and stars, I bind your souls.
The gods bear witness to your union.

Fabian and Jeremiah knelt, their foreheads pressed together as Desiree said a final prayer. Relaina caught Darren's eye from where he sat at one of the tables closest to the front with Nehma, Rhea, and Bracken.

"...May their bond remain steadfast..."

The word Darren had mentioned two nights prior drifted through her mind as he held her gaze. *Calirhán.* Chosen bonded. Without even meaning to, he had chosen her in some ancient, sacred way, giving her some of his power. Calixtos's power.

Though she wasn't some god's heir, she couldn't help but feel she'd chosen him just as profoundly.

Cheers erupted from the gathered crowd as Fabian and Jeremiah stood and kissed. She grinned, joining in the shouts of celebration. Before others converged on them, Jeremiah turned to pull Relaina into an embrace. Fabian embraced her, too, and she wiped tears from her eyes and melted into the approaching crowd. Nehma stood from their table, nudging Relaina.

"Is there magic involved in healer weddings?" Relaina

asked, watching as Darren offered his congratulations to the two kings.

"Yes," Nehma said. "We bind their hands with light instead of a scarf."

"I see."

Nehma started to speak again, but Darren approached them and took Relaina's hand, and she rejoined Rhea and Bracken at their table, throwing Relaina a raised eyebrow.

"What were you two discussing?" Darren asked, one corner of his mouth lifting.

"Healer wedding ceremonies." Relaina hoped her expression was more measured than her voice.

"Come join us, you two!" Bracken called, and they did, settling in as Lyneisians brought out food. A fiddle player and flutist struck up a lively tune.

They celebrated well into the evening, and though Relaina enjoyed watching others drink themselves into oblivion, she was satisfied with only one cup of wine. Their table was quiet but content among themselves.

"I'll miss them, and all the Evarians," Bracken said, and the rest of them agreed. "But I'm glad we'll all be together."

Relaina was glad herself—she had missed Bracken, and knowing that he, Nehma, and Rhea would be with them as they ventured into the heart of Terrana gave her courage. But a thought still nagged at her, ever since Fabian had voiced his reasoning for hastening his marriage to Jeremiah.

After her nerve had built and faltered a number of times, she finally leaned over to Darren and told him what had been on her mind for days. His eyes widened.

"Tomorrow night?"

She nodded. "Before we leave."

His answering expression filled her with warmth.

Chapter 47

To Carry in the Morning

Darren wasn't sure after the ordeal with the Order if he'd ever feel joy the same way, but tonight had proved him wrong.

Tonight was better than the night Relaina had told him she loved him.

It was better than the night she'd agreed to marry him.

Beneath the sun and stars, I bind your souls.

After returning to their room in the inn, they left a trail of clothing from the door to the bed and fell upon the mattress in a tangle of heated kisses and gentle touches. He lost himself entirely in her, surrendered every piece of pain and brokenness, at least for a little while.

Relaina gasped as he kissed her neck and pushed inside her, wrapping her legs around his waist. With each thrust, she stifled a whimper, and he reveled in the pleasure he drew from her. He let his power flow freely from his hands.

Shadows appeared around her in response to his. Their darkness drifted around them softly as they moved together, connected so completely that Darren wasn't sure where he ended and she began.

The gods bear witness to your union.

Relaina's body tensed, and she gripped him tighter. "Darren," she said, breathless, and he met her eyes as her brow furrowed. "I love you."

"I love you, Relaina," he breathed.

They ran a bath after, catching their breath for a few minutes, and before they submerged themselves, Relaina was straddling him and guiding him inside her again. After everything they'd endured, this night, this closeness with her allowed him some measure of peace.

Still, when they finally settled down to sleep, Darren's mind began to drift to darker places, and he tried to push the thoughts away, tossing and turning.

"Set it down, whatever it is that plagues you," Relaina murmured, drawing circles on his chest. "It will be there for us to carry in the morning."

"WRITE AS SOON AS YOU ARRIVE," Fabian said, and Darren nodded, clasping his forearm before Fabian pulled him into an embrace. Tears pricked Darren's eyes as the morning breeze wove through his hair. To his left, Relaina and Jeremiah were exchanging a tearful goodbye of their own. They'd all agreed on this plan, but it didn't make it any easier.

Relaina and Darren would make their way to Lues, stopping by the Caspian healers' sanctuary on the way to retrieve Catrin and speak with the elders. It was a relief that Nehma, Rhea, and Bracken had agreed to come with them, alongside the Terranian Elite.

"The moment you need us, we will come," Jeremiah said, addressing both Relaina and Darren. "Stay safe."

"And you as well," Darren said. After a moment of hesitation, Jeremiah pulled Darren into a tight embrace himself.

"We are not our fathers," he said quietly. "You most especially."

Jeremiah released him, and he joined his companions, mounting his horse.

"I love you both," Relaina said to Fabian and Jeremiah.

"And we love you," Fabian said, smiling. He bowed to her, and the Evarians and Lyneisians around them followed suit. "May the gods be with you, Relaina Andovier, Princess of Maremer. Queen of Terrana."

Relaina bowed in return, making the gesture Darren had taught her that was the highest form of respect in Terrana. He made it as well.

"And with you, Darren LaGuarde, King of Terrana," Fabian said.

As they rode at a leisurely pace through the streets, Relaina leaned toward Darren in her saddle.

"Do you think they know?"

Images of the night before flooded his mind. The dark quiet of the woods they'd snuck off to, Relaina's hands in his, surrounded by light magic. Her face as Rhea, Nehma, and Bracken stood by them. He shook his head.

"No," he said. "But we'll tell them soon."

She grinned and faced forward again, Amariah picking up her pace as they neared the southern edge of Ellyr. With one last glance at the Evarians behind them, Darren urged his horse onward, following his wife.

EPILOGUE

Acantha prided herself on her power, but also on her intellect. She was clever, and cunning, and always solved her problems. *My little white fox*, her mother had called her.

But today, the white fox's teeth were bared. That fool Archan had fumbled the Lyneisian coup before his even more foolish cousin's capture, and the Pretender was now a much larger problem.

When she'd arrived at the healers' sanctuary, Acantha had sensed the dark magic on her. It made no sense—she was Talea's daughter, a healer, and a Seer. Acantha had a high tolerance for many things, but surprises? She loathed them.

Hedda and five of her Flameguards trembled before her in the empty dining hall of the Artea manor, their heads touching the floor in low bows.

"I trusted you to find the Heir of Calixtos and convert him to our cause while I found out more about the Pretender," Acantha said, stepping between the crouched figures. "We even had the onyx bolts to aid your success. But you took it too far. Your devotion to me is admirable, but your foolishness in attempting to bait and silence the Pretender cost me the one ally that would ensure our victory."

"I...I am so sorry, my lady," Hedda said, her voice brittle. Acantha remained silent for a moment, pausing by the farthest left Flameguard where he silently wept on the floor. His shame at disappointing her softened the raging anger within her somewhat.

Acantha walked over to the dining table where the three Arteas were bound and gagged. Their eyes were wide with terror as they beheld her.

"Hedda," she said.

The healer lifted her head. "My lady?"

Acantha took her time walking back to her followers.

"I've tried," Acantha said softly. She crouched in front of Hedda, taking her chin gently in her hand. "I've tried to lead with compassion. I will always prefer devotion to fear."

"You have led with compassion, my lady," Hedda said, her eyes wide in appeal. "We are endlessly devoted to you."

"I know," Acantha said, smiling softly. She gripped Hedda's throat in her hand, and the healer choked. "But I am deeply fucking displeased."

She let Hedda's face turn several shades of red and purple before she finally released her. Hedda gasped and coughed, trying to speak.

"I know you're sorry, Hedda," Acantha said. "Which is why I know this will not happen again. First it was Kalmali, and now...*this*. You've made my aim to convert the Heir of Calixtos to our cause far more difficult."

Hedda bowed on the floor again.

"You will come with me," Acantha said. "The Flameguards will remain here with our gracious hosts." The Arteas shifted, looking at one another and then back at Acantha. "We'll find another way to take Parea, but for now, we must set our sights on what's most important."

She strode back to the Arteas, leaning down so her face was right next to their youthful daughter's. "In war, if it cannot be devotion with which I lead...then fear will do."

Corta Artea trembled, and Acantha smiled.

"Take them back to their holding room," she said, and the Flameguards moved at once. "Hedda, we leave at dawn."

Once they had all vacated the room, Acantha crept up the steps to the master's chambers, making herself comfortable upon the massive, plush bed. She closed her eyes as her arms lit up with her magic and touched her own forehead, falling into unconsciousness.

She landed in the Grove of the Gods, surrounded by lush trees. Strange. Last time it had been winter here, when the Pretender had abruptly appeared. Perhaps the seasons changed differently in this realm.

Iros, she called.

The god materialized before her, his dark green eyes cold and calculating.

What's happened? he asked.

My foolish followers have pushed the LaGuarde boy right back into the Pretender's hands.

Iros frowned. *This is grievous. She will corrupt him.*

I will find a way to convince him. But it won't be easy.

Elenia wills it, Iros said. *It's your duty as the keeper of her power to ensure that the Heir of Calixtos does not fall prey to heretics. It's in his nature to let darkness consume him, to allow evil and death to befall the world. He needs a guiding light.*

Acantha knelt before him, her fists clenching. *Shouldn't I have greater power as the Heir of Elenia? I am strong, but I do not command the same power as the Heir of Calixtos.*

You question the power I bestowed upon you in Elenia's stead? The power I bestowed upon all mortal healers?

No, of course not. Forgive me.

Esran needs you, Acantha. You and the Heir of Calixtos are meant to lead it into a new age, where mortals follow the will of the gods with reverence and unyielding devotion. Find him. Complete the ritual at the Eternal Fire.

The wind in the Grove picked up, and Acantha shivered as Iros's presence began to fade.

I am your servant, and Elenia's, Acantha vowed. *Your will is mine to uphold.*

Acknowledgments

An absolutely HUGE thank you must go to those who helped me take TPOM from first-draft monstrosity to published book. Holli, my fearless editor/sensitivity reader/dear friend. Amie, my proofreader. Maggie, my alpha reader. Sydney, Maggie, Sierra, and Katie, my beta readers. Shar, who answered sensitivity questions and was always patient and encouraging.

I'm so thankful to all the author friends I've made along the way, but especially to Hannah, who showed me endless support and unwavering friendship through all the highs and lows of this past year. H&H chat gets me through the hard days and keeps me sane.

Thank you to my mom, who listens to me explain plot points out of context like a conspiracy theorist and never makes me feel ridiculous about it.

Thank you to each and every friend who has encouraged and supported my author endeavors. The fact that I'd be kicked off the stage at the Oscars if I listed all your names is something I don't take for granted. You all have my heart.

And to my readers - you are absolutely the greatest people on the planet. Your kind messages, eagerness to apply for ARCs, and simple willingness to read the books I've poured my soul into are why I do what I do. I'm so glad you're along for the ride. HOEs for life.

Character Glossary

A glossary of named characters in the
Heirs of Esran series

Lyneisian Royals

King Stephan Gienty
Queen Christine Andovier Gienty
Prince Aronn Gienty (Crown Prince)
Princess Annalise Gienty
Princess Relaina Andovier (Gienty), biological daughter of Jeremiah Andovier and Talea, adopted in secret by Stephan and Christine

Lyneisian Nobles

Loyalists
Lady Justinia Elke
Hektor Elke, Lady Elke's brother
Misenia, Keeper of Law (noble by merit/station)
Torrence Doldren, Keeper of Records (d.)
Lord Fie

Lord Tira
Bracken Averatt, best friend of Relaina Andovier, one of King Fabian's Shadows

TRAITORS
Archan Conclave, son of Lady Vesta Conclave, Keeper of Coin
Zarias Conclave, cousin to Archan
Erine Tarod
The Norhens

OTHERS OF NOTE

Saheer, leader of Evarian forces sent to aid the loyalists
Mazin, Lynx Guard
Varun, Evarian guard
Ericka, Elder of the healers' sanctuary near Parea
Karra, Annalise's temporary guardian
Maya, a mysterious healer
Shojen, Evarian healer

EVARIAN ROYALS

King Fabian Thereux
Jeremiah Andovier, betrothed to King Fabian, heir to the Andovier house, Captain of the Lynx Guard (Lyneisia)

EVARIAN NOBLES

Lord Paulus Vontair, Keeper of Coin
Lady Clarisse Vontair

Lady Jiteya Abara, Keeper of Records
Lady Kenna Granger
Lady Tyla and Lord Elowen Rhoe
Lady Rhonea Andovier
Captain Desiree Fontaine
Lord Henry Swanson
Lord Harnow
Lord Fennel
Lady Guerraine
Lady Drennal

Others of Note

Nehma, Desiree's niece (Caspian Forest healers)
Rhea, twin to Thea (Caspian Forest healers)
Thea, twin to Rhea (Caspian Forest healers)
Catrin (Caspian Forest healers)
Nadia, Saheer's sister, healer

Terranian Royals

Prince Darren LaGuarde, son of the Tyrant King, former assassin
King Gabriel LaGuarde, the Tyrant King (d.)
Queen Kacelle Gerratt LaGuarde (d.)
Prince Lucas LaGuarde (d.)

Terranian Nobles

Lord Leonardo and Lady Mariana Delimont
Katarina Delimont (d.)

Lady Ines Tryali
Lady Ihara and Lady Lucia Eyern
Lord Gio and Lady Kala Artea (potential claimant/usurper)
Corta Artea
Lady Reyes
Lorina Reyes
Lord and Lady Maez (potential claimant/usurper)
Lord and Lady Kratos (potential claimant/usurper)
Lord Gerratt (d.), Darren's uncle (killed in book 1)
Lady Carmen and Lord Kastor Gerratt, Darren's maternal grandparents

OTHERS OF NOTE

Acantha, a mysterious and powerful healer
Kalmali, Acantha's subordinate, tenebrae
Hedda, Acantha's subordinate, healer
Captain Vrana, head assassin of the Terranian Elite
Heris, pub owner in Ryos and one of Fabian's Shadows
Alaris Onnea, an old tenebrae

THE GODS OF ESRAN

MAJOR GODS
Elenia, Queen of the Gods, Goddess of Light, Sky, and Seas
Calixtos, God of Darkness and Death
Saeva, Goddess of Animals and Nature

MINOR GODS
Iros, God of Healing
Praelia, Goddess of War
Ashima, Goddess of Wisdom

Oara, Goddess of Storms
Elodeus, God of Horses

Caliena, the first Queen of the Gods, now Divine Spirit of the
earth

Spice Rack

For you to easily find or avoid scenes that depict explicit sexual content

You'll find spicy content in:
Chapter 3
Chapter 18
Chapter 23
Chapter 27
Chapter 47

The first four scenes are multiple pages long, but don't take up the entire chapter.

Hayley Turner is a writer and composer from North Carolina. Her favorite stories blend fantasy, magic, romance, and epic adventures for an overall "fairytale for adults" feel, and that's exactly what she seeks to capture in her own books. When she isn't writing books or music, she can be found playing videogames, eating good food with even better friends, or cuddling with her dog, Leia, or her void goblin cat, Nyx.